THE VOICE IN HIS HEAD

Suddenly, Bev felt it.

It was coming: a chill at first, as if ice crystals had formed in his bloodstream. Then, a tugging at his head: the fingers. They had returned. *Digging, digging, scratching,* seeking more space between his skull and brain, the scraping sound echoing in his brain. His head shivered. Eardrums vibrated. He dropped the roll and clutched his head with both hands. "Why!" he shrieked. "Why me?" He shuddered with fear: his voice had changed. It was low. Deep and hoarse. His hands trembled, the tender lacerations in his palms throbbing more intensely; breaking open; bleeding. Anger welled in him. His heart rate sped. His skull felt as if it was going to crack. He began to kick and buck uncontrollably, spilling the hot coffee on the car seat. He heard himself howling in pain, body writhing on the front seat, arms flinging, tearing at his hair. He heard a deafening scream in his head, deep, pain-filled; and then, clamorous laughter. He pressed his hands harder against his ears in an effort to blot it out. The laughter faded. Then, the voice:

Come to me....

Other *Leisure* books by Michael Laimo:

DEEP IN THE DARKNESS
ATMOSPHERE

THE
DEMONOLOGIST

MICHAEL LAIMO

LEISURE BOOKS NEW YORK CITY

*This novel is dedicated to my parents,
Stellario and Josephine Laimo.*

A LEISURE BOOK®

May 2005

Published by

Dorchester Publishing Co., Inc.
200 Madison Avenue
New York, NY 10016

ISBN 0-8439-5527-9

The name "Leisure Books" and the stylized "L" with design are
trademarks of Dorchester Publishing Co., Inc.

Printed in the United States of America.

Visit us on the web at www.dorchesterpub.com.

ACKNOWLEDGMENTS

I'd like to send a special thanks out to those bands who've provided me with so much guilty pleasure over the years:

Marillion, The Flower Kings, Transatlantic, Dream Theater, Spock's Beard, Neal Morse, Queen, Uriah Heep, and Yes.

And of course, thanks to you, faithful reader, who's still got faith in the new kid on the block.

THE
DEMONOLOGIST

Prologue: Israel
The Six-Day War

The beast shall ascend from the gates of Hell and gather up with thy hand the child that has been cast aside like a thorn . . .

The car, barely running, shook along the dirt road. Clouds of dust encapsulated it, like a swelling storm. The boy sat in the back seat, one of six occupants. Beads of sweat sprung from his brow and dissolved into the hot, arid air. In spite of the heat, he shivered. The same feeling had struck him two hours earlier in the moments before his family was executed.

War had begun. Bloodshed clung to the Middle East like a parasite. Syrian aggressions had coerced Israeli jets to shoot down six fighter planes. Syria, in response, prepared for battle along the Golan Heights. Israel attacked, driving the enemy forces back into the Sinai. Homes were destroyed, many civilians killed. Others found themselves driven south into the Negev desert with very little food or water.

The desert offered an escape from the bloody combat in the north. A rock-strewn road led the way south, deep into the country's no-man's-land, east of the Jordan Rift Valley. The boy was in need of washing, food, and water. The Samarian hills offered fertile valleys but lay two hundred miles away. Was this the driver's destination?

He could smell the stench of ripe bodies. His gaze followed the barren waste beyond the slow-moving vehicle, his weak form pressed against the door alongside a woman shrouded in a black burka. Next to the woman, an old man stretched his legs and prayed, staring at the blood and soil on his hands.

The boy's thoughts wandered: of his parents being dragged away, shot by soldiers while he watched; of being tossed atop their warm corpses like a strewn sack, a hot barrel pressed against his skull; of explosions in the house next to his, the soldiers covered in ash, pulling away from their victims.

In the front seat, a man gagged and spit onto the floor. His coughs resounded, like the gales of sand blasting the cracked windshield. His head leaned forward, and sudden words fell from his lips in jabs:

"Death awaits us. Death, and then beyond, more death."

The car ground to a sharp stop. Dust and dirt rose. Quick shadows loomed. Shouting. Savage dogs barking in the distance. Gunfire.

The driver glanced back. The boy watched him. The driver opened the door, stepped outside. His robe billowed in the desert wind. He raised a pensive hand. Shouted in Hebrew: *"We are not the enemy!"*

A lone gunshot filled the still desert. Blood burst from the driver's chest. His form, petrified for a horrible moment, collapsed to the dry earth.

Screams erupted in the car. The boy hunkered down. The woman next to him crawled over him out the window. Hands grabbed her. Guns pointed. Fired. Blood sprayed, spattering the torn seat, falling against the boy's skin, warm and wet.

Raw hands reached into the front seat, dragging out the remaining occupants. The boy gazed up momentarily. A rebel soldier stood defiantly. He grinned, teeth brown with decay. He shot the men whose faces the boy had never seen. They slumped to the desert floor, sobbing. Further gunshots silenced them forever.

Another soldier came, wrenched the old man from the back seat. He continued his prayers until the moment of his death.

And again, the boy was alone. He prayed. Shadows shifted. Feet shuffled. The moments ticked by painfully.

The soldiers did not take him. Had they not seen him?

Silence. Then a soldier screaming. Swearing. Shouting.

And then prayers of desperation.

Smelling fresh blood, dogs ran from the outer-city wastelands, their urges savage and brutal upon those they attacked. The boy rose up and peeked out. The rebels were four strong. The dogs ten or twelve. He watched as two beasts fell to gunfire. The rest were too many for the soldiers and were soon feasting upon them, hungrily tearing limbs and face and bowels away.

The boy sank down, listening to the dogs' growls, their fighting over the scraps of rebel flesh torn free. He prayed to God and waited for an answer. None came.

Moments passed. The wind hurled sand into the car,

and grains caught in sticky blood. Suddenly, one dog leaped up to the open window—snarling furiously, teeth shredding rubber stripping, spittle and foam leaping from its muzzle.

The boy cried, sliding across the seat in a backward panic, eyes fixed on the dog's bloodstained teeth. The dog's claws fell into the car, tearing at the fabric, the shredding sound echoing its fierce barks.

The boy screamed. He kicked at the dog's face.

The dog leaped back outside, yelping.

Wind-filled silence dominated.

"Thank you, God," the boy prayed.

Minutes passed. Tentatively, the boy stretched up and peered outside. He glimpsed the mutilated body of a rebel soldier. Alongside it, the body of one of the men from the car. Sand had begun to drift over it, the last remnants of his place on earth soon to be extinguished forever. Looking out the rear window, he could barely see the city of Jerusalem in the distance.

More bodies lay in the blood-drenched sand. A dead dog, sprawled next to a woman whose open burka flapped in the desert wind. Blood pooled from the bullet hole in her head.

The boy looked up. The dogs were clustered a hundred feet away, looking back at him.

He squinted at the dogs, their threat dwindling as some settled down on their haunches. Around him, carnage. Nine human bodies partially devoured, flies buzzing around them in droves. The boy opened the door and stepped from the car. His feet sank into the hot sand. The wind whipped at his face. He shrugged away the bloodbath and paced in the opposite direction of the dogs, along the side of the road, looking over his shoulder as he walked.

One dog rose, separated itself from the pack. The boy contemplated the dog, dry earth and deathly remains between them.

God is watching.

Slowly, the dog trotted over to the boy, barked, then moved away, as if beckoning the boy to follow. The boy tailed the mangy animal in a westwardly direction, off the road. They traveled into the desert for hours. The sun beat its poisonous rays down upon them, the air vibrating.

Eventually, they fell upon a muddy stream, reaching through the desert like a vein.

The two drank, then paced unsteadily, following the water's flow as it fell into a depleted ravine. The boy followed the dog down fifteen feet beneath the earth.

At the bottom the dog fell on its side, dead. The boy slept.

Hours later, the boy was awakened by a gentle, intermittent scratching sound. Darkness had arrived. Guided only by the light of the moon, he followed the noise to the side of the ravine. He scraped at the sand and unearthed a limestone marker, indecipherable hieroglyphs etched upon its surface. Slowly, he sifted away the surrounding earth, revealing a carving of a scarab. At the top of the five-foot marker, he discovered a face deeply engraved in the limestone: cavernous eyes, flat nose, bulbous lips pulled into an angular grin. An ancient gaze free at last.

God.

From behind the marker, he heard more scratching.

He kneeled down and prayed, hands pressed together, eyes tightly shuttered, devoid of the tears they wished to release.

Shadows danced as dark clouds rushed in. The

moon fell behind their dark shroud, and the rains fell, softening the earth around the stone. A breeze sprang up, cooling him, offering him strength.

His heart beat soundly with the conviction of knowing that soon he would come face-to-face with God.

He fell forward against the marker. Quickly ran his fingers around the edge of the stone.

And began to dig.

I

And So It Began

Los Angeles: Today

One

It evolved like the slow birth of a reptile through an egg's membrane. Evil had finally matured. A torturous cry of horror ensued that sounded out in a place where no one could hear; the great tree in the woods had finally fallen, with no soul present to become its witness. And then normalcy returned, not a human aware of the event. Though some animals knew. And they hid.

Sixteen miles away, the L.A. Forum was packed full of screaming teens, and even some folks in their twenties and thirties. The rafters shook. Spotlights swirled crazily from eight uppermost points, smoke spiraling lazily in their beams. For over two hours Bevant Mathers performed his heart and soul out. It was a homecoming of sorts; the local boy's second CD, *Beneath*, had gone platinum, thanks to the number-one single "Blush," which still rode the top twenty-five on the *Billboard* charts after eighteen weeks. He'd toured

America for nine months and had returned home to the wanton screams of fans his daughter's age.

On this evening, Friday, November 8, Bev rocked the Forum with nearly every original song in his repertoire, plus a few covers thrown in as surprises, like the Floyd and Zeppelin numbers he'd played night after night in the clubs for over twenty years. Bev waited in the hallway leading from the stage, soaked in sweat, listening to the unrelenting roar of the crowd who waited in hope for one more encore. He'd had one more for them, too, a cover of Marillion's "Kayleigh," a lighter song that was written and recorded back when most of these concertgoers were still in diapers. A perfect end, he felt, to a perfect night.

Surrounded by his band, he went back onstage to the frenzied delight of the crowd, the wavering spots focusing on his brazen presence. He thanked them all for coming, then launched into the song with no introduction.

At some point after the second verse, during the guitar solo, he felt an odd sensation: The music sounded muffled, the beat of the drums offset, the instrumental pieces falling away from one another, creating a dissonance in his mind. After his guitar lead, he sang the third verse, feeling distant from the music—in more than twenty years of playing live, he'd never experienced anything quite like this. It felt as though the music was trying to separate itself from him. He couldn't concentrate. He stepped back from the microphone, the third and final chorus unsung. Did anyone in the crowd really know how the song was supposed to be played, anyway? The song finally ended. He waved to the delirious crowd, then walked off the stage.

Like magic, the houselights came up. The crowd

stopped screaming and started dissipating. Now they would all have to take their fading buzzes back home and lie in the quiet darkness of their bedrooms.

He paced down the hall, shrugging off the looming music reporters. Bev and the four musicians in his band waved a few times, then closed out the imposing world behind the safeguarded door of their dressing room. Not that it was any less crowded there: Family members and friends and music execs awaited.

Slyly, Bev skirted the crowd and padded down a short hall into the bathroom. He shut the door behind him, muting the noise; he could hear the familiar thump of "Blush" surging from stereo speakers. Taking a deep breath, he ran the water and splashed it onto his face, then looked at the tired man in the mirror. *Man, what just happened out there?* He had no clue. He felt a painful vibration in his head, as though someone were running a fingernail across the inside of his skull. The bathroom took on an oblong shape. His stomach twisted and he felt suddenly nauseous. He gripped the porcelain sides of the sink and held on. *I'm getting too old for this. Man, why did I have to break out at such a late age?*

He thought of Kristin, his daughter, who was here somewhere. His twenty-one-year-old was probably mixing it up with the celebs and reporters. The tabloids had it right. Rock stars' kids grew up fast.

He wiped his face with a paper towel, feeling better now; only a ghostly echo of the sensation remained. *What was that? Felt like something crawled into my head. Better get out there and mingle*, he thought. After all, most of the people had come to see *him*.

He banded his shoulder-length hair into a ponytail, exited the bathroom, and moved into the crowded

Michael Laimo

room. Feeling a bit tense, he attentively lobbed his glance around. Everyone was caught up in conversation, alcohol, and cigarettes. The bright lights from above cut into their wearied looks and ignited their bloodshot eyes. His drummer, Ian Hogarth, talked to a male reporter but kept his gaze pinned on a young blonde who returned his attention with a coy, accepting smile. People milled about, laughing, chatting, shouting. There were girlfriends, cousins, neighbors, more girlfriends, and a few attractive wallflowers who had used their assertive sexuality to coax their way backstage. These women, usually named Tiffany or Samantha, were present at every show, wearing outfits more suitable for pole-swinging at strip clubs. Like ferrets, they'd crane their necks seeking Bev, and upon finding him, would wander over and seductively offer their wares to him—sometimes two or three at a time. After nine months on the road, even that grew old, especially for a forty-three-year-old who could barely keep it up on a nightly basis.

Tonight, he just wanted to see Kristin. He searched the growing crowd. *Who are all these people?* He didn't see her.

"Bev! Bev, my *man!* Fucking brilliant, fucking brilliant!" His manager, Jake Ritchie, overweight and jovial, eyes glimmering with mischief, wrapped his pudgy arms around Bev's body. For a moment Bev thought he'd suffocate. Dark remnants of Bev's sweat marred Jake's blue silk shirt. "What a stellar performance!" he sputtered, breath reeking of vodka.

They were suddenly framed by the crowd, who'd taken apt notice of Bev's presence. Adoring women ogled, even those with partners. A few cameras flashed, and a videographer zoomed in on him. Beyond, folks shouted their approval of tonight's performance. No one seemed to have noticed his breakdown during the final encore; if they had, it wasn't evident.

"Really, Bev, this was a magnificent end to the tour! Now . . . uh, not to mix business with pleasure, but I have to remind you that Epic wants you in the studio next week. I do hope you've written a good deal of new material while on the road."

"It's all business, Jake."

Bev loved Jake. He'd been there since the beginning, when Bev started out in the clubs with the various incarnations of bands he played with. Jake had found success in his twenties after his first client, Lionheart, went into the top fifty with the single "Back to the Light." He'd managed them for six years. After their decline, he moved on, earning a number of bands varying degrees of commercial success. Through it all, Jake had never stopped shopping Bev's demos. Everyone else had written Bev off as a washed-up club musician. But Jake had seen the talent and drive in him and got Epic to take a shot with his first CD, *Re-Birth*. It went gold, and laid out the red carpet for the platinum *Beneath* and the top-ten "Blush." Bev Mathers had finally become a star.

Jake fumbled for a cigarette in his shirt pocket, then a lighter. "So've you penned some killers, shithead?"

"A couple of real good ones."

"A couple? A couple? Are they thirty minutes long?" He swayed like a buoy.

"More than a couple."

"I damn well hope so. It's expected of you."

"Put the pressure on, why don't you."

"Like you said, it's all business." The music industry was like that. Give them an inch, they take a mile, and expect you to run it even faster, especially when you've tasted success.

"You see Kristin anywhere?" Bev glanced around, feeling a bit odd again. He waved to some familiar faces while Jake playfully called someone a douche bag, his pudgy hands grabbing a beer from a waitress's tray.

Jake swilled the beer. Some spilled down his chin, adding to the assortment of dark splotches on his shirt. "Naw, ain't seen the bitch anywhere!" He guffawed, then melted into the crowd, shouting at Bev's bassist, Pete Morse. Pete grinned uncomfortably. Bev chuckled, then circumvented the room, looking for Kristin. He couldn't travel two feet without being stopped.

While in conversation with *Rock Hard Magazine* publicist Rebecca Haviland, Bev shot a subtle glance across the room to a dark, middle-aged man standing against the wall. Tired-looking. Chiseled features. Shadow of a beard. He had his hands behind his waist and stared at Bev, eyes contemplating him intensely. The man wasn't at all familiar. Bev returned his attention to Rebecca.

"Douche bag! There's someone here you should meet," Jake said.

Bev turned away from Rebecca, suddenly disengaged. "Excuse me," he told her, grinning.

Jake brought over a thirtyish, suit-wearing man with a grin as wide as a city bus. "Let me introduce you to Bobby SanSouci." Jake leaned over and whispered with sour breath in Bev's face, "He's with Epic. They're talking about renegotiating your contract for three more albums." Jake grinned.

Bev smiled. This *was* good news. "Pleased to meet you, Bobby."

Bobby kept on smiling, didn't say word. Couldn't, really. Jake was all over it. "We'll call tomorrow and arrange a meeting. Sound good, Bobby?"

Bobby nodded.

"Now go get laid. We're not talking any more business tonight!" Jake winked at Bev, leaned over, whispered, "He's a piece of fucking cake, Bev. You're gonna be richer than rich!" Jake's lips were wet with drool.

"Thank you, douche bag," Bev said sarcastically, and again, Jake filtered into the crowd, cheeks glowing red, spewing more innocent abuse around. The man really enjoyed being outlandish. Just this last tour, Jake had gone on a binge in Kansas City and ended up trying to take on the entire Royals baseball team, calling them a bunch of ass-slapping faggots. Luckily, some of the road crew were there to bail Jake's ass out before any real damage could occur.

"Bev?" Rebecca Haviland, still waiting. Smiling adoringly.

"Oh . . . I'm sorry," he said, tossing a glance over to the spot where the dark man had stood. Gone. "Any chance we can do this another time? I haven't seen my daughter in nine months, and she's supposed to be here."

She nodded, as though expecting him to shrug her off. "Call me on Monday. We'd like to get the story done for—"

"Daddy!"

She appeared from the crowd like an angel. She'd grown since the last time he saw her. Gone were the pudgy cheeks, the innocent eyes, even the dark freckles. His little girl had turned into a woman, just like that. She ran over and wrapped her arms around him and hugged him tightly. He kissed her soft cheek, just as he'd done a million times in the past, and even now, it felt no differently than it had when she was a baby.

They broke the clutch, holding hands. He stepped back to admire her. Five-four. A hundred fifteen pounds. Blond hair, walnut eyes, a beautician's make-over. She wore low-rise jeans and a tank top that revealed too much of her breasts. Suddenly, his admiration turned to offense. This was his *daughter*.

"I missed you so much!" she cried, bear-hugging him again. More smacking kisses. Morbidly, he thought of some of the girls he met backstage while on tour. Was his daughter just like them? No . . . Kristin was *classy*. Driven. They may have looked the same, but there was a marked distinction. All you had to do was peer a little deeper into their intentions. *There's* where you'd find the difference.

"How've you been, hon?" Bev beamed, unable to control the flow of love for his girl.

"Oh, so busy. There's so much to talk about! I finished another article for *Rock Scene*."

"The one about . . . uh, I know you told me about it . . ."

"The decline of the L.A. rock band."

"Yeah, that one. When's it coming out?"

"Next month's issue."

"Wonderful. Any new projects?"

"Well . . . yeah . . ."

"Tell me about it!"

"I will . . . but not now, Dad. This is *your* party!" Her eyes widened with genuine excitement. "We'll talk about it soon. Now that you're back, we'll have plenty of time, I hope. How long are you gonna be home for?"

"At least until spring. I wrote some songs on the road, but need to get into the rehearsal studio pronto.

Epic wants me to start recording in a few weeks. Plus, they're talking about extending my contract for three more CDs. Jake's working on it."

Her face lit up. "You serious?"

"Yep," he smiled, hugging her again. She smelled amazing, like rose petals. *Just like Julianne used to smell.* They broke the clutch. He eyed her pierced navel, then asked, "So what's with the outfit?"

She smiled. "Dad . . ."

"I'm serious . . . you look great and all, but damn, you're my daughter."

She did a pirouette, then said jokingly, "You know what the tabloids say."

Nice way to skirt the subject.

"Well, I'll be a nun's tit!" Jake barged in like a storm cloud, throwing lightning bolts. "Damn, you look *fine!*" he said to Kristin. "Bev, if I were you, I'd take her out on the road with me. Girl like this should never be left home alone."

Bev winked playfully at Kristin.

"Hi, Jake," Kristin said.

They remained in conversation for a few minutes, Jake close-talking with vodka-beer breath, Kristin nonchalantly leaning back, smiling, doing her best to avoid contact with the overbearing man. Bev did his best to pay attention to the unimportant conversation, but his gaze was suddenly drawn across the room to the dark man again, who was now standing near the doorway. He peered back at Bev, eyebrows downcast, then bowed his head and exited the party.

". . . isn't that right, Bev? Bev?"

Bev focused back to the conversation at hand, at once concluding that he didn't miss much. He nodded. "Absolutely."

Jake roared something close to a laugh, then staggered away. Kristin smiled. "How do you put up with him?"

"It's all business."

Bev felt sleepy. His shoulders were knotted and slumped, his eyes red and itchy from cigarette smoke. He paced away from the cluster of people near the door and checked his watch. Nearly one A.M. The party had finally thinned some, and the man of the hour was more than ready to head home. He'd said his hellos to everyone, chatted with all the important people (and more than a few unimportant ones), and now looked forward to sleeping in his own bed again. Hadn't done that in nine months.

Jake was still on his feet, but no longer going strong. He wore his last drink on his pants and had chewed his fingernails until they bled. Two road assistants had him supported, each with a burly arm over their shoulders, leading him out the door.

Bev yawned, finally alone. He glanced fondly at Kristin across the room, engaged in an enthusiastic dialogue with Rebecca Haviland. Kristin had aspired to be a music journalist from a very young age. Her love for the music that Daddy played seemed intuitive, coupled with a predominant desire to create. Bev had offered her guitar and piano lessons, but she showed limited interest in making music. Instead Kristin wanted to know about the people who made the music and who worked behind the scenes. Tirelessly, she researched every nuance of the business, and, by the time she entered high school, was penning reviews of her father's music and publishing them in her school paper and the local city rags. When Bev signed with Epic,

Kristin immediately landed a job at *Rock Scene,* a newly published zine with a seminational circulation. Her articles found an audience among the mostly male readership, who probably were taken with her looks, too. *Rock Scene* didn't pay very well, but it served as the perfect stepping-stone to magazines such as *Spinner* and *Rock Hard Magazine.*

He winked at Kristin. She smiled. Rebecca smiled.

Scratch . . . scratch . . . scratch . . .

His head again. Jesus. That feeling. Like persistent fingers probing his skull. He gripped his temples.

Then a voice.

In his head.

Bevant Mathers . . .

Deep. Whispering. Distant. It echoed and faded. The scratching then stopped. Soon thereafter, he felt fine. Just tired. But the voice. Something . . . something bugged him about it.

It wasn't until thirty minutes later, while he rode in the quiet cruise of the limo, that he realized what it was.

It had an accent.

Two

At 1:37 A.M., Bev asked the limo driver to stop at the Ocean Crest Diner, a quarter mile away from his home. Bev lived in an adobe-style rental home south of L.A., in Torrance. He realized that he could very well afford a million-dollar home, but hadn't had the time or energy to pick up and move. And besides, he really *liked* his place. It had that lived-in, struggling-rock-star feel to it, gloomy and tight with CDs and amps and guitars. He also knew that in the music business, as quickly as fame and fortune came, it could disappear as well, and at his age, he wasn't quite certain how long the ride would last. One bad album and you were toast. He'd decided to be prudent, play his cards safe, and stay in the modest dwelling until his fortune reached disposable levels.

The diner was empty save for a young couple sharing one side of a booth and four teens who might very well have been at the concert tonight. He hoped not—he wasn't up for any attention. He sat at the counter, ordered a fresh turkey wrap and fries, then rubbed his tired eyes and thought of the sounds inside his head. He frowned, worried. The scratching had come first . . . muffled, yet striking enough to be heard above the blare of music emanating from the speakers on stage. Then came the ponderous desire to flee the stage. Fatigue, he told himself. Exhaustion. Nine months on the road will do that to a man.

The waitress, birdlike and demure, brought his food with no smile. She trudged away and sat in a corner near the kitchen, counting her meager tips. He ate his wrap, staring at the her. She looked up.

"Get ya something else?"

"No. No, thank you." She went back to estimating her net worth for the evening.

Bev heard the door creak open behind him. Tapping footsteps approached.

The waitress looked up. "Take a seat anywhere. I'll be right with you."

The unseen patron remained silent. Bev nibbled on a fry. The footsteps crossed behind him. A dark silhouette appeared in his peripheral vision and sat three stools away.

Bev rubbed his eyes, ran his hands through his hair. *There's fifteen damn stools and the guy has to sit three away from me?* The waitress walked over. Bev, focusing on his food, heard the man order black coffee. Bev ate. The man sipped. Neither looked at the other. In a minute, the man stood to leave, leaving money on the counter.

Casually, Bev glanced up.

It was the dark man from the Forum's backstage

party. Middle-aged. Tall, legs like stilts. Short hair, tousled. Defined. Eyes dark like charcoal, staring at Bev.

Bev felt a sense of uneasiness. The man stood there unmoving, looking at Bev intensely, as if at that moment he'd planned to break the law and would let nothing get in his way.

He nodded once at Bev, and it was at this moment that Bev saw the man trembling. "Good show."

Bev nodded back. "Thanks."

And then the man discreetly slipped a plain beige envelope onto the counter between them . . . not close enough so that Bev could easily reach out and grab it, but not too far away, either.

Quickly, the man paced away and exited the diner. The door creaked shut behind him.

Bev glanced toward the door, saw the man's shadow vanish into the black night. The young couple in the booth stood to leave. Bev put his head down so he wouldn't be recognized, and his eyes caught sight of the beige envelope. On it, inscribed in handwritten block letters, was his name:

BEV MATHERS

He rubbed a hand on his cheek, looked out the door, back at the envelope, then at the waitress, who was sipping coffee and trying to stay awake.

Bev looked at it again, then leaned forward and grabbed it. Crisp, sealed. He ran a finger along the pointed edges, staring at his name written in dark, hard contrast.

The door burst open. A group of young adults entered, disrupting the interior calm and startling Bev. He spun on his stool and looked up at them.

They looked at him. The recognition was obvious in their widening, disbelieving eyes.

"Holy shit, it's Bev Mathers!" one girl cried.

"Where?" asked another at the back of the group. They fanned themselves so all could witness the sudden miracle. Bev could do nothing but smile. He tucked the envelope into his back pocket and stood to leave, hoping to avoid the inevitable. He nodded an acknowledgment at their grinning faces.

"Great show tonight, Bev!" a young man lauded.

"Yeah!" the others agreed in near unison.

"Thanks, guys," Bev replied. "Glad you enjoyed it."

"Yeah!" they all extolled. Finally, one added, "Can we get an autograph?"

Bev nodded, reluctantly complying, signing odd items like brown paper bags, T-shirts, and white paper place mats pinched from the counter. The waitress and a cook looked on with curiosity, clearly not knowing who Bev Mathers was. While signing, Bev answered their impromptu questions, then shook hands with them, paid his bill, and fled the diner to the secure refuge of the limo.

Ten minutes later, the limo dropped Bev off in the driveway leading to his home. As he exited the back seat, a newspaper truck ripped by, breaking the deadened silence of the night in its promise to deliver the most up-to-date details of the nation's events. He paced up the stone steps leading to the front door of his house; below, a slate embankment fell fifteen feet to an adornment of azalea bushes. Behind the house, a half-mile of undeveloped woodland extended all the way to the freeway, a hidden symphony of crickets proudly performing their anthem. At his door, he waved to the limo driver, who returned the gesture and drove off into the night.

In the distance, thunder rumbled. Sheet lightning immediately flashed. He looked to the sky. Dark purple clouds roiled in the distance.

For the first time in nine months, Bev Mathers entered his home.

Just as he'd left it. Clean. Neat. Kristin had a cleaning service come once a month to take care of the dust and cobwebs. The bay windows overlooking the woods glimmered; the raised brick fireplace and pine walls absorbed the color of the throws; in his bedroom, the crisp whiteness of the bed's comforter invited him. He used the bathroom, then investigated his "office," a makeshift studio with foam-padded walls packed tightly with amps, stereos, guitars, and sixteen-track recording equipment: a reunion with old friends.

Back in the bedroom, he tossed his clothes on the floor and crawled beneath the covers. He shut off the light and stared into the darkness. In the familiarity of his home, his ears rang, nearly drowning out the rain now pelting the roof. His mind raced over his near-perfect performance tonight, all the people he'd talked to at the party, and Kristin. He'd never gotten a chance to say goodnight to her. Where had she gone? More than likely idling the hours away with Rebecca Haviland, the *Rock Hard Magazine* gal.

And then he thought of the dark stranger, milling about the party, eyeing him, showing up at the diner. The eerie reality of the situation set in, Bev realizing now that he'd been *followed*. He remembered the envelope—the stranger's obvious intent had been to deliver it to him. And that objective had been successful. It was wedged in the back pocket of the jeans he'd worn, strewn on the floor alongside the bed. He considered getting out of bed to retrieve it, but his weary body stifled his curiosity. *It'll be there in the morning,* he told himself.

He closed his eyes and in seconds was asleep.

Three

Bev dreamed.

Hot, boiling lava flowing around his buried knees, he waded through the molten asphalt; it spit at him, glowing red beneath a shifting layer of black crust. Around him, hundreds of poor souls were being taken down by the brutal tide. He approached a small, barren beach where he saw Kristin and Jake. The two stood naked on the rocky shore, holding hands, shouting, "Come here! Come to us!" He tried to move forward, but the tide of lava held him back. Skeletal arms wrapped in liquid flesh reached out from the depths of the flow, grasping at his waist, his chest, his arms. His head swelled, and from deep within he felt the scratching, persistent fingers burrowing beyond the surface of his skull into the tender matter of his brain. The melting hands rooted into his skin, blood pooling out from his chest, ripping his beating heart free from its cavity.

He stood, only feet from the rock shore where Kristin and Jake waited in glistening nudity, outstretched arms falling to their sides in defeat. They turned and padded away into the darkness, leaving Bev alone to die . . . .

He awoke, eyes wide, heart pounding. *Jesus, what a nightmare!* For a time he lay still, breathing heavily. He shifted his legs and felt a hot, moist sheen on his body, as if he'd just emerged from a sauna. He kicked the covers off with one leg. He saw raindrops clinging to the bay window like ornaments, gray light filtering through them in dull slivers.

His cell phone rang.

Startled, he crawled sideways across the bed, stomach heavy and knotted, head banging fiercely. He followed the ring. Somewhere on the floor . . . there, still clipped to his jeans, the soft green light from the display signaling him like a tiny beacon. He reached down and grabbed the phone, pulling his jeans up with it. A few coins jingled to the floor.

From the back pocket, an envelope slipped free and landed amid the coins. He pressed the Send button on the phone. "This is Bev."

"Wake you up?" Jake said.

"Uh, yeah. I guess."

"You guess? C'mon, douche bag, either I did or I didn't."

"I'm awake now. What time is it?"

"Almost noon. How you feeling?"

"Well, considering that I just woke up . . ."

"I didn't puke, so I'm ahead of the game."

Bev laughed. "To what do I owe the pleasure?"

"We've got dinner at six. My place. Gonna discuss your future. Then a party at eight."

"Jake . . ."

"Don't 'Jake' me. Epic is very serious about keeping you on board for the next few years."

"Jesus, Jake, it's my first day back in nine months. Make them wait a week."

"Listen to me, we can't let them sit on it. They might change their minds, I'm telling you—"

"If they want me, then they can wait a week. I'm officially on vacation."

"Bev, this is serious shit, and I—"

"I'm serious too, Jake. I need to spend some time with my daughter. No distractions. No ongoing negotiations. Got it? I'm freakin' tired and I need a break. Make an appointment for next week sometime."

"Jesus Christ, you're fucking nuts," he rasped. "Success has mushed your brain."

What a pain in the ass, Bev thought, then remembered his dream and changed the subject. "Hey, you see Kristin leave last night?"

"Kristin? Oh . . . you mean that hot little—"

"Watch it, Jake . . ."

"Fine," he murmured. "No, I didn't see her leave. Frankly, I don't remember much of anything from last night other than Epic's proposal—and that I didn't puke."

"You're such a charmer. Listen, I gotta go."

"Well . . . what about Epic?"

"Next week."

"Jesus, you're mad."

"I'm a rock star. I have to be."

Jake laughed, defeated. "Fuck. You make my job so damn hard."

"Gotta work hard to earn the big bucks, my man."

"Yeah, yeah, whatever. Forget about dinner, then. Just try to make the party. Okay?"

"I'll try." Bev disconnected the line. He ran a hand through his hair, rose from bed, and staggered into the bathroom. He showered and shaved, and a half hour later was a new man, no headache, no fatigue. And no odd finger-probing sensation in his head.

His stomach rolled with hunger, though. Nine months out of the apartment had left him with nothing to eat; he hoped Kristin would be available to meet for lunch soon.

Back in the bedroom, he got a cigarette out of the pack on the nightstand, lit it, then went to the sliding closet. Folded atop the white wicker hamper were three pairs of jeans; his suitcase was still in transit along with the guitars he'd taken on tour. He pulled the boot-cut denims from the top of the pile, grabbed them by the waistband, and shook the stiffness out of them.

A beetle the size of a prune fell from the jeans and dropped to the wood floor with a tiny audible *clack*. It quickly righted itself and skittered away toward the bathroom.

"Jesus!" Bev dropped the jeans. In a hesitant panic, he reached into the closet, grabbed the closest shoe, and dove after the fleeing insect. With a quick instinctual swing, he brought the shoe's heel down on the vacating bug. It made a wet crunching sound. He ground it back and forth, doing his best to finish the job. Once satisfied, he raised the shoe. Yellow custard oozed from the beetle's shell. Two of its six or eight legs were stuck to the heel. Still, amazingly, it wasn't dead. It continued on in a slow, staggering amble—a last-ditch attempt for survival. *This is the reason why cock-*

roaches and beetles have been around since the dinosaurs, he thought. With a flick of the wrist, he whacked at it again, then plucked the cigarette from his mouth and put it out on the beetle's crushed back. It wasn't going anywhere now.

He hurried into the bathroom and grabbed a handful of tissues. He used them to clean away the soft carcass from the floor and the shoe. After flushing the tissues, he went back and picked up his strewn jeans.

Another beetle fell out and raced across the floor, its sanctuary disturbed. "Son of a bitch!" Bev shouted, throwing the jeans down again. He watched with dismay as the bug quickly sequestered itself in the dense safety of the closet.

Bev's heart pounded, his breathing quickened. "What's with the fucking bugs?" He slid the doors to the closet fully open, exposing his entire wardrobe.

He leaned down and peered into the dusty darkness beneath his hanging clothes.

Six or seven large beetles like the ones he saw were walking on the back wall of the closet. Antennae flickering. Legs racing. Shells fluttering like wings. Some disappeared behind his clothes; others came back down to replace them.

He shouted out. Staggered back. His skin crawled. At once he felt as though they were on him, and he slapped his hands all over his exposed skin. *What the fuck?*

The apartment was infested. And he'd *slept* here last night. Suddenly, his skull itched from within, the invisible fingers digging along the thin area where brain met skull, as though they were creating a space there to settle. He quickly grabbed the jeans from the bed, the ones he'd worn last night, and shook them briskly. No beetles. He jumped into them, then checked his shirt, which reeked of smoke and sweat, and put that on, too. He peered at his shirts hanging in the closet, considered grabbing a fresh one, then decided against it.

Compulsively, he got down on his hands and knees again and peered into the closet. Beetles raced everywhere—on the back wall, on the floor, in his shoes. They seemed to really like it in there: cool, dark, dusty. Safe.

Suddenly, the room grew hot. Oppressive. A sweat coated his forehead and back. His armpits dripped. He stood, slightly dizzied, those phantom fingers still digging. He walked to the wall and put a hand against the central air vent. Cool. *What the fuck? I must be getting sick. And my apartment . . . it's infested!*

He grabbed his cell phone from the bed. His keys and wallet were still in his pockets. The air suddenly kicked off. The apartment fell into a strange silence. He shivered—cold despite the sweat on his body.

Then he eyed the envelope on the floor. His handwritten name hypnotized him: *Bev Mathers*. He picked it up, then fled the odd infestation that had become his home.

The door closed behind him. He stood on the cement landing in the gray drizzle of a Saturday afternoon, taking in long deep breaths. By the time he reached his car parked in the detached garage a hundred feet away, the scratching in his head had vanished.

Four

In a room laden with darkness, the man prayed. In his heart, a great ache loomed. In his head, the profound beat of the blood pumping fearfully through his veins. He searched the gloom for a guiding light but found only desolation. Loneliness.

Behind him, a quiet clearing of a throat. He turned. Bathed in the flickering gold of a candle's flame, a teenaged boy. Used. Forlorn. *Searching*. The front of the boy's pants were stained with urine; he seemed not to notice or care. The boy walked over, placed a four-fingered hand out. "It is time." His breath reeked of putrification, of things charred.

The man shuddered under the weight of the boy's message, closed his eyes in search of salvation, for himself and for the boy. Like many others, he'd found his God, a God who weighed him down with foul intent: a savior who accepted a host of menstrual blood and bile, who drank from a chalice formed of excrement.

Within their proximity, a vibration in the walls commenced. A calling of all souls. The man rose to his feet. With blind fury, he seized the boy by the collar and dragged him to a chair across the dank room.

"Who is your God?" the man rasped, eyes burning.

The boy cowered. Perspiring. Sour stench. Through clenched teeth, he replied, "Allieb."

The man released his hold, eyes boring holes into the poor young soul. "Go and pray." The boy quickly fled the room.

The man wiped his brow with an unclean handkerchief, then exited the room.

He roamed the dark, quiet hallways of *In Domo,* gingerly passing unoccupied rooms, peering in with disgust as if they were open wounds. As he moved closer toward the darkness, a tremendous weariness beset him. He prayed for strength. The vibration in the walls grew deeper. In its wake, a chanting began. He forced himself up a flight of stairs, into an antechamber where nearly fifty people prayed in icy, bitter unison. In his heart, he kissed his God and moved off to feign prayer to another.

Two hours later, the man was alone in his room. Exhausted, he carried his burdenous weight into the bathroom, stared at the mold in the sink. He lodged a finger down his throat and vomited blood.

On the floor by his bare feet lay a towel reeking of mildew. He grabbed it and wiped his mouth of the taint. He stood unmoving, catching his breath. His wits. He rubbed his weary eyes. Waited for the world to stop moving. Pink saliva pooled from his mouth to the broken-tiled floor.

Back in his room, he reevaluated his mission. He doubted himself and his ability to perform what seemed an impossible task.

Faith alone could not defeat true power, he knew. There needed to be a spirited adversary with strength enough to fight.

He knew just where to find it, but getting it would be a daunting task.

Five

A few minutes after leaving his house, Bev Mathers called information and got the number for an exterminator in Torrance.

"What's the problem?" the woman, a receptionist, asked.

"Beetles. Big ones. In my closet," he explained.

"Beetles? Not cockroaches?"

"No. Definitely beetles. Hard shells. Roundish. Lots of legs."

"Probably water bugs. You got a leak?"

"No . . . Jesus, what the hell difference does it make? Just get someone over there to take care of the problem." He gave the woman the address. He'd left the door unlocked (a would-be burglar wouldn't be too smitten with the occupants, he figured) in hope of an exterminator's quick arrival. She promised someone would be there within the hour.

"Bugs'll be dead and gone by the time you get home, Mr. Mathers. There'll be a strong odor from the chemicals, so I suggest sleeping someplace else, just for one night."

"Thank you."

After hanging up, he dialed Kristin's cell phone. While on tour, Bev would call his daughter regularly, sometimes twice a day. Just hearing her voice for a few seconds would give him the strength to carry on when the grind of touring seemed an impossible task. At times, when he called late at night as he lay in his dark hotel room with his ears still ringing, her voice sounded so much like Julianne's used to, soft, pleasant, loving, triggering welcoming memories of his youthful past.

"Hello . . ."

"Just wake up?"

"About a yawn ago."

"You sound awful," he said.

"Probably look awful, too."

"How was the rest of your night?" he asked, looking at his watch. Almost one. *Rock star kid.*

"Great. I'm sorry I didn't get a chance to say goodbye. I looked but couldn't find you, it was so crowded. I ended up leaving with the *Rock Hard* publicist."

"Yeah? You hit it off with her, huh?"

"Uh . . . yeah, I guess."

"Where'd you go afterwards?"

"Her place."

"Her place . . ."

"She had a small party there."

"Uh . . . I don't think I want to know."

Silence. "Dad . . ."

"Kristin, you're only twenty-one."

"And of legal age to make porn—but I don't."

Stomach turning, he decided to change the subject. "We on for lunch?"

"Sure. Can you give me half an hour?"

"Yeah, of course. Meet you at Danfords?"

"Danfords in thirty."

"Great. See you then. Ciao, babe."

While he was speaking to Kristin, the drizzle had stopped. The gray clouds above were thinning. Soon, Bev figured, the sun would begin to spread its temperate rays upon Los Angeles and fill the beaches and parks with people. Bev drove west toward the beach, then north on the San Diego Freeway. Kristin lived in Manhattan Beach, just north of Torrance, where Danfords was located. Lunch at Danfords had become a ritual for the two of them, where they could sit outside on the pier in wooden booths and enjoy seafood while gazing out at the Pacific's soothing waves crashing upon the shore.

While turning onto the freeway, Bev felt the ghostly fingers in his head again.

They'd returned with a vengeance, it seemed. The scratching sensation turned to digging. His chest tightened. He labored to draw in a breath. His hands were white-knuckled on the steering wheel.

And then, the voice.

Bevant . . .

The same voice he'd heard last night. Foreign. Deep. Soft, but intense.

I know that accent, he thought.

At first, the voice had alarmed him. Now he felt anger. He felt a sudden, overwhelming desire to pick a fight. He wanted to scream, to punch, to hit, to *attack*. He slammed his fists against the steering wheel, once, twice, three times. Then, instantly, he became overpowered by a feeling of free falling, as though the road beneath the car had fallen away, leaving him to plunge infinitely into a bottomless pit.

He felt his foot pressing down on the gas. The car sped forward.

Digging, digging, digging.

Crumbling.

An odd odor rose into his nostrils. Burning charcoal. In his sights he saw red embers glowing, flitting across his vision like flies on a television screen. His body began to tremble. He noticed his car closing in behind a black BMW. His mind told him to decelerate, but his body remained frozen in position, feet unable to shift from gas to brake. He could see the driver in the BMW glancing irritably in his rearview mirror, his hands raised briefly in frustration. Nausea twirled in Bev's gut. His head spun. He spoke aloud, "Please don't faint, don't faint." His voice sounded distant, as if coming from far away.

In the next moment, the mind-fingers stopped their scratching. Soon thereafter, the burning odor vanished. At once he regained control of his body and was able to slow the car, the speedometer's needle diving from eighty to forty in ten seconds. Ahead, the BMW sped off in the distance.

Now the drivers behind him got pissed. Horns sounded and tires screeched as cars and SUVs sped by him. More hateful glances came his way. Carefully, he crossed the lanes and rode the tar-notched shoulder for a half-mile until he reached the next off-ramp. He exited the freeway, then pulled into a gas station on the corner, one exit away from the restaurant; he could take Redondo Beach Boulevard from here, no problem.

The car idled. He squeezed his fists. Sweat. *Anxiety.*

"What the fuck is happening to me?" he said aloud, wiping his brow. A chill ran through his body. He wondered, *Am I sick? Am I crazy? Jesus, am I having a heart attack?* Impulsively, he picked up his cell phone, called information, and got the number for his internist. *Haven't been to the doctor in a few years, anyway.*

"It's a . . . a mild emergency," he told the receptionist, who picked up on the first ring.

She put him on hold. He listened to canned Neil Diamond. She came back on: "The doctor can see you tomorrow at noon."

"Tomorrow's Sunday."

"Yes, the doctor keeps Sunday hours, twelve to five. He's closed on Mondays."

Bev thanked her. Crazily, in this short time, he felt better. No more scratching; no anxiety; no anger; no *voice*. No other odd sensations.

What the fuck is happening to me?

The sweat on his face dried. He looked through the windshield. A station attendant eyed him curiously. Bev nodded, then put the car into drive and slowly made his way to meet Kristin, feeling as good as he had yesterday before all this insanity started.

Six

The drive off the San Diego Freeway took him along Redondo Beach Boulevard and Alondra Park. Alondra Park offered 315 acres of native plant gardens, landscaped forest glens, a fishing lake, and a massive sprawl of woodlands made up of trees and meadows. After Julianne died, Bev would come here to lament, wheeling his two-year-old baby around and watching the more than 350 species of birds that made Alondra Park their home. At times he used to imagine that out there among the millions of birds flew a solitary envoy with a message from Julianne—one that would transcendentally guide his directionless life toward an acceptable level of happiness. He walked the park nearly every day, soul-searching, hoping to find some kind of psychic connection with a winged spiritual shepherd.

At a time when he was willing to write off his prayers as frivolous and impossible, his message was delivered. He'd been walking stiffly along the lakeside, pushing the stroller, probing the calm waters and the families of fowl diving for fish, chanting *Ohm-Nama-Shivaya,* a tantric drone that, according to Buddhist teachings, brought good fortune to those who sought its "inner serenity." A single white swan swam gracefully to the shoreline, climbed out, and stared at Bev. In his mind he heard Julianne's voice telling him that she rested comfortably in a beautiful place blessed with goodness, and that she would continually watch over him and Kristin until the very moments they came to be with her. The swan continued its hypnotic stare, head bobbing, wings fluttering. It then paced gingerly to Bev and rubbed its feathers against his weakening legs. Julianne's voice returned to his mind and told him to take his talent to the skies.

The swan, suddenly out of trance and seemingly frightened of its unexpected location, quickly waddled back into the safe haven of the lake.

Upon the swan's retreat, the voice left Bev. Darkness immediately consumed him, and he fainted to the ground. Some nearby park-goers assisted him until he regained consciousness a few moments later.

Within a month's time, Bev had discovered a newfound interest in music. He'd never sung a note before in his life, but now had the ability to carry a tune across three octaves in a voice comparable to the seventies rock gods that he and Julianne enjoyed listening to so much. Soon thereafter he began music lessons, and in a year had mastered the guitar and piano. Not once did he ever consider himself a prodigy; he'd struggled daily for months with his instruments and his voice, determined to learn the art of rock and roll so he, too, could entertain like Robert Plant or Jimi Hendrix had during the sixties and seventies. The message from Julianne had not been a gift of talent, but instead a catalyst leading him in a rightful direction, giving him *drive,* just as he invoked while meditating.

Later, Bev would convince himself that he had not made contact with Julianne, that he'd made contact with his inner soul, and thereby discovered his true purpose in life.

Still, there was the swan . . . and her voice.

Driving by the park, he couldn't help but think of the hundreds of walks he'd taken there, and of the day his life changed forever. He remembered the flush of joy he felt after leaving the park that day with Kristin in tow, how he'd told the then two-year-old that things were going to change for them now that Daddy had "found himself." These memories had some mystical purpose behind them. He'd lost Julianne, but gained a goal and the drive to reach his newly found ambitions, that of a devoted father and aspiring musician.

Ten minutes after passing Alondra Park, Bev pulled into the parking lot at Danfords Restaurant. The sand-strewn blacktop abutted Manhattan Beach, which ran a hundred yards to the crashing ocean. The shore glowed whitely beneath the high sun, scatterings of sunbathers and surfers and picnickers enjoying the afternoon's pleasantries. Bev got out of his car and paced across the lot, hidden behind the nondescript privacy of Ray-Bans and a Dodgers cap. Celebrities in L.A. kept this tandem disguise handy. When wearing these, you didn't necessarily hide the fact that you were a celebrity, just *which one* you were.

A few children burst through the door of the restaurant as Bev walked in. Their playful shouts hit a shudder within him. He thought for a moment that the brain-fingers were returning. Thankfully, they weren't. But the piercing voices of the three kids and their mothers aggravated the looming headache he'd been trying to stave off.

Kristin was here, waiting inside. She greeted him in white nylon running shorts, a black T-shirt, and sneakers. She wore no makeup, and her hair was tied up in a scrunchie. The thrown-together outfit reflected her frame of mind: tired and not in the mood for anything too important.

"Hi," she said with a thin smile.

Bev beamed. They shared a hug; she retained an odor of last night's party, too. A chip off the old block.

"Guess I really did drag you out of bed."

"It's okay, it's worth it. . . . I'm so thrilled to have you home now."

"Good to be home."

A young hostess escorted them to one of two dozen booths on the outside pier. They ordered a bucket of mini-Coronas and faced the healing vista of the ocean. Cool, salty wind escaped the ceaseless motion of the surf and kissed their silent faces—nature's rhythm, offering its comforting welcome, which they embraced. A waitress came and took their orders. While they waited, they drank and spoke of their careers, Bev asking Kristin questions about her writing and then her personal life. She revealed as much as she'd been willing, or so it appeared, until he brought up the night before and Rebecca Haviland.

"Dad, please . . ."

The waitress returned with their meals. Bev stayed silent until she finished serving them. Then he said, "Look, you're my daughter. I raised you all by myself since you were a year old. . . . I'm only looking out for your best interests, as much as I can."

"You've mentioned that. A few times before." She raised one eyebrow.

"Just want the best for my girl."

"Understood. And I want the best for my dad. So . . . any women in your life?"

"How'd this get turned around?"

"Answer my question, and I'll answer yours."

"Wiseass!"

"I can be. Sometimes. So . . . have you hooked up with anyone, or what?"

"No—no one special."

"Just your road hos, huh?" She giggled.

"Kristin . . ."

"Woo-hoo, Dad!"

"All right, enough. I don't do those things. Anymore. Frankly, I can't handle it."

"You oughta take out Rebecca Haviland."

Bev eyed her suspiciously. "Rebecca?"

"Yeah . . . she's available, you know."

"Well, I didn't know that, nor do I really care. Actually, I thought that you—"

"Why not? She's pretty. And she kinda looks like Mom, you know, from the pictures."

Bev thought about it. The publicist *did* resemble Julianne a bit. Maybe just in the eyes. He wondered how he hadn't noticed this until Kristin brought it up. "No one could ever replace your mother."

The somber note segued into a few moments of silence where they enjoyed their meals. Bev ate a seafood salad while Kristin attacked a cod sandwich and fries. The food, the cool wind, and the fresh air seemed to have revived Kristin a bit. She ate and smiled and chatted pleasantly between bites. When they were finished, they lit cigarettes and stared back out into the ocean blue.

"That was good," she said, and the way the sun hit her at that moment made her look more like Julianne than ever. The ache it brought struck him hard, and he looked down into his empty plate.

"Last night, at the party," Kristen said, changing the subject, "there was a man looking for you. Said he had something important to give you."

Bev looked up at her. With all the day's distractions, the bugs and the odd physical discomforts, he'd forgotten all about it. He slid his hand into his back pocket. The envelope. Still there. "Son . . . of . . . a . . . bitch." He pulled it out. Crisp. Beige. He unfolded it.

His scrawled name met his hesitant gaze. His stomach fluttered uncomfortably.

"What'd he look like, this man you spoke to?" His gaze was still on the envelope.

"I don't know—didn't really look at him too closely. Tall, serious. Kinda disheveled. Didn't look like he was there to have a good time like everyone else." She gazed inquisitively at the envelope in his hand.

"It's the same guy."

"Who?"

He shook his head. "He . . . this man you're talking about . . . he followed me to the Ocean Crest Diner last night." He held up the envelope. "He gave me this."

"What is it?"

"A note, I suppose. Has my name on it." He held it out for her to see.

"What's it say?"

"Don't know. Didn't open it. Honestly, I'm not sure I really want to."

"How come?"

"It's kinda creepy. Wouldn't you agree?"

"Well . . . I suppose. But then again, it's probably just a piece of fan mail, you know? Guy figures that if he sends something to the fan club address, it's gonna sit in a pile with a million other letters until some poor temp is hired to dig through the mountain and mail back Bev Mathers carbon-copy photos. That's pretty much the drill, isn't it?"

"I resent that. I read all my fan letters and respond to each one personally." He grinned.

"Yeah, and I'm the President's daughter."

He frowned and tucked a finger under the flap of the envelope and ran it underneath. The folded edge of a letter peeked out. Simultaneously, last night's scenario filtered back in flashes, the stranger and his low-profile delivery of the envelope. *Too strange.*

Bev shivered.

Did he really want to expose the contents?

Kristin waited, eyes roaming back and forth between Bev and the envelope. He reached in, pinched the beige parchment, pulled it out. It was folded in thirds. He opened it. It read:

BEVANT MATHERS

YOUR PRESENCE IS REQUESTED FOR AN
EXCLUSIVE GATHERING
SUNDAY, NOVEMBER 10
A LIMO WILL ARRIVE AT YOUR RESIDENCE
AT 6:00 PM

BE AVAILABLE

Kristin leaned forward, eyes narrowed. "So . . . what's it say?"

"Looks like an invitation," he replied, staring at his name. *Bevant Mathers.* Nobody ever called him by his full name. Nobody.

Except that voice in his head.

He stared at the paper. Frowned. He didn't like that last line. *Be available.* The invitation had requested his presence, but seemingly *demanded* he be available. It almost read as a . . . threat.

"C'mon . . . what's it say?" she persisted.

He handed her the parchment. She read it in silence. "Strange."

"I agree, considering how it was delivered to me." He explained how the man, after following him to the diner, had discreetly slid the envelope across the counter to him before leaving.

"That *is* weird."

"Think he's a stalker?"

"If so, a very creative one." She exhaled a plume of gray smoke into the wind.

"The man who asked for me last night—did you speak with him at all?"

She shook her head. "No, not really. I was walking around the room looking for you, and he just came up to me and asked if I'd seen you yet, and I said 'no,' and then he told me that he had something important to give you, and when I asked him what it was, he just walked away. That was really it. After that, I got distracted and forgot about him."

"You think he knew you were my daughter?"

"Hmm, not sure. Probably not. If he had, I suppose he could've just asked me to give you the envelope."

Bev was unconvinced. "I don't like this. Maybe I should call the police."

She shook her head. "I don't think that's necessary. There's been no threat. And besides, if you do, the tabloids'll catch wind of it and show up on your porch snapping pictures for their next issue, and then all your fans will come out from under their rocks and start stalking you for real."

"C'mon, I'm not *that* famous."

"I'd still steer clear of bringing it out into the open until . . ." She hesitated, then added, "You know, it's probably only what it appears to be: an invitation. It says that they're gonna send out a limo to pick you up at your place."

"Which means they know where I live. Kristin, listen to me: This guy *followed* me last night, tailed me from the Forum to the diner. And let's not forget that he managed to make his way backstage. That right there tells me he's not working alone. Clearly, he's got some pretty resourceful connections, ones that gave him access to the Forum's restricted areas. I mean, as far I know, there could very well be someone here right now keeping tabs on me." He gazed around the pier at the people dining in the booths, and then toward the bar, where casually dressed men and women were clustered socially around every occupied stool.

She shook her head, grinned, then looked around. "I don't think you have to worry about anyone here . . . except for maybe that guy." She pointed, and Bev turned around. Standing at the pier entrance was Jonas Stolt, the lead singer for Pathway, another local band making their mark with a recent top-forty hit. He recognized Bev and waved. Bev returned the gesture and turned back to Kristin; each respected the other's privacy.

"Ha-ha. Funny."

She handed the invitation back to him. "Well . . . it's not like you've never gotten invited to a party before. Hey, Dad, maybe you'll get lucky and it'll turn out to be one of those ultrasecretive, high-class sex romps. You know, orgy of the stars!" Bev rolled his eyes. She added, "This is L.A., Pops. They go on all the time."

"How would you know?"

"I work for a music tabloid, remember? I know everything that goes on in the business, maybe even more than you." She grinned slyly.

He ran a hand through his hair. "Maybe I'm overreacting. Maybe it is just an invite."

She took a sip of beer. "I wouldn't worry about it too much. You haven't been threatened. Nobody's held a gun to your head."

After a silence, Bev said, "Yeah, I guess you're right. It's just . . . well, I haven't been feeling all that well since I got back, and I guess it's got me a bit worked up." He rubbed his eyes.

"What's wrong?"

Bev explained. He told her about the odd, lightheaded sensation that had come and gone, the disassociation with the music on stage last night, and the episode that occurred while driving on his way here, how he'd felt inexplicably angry and hostile. Plus the sudden anxiety. The out-of-body feeling. He even told her about the bugs in his apartment, and she responded with a look of horror.

He told her everything . . . except one thing.

The voice.

Too serious to discuss, he decided. Institutional stuff. Better left unsaid.

"I made an appointment with the doctor."

"When are you going?"

"Tomorrow. Noon."

"Good. Please let me know how you make out, okay?"

"I will." He stretched his legs out beneath the booth, then chanced another look around at those minding their own business. "What are your plans for the rest of the day?"

"A little R and R. Nothing important. And then Jake's party tonight."

"Jake's party?"

She smiled, her eyes narrowed with disbelief. "He forgot to invite you?"

"I guess . . . then again, maybe he did mention something to me earlier. Can't remember."

"Well, today's his birthday and he's having a party at his house at eight. He mentioned it to me last night. Said you were coming."

"I don't remember him saying anything to me about his birthday."

"Well, you better be there. I was hoping we could spend some more time together. And Rebecca Haviland will be there."

"What is it about Rebecca?"

"She likes you, Dad. And she's a wonderful woman."

Bev laughed uncomfortably. "Drop it, okay?"

Kristen shrugged, sullen. "Okay, okay."

Bev heard a close shuffling of feet behind him, a slight stir of something brushing by. He darted around, looked.

No one was there.

He turned back, audibly breathing out. "What do you say we take a quick walk on the beach?" Suddenly, he wanted to flee the restaurant.

"Sure."

He stood from the booth, stretched his limbs, feeling as though someone was standing right next to him.

Brushing up against him.

He shuddered.

Scratch. Scratch. Scratch. In his head. And then, in a flash, it was gone.

Seven

Bev and Kristin bought plastic bottles of Evian water at the bar and took them along to the beach. White sand glared beneath the sun's rays, splaying a blanket of warmth for the crowd: sunbathers, lifeguards, athletes flexing their muscles for strolling bikinis. Pacific Ocean waves crashing against the surf, into the bodies of waders. They walked northward toward a less populated point, nestled themselves in the sand, and took in the vista.

Silence dominated the moment; Kristin pressing her face to the sky to worship its offer of warmth, Bev taking this time to think of Julianne. They'd met in their late teens after graduating from high school, each of them working cashier shifts at an L.A. Bi-Mart. Quickly, they'd discovered that they'd shared some interests. Like a taste for the hard rock music that had come in from England in the sixties: The Who, Led

Zeppelin, Pink Floyd, Cream. Both had been brought up by aunts after losing their parents at a young age; they couldn't afford college, and yearned to work enough hours to afford small apartments. After a week, they'd started dating steadily, and in two months had pooled their narrow resources and moved into a south L.A. apartment together. After two years of sinful, blissful, faithful, and rather meager living, Julianne got pregnant. It was an unplanned shocker for the teens, who'd always played their lovemaking cards carefully. With no one else to talk to other than themselves, they'd discussed their options and come to a quick conclusion: Their love was special and would last a million lifetimes; their baby was a gift to treasure, and they would keep it and raise it to the best of their abilities. They'd arranged a quick trip to Las Vegas, pledging their vows to each other in a small church off the south end of the strip. Eight months after the young lovers received their license, Kristin was born.

And, as always, when thoughts of Julianne filtered into his mind, Bev flashed back to the accident. How he'd waited at the red light at the not-so-busy intersection of Crandon and Wolfland Road, how there hadn't been any cars at all passing through the green light. And when his signal turned green, he looked both ways anyway because one couldn't be too careful, especially with a baby in the car, and when all seemed clear, he inched out into the intersection, but how could he know that coming down Wolfland Road at sixty miles an hour was a car being driven by a girl who'd just hours earlier drowned her miseries in a bottle of Jack Daniel's and had decided on taking her own life, and what the fuck, how about a couple of innocents along with her? Every cell in his body flinched when he recalled the howling shriek of the tires on the road—an instinctual response from the girl, who might have had second thoughts in the last moments of her life—and he remembered turning, looking past Julianne, who'd just echoed the scream of the tires herself, hands raised in defensive terror as the out-of-control car leaped at them like a shot from a cannon. For a split second he could see the girl behind the wheel of the car; her face had no discernible features, just a black void of nothing in the moment frozen in time, and then there was a different kind of shriek, that of tearing metal, and his world spun away into a black vortex. The next things he recalled were the ambulance sirens and the pain that rose up into the agony of knowing that he'd lost his one and only true love. "What about my daughter?" was all he could say, over and over again, before his blurred vision pooled back into focus and he could see the mangled car, the shattered glass, the blood on the pavement.

The impact had been devastating for Julianne, who'd become instantly unrecognizable in the crushed carnage of their car. And the cops had been correct in their immediate assumptions—miraculously, Bev had managed only bruises from the accident, and thank God for the car seat that had held one-year-old Kristin Mathers; she'd cried terribly but had only internal injuries, resulting in a three-day hospital stay, and she'd made it home just in time for her mother's funeral.

And thus began Bev and Kristin's lives, minus Julianne Mathers.

It always took great strength for Bev to put these hideous memories of catastrophic agony into the appropriate recesses of his mind where they could do no additional damage. To counteract the pain, he utilized another branch of strength to drum up the more mystically pleasurable recollection of his day in Alondra Park, when the swan came to deliver his message from Julianne.

A barking dog shook Bev from his reverie. He and Kristin adjusted their positions on the sand. Two shirtless college-age men ran down the beach, tossing a Frisbee back and forth, splashing in the tide's crescents, and diving into the shallow water to make great catches. A mixed-breed dog with a red bandanna around its neck splashed along the edge of the rushing waves, barking gleefully, hopeful to catch the flying disk in its jaws. In between throws, the two guys, tanned and toned and flexing, peeked over at Bev and Kristin, who were doing their best to avoid their overt gazes; they'd either recognized Bev beneath his hat-and-shades cloak, or were checking out Kristin. Maybe both.

Or, maybe, they were *watching* him.

Finally, the Frisbee was overthrown. Bev blew out a deep breath. Predictable. It landed a few yards from Bev and Kristin.

"Here they come," Kristin said expectantly. "The male species at work."

"They've been looking over here since we sat down." Bev didn't want to press the issue any further: that these guys, expertly camouflaged amid the sunny environment, may very well be keeping tabs on him. *Something isn't right here.*

The dog darted over and clutched the Frisbee in its jaws. Shook it about. Sprayed some sand on Bev and Kristin. The Frisbee throwers rode the dog's wagging tail, both of them male lions, chests out, pearly teeth bared. Their boardshorts rode low on their slender hips; one wore a matching red bandanna around his neck; the other, a seashell necklace.

Bev nodded upon their approach; this simple acknowledgment would hopefully send them on their way.

The guy with the bandanna leaned down, grabbed the Frisbee from the dog. "Here ya go, Garcia." He flung the Frisbee to the left of Bev and Kristin, a hundred feet away, toward the dunes.

The guy with the seashell necklace said, "Bev Mathers, right?"

"That's right," Bev answered impatiently. Kristin smirked, covering her mouth with her right hand.

"Don't mean to bother you, man . . . actually, I'm really not a fan of your music, but I just thought you'd like to know that there's a guy up there in the dunes checking you out with a pair of binoculars. We've been watching him ever since you got here."

"We're guessing he's the press or something," the guy with the bandanna said.

"Where?"

Kristin pulled her hand away from her face. She peered up at the two guys; they eyeballed her up and down and sideways, grinning, vying for her attention. They didn't get it.

The dog returned with the Frisbee and dropped it at Bandanna's feet. He picked it up, flipped it end over end, allowing the sand to spill out. "Don't look now . . . I'll toss the Frisbee toward him. He's up on the dunes, near the restaurant. Under the pier."

Bev eyed Kristin; his quiet apprehension was obvious and seemed to say, *Told you so.* She acknowledged him silently.

Bandanna tossed the Frisbee to the left of Bev, over the heads of two male sunbathers and into the sand alongside the edge of the dunes. The dog took off like a greyhound, racing along the beach, spraying sand and shells in its wake. Bev pretended to watch the sprinting dog, glancing up toward the pier instead.

Indeed, a man was there, standing in the dunes beneath the pier about fifty yards away. He wore sunglasses, khaki slacks, and a black tee. In his hands was a pair of binoculars. He shifted his sights toward the surf.

"Son of a bitch. It looks like the same guy from last night."

The dog raced back with the Frisbee, dropped it at Bev's feet, then ogled him, happily panting and eager for another sprint. Bev reached forward and grabbed it, then stood and faced the ocean. He nodded. "Thanks for the heads-up, guys."

"No problem," they replied, almost in unison, eyes roaming all over Kristin as she stood and brushed the sand from her hips.

Bev held the Frisbee out in front of him. "May I?"

"Go for it," Bandanna said.

He tossed the Frisbee toward the water. The dog and its masters took off after it as it sailed away, caught in the wind.

Kristin, eyes once again targeting the man, said, "Are you sure it's him and not a reporter?"

"Like I said before, I ain't that famous."

"So who is he? A fan?"

Bev glanced up. The man began walking along the dunes, eyes toward the surf. "Nope." He looked at his feet, nervously shifted some sand. "I don't like the smell of this. Why don't we walk down by the water . . . just pretend that you don't know he's watching us."

Lazily, they strolled toward the surf. They passed the

Frisbee throwers, then headed back south along the beach.

Discreetly, Bev peered up toward the pier.

The man was gone.

"He's not there anymore," he said.

Kristin looked around the beach, which grew more crowded as they headed farther south. "Where'd he go? I don't see him." The waves broke against the surf and churned the sand inches from their feet. The crisp contact of ocean on sand, the gentle squawk of the gulls, the ambience of the crowd, usually set Bev at ease. Now it distracted him, seemingly incapable of rescuing his turbulent mind.

Scratch . . . scratch . . . scratch.

Crumble.

The fingers. They reappeared. But unlike their approach at the restaurant, when they quickly vanished, they now persisted, chipping away at the inside of his skull like tiny picks against soft limestone. And like earlier, when he was driving, his nostrils stung with the stench of something burning. Charcoal, or smoldering wood.

He stopped walking. Grabbed his head at the temples and attempted to counter the internal grope. With his palms, he massaged the pressure points. His skull felt numb beneath his grasp, as though anesthetized.

"Dad . . . you okay?" Kristin's voice sounded muted to Bev, as if she'd spoken to him from behind a thin wall. *Like the music while I was on stage.* He tried to answer, but his voice sank into his lungs. An oppressive hot flash washed over him, as if he'd instantly acquired a fever of 104 degrees. His veins pumped, his heart pounded, a surge of adrenaline racing through them.

Then, like earlier, an overwhelming anger rose in him. His mind instantly rejected everything that he knew and felt, the love for his daughter, his friends and acquaintances, his musical talents.

"Dad? What's wrong?"

A distant echo of her voice. His sensible mind fought hard to counter the horrible feelings blooming within him, but what remained of his inner strength sank deeper into the bowels of his body.

"Get away from me!"

"Dad!" Kristin hollered, her voice a distant echo—a call from a mountaintop. "What's wrong with you?"

Bev fell to his knees. Squeezed his head. His feet burned. His legs trembled. The ghostly fingers in his head continued their tenacious digging. And now, more than ever, the sensation of *crumbling* rose in him, as though sediment from his skull was falling away.

Kristin placed a faltering hand on his shoulder. He could feel his head slowly turning toward her, his face contorted into a rageful scowl: eyes pinning her with foul hatred; lips stretched wide and hot with saliva. He felt his mouth part and heard himself speaking in a voice that wasn't his: "Don't touch me!"

"Dad!" she screamed, her voice breaking through his consciousness. The fingers at once ceased their mental excavation, and he could feel himself quickly getting back to normal. Tears sprouted uncontrollably. The pressure of those terrible moments had distressed his body: muscles wearied; shoulders joggling; mind fraught with shame and disgust.

"Dad?" Kristin. Quieter. Tentative.

"Jesus, what just happened to me?" Bev could *feel* again: the mist from the ocean against his face, the wind and the sand in its grasp.

"Dad . . . are you okay?"

"I . . . I am *so* sorry. I can't . . . I can't explain what just happened to me."

Voice still shaking, Kristin asked, "Why did you say those things to me?"

"I don't know . . . baby, it wasn't me . . . it . . . was something in me. I can't explain it." He looked up at her. In spite of her tan and the rosy glisten of her cheeks, she was scared to death—eyes sallow, the whites bloodshot; mouth trembling. Bev felt a huge welling of emotions, of fear, shame, remorse. He thought, *I am not responsible for my actions. I didn't do it . . . I had no control. I was buried deep below . . . in my lavas.*

My lavas?

"I told you earlier that I wasn't feeling well . . . remember?"

She nodded, taking notice of the people walking by. Many, from their safe distance, inspected Bev's troubled posture. No one offered any assistance.

Slowly, he stood up, then held her hands. Squeezed. Despite his trepidation, he now felt physically fine. "I'm not sure what's going on with me. This is the fourth time it's happened, I think."

"Jesus, Dad, I'm worried about you."

"I am too, Kristin. I am too."

Eight

Slowly and carefully, Bev and Kristin retraced their path across the beach, weaving in and out of those lounging on folding chairs and towels. They kept their glances attentive. The Sunday-afternoon crowd had multiplied. Spotting the man who had watched them wouldn't be easy. He could be anywhere.

They climbed the steps to the busy pier. Bought two more bottles of water from a beverage cart on the pier. As they drank, they took notice of the throngs of people around them, basking in the buttery sunlight, roller-skating, jogging, just plain having fun. After a minute, they tossed the empty plastic bottles into a steel-mesh trash container, then walked across the Danfords parking lot to Kristin's car. Bev did his best to convey a sense of ignorance to whoever may be watching him—in his gut he *knew* that he was still being watched, but he didn't intend to alert the one monitoring his actions that he was aware of him.

"Are you sure you don't want me to take you home?" she asked.

Bev looked at his watch. 3:15. "No, you go. I'll be fine." He did have some concerns about another "episode" occurring while driving; he'd planned on going straight home from here, a short ten-minute drive. If history repeated itself, it wouldn't happen again so soon.

"You sure?"

"Yes. Go along."

She kissed his cheek, then got into her car, an '03 Ford Mustang he'd bought for her when she turned nineteen. He walked around to the front of the car, staring at his reflection in the car's glossy red exterior.

His distorted face stared back at him.

And then, for a split second, it changed: a malevolent mask, scowling at him. He shuddered with terror.

And then his normal reflection returned.

But it was there. A change. Eyes, wide like saucers, yellow irises set in glimmering black. Skin, bone white, mottled with patches of gray. Lips, red like fire, spread wide to show brown stumps for teeth.

"See you tonight at the party?" she asked.

He started. "Sure," he replied with feigned enthusiasm, the demonic image lingering in his distressed mind.

"Don't push yourself. Come only if you feel up to it."

He didn't want to disappoint his daughter. Yet he told himself that if he had one more episode, he'd have to promise himself a good night's rest, Jake's birthday or not. *It's anxiety, that's all. Panic attacks. They come in many different forms, and I've got myself a real bad sort.*

Then explain what you just saw. Explain the voice. Is that anxiety? Or maybe it's delusional schizophrenia?

"It's Jake's birthday," he answered. "He'll be passed out by ten. It won't be a long night."

"Call me later."

"I will."

She smiled. Waved as she closed her window. Drove away.

Bev stood there for a minute, leaning against a white Pathfinder. He rubbed his eyes. Wondered if he should have accepted Kristin's offer of a ride.

The sudden need to relieve himself forced him to move—two beers and two bottled waters will do that. He paced back into Danfords, looking around and not seeing anyone suspiciously eyeing him. The hostess recognized him as an earlier patron. He told her he needed to use the restroom, and she responded with a soft assenting smile.

He entered the restroom. It stunk of grape disinfectant. He used a urinal, staring at the wall, counting the lines of grout between the tiles. When he finished, he washed his hands and splashed cold water on his face.

He looked into the sink.

A beetle, like the one in his apartment, wriggled out of the drain.

Jesus!

He backpedaled away from the mirrored wall, breathing in gasps, head shaking with apprehension. Slowly, he leaned forward and peeked back into the sink.

White porcelain. No beetle. *Must've slipped back down the drain.*

Was it ever there?

He turned, confused. Stared at himself in the mirror. Lines of worry, carved into his face; coarse; chiseled. Still wet. Impulsively, he raised a hand and touched his reflection. An index finger against itself.

It touched him back—not the cold spotted surface of the mirror, but the smooth warm tip of his own finger.

He shivered, keeping dreadfully still and silent. Feeling his finger.

With the rapidity of a snakebite, his reflection morphed itself into the offensive face he'd visioned in the car's glossy finish. It produced an audible bark and snapped at his finger.

He cried out, jerking his hand away as if he'd been burned.

He gazed down at his hand in disbelief—then, with a reflexive jolt, back into the mirror.

His own reflection stared back at him—but not the same reflection he knew. This stranger in the mirror had witnessed something unexplainably terrifying—this man in the mirror was trembling with fear and pain.

Someone walked into the bathroom. A young man, perhaps sixteen or seventeen. Crew cut. Tan. Earrings in both ears. He gave Bev a quizzical look. "You all right, man?"

Breathing heavily, face still wet, Bev nodded. He gazed sideways at his normal reflection one last time, then fled the bathroom.

Leaving a smear of blood on the doorknob.

Nine

The lava had risen to his chest. He pressed forward, skin sloughing off his body in visible chunks, sizzling on the surface of the flow as it floated away like slabs of debris from a downed boat. The flow pushed him, and he reached forward with arms melted to tendon and bone. Kristin and Jake were still on the shore. Kristin was clothed now. Jake stood fully naked, utilizing one raw-knuckled hand to stroke a hideous, spaded erection. He bounced up and down like an impatient child, fisting his deformed staff, masses of cellulite moving on his body like water balloons. In a coarse, guttural voice, he yelled, "Hey, Bev, I'm gonna fuck your slut daughter now. Gonna drive it up her ass so far it'll gag her." Bev screamed "NO!" the hot acidic vapors rising from the lava searing his lungs, and in a move of pure panic tried desperately to wade forward, but skeletal hands thrust up from the flow and held him back, and he could do nothing but watch as a smiling Kristin pulled her jeans down to her ankles, got on her knees, pressed her face to the soil, and used her hands to spread her ass cheeks wide. Jake laughed deeply, his voice suddenly accented and bristling with venom, face morphing into the demonic visage that had snapped at Bev from the bathroom mirror. A rotting stench filled Bev's nostrils, and despite the lava and the sweltering flow that had rent his flesh from his body, he felt an inner chill running deeply through his veins. Jake, or the demon that had replaced him, fell to its knees. Abruptly, its bare pink flesh turned black, sprouting random patches of rotting feathers, flaring scales, and dripping excrement. The Jake-demon laughed, then filled the room with a cry of triumph, fueled with indifference and fury. It pulled Kristin's hair back, exposing her throat and thrusting its black misshapened penis into her anus. It pumped ferociously, jerking her hair, screaming, "She's mine now! The pig is mine!" Bev stood rooted in the lava flow, screaming in defeat. He brought his melting fingers to his face and tore away bits of flesh from his cheeks, watching with horror as his daughter tilted her head and smiled stupidly at him, all the while sticking her fouled ass into the air with true, feral acceptance. Ash-laden tears burst from her bulging eyes. Bev reached out to her.

She kept on smiling.

Until she opened her mouth and gagged on the black-mottled penis that wriggled its way out from between her swollen lips.

Bev awoke with a start. Sweating. Arms and legs curled inward. Numb. For minutes, he remained still as the blood worked its way back into his limbs and the image of the terrible nightmare faded. Soon, the numbness was gone, and so were the horrendous memories of his dream. He stretched out, bones popping. His feet touched the soft edge of the couch.

Where am I?

Not in bed, he told himself. And not in the studio; the love seat there was tiny; his legs would have hung over the edge.

He rubbed his eyes. Opened them. The room, pallid gray. Dali prints, candelabras, and drab draperies haunted the gloom like tree shadows in a dark forest.

Jake.

He propped himself up on his elbows, then gazed around the room. Silk black curtains were pulled, drowning out most light. He twisted his body around and reached over the sofa's armrest. Felt out the end table. The lamp. He located the switch.

Light burst into the room.

He *had* been here before. He was in one of Jake's guest rooms.

Jake Ritchie lived more elaborately than Bev. He'd applied much of his fortune toward his lifestyle, and it showed; as crude as Jake was, he had a soft spot for art and sculptures and even candles and amenities like incense and potpourri. The house was a modern five-bedroom, five-bath multilevel anchored into the side of a mountain in Beverly Hills. It had the mandatory pool and Jacuzzi outside, along with a pond and topiary collection that corralled the backyard for privacy.

He sat on the edge of the leather sofa and rubbed his eyes, wondering, *What the hell am I doing here? And how did I get here?*

Memory loss. Add that to the list of sudden symp-

toms. He ran his feet through the plush leopard-skin rug, taking slow, calculated breaths in an effort to calm his nerves. It was so easy to let one's fear of the unknown take control. He took another look around, then heard a faint doorbell chime.

In the distance: "Traci, you gorgeous creature you! Come in. You're the first to arrive, you lucky bastard!"

Bev smiled woefully, shaking his head and rolling his eyes as Jake barked another playful obscenity at an arriving guest. Bev stood and stretched out his weary muscles, wondering with dismay as to when, how, and why he'd come here. *A good nap will confuse the heck out of you.* Beyond the closed door, he heard thundering footsteps attacking the oak stairwell, and in seconds Jake Ritchie burst into the room. He was clutching a glass of amber liquid. There was a small wet stain on his black silk shirt: the first of many, Bev predicted.

"Well, hello there, sleeping beauty. I was just coming to kiss your ass awake."

"Jake, what am I doing here?"

"You're here for the party."

"I mean, how did I get here?"

"How? You drove, mon douche."

"Drove? When?"

"Bev, you've got a funny look to you. You been taking anything?"

"No, no, please." He waved Jake's words off adamantly. He stood and paced the room, arms swaying nervously. "I'm just a bit confused. Last I remember . . . I . . . I had lunch with Kristin at Danfords, was planning on heading home afterwards. We said goodbye in the parking lot, and then I really don't remember anything after that. Last thing I remember was . . ."

. . . was that hideous face staring back at me from the mirror.

He looked down at his index finger.

It was cut. Half an inch. Across the tip. The injury was soft and tender, but not bleeding.

Jesus Christ. No . . . no . . . I cut it on the doorknob of the bathroom. That's it. I remember the slight pain . . .

". . . was standing in the parking lot, kissing Kristin good-bye."

"Jesus, Bev. You telling me you blacked out?"

"I—I don't know. This is too weird, man. Scary."

"Well, how're you feeling now?"

"Not bad, I suppose. Other than being a little confused. And nervous."

"Well, it only makes sense to feel that way. I would, too, if I had some memory loss . . . but then again, I can't remember much of anything when I drink, which is most of the time. See, you don't have it so bad after all!"

"When did I get here? How long was I sleeping for?"

Jake shrugged, looked at his watch. "Well, it's eight-fifteen now. And you got here around four. When I let you in, you told me you were tired and wanted to rest up, said you weren't feeling too well. You also said something about not being able to go home because there were exterminators there spraying the place. What's that all about?"

"Shit. I forgot about that."

"So I brought you up here and in a minute you were passed out on the couch. You sure you ain't taking anything?"

Bev shook his head. "No, Jake, no. I wasn't feeling well earlier today. What freaks me out is that I actually drove all the way here—and don't remember any of it."

Jake paced across the room. Pulled aside the curtain and peeked out into the backyard. "It's called autopilot. I do it all the time. You drive from Point A to Point B while you're mind is off in la-la land. Next thing you know, you've arrived at your destination without even realizing it." He turned back and spread his arms. "But enough of that. Go on and take a long, hot shower. Then get yourself dressed and haul your hairy ass down to the party." The doorbell chimed. Soon after, gleeful shouts of recognition rang out. "Gotta get back downstairs—more guests are arriving. There're some guest clothes in the closet—God knows I've had my share of drunk guests needing them!" Jake winked and strode excitedly from the room.

Bev sat back down, and for a few minutes thought, *It's exhaustion. Nine months on the road has taken its toll on me, and it's bringing with it a whole bevy of intimidating symptoms: fatigue, dizziness, voices in my head, blackouts. Man, it's bad. Thank God I made a doctor's appointment. I'm starting to erode.*

He rose from the couch, searched the closet (filled with casual wear for both men and women—all Tommy Hilfiger—and Bev remembered Jake once telling him about a connection at the company that filled his closets for free), and found a pair of vintage-wash jeans his size and a black knit shirt. In the drawers of the pine armoire he located packages of cotton briefs, boxers, and athletic socks. An example of how Jake was prepared for every occasion. *This* was why the man was so successful.

Bev showered, then shaved. The hot water felt great against his skin and seemed to revive him, to wash away the dreadful symptoms harassing him. After getting out, he toweled down, then chanced looking into the bathroom mirror. Thankfully, no monster stared back at him—only a healthy pink hue in his face that had replaced the anemic gray. He felt remarkably well, refreshed, clearheaded, and energetic. What a difference a little rest makes.

He got dressed, then checked his cell phone for voice mails. There were none. He tied his hair back into a ponytail, then remembered something: his jeans, strewn on the couch.

He tucked his hand into the back pocket and removed the invitation. He gazed at it briefly, then slid it into his front pocket and went downstairs to join the party.

Ten

The grandfather clock in the foyer struck nine as he made his entrance into the smallish crowd totaling perhaps twenty-five. He immediately saw Rebecca Haviland near the entrance of the kitchen. She wore dark brown jeans and a beige long-sleeve top that hugged her trim waistline and curvy breasts quite well. The sight of her dissolved what remained of his daylong concerns. *Kristin's right. She does look like Julianne.*

Bev knew a handful of people here. Peter Froberg, music reviewer from the *L.A. Times.* Jamie Zetlin, *Music On Air* correspondent. The kid from Epic, Bobby SanSouci. There were also a few of the guys from Holloway Girl, a new band under Jake's management. They milled about, chatting happily among themselves and their girlfriends. For the most part, the party was small and quiet, very un-Jake-like.

"Only my closest friends tonight," Jake said, sidling up, strangely reserved.

"You forgot to call me douche bag."

"I'm feeling melancholy. Birthdays'll do that to you once you hurdle thirty-five. Being forty-four, well, I'm damn near bilge at the bottom of the boat. Figured a small get-together with my friends might cheer me up some."

"I've never known you to be so serious, Jake."

"Fuck it."

"That's better." Bev smiled, then asked, "Got any coffee?"

"Ask one of the waitresses. In the kitchen."

"Thanks." Jake headed off as the doorbell rang and a few more people arrived. Bev slid into the kitchen, trading smiles with Rebecca in passing. He found some already brewed coffee and fixed himself a cup.

In an hour, the party had grown to a vibrant forty. People were drinking and eating, tying themselves into knots of conversation. Strangely enough, none of the members of Bev's band had come, and neither had Kristin, whom he'd expected. He phoned her apartment. Got only her machine. Left her a message. *Where are you, baby? I came to this party just for you.*

Or did I? If only I could remember . . .

He mingled about, helping himself to hors d'oeuvres offered on platters by two well-dressed servers-for-hire. He talked to T. J. Fleming, a balding, freckle-faced L.A. radio host who gently hinted to Bev about doing a live on-air performance. Bev agreed to it, asking him to arrange a date with Jake. Fleming responded with a mirthful grin. Bobby SanSouci cornered Bev, too, and took as much time as Bev was willing to allow: about ten minutes. Rebecca Haviland kept mostly to other conversations, but not without answering Bev's guileful glances with a few sidelong smiles of her own.

Also in attendance were people Bev didn't know. One man in particular, seated on a couch by himself wearing gray dress pants and a black shirt, piqued Bev's curiosity. Perhaps in his early fifties, he had dark features, graying hair, with thick creases in his brow. Bev could see something desperate in his eyes—yet, at the same time, a sense of warmth emanated from them, a quasipsychic reassurance that everything would be okay.

"You look familiar," the man remarked, eyes narrowed, voice cradling.

"Bev Mathers. I'm a musician."

"Father Thomas Danto. Pleased to meet you." He held out the hand that wasn't busy with a glass of brandy. Bev accepted it. Cold. Tense. There was a shudder in it, and then he let go.

"Likewise. Are you friends with Jake?" He'd never known Jake to be the religious type.

"Jake is a new member of our congregation at St. Michael's."

"St. Michael's. On Caliendo Street."

"Correct." The priest smiled, then commented sarcastically, "I thought it might be interesting to see how you rock-and-roll people live." He laughed mirthfully.

"Don't believe everything you hear. We're a tame bunch." Then he added, with a wink, "For the most part."

"There are worse sins in the world than indulgence," Father Danto said. "And I'm not one to judge. Even we priests take to drink much too often, I'm afraid."

Jake walked over and joined the pair. "I see you've met Father Danto, Bev."

Bev nodded. "I have."

"In addition to being a priest, Father is also an archaeologist."

"Really?" he answered, feigning interest.

The priest shrugged modestly. "Nonpracticing for the last twenty years—no time beyond my call of duty."

"Ah, well, mon . . . *monsieur* . . . Father needed a place to stay tonight. They're doing a bit of cleanup at the church."

Bev cast the priest a questioning glance.

Father Danto nodded, speaking reluctantly, it seemed. "Well, unfortunately, a disgraceful crime occurred at the rectory last night, forcing us all to relocate temporarily."

"Oh . . . that's terrible," Bev said. "What kind of crime?"

He hesitated, then answered, "One of a most deplorable nature. Unfortunately, we share this world with many sick people who have no qualms about committing blasphemies, for whatever selfish reasons they claim." His voice rose in volume, showing a bit of anger and perhaps fear.

Judd Schiffer, a reporter for the *L.A. Times* who'd done an Entertainment Page story on Bev's "late-age" rise to success, moved in on the conversation. "Father Danto? Judd Schiffer. We spoke this morning on the phone. I did the story for the *Times*."

"Mr. Schiffer . . . hello. My, this is a coincidence."

"Indeed. Pleased to meet you, and thank you for the information."

Danto nodded. "You're welcome."

Bev interjected, "I seem to be the only one in the dark here—can someone fill me in on what happened?"

Schiffer answered. "Last night, someone performed a Satanic ritual on the lawn outside St. Michael's."

"Well . . . not really," Father Danto interjected, correcting the reporter.

"Pardon?" Schiffer's incredulity shined like a beacon.

"It wasn't exactly a *Satanic* ritual."

"Father, it certainly appears that way—"

"Appearances can be deceiving, Judd. The ferocity of the act committed last night shows more of an influence of *demonic* worship." Schiffer nodded, in understanding now. "There are vast differences between Satanism and demonology, and even witchcraft. The kind of extreme conduct we saw last night doesn't carry any Satanistic hallmarks." He took a sip of brandy. "Demon worship, yes. But not Satanism."

Bev found this sudden conversation riveting—especially with a priest involved. Schiffer sipped his drink, his gaze deadpan. "What's the difference?"

"There's a big difference. Satanism is a formulated religion based on a crude set of self-serving morals. Satanists, or members of the Church of Satan, worship Satan as a god, and under his guise and so-called rule act in immoral and selfish ways. But Satanists . . . they are also very secretive in their enterprises, and are considered to be merely harmless atheists. Yes, animal sacrifices are rumored to be made, but only within their private confines, and only during black masses, which are conducted solely on their appointed holidays. It's a systemized and widespread organization that focuses, really, on parodying the Catholic religion, with no true harmful intent.

"Demon worship, on the other hand, which is also in

its own way systemized—albeit among smaller cults—carries a much larger threat with it. Demonologists and their followers take their ancient craft very seriously, utilizing the enigmatic powers of black magic in an effort to raise demon spirits from their slumbers. Demon worshipers are not merely atheists. They are individuals who knowingly and willingly choose to worship evil spirits and fallen angels instead of God. They seek only darkness and death, and are more than willing to go to any extreme to attain their goal. Hence the sacrifice at the church."

"Sacrifice?" Bev asked, stunned.

Jake, uncustomarily demure, asked, "Father, it sounds as though you're a bit of an expert on this stuff—black masses and devil worship and everything?"

Danto shrugged, as if embarrassed. Swirled his drink. "I've done my fair share of research on demonology and its history in religion."

Bev asked impatiently, "Please forgive me for prying, but what exactly happened at the church?"

Schiffer, asking permission: "Father?"

The priest nodded.

"Last night, someone sacrificed a goat on the lawn outside the rectory. It had been decapitated, its carcass gutted and impaled on a large crucifix. Its entrails were laid out into a pentagram shape beneath the cross."

Danto added solemnly, "The individual—or individuals—who did this somehow made their way inside the rectory during the night. All of the priests, myself included, woke up this morning with goat's blood on our hands. On one of the walls in the rectory, someone scribbled in blood, *Baphomet has risen.* History tells us that Baphomet was a bearded demon with a goat's head."

"Jesus." Bev was stunned.

"And the goat's head," Schiffer added unobtrusively, "was found perched upon the altar of the church, wrapped in sacred cloth."

"The most alarming part of all," resumed Father Danto, "is that there were no signs of forced entry. We have no idea how the person got into the rectory, or the church, since everything was locked up at ten P.M. Father Sandi was on duty last night, and he insists that all the doors were locked when he made his rounds."

"Which means that the person who committed this act either has a key or was already on the inside."

"An inside job." Jake shrugged. "Sounds like something out of *NYPD Blue.*"

There was a wave of uncomfortable laughter. Father Danto said blandly, "It's certainly reason enough for us to sleep elsewhere for now. Masses will still be performed, of course, but we'll have to stay away until the smoke clears."

Bev took a sip of coffee. Strangely, he felt invigorated. *No headache. No ghostly fingers.* "Father Danto . . . you mentioned earlier that you've done research into Satanism. Is there any truth to all this black-magic stuff?"

"Not Satanism," he corrected. "Demonology. And yes, there is a great deal of validity to it. I attended the Institute of Archaeology in Jerusalem during the late sixties. I'd had a great deal of interest in the beginnings of Christianity, and the course curriculum at the university included an in-depth study of the archaeological finds from the first millennium B.C.E., at a site located just beyond the outskirts of the city. During the Six-Day War, some errant shellings in the desert unearthed a burial ground near the site from the lower-city section of Hazor, also dating back to the biblical era. There'd been a great deal of excitement at the time, as many of us had thought the discovery might be that of Jesus's burial site. But eventually, after the hieroglyphs on the tomb were translated, we found our expectations to be misguided. What we'd found was no holy ground at all—it was the site of a massacre where thirteen children had been slaughtered by a man who called himself Allieb, son of the demon Belial. According to the story, Allieb was caught and punished for his sins, buried alive by the townspeople in the very same tomb he constructed for his sacrifants. For months we studied the bones of the children, and we discovered that they'd all been flayed. Each of them had been decapitated, with their heads positioned atop their groins, hands holding the skulls in place. There had been some attempt at mummification, but as we all know, only the Egyptians had mastered that craft, so there wasn't much left of the children's bodies to study, save for their brittle bones and some bristles of hair."

Judd Schiffer asked, "How did you know that they'd been flayed?"

"What remained of the children's bones contained deep gouges consistent with that of a sharp stone tool. It stood to reason that the angles of the gouges showed a successful effort to remove the flesh from their bodies. The story on the tablets found later revealed that Allieb had successfully summoned the spirits of thirteen demons, his father Belial being the first, each of which had possessed the bodies of the thirteen children. One by one, he ate the flesh of the children— while they were still alive—in an effort to possess their demonic souls and grow stronger in his battle to dethrone Christ."

"The Antichrist," Bev said.

"Precisely. Or his attempt to become the Antichrist."

"Sick," Bev commented.

"From what we've gathered, Allieb carved the hieroglyphs while trapped in his dark catacomb. He'd survived a fortnight with no food or water before succumbing."

"How long were you at the dig for?" asked Jake.

"Almost a year. It was an amazing discovery, and I'd learned that the ability to possess one's body with the souls of demons was in fact a true belief of the ancient Israelites, and not just Bible stories of Jesus casting demons out into the desert. It was soon thereafter that I left school and turned to the priesthood in an effort to rinse my soul of any taint I might have picked up while at the dig."

"Taint?" asked Schiffer.

The priest nodded. "The site was discovered about a mile from the scene of a mass murder. Nine bodies had been found outside an abandoned vehicle—nothing too uncommon, considering the sudden onset of the war. The bodies had been dead about two weeks when found, and had not survived the elements: the heat, the wind, the scavenger dogs. We eventually located the exposed tomb. Inside we made the discovery. But . . . we found something else as well. A young boy. Alive. Inside the tomb. Apparently, he'd escaped the attack on the car in the desert—or so we'd presumed—and had found his way across a ravine into the shade of the tomb. In shock, he'd hid inside alongside the bones of the slaughtered children. When we asked him how long he'd been here, his only reply was "A fortnight."

"Odd," Bev said, "considering what you found in the writings."

"Right . . . but remember, we didn't have those writings translated until about six months later, after we were well into the dig. By then, the child had been sent by the Israeli government to live with a family in America. All we found out from him was how long he'd been there, and that he'd survived that time by consuming the carcass of a dog he'd dragged into the tomb with him."

"That's enough for me," Jake said. "My stomach can't handle this." He thumped away to engage in a conversation with Jamie Zetlin.

"I'm sorry . . ." Father Danto said. "I shouldn't have elaborated so much. Brandy loosens my tongue too much for my own good."

Both Bev and Schiffer waved him off. "No, not to worry about Jake," Bev said. "He's got a weak stomach for anything horror-related. Shoulda seen him bailing out of the theater during *The Blair Witch Project*."

"Please continue, Father," Schiffer pleaded. "This is very interesting."

"Well, to make a long story short, I worked at the dig for about a year, all the while studying ancient religion in school. I became alarmed after locating some additional texts analyzing Allieb's scriptures, and felt no alternative at the time to enter the priesthood."

"What did they say, these scriptures?" Schiffer asked.

"You have a year? I could go over it with you." He took a sip of brandy, then said, "Let's just say that Allieb was indeed the demonologist the tablets proclaimed him to be, and had spent his entire life making sacrifices in an effort to hone his skills in raising demon spirits and possessing their souls. There'd been a lot of trial and error, resulting in the deaths of many at his hand. Eventually came the child sacrifices—it is said that Belial had somehow escaped the bonds of Satan and guided his son toward the proper course of action."

At that moment there was some loud laughter in the background, and the clutch dispersed before Father Danto was able to continue. Bev got the impression, by the apprehensive look on the priest's face, that there was much more to the story than what he'd just told. Perhaps it had triggered a distinct anxiety from the crime at the rectory? A few people, readying to leave, came over to say good-bye. Bev noticed that Father Danto had grown suddenly pale. He gazed intensely at Bev, then kindly excused himself. "I have a mass at eight-ten." He ambled away and located Jake, who immediately escorted the priest upstairs to one of the bedrooms. Bev watched as the priest disappeared behind the hallway wall on the landing. He then looked at his watch, noticed the time: 11:30. *Where's Kristin?*

Bev again dialed her number on his cell. No answer. When he disconnected, Rebecca Haviland drifted over. She smiled, her lips full and pouty, *like Julianne's,* her blue eyes twinkling, *like Julianne's used to,* her blond hair flowing smoothly to her shoulders.

Just like Julianne's.

Jesus.

"Hi, there . . . enjoying the party?"

"Rebecca, it's about time you came over to say hello."

"The guys from Holloway Girl had me cornered."

"Did they impress?"

"Their music speaks well for them. Their personalities . . . different story."

"Yes, the party has been interesting. I was speaking to a priest whose expertise is demons and witches."

"Really?"

"Well, sort of. Interesting fellow, to say the least."

"Where's Kristin?" she asked.

"No clue. I just tried calling her cell. No answer."

They locked smiles, then spent the better part of a half hour, maybe more, engaged in conversation. They stood against the wall by the kitchen, talking about their careers, comparing musical tastes, and Rebecca even mentioned to Bev that Kristin might be a good fit at *Rock Hard Magazine* as an assistant writer. Bev made a mental note to mention that to her, and wondered again with dismay as to her whereabouts.

More comfortable now, Jake reverted back to his usual self: extroverted and caustic. The whiskey flowed continuously into him, and by the time midnight rolled around, Jake was staggering about the place like a three-legged bull, spilling his drinks and drooling and accusing the servers of watering down the whiskey. The guests had begun to filter out, headed for the clubs on Sunset Boulevard.

By one A.M., the last of the guests had left and it was just Jake, Bev, and Rebecca, sitting at the kitchen table. The servers had cleaned all the rooms and were now gone. Jake held his head in his hands, complaining incessantly about a headache and the "douche bag servers who slipped him Wild Turkey instead of JD." Bev and Rebecca sat alongside each other, their knees touching beneath the table, grinning playfully at each other over Jake's drunken demeanor. Cool shivers raced continuously across Bev's skin. It felt good being this close to her.

Soon Jake went silent and his eyes began to close. Bev and Rebecca helped him to rise and moved him to one of the living room sofas—a feat not so easily accomplished—where he plopped down, shirttail out, white stomach exposed. In seconds he was snoring.

"It's late, and I've had a very long day," Bev told Rebecca, leaning against the banister leading upstairs. "I'm gonna spend the night here. Got a bug problem at my place."

"Bugs? Ecch."

"Yeah, I know. Exterminators sprayed today. Should be okay tomorrow, though."

Rebecca, expectantly, placed her hands across her waist. "I left my jacket upstairs," she said.

"Which room?"

"To the left of the stairs."

"I'll walk you up."

Eleven

In five minutes they were both sitting Indian-style on a made bed in one of Jake's guest rooms.

Facing each other. Hands locked. Staring into each other's eyes.

Leaning forward.

Touching lips.

He glanced away from her face. In the darkness, it gave him the haunting impression of being with his wife again. In this moment of distraction, he saw a long tear in the dark curtain. The moon's beams branched through it, into the room, onto the bed. Bev caressed Rebecca's tossed hair as she fell upon the pillow. He remained silent. She caught him by the arm. Her touch was tender, warm, and caring. Not lust-driven, like the girls he'd met on the road. It was gentler. Kinder. It pulled him down to her.

She pressed against him. He could feel her heartbeat, a rhythmic pounding filled with passion. He accepted her approach. Pressed back against her.

They removed their clothes, piece by piece, taking turns, until their naked heat blended into one.

He made an impulsive turn to face her. She pulled away, pressing her warm posterior against his groin. With a fitted thrust, they became one. He, within her. She, filled with him.

Bev was filled with a fresh and exhilarating sense of awareness. All his physical and mental pain instantly vanished, the negative memories of the day washed away. He relished in the pleasure, every beat and rhythm between them. The moment was perfect. Bev felt as if he were in a chamber of pleasure floating amid the harsh reality of the outside world, this moment of ecstasy a shroud of protection from the pains of the day.

In an adept move, Bev grasped Rebecca's thigh and brought her leg over his waist, twisting himself on top of her without breaking their slick connection. Here in this position he could see her face clearly, her eyes shut, her mouth drawing tiny gasps that progressed into deeper inhalations as their tempo increased. Her familiar facial features triggered an indescribable eroticism in him, lips pouting, eyes closed, nose quivering with pure want and desire.

Perhaps sensing his burning desire for her, Rebecca finally opened her eyes. Gazed deeply into his. Bev felt energized at this level of intimacy. He looked away from her perfect face. Lifted himself up so his eyes could explore her damp body: svelte shoulders, smooth breasts, taut waist. Their lovemaking grew more intense, both of them gasping across each other's cheeks. They both cried out in unison, their tiny slice of the world jumping and quaking as Bev thrust one last time and released himself into her.

Soon, everything that made up their world flowed away into quiet heaven, setting the room into a breathy silence. They remained in an unmoving position for a period of time. Eventually, he withdrew from her and turned on his side to face her, his head touching hers. Their breaths commingled. Neither of them spoke, and in time they drifted off to sleep.

Twelve

The flow of lava strengthened. Skeletal hands blocked the way like entangled tree limbs in a tar pit, fingers drilling deeply into his flesh, bone touching bone, keeping him immobile as the wicked play commenced on the shore. The Jake-demon backed away from Kristin, gripping his swollen black staff, squeezing it tightly as acid-semen pooled out from the tip and sizzled on the ground. Kristin, still smiling, stood and waved to Bev, blood and excrement pouring down her legs. "Come to me, Daddy!" she cried happily. Bev tried to move, but the skeletal hands restrained him.

"Go to her, Bev. She needs you," came a reassuring voice from beside him. Bev turned. Father Danto stood in the lava, unruffled by the searing flow. He wore his collar and robe, a silver crucifix centered on his chest, glimmering despite the gloom. "She needs you. We need you. There is a long battle ahead."

Bev looked toward the shore. Rebecca Haviland was there now—she, too, naked—standing beside the Jake-demon. The Jake-demon stroked its staff, working it back to full erection; blood coating it; yellow smoke geysering from the head. Kristin continued to wave, robotlike, with no purposeful awareness. The Jake-demon took one step forward, shook its body like a wet dog. Black feathers fluttered away, burning as they hit the ground, like straying embers from a campfire. "Bev!" it shouted, voice coarse and guttural. "Round two. Gonna fuck this one in the mouth till it comes out her ass." It growled and plodded toward Rebecca, face contorting, head gyrating, swollen tongue lolling animalistically from its mouth. Rebecca, smiling and waving at Bev, got down on her knees. She opened her mouth wide, fully willing to accept the Jake-demon's huge staff. Spasms of rage riddled Bev, and he pressed forward, breaking the skeletal bonds that blocked him. He stretched his hands forward. "Wait!" came a voice from behind. He turned. Father Danto gazed at him, tears of blood trickling from his eyes. "It's good that you came," he uttered, hands gesturing forward, stigmata in his palms. "There are two souls invading you," he said, thrusting his bloody palms forward. "A man's, and a beast's. It is the man's soul that torments you. You must follow the beast." Bev turned away from the priest. The Jake-demon, witnessing this exchange between them, staggered toward the surf. The Jake-demon slammed down into the shallow lava, limbs flailing, throat breaking open, blood gushing out onto the shore. The coarse hide of its scales and feathers burned away, leaving behind a smoking mound of pink flesh that drowned in the shallow lava. Rebecca and Kristin stared toward the red skies, oblivious of the strange event. Bev turned back to face Danto. The priest was gone. In his place stood Julianne. She, too, was unaffected by the blistering flow. She stared at Bev, her face an expressionless mask. Crying, Bev reached for her. She reached for him. Like quick blasts from a furnace, thin strands of metal wire thrust up from the lava. They danced in the air between them, as though charged with electricity, then attacked Bev, wrapping around his hands like coiling snakes, digging into his palms and pulling his arms back until his shoulders snapped. The pain was excruciating. Blood fell from his hands into the fiery lava, riding the flowing surface toward Julianne. She peered down, her face morphing into the demon visage Bev had seen in the mirror . . .

Bev opened his eyes. Dark. The bed beside him, empty. He shivered, cold from sweat. He rose up in bed. Looked around the dark room. Where was Rebecca?

The curtain billowed. The sliding doors, open. In the moon's light, a figure appeared. A female form. Naked. Rebecca? Yes. But she spoke in Julianne's voice:

"You killed me . . . you killed me . . ."

"No," Bev answered, weakly. Ineffectively.

"You knew the car was coming," Rebecca said in Julianne's voice.

"No," he answered more loudly. "The swan . . . the swan . . ."

"You saw the car coming, and still you pulled out into the intersection."

"But the swan!" he screamed.

Rebecca backed out through the sliding doors and leaped off the balcony.

Bev screamed.

Beside him, screaming. A woman's voice.

He twisted around, heart pounding, to face Rebecca.

She sat up, breathing heavily. "Jesus, Bev! What's wrong? Are you okay?"

He looked at her. Gasping. Sweating. The room, now instilled with thin streaks of daylight. He looked toward the curtain. Partially open. The sliding doors: shut. "I . . . I just saw you . . ." he said, pointing toward the balcony.

She tilted her head, pulling the sheet up over her breasts. "Saw me where?"

"By the sliding doors . . . They were open and you were standing there and . . . Jesus Christ, thank God you're okay!" He hugged her head, pressing her against his chest.

She hugged him back, halfheartedly. "You must've had a bad dream." She pulled away. Looked at him. Her expression turned from concern to fear. "Bev, my God, your hands."

He looked down at his hands. His heart pounded ferociously.

There were deep gouges running across his palms.

As though thin metal wires had dug into them.

"Oh . . . my . . . God . . ."

"Bev, what happened?"

"I don't know," he lied, remembering the dream. Of Julianne, wading in the lava, the wires jutting out from the searing flow, attacking his hands. "I think I'd better leave now. And you should, too."

"Bev?" Her expression shifted from fear to disappointment.

"What time is it?" he asked.

She peered at her watch, the only item still on her body. "Nine-fifteen. Bev, what's going on?"

He leaped from the bed and got dressed in a huff, trembling, ignoring Rebecca's pleas. Finally, he faced her, on shaky legs. "I have to leave now. I haven't been feeling well lately, and . . . and . . . I just need to leave." There was really no logical way to explain what had just happened. The continuing dream was an extension of something bigger, something incomprehensible, branching off from the root of the problem, just as the digging fingers had—just as the hallucinations and delusions had. And now, extending farther from his dream, a shove into the real world in the form of something material—something painful that would stay with him long after the physical wounds had healed. He leaned and kissed her forehead. "Thank you for a wonderful evening, and I promise, I will call you later."

He fled the room, trying to ignore the stabbing pain in his hands, thinking of his dream and what Father Danto had said: *There are two souls invading your body . . .*

Thirteen

Bev located his car in one of the eight parking spots reserved for Jake's guests at the forefront of the driveway. He staggered into the driver's seat, reached into the glove compartment, found a pack of stale Camels and tapped one out. He lit it, using the car's lighter; the cigarette jumped in his trembling hand. His entire body fidgeted, sweated. Shutting his eyes, he inhaled and exhaled deeply, drag after drag until tobacco became filter. He lit another, then started the car and ran the air-conditioning. He thought of Kristin. Quickly dialed her number. No answer. Left her a message, his voice wavering, sounding distant and weak in his head, as though stuffed with cotton. Frowned. Not like her to break touch like this. He made a mental note to stop by her apartment ASAP.

He looked at the car's clock; 10:07. His doctor's appointment was at noon. Then he remembered the invitation: *Sunday, November 10. A limo will arrive at your residence at 6:00 P.M. Be available.* He tucked a hand into his back pocket. Not there. Then the front pocket, where he felt the folded envelope. *Why am I so concerned about it? I should be focusing on my health. My sanity.* Bev drove away, slowly, nerves jangling, helplessness floating errantly about him. *Will a limo really show up at my place tonight?*

He drove carefully, trying to not rub his injured palms against the steering wheel. He avoided traffic by taking only the winding neighborhood roads instead of the highway. Along the way, he smoked three more cigarettes. Snuffed them out in the car's ashtray, knowing and not caring at all that the doctor would smell the smoke on his breath. The nicotine helped calm his nerves for now.

At 10:55, he pulled into a 7-Eleven. Bought black coffee and a roll. A lingering sense of unreality surrounded him while he completed this mundane task, waiting in line behind others who were going about their routines with utter normalcy. It felt as though he were in a dream, floating through his actions with no promise of self-command. He returned to the car and sat quietly in the driver's seat, nibbling at the roll, sipping coffee, hiding behind sunglasses and wondering how in the hell he'd felt so fine last night at the party, only to wake up feeling so freakishly lost in his own mind. Nothing right now seemed to make any sense.

Suddenly, he felt it.

It was coming: a chill at first, as if ice crystals had formed in his bloodstream. Then a tugging at his head: the fingers. They had returned. *Digging, digging, scratching,* seeking more space between his skull and brain, the scraping sound echoing in his brain. His head shivered. Eardrums vibrated. He dropped the roll and clutched his head with both hands. "Why!" he shrieked. "Why me?" He shuddered with fear: His voice had changed. It was low. Deep and hoarse. His hands trembled, the tender lacerations in his palms throbbing more intensely; breaking open; bleeding. Anger welled in him. His heart rate sped. His skull felt as if it was going to crack. He began to kick and buck uncontrollably, spilling the hot coffee on the car seat. He heard himself howling in pain, body writhing on the front seat, arms flinging, tearing at his hair. He heard a deafening scream in his head, deep, pain-filled; and then clamorous laughter. He pressed his hands harder against his ears in an effort to blot it out. The laughter faded. Then the voice:

Bevant . . . come to me . . .

The voice quickly vanished, the accent echoing in his head. Then the anger dissipated. A weak lethargy at once consumed him as his consciousness returned to his mind, and he curled up on the front seat of the car, crying, reeking of coffee and smoke, gasping for breath.

He sat up, terrified. Hurting. Tears streamed down his face, blurring his vision. He used his sleeve to wipe them away. In minutes, his heart rate slowed back to normal. He stayed unmoving for a period of time, hands on the steering wheel, leaving sticky streaks of blood behind. His thoughts ran amok during this time, not making sense, seeming to simply reorganize themselves. When all the waters seemed calm again, he started the car.

There are two souls invading your body . . .

The clock read 11:48.

Time to see the doctor.

Fourteen

Doctor Richard Palumba's office was north of Torrance, in Marina Del Rey. Again Bev drove the back roads, very slowly, very mindfully, set to pull over should another attack occur. Thankfully, all remained calm. He only had to deal with impatient tailgaters, and his trembling fear: the anxiety of what had just occurred, and if it might happen again.

A middle-aged nurse accompanied him to an examining room. She seemed to notice his unkempt appearance, the injuries on his hands, but made no mention of it. She took his temperature and blood pressure, questioned his reason for the visit, to which he replied, "Personal," then left.

After ten minutes, Richard Palumba walked in. He wore brown poly/rayon pants, a tan dress shirt, and a striped tie beneath his stethoscope. He possessed an uncommonly full head of hair for a man in his sixties. He grinned professionally and opened a blue folder on the steel supply table; scanned it briefly.

"Mr. Mathers. Been a few years. Success takes up most of your time, I suppose."

Bev nodded. "It does."

"So, what brings you in?"

Bev summarized what had happened, narrating the same list of events he'd shared with Kristin the day before, starting with the onset of everything while on stage, right through all the odd physical elements that still beleaguered him. He elaborated in more detail how he *really* felt: scared, tired, quarrelsome. For the moment he left out the odd hallucinations he'd experienced before coming here, and the voice in his head. "Two days ago, I was feeling fine. Today, I feel as if I've lost my mind." He kept his hands facing downward, keeping his fresh injuries to himself.

"You have no temperature. Your blood pressure's fine."

"That's good."

"Any insomnia?" Palumba asked.

"No, no, I sleep fine." *Except for the dreams, and these damn lacerations on my hands. Got those while sleeping.*

"You mentioned that you've been feeling angry. Are there any personal issues that might be driving you to this?"

"No . . . everything is fine. I've never been happier, really, up until all this started happening—over the last forty-eight hours or so. It feels as though I've been hit with some terrible disease—it came on that suddenly. And honestly, it's scaring me."

Palumba took notes in the folder. "Appetite?"

"Fine, I guess."

"You mentioned this *scratching* sensation in your head. Any headaches?"

Bev shrugged. "Nothing out of the ordinary."

Palumba nodded, unimpressed. "You drink regularly?"

"No. Only on occasion."

"Smoke?"

"Yeah."

"Drugs?"

"Doc?"

"Process of elimination. Everything's confidential."

"Nothing. Well . . . your occasional puff on a joint, but even that's more not than often."

"Did you take any pills within the last few days? Prescription medication? Anything?"

"No. I don't even think I've had anything to drink, outside of a beer at lunch yesterday."

The doctor walked over, felt Bev's glands. Checked his ears, nose, throat, eyes. He ordered Bev to lie down, then ran the cold stethoscope over his chest.

"What is it, Doc? What's wrong with me?"

"Well, I'm not sure yet. All those things you've experienced are strongly symptomatic of panic, anxiety, even depression. However, as an internist, I need to rule out all possible physical ailments first before heading down that road. Anxiety and panic can mimic a great deal of true physical ailments, most commonly heart attacks, brain tumors, fybromyalgia, even schizophrenia—you know, all the bad stuff that's very easy to worry about. So we have to be careful. However, considering the sudden onset of your symptoms,

I'd venture to guess that all those possibilities are improbable. We can go ahead and treat you for anxiety and panic, see what happens, but still have to be certain that it isn't anything else. Even dehydration can cause many of the symptoms you've described, especially the 'feeling of being out of control.'"

Bev sat up. Felt a slight wave of relief, but still wasn't wholly convinced. "What's next?"

"The nurse will come in and draw your blood. The lab will run a standard workup to check your cell counts, cholesterol levels, thyroid activity, and diabetes, too. We'll also need a urine sample to test your liver and kidney functions."

The doctor excused himself and a different nurse came in with a plastic cup and a syringe. She drew his blood and afterward waited outside the room while Bev filled the cup in an adjoining bathroom. After all samples were collected, she left and Palumba returned.

"How long have you been away, Bev?"

"Nine months."

"I'd gather that touring the world in a rock-and-roll band isn't very conducive to a healthy lifestyle. Late nights, constant traveling, poor diet, not to mention being away from home and your loved ones. The parties at night, the public appearances, and the ongoing pressures of being expected to perform at the top of your abilities night after night. That'd get to anyone, and you have to remember, you're only human just like the rest of us."

Bev nodded. It did seem to make sense.

"Doc?"

Palumba was scribbling in the folder. "Yes?" He didn't look up.

"There's something else."

Palumba finished what he was writing, then put his pen down and looked at Bev.

"I've been, well, I've had some . . . some hallucinations."

"Hallucinations? What kind exactly?"

"I'm scared to admit this for fear that you might think I'm nuts, because I'm not . . . but . . . I've been hearing this voice in my head, and then, well, yesterday I saw a face."

"A face?"

"Yeah . . ." He rubbed his hair; pressed his cheeks; eyed the doctor seriously. "In the mirror. This is gonna sound crazy, but for a split second the person staring back at me wasn't me. It was someone else." He'd wanted to say *something* else, but refrained from doing so.

Palumba nodded as if he understood, as if the advent of hallucinations was significant to his pending diagnosis. He went back to taking notes, remaining silent throughout. Finally, he began tearing sheets of paper. "First things first. I am going to recommend an immediate change in your lifestyle. Any travel plans coming up?"

"No."

"Good. Get some rest. Change your diet, eat only healthy foods. No parties. No traveling, and above all, no work. I'm not recommending a vacation yet, although one might be good for you once you get your nerves all settled."

"Nerves? Is that what this is?"

"I suspect so. Ten years ago, it would've been the very last consideration on a long list of probable physical ailments. However, these days, with the economy the way it is and the pressures it induces upon everyday life, nearly half my weekly visitors complain of ailments that are directly related to the stressors of their routines: their jobs, situational problems with the family. I've seen it enough to know that what you're probably experiencing is a nervous breakdown. Generalized anxiety disorder coupled with severe panic attacks."

"But why all of a sudden?"

"Oh, it hasn't been a sudden onset. It's been there all along, for years maybe, building up in you—kind of like water behind a dam. You just didn't know it was there. When you were on stage the other night, for some unknown reason that was the catalyst causing your dam to finally burst—and you had a full-blown panic attack. Now the anxiety is unleashed, racing through your bloodstream. In actuality, we're talking adrenaline here, and you've got copious amounts of it squirting through your body, more than you can handle. Hence all those irritable symptoms you're feeling. You see, your mind *thinks* your body is in trouble, and as a result your fear/response system is working overtime to compensate, when it really shouldn't be working at all. It's apparent just in your demeanor . . . you haven't stopped fidgeting since you got here. That's an involuntary physical response to the surge of adrenaline."

"Then what about the hallucination? The voice in my head?"

"All symptoms of a hyperactive mind . . . and common ones, I might add. Ever get a song in your head for days at a time and it just won't leave?"

"Of course. Part of the job."

"Well, that's your mind working nonstop when it really should be at rest. That voice in your head is a memory engram in your subconscious that found its way out when the dam broke. Now, uncontrollably, you've got a little green man in there making your life miserable, tossing words your way at any given moment—just like that song in your head that won't go away."

"Well, I suppose that makes sense. And the hallucination?"

"Not so bad, all things considered. You've only had one episode, correct?"

"Yes."

Palumba nodded. "I've had folks come in complaining that their furniture was sliding across the room, that their walls were breathing. Everyone's different, but the cause is usually the same. Now, don't get me wrong, we will check for any possible physical causes for your discomforts, but we'll treat you for your attacks in the meantime. Frankly, there's no physical ailment we know of that can cause a cocktail of all the symptoms you're describing in so short a time, other than panic. And if you were suffering from something on a psychotic level, then you really wouldn't be having such a coherent conversation with me right now."

Bev nodded. "Should I go see a shrink?"

"It wouldn't hurt to talk to someone in more detail about what's ailing you. If anything, it might help relieve some of the pressure. In the meantime, I'm giving you a prescription for Celexa."

"What's that?"

"An antidepressant. Twenty milligrams, once a day. It'll take some time to kick in. Until that begins to work, here's a prescription for Xanax, a mild tranquilizer. Two milligrams, twice a day, as needed. The results of your blood tests will be back tomorrow, but I'd venture to guess that you're physically fine."

"That's good news," Bev said, taking the scripts from the doctor. "Thank you. Does this mean I'm not crazy?"

Palumba shook his head and smiled warmly. "No, I don't think you're crazy. I do suggest going home and getting a good night's rest. And try not to worry about anything."

"Thank you, Doc."

Fifteen

When he got to the car, he called Kristin. Again, her answering machine. He left another message. Told her that he'd visited the doctor and that it was all nerves. Nothing else. He apologized again for his outburst at the beach, then hung up, feeling utterly alone and lost. *Where is she?*

He started the car and began to drive, wondering how on earth it had come to this. *The doctor was right. I'm only human, and nine months of touring will do that to a person.*

He again opted for the back roads, keeping his pace slow. He was starting to feel better, actually, as he had at the party, as though the holes in the dam had been plugged. Perhaps knowing what was wrong—that it wasn't anything life-threatening—was already aiding in his recovery. After all, anxiety isn't a physical illness, it's a negative result of stress and the improper thinking patterns that arise from it. *The best medicine is positive thought,* he told himself. *Mind over matter.*

He stopped off at the Eckerd's Drug a mile from his home. Left the prescriptions with a short, bald man named George. He bought a copy of *Men's Health* magazine, a few protein bars, two packs of cigarettes, and a small register-side pamphlet on combating anxiety.

Back in the parking lot, the fingers came back. Quickly. Suddenly. But not as powerfully as before. This time it was more of a little tease. *Scratch, scratch, scratch.* No digging. And then they at once settled down. As if they meant to say, *Don't forget about us, we're still here.*

He stopped and thumbed his temples as the feeling faded. Then, suddenly, a terribly rotten smell hit him. Like meat gone afoul. Nausea rolled in his gut. He sniffed the air, searching the vicinity for a Dumpster, then instinctively placed a hand to his mouth, realizing with utter dismay that it was his breath. He ran back into the drugstore, bought some gum and mints and filled his mouth.

He returned to the spot where his car was parked.

Stopped.

Stared.

Clutched his leaping heart.

On the windshield.

Drawn in white marker.

6:00.

Sixteen

Bev looked at his watch. 2:13. He gazed around in a paranoid fashion, just as he had at the beach when he'd discovered that someone had been watching him. He saw no one suspicious nearby. A heavyset woman stood before a Jeep Cherokee, loading a child into a car seat; a man wearing a Spock's Beard T-shirt stood by the entrance to the drugstore, opening a pack of cigarettes he'd presumably just purchased. A girl with green spiked hair sailed by on a skateboard.

"Hey," Bev called to her.

She glanced around, then one-eightied on her skateboard, rolled over, and stopped a few feet away from him. With a flick of her foot, she kicked up the skateboard and caught it with one hand. She waited in haughty silence.

Bev eyed her various piercings: nose, eyebrow, lip. He said, "You know who I am?"

She shook her head.

Not that famous.

"My name's Bev. Bev Mathers."

She looked at him quizzically. "So?" Arrogant youth. Not one of his crowd. More in tune with the Sex Pistols, or the Misfits.

"Well . . . I guess it's not important."

"What do you want?" the girl asked, tossing her skateboard back to the blacktop.

He pointed to the windshield of his car. "See that? The six o'clock? You didn't happen to see who wrote that there, did you? It had to have happened within the last five minutes or so, while I was in the store."

"Actually, yeah, I did."

Bev's heart sped. A lump formed in his throat. "Mind telling me?"

"Nope. I did it."

"What?"

"Yeah. Sorry about that. It'll come off with water."

"I'm not worried about it washing off." Bev stepped forward, ready to grab the girl should she try to flee before he had an answer. But the girl remained steadfast, living up to her arrogant appearance. "Who are you? Why'd you put that there?"

"Hey, man, don't shoot the messenger, okay? Some guy paid me twenty bucks to do it."

"Some guy? What'd he look like?"

"I don't know. Kinda geeky, I guess. Said it was a joke. I didn't care. Got me twenty bills out of it."

"Where is he now?"

"Drove away after I did the deed."

"What was he driving?"

"Uhh . . . white car. Kinda small."

This meant one thing: that the man from the Forum

party, the one that left the invitation, the one who followed him at the beach, was *still* tailing him. Bev shivered, considering all the unanswered questions: Who was this guy? What did he want from him? Was it really just a party, as Kristin suggested? Or was there some other kind of sick motive? One thing was for certain: The guy was determined.

"Can I go now?"

The girl fidgeted with the loop in her nose, thrust a tongue stud forward with her teeth. She looked impatiently bored.

"Yeah, you can go. Thanks."

She nodded, and skated across the lot around the side of the building, out of sight.

Bev peered back at his windshield.

6:00.

He felt in his pocket for the invite. Took it out. Stared at the typewritten words:

A LIMO WILL ARRIVE AT YOUR RESIDENCE
AT 6:00 PM
BE AVAILABLE

He looked at his watch.

2:28.

Be available.

Seventeen

The man went into his room, sat on the edge of his soiled bed. He folded his hands in prayer.

His invocations were interrupted by harsh memories. The past. Thirty-four years ago. When the call came.

We have a child for you. A six-year-old Israeli boy whose parents were killed in the war. He was rescued by a team of archaeologists in the desert, and has been nursed back to health. We believe that you and your wife are the perfect parental candidates for him. His name is Allieb.

The lengthy application process had asked a seemingly never-ending list of questions, from religious preferences to dietary practices to political beliefs. One question in particular carried a great deal more weight than the others; it had asked if the applicants had desired only an infant child. A humorless woman at the adoption agency explained to them that most eager parents preferred to start from scratch, so to speak, regardless of the long wait for a newborn. But, if they would agree upon a child up to the age of ten years, then the wait would be much shorter. *There are many parentless children in overseas camps waiting for an opportunity to come to America.* Feeling pity for the thousands of faceless children the agent had so sorrowfully referred to, the future mother and father agreed to this arrangement, knowing that soon they'd become the proud parents they'd always dreamed to be.

Three months later, the call came to notify them of the good news. A child had been chosen for them. They'd rejoiced in prayerful song and feast, their dark world falling beneath the beams of a previously impenetrable light—the man's curse of sterility, now offset with a gift from God. There had never been a happier moment for the two of them.

Papers filled. Signed. Then . . . a son.

On December 25, 1968, they met him at the L.A. International Airport. Dark curly hair. Olive skin. Large unflinching eyes. The man recalled the undying emotion of the moment, heart pounding with joy, of proud anticipation racing through his veins upon first sighting his son. He remembered how they'd locked gazes for the first time. And how he'd felt a fleeting second of a headache, a unique scratching in his head like a fingernail on limestone, and then a faint burning smell like charcoal that seemed to have come from nowhere, and with all of this a slight stir of hesitancy washing over him, disturbing the happiness of the moment that faded as soon as the boy smiled and raced forward, hugging him around the waist.

They showered him with affection from that moment forward. Hugs. Gifts. A new home to sleep soundly in. All had seemed perfect—a grand start to a wonderful life together. What more could they have asked for?

Soon, however, they would realize something was wrong.

For weeks thereafter the boy remained silent, tentative in his new surroundings, unwilling to do little more than eat raw vegetables and sleep during the day and pray silently in his room at night. He spoke very little, mumbling only in prayer and acknowledging his parents with curt whispers and nods only during brief respites. Despite this reluctance to communicate, the man and his wife still poured their heart and soul out to him, making sure that he was fed, clothed, protected, hoping that soon he would open up to them and return the love that they were so willing to give.

Months passed. In time the boy had indeed begun to open up, to show some willingness to speak, and even took an interest in primary education. It seemed as though the new parents' hard efforts were beginning to pay off. As a minister, the man made every effort to raise the boy a Christian, despite Allieb's intrinsic Hebrew upbringings, and his odd silent prayers. The boy consented to the man's indoctrinations, attending his father's sermons, although the man suspected the boy might not have paid attention to the daily teachings instilled upon him. Still, he brought the boy to church every Sunday and continued to school him at home, religiously and educationally.

By the age of nine, the boy spoke fluent English.

By ten, French.

And soon thereafter, Italian. And Latin. And German. The boy exhibited a proficiency not only for language but for math as well, able to decode even the most complicated formulas, whether in algebra, trigonometry, or calculus. Even stranger, the boy retained knowledge of affairs that required research beyond his restricted capacities, from events in Russian history to the man's own genealogical background.

With this sudden and rather alarming proficiency, the man and his wife, driven mostly through religious influence, grew very concerned.

On an instinctual whim, the man began to research the history of the boy's name: Allieb. No mention of it in the Bible, although there was a passage in the Old Testament that stated, *Removing the lie shall reveal a demon in disguise.* It had stood out for weeks in the man's mind, pestering him like a persistent itch, until the pieces of the puzzle finally fell together.

On a piece of paper, the man wrote down his son's birth name: Allieb.

Remove the lie. He crossed out the word "lie" in his name. That left A-L-B.

Rearranging the letters, he spelled out: B-A-L. He shuddered, then looked at the remaining letters, L-I-E. He mixed them up, then one by one placed them back into his name.

"Dear Jesus, help us," he said aloud, staring at the letters written on the paper.

B-E-L-I-A-L. The demon.

Feeling helpless, the man continued his daily routine of preaching and teaching and supplicating, watching over his son carefully as the boy continued to exhibit an intelligence far beyond his schooling and development. The boy went about his odd routines, keeping quietly to himself at all times, even when his father out-

112

wardly probed his behavior. Arguments arose. Fights ensued.

Then, on the morning of his first communion—a special day his parents had looked forward to for years—the boy's true persona emerged. They found him on the bathroom floor, naked, peering up at them, a razor clutched in his hand. Mother had dropped the blue suit she'd been holding and run from the room, sobbing uncontrollably at the sight of her son. The father had stood there motionless, making the sign of the cross, praying for his son, who'd shaved his head and eyebrows and sat smiling idiotically on the floor.

The communion commenced, the man unwilling to allow the spawning darkness to consume his only child. The procession of children went fifty or more long. Allieb had stood in the middle, fidgeting uncontrollably as he neared the front of the line. Unexplainably, the church organ blared loudly upon his turn to accept the host.

The boy closed his eyes. Opened his mouth. The priest placed the Body of Christ upon his tongue.

Immediately, Allieb gagged and collapsed to the floor, clawing at his lips, screaming, "It's choking me! It's choking me." His eyes rolled up into his sockets, exposing bloodshot whites, and when the priest kneeled down to assist him, the boy jutted up as if tethered on strings, arms outstretched, mocking crucifixion. He spit a wad of phlegm at the priest, laughing as he did so, taunting his stunned parents with cold, vicious eyes.

This, the man realized, eyes heavy with tears, *is the beginning of the end of it all.*

God help us.

* * *

In tears, the man stood up from his bed, shaking the invading memory from his mind. He paced unevenly to the wooden nightstand alongside the bed and fumbled out a silver crucifix. He kissed the cross and continued his prayers until a knock came upon the door.

He looked up, shoving the cross back into the drawer. "Enter."

Slowly, the door creaked open. A thirty-something woman appeared. She wore a hooded black robe and sash. A silver pentagram sat against her heart from a beaded chain around her neck. Her skin was pale and peppered with acne. Her blue eyes bristled with nervous anticipation.

"Additional vehicles have arrived," she said, cocking her head curiously. The tears in his eyes.

"How many?" he asked.

"Three. A man, and two women."

"How did they get here?"

"By calling."

He nodded. Like the last one that had come. *Baphomet.*

He hesitated, then asked, "Who is your God?"

"Allieb," she answered, bowing.

"Go and pray," he commanded, and the woman fled the room. He gazed at the clock on the wall. Through the cracked face, he saw: 2:45 P.M. By eight, twelve of the thirteen would have arrived. He reached for the bottle of scotch on the table in the center of the room. Drank in the darkness.

The last one. Number thirteen. He wouldn't be here to begin the ceremony, he knew. His presence, though, was required. His acceptance, however. . . . He still hesitated. Additional influence was needed.

6:00. Would there be enough time for him to gather his force?

The man continued his prayers.

The thirteenth was his only hope for survival.

Eighteen

"Kristin, if you're there, please pick up."

2:57. No answer on her home phone. Her cell had also gone unanswered since last night. He'd been waiting in his car in the Eckerd's parking lot for a half hour now: waiting for the fingers to return, waiting for Kristin to return his calls. *Please.* He'd phoned her six or seven times now, worrying more and more with each unanswered call. He placed his cell phone on the passenger seat, started the car, feeling caught in the closed confines, as though caged underwater. *Anxiety.* He opened the window, took a deep breath. Common sense told him that he should head home, nestle himself in bed, get some rest just as the doctor had ordered. But his fatherly instincts had him doing otherwise: driving out of the parking lot in the direction of Kristin's apartment, taking the roads slowly and surely just in case another panic attack should arise.

He gripped the wheel tightly, easing the clutch of panic that seemed to roll in even without the onset of the skull fingers. Deep breaths; inhale through the nose; exhale through the lips. *Ohm-nama-shivaya.* Keep calm, keep calm.

Ahead, on a hill, the brownish facing of Kristin's gated complex came into view. He pulled in through the security entrance, gave his name to the guard as Kristin's permanent guest, then drove over the small stone bridge to town house 1034.

Kristin's car was parked out front.

He parked alongside the red Mustang. Grabbed his cell phone and got out of the car. The sun cast a blanket of warmth upon him as he strolled nervously up the walkway leading to her residence. He tried to peek through the front window but couldn't see past his shadowed reflection in the panes. When he cupped his hands on the glass, he glimpsed only an unoccupied living room.

A door creaked open in the attached town house next door. A middle-aged man wearing jeans and a golf shirt emerged, holding a Mervyn's bag. He eyed Bev suspiciously. Bev smiled weakly and shoved his hands in his pockets, feeling, and probably looking, guilty.

"Help ya?" the man asked, an eyebrow raised, the eye below probing him.

"My daughter," Bev answered, defensively. "I'm looking for my daughter."

The man grinned, as though impressed. "Ah, you must be the rock star."

Bev returned the grin, fingernails probing the dust in his pockets. "That would be me."

The man drifted forward, offered a handshake,

which Bev accepted uneagerly. "Joe Caputo. Pleased to meet you."

"Bev Mathers."

"I've heard so much about you from Kristin."

"You see her often?"

"Often enough. We are next-door neighbors, of course."

"Any idea where she is right now?"

Joe shrugged his shoulders. "Saw her getting into a limo last night. 'Bout seven or so. Last I've seen her."

"A limo?" His heart started pounding. *Be available.*

Joe nodded. "Yep. Nice big fancy black one."

"You see anyone else get in?"

"No . . . Is there something wrong?"

Bev shook his head. Ran a sweaty hand across his face. "No, just being a parent." His voice wavered.

"Gotchya. Got two of my own. Both married for years. And I still worry."

Bev peered about the manicured complex. A flock of black birds flew overhead and landed in a cherry tree across the street, filling the branches. An uncomfortable silence emerged. Finally, Bev said, "I'm gonna wait out front a bit. Hopefully she'll be home soon." *A limo will arrive at your residence at 6:00. Be available.* Had Kristin received the same invite? No, impossible, Bev thought. They'd talked all about it at the restaurant yesterday. She would have mentioned something to him.

Joe nodded, said, "Well, nice to meet you," then walked to his car.

Bev watched Joe Caputo get into his car, back out, and drive away.

He poked out a Camel, lit it, diverting his attention to the motionless birds in the cherry tree that seemed to be staring down at him. He rubbed his tired eyes, then stared back up at the birds and thought with dismay how awful he felt, both physically and mentally, as though he were on a slow-sinking ship, the water now up to his waist.

The lava . . .

Five minutes passed. The birds remained strangely quiet, not a squawk or a rustle of feathers to be heard. He tossed the half-smoked cigarette to the floor, snubbed it out, then walked back to the town house window and gazed inside. Nothing different. Only his tired reflection staring back at him as he backed away. On a whim, he tried the door.

The knob turned.

He pushed the door. It creaked as he entered in silence. A sense of unreality immediately consumed him, thoughts of actually having to discontinue his career as a musician taunting him; his mind, rightly so, was devoid of any creative inspiration at the moment. *Ain't doing nothing until I find Kristin, and until I get myself feeling better. Wouldn't be the first time someone in my position had to take some time off for mental health.*

Closing the door behind him, he felt a chill . . . a tearing premonition that seemed to fill his heart with shards of ice. He turned around and gazed about the empty town house. For a moment he stood still, studying the untouched living room, sniffing the stale air. Then he stepped forward, overcome with an eerie sense of anticipation. He shivered. *Something,* he thought, *is about to happen.*

He paced across the living room, checking out the coffee table, the sofa and love seat, wondering for the first time why Kristin had left the front door open. *Unlike her to be so careless.* The room—it was undisturbed, everything clean and neat as though she'd been expecting company. *A limo? Yep. Nice big fancy black one.* Arms folded to counteract the invading chill, Bev crossed into the small eat-in kitchen, which was just as immaculate as the living room, oak table polished, the sink's surface sparkling white.

On the wall over the table, Bev gazed at a series of photographs framed in a montage: pictures of Kristin at various ages, most of them with Bev. One photo on the bottom was of Bev and Julianne seated on a sofa, smiling as they cradled an infant Kristin. Bev placed a finger against the photo of Julianne. *She does look like Rebecca Haviland,* he thought, smiling, thinking of their time last night.

Feeling a sudden, remorseful need to apologize to Rebecca for his hasty departure this morning, he grabbed his cell phone.

Started dialing her number.

As he did so, he gazed at his hands.

And froze. The phone fell to the floor.

Because they'd stopped hurting him, he'd forgotten about the mysterious scars he'd obtained while sleeping. Now, looking at his hands, he saw that the scars had healed over. Once red and sore and bleeding, the deep gouges in his palms were now dried and scabbed. What should have taken a few days to mend had taken only a few hours.

Shaking his head with confusion, flexing and staring at his hands in disbelief, he picked up the phone, then slowly paced out of the kitchen, stopping in the foyer to stare at his hands and reaffirm the fact that the scars were nearly gone. In a cloud, he made a left down the short hall into the first of two bedrooms.

Here the walls were painted off-white. Curtains,

drawn, blocked the view of the courtyard out back. The twin bed had been made, throws placed carefully atop the fitted spread. The bathroom door in the far left corner was ajar, brilliant white wall tiles gleaming beneath the skylight.

Finding nothing of interest here (and feeling a bit uncomfortable snooping in his daughter's bedroom), he exited back into the hallway and stood before the closed door to the second bedroom, which Kristin used as an office for her work. He pushed the door open and stood attentively in the entranceway, gazing in sudden bewilderment at the contents of the small room.

In stark contrast to the rest of the house, there was a major clutter of items, although everything seemed to be situated in its own respective area, as if, despite the presumed chaos, Kristin knew exactly where everything belonged. Magazines and newspapers were piled three feet high—rows that ran the entire length of the far wall. A desk was situated against the right wall beneath the curtained window, a computer, reading lamp, and telephone nearly buried beneath a mountain of textbooks and papers. Her closet had been left open, and from within more books spilled out. It had been perhaps eight months since he was here, and at that time the office had been kept as immaculate as the rest of the home. *So what happened?* Bev stepped over a crooked pile of data folders to the desk.

He flicked on the lamp and eyeballed some of the papers there, mostly scattered writings of recent articles, interviews, and notes for her work at *Rock Scene*. Alongside the desk on the floor sat piles of books stacked at various angles, their bindings bragging a myriad of topics: *Rock Hard Magazine's 100 Greatest Live Albums, Conducting Interviews With the Fa-*

mous, How to Write a Bestselling Novel, Research in Demonology . . .

"What the hell," he muttered, crouching down to make sure he'd read the book's spine correctly. He had. And, reading farther down the pile, he noticed many more odd titles mixed in with the more common journalistic publications expected of Kristin: *Summoning the Dead, The Harsh Spirit World, Paranormal Studies*. He picked up the first book he spotted, near the top of the pile, *Research in Demonology*, and quickly thumbed through it. Nearly four hundred pages of text peppered with artist's renditions of historic people, as well as black-and-white photos of archaeological sites and the curios discovered in them. Portions of the text had been highlighted throughout.

Impulsively, he turned to the book's index. Ran a finger down the A's to . . .

"Here it is," he muttered, surprised, as well as a bit shaken. "Allieb. Page 238." He turned to the indicated page. On it was an undated pencil sketch of a man wearing all black clothing. He was completely bald, with a black goatee and thick black eyebrows that curled up at the outer edges like handlebars. His piercing eyes, sharp and narrow and almost reptilian in nature, stared up at Bev from the yellowed page. Beneath the picture ran a few lines of text:

Artist's rendition sketch of Allieb, a demonologist from Israel, and the self-proclaimed son of the demon Belial. Stories date back to the first millennium B.C.E. Purported to have slaughtered and cannibalized thirteen children in an effort to embody demon spirits from the underworld. Was later captured and buried alive by the people of

*Jerusalem in the very tomb he created for his
sacrifants.*

Bev shuddered, feeling suddenly cold. Alarmed. The
story . . . it was the same one Father Danto told at the
party. *Christ, what are the odds?* Bev closed the book,
disconcerted with the coincidence. *Too coincidental,
too crazy. First the priest, and now my daughter.*

Judd Schiffer's words came back to him like a sudden shot in the arm: *Last night, someone sacrificed a
goat on the lawn outside the rectory. It had been decapitated, its carcass gutted and impaled on a large
crucifix. Its entrails were laid out into a pentagram
shape beneath the cross.*

What the hell is going on? Bev wondered, confused,
feeling suddenly weak in the knees. *Nothing. Nothing.
Don't be alarmed. It's your anxious mind making
mountains out of molehills. It's nothing more than
some crazy, nutty coincidence.*

He gazed around the room some more. As his eyes
adjusted to the mess, he began to notice even more
textbooks and magazines and tear sheets on subjects
concerning the occult, psychic phenomenon, and demonology. He picked up a folder from the floor and
within discovered a stack of handwritten pages. He
skimmed through them, noticing paragraphs pertain-
ing to black masses, séances, and the occult.

"What is all this?" Bev asked himself aloud, reading
a passage scrawled in Kristin's handwriting:

*Proper performance of demonic worship is
most suitably effected during the black masses
of numerous individuals, although demons can
still be exhorted from afar with the assistance of*

other demons that have already been assembled beyond their strickened confines. "Evil" is then perpetrated upon the worshiping masses in the form of copulation and other commissioned desecrations of an extensively lecherous nature. Necrophilia and zoophilia are common practices among cultists, alongside additional extreme sexual acts that utilize statuettes of Christ and the Virgin Mary as phalluses. These phalluses are lubricated with the menstrual blood of virgins and inserted into the mouths and anuses of those conjugating with the bodies of those sacrificed.

Bev flipped to another page dealing with ritualistic murders. He read it slowly, frowning and shaking his head with utter disbelief, thinking of Kristin and recalling his conversation with her at the Forum party:

"Any new projects?"

"Well . . . yeah . . ."

"Care to tell me about them?"

"Yes! But not now, Dad. This is your party! We'll talk about it soon."

Was this what she was referring to? If so, then she'd apparently been wrapped up in it for quite some time. He gathered an armful of folders from the floor and sat at the desk. Racing through them, he found pages and pages of minutely detailed pencil sketches, indiscernible symbols of an astrological nature interspersed with pentagrams and ram's horns and other representations of a dark sort. Paper-clipped to many of the drawings were pages of handwritten text describing each piece in utter detail, including its history, meaning, and purpose. Bev flipped to the page attached to a sketch of a woman figure seemingly crucified on a life-size statue of the Virgin Mary. He read:

> *Rituals during the holy time of Sabbat use the Virgin Mary as a role model, whereas her form would be erected at an altar. In one known sacrificial ritual, a pregnant woman would be fettered to the statue, her legs wrenched open wide with ropes or chains tied to brass cherubim on the altar. Members of the congregation would engage in oral sex with the woman. Ivory phalluses would then be blasphemously inserted into her anus and mouth while the priest masturbated on her vagina. After his ejaculation, the priest would batter the woman's swollen belly with a crucifix until the dead fetus fell out, which was subsequently gathered in a chalice and fed upon by members of the congregation as an offering of the Host.*

"My God, Kristin," Bev uttered in an anxious tone. "What are you into?" He dropped the folder on the desk and picked up another. His eyes searched the papers frantically. He read various essays on black masses and the actions of its willing participants. In a short time, he fell upon some rather troublesome lines of text:

> *The goal of the Master Demonologist (in addition to summoning malevolent spirits, his arts also include magic, abstract sciences, alchemy, language mastery, communication with animals, as well as numerology and pneumatology) is to incantate demon spirits from the netherworlds*

through the art of self-possession, or, as discovered in many cases, the purposeful possession of others. During "projected" possession, the recipient of the demonic soul will not immediately become aware that he or she has become "possessed," as time must pass for the demon to "find" its way out from the bowels of the individual into the physical body, or "vehicle," of the person under possession. Eventually, all physical and mental functions are retained through what is referred to as "demonic invasion," that being the time from initial conception to full-bodied possession. An immense alteration of personality takes place during the time of invasion, to a point where others around the possessed individual and perhaps the individual themselves will feel that a terrible mental sickness has set in. More of the common traits of an individual under possession are the mimicking of other people, dead or alive, the speaking of tongues previously unknown to the person, and the ability to calculate complex mathematical formulas. In more advanced stages, the person under possession may bear telekinetic capacities, or the ability to move objects without the use of physical coercion. The demonologist's goals appear to emulate the abilities of the demon itself.

Bev ran a hand through his hair, then pulled another page of text and read it, fully absorbed:

It can only be speculated as to what an individual may experience while under demonic possession. At first, they may feel suddenly ill,

*nauseous, and dizzy. Tired, yet unable to sleep.
When sleep does come, it is usually fitful and
may be filled with surreal, enigmatic nightmares.
Other physical symptoms may include those
which suggest schizophrenia or epilepsy. These
include hallucinations, delusions, convulsions
and/or seizures, combativeness, automatism,
and somnambulism. No less daunting are the
physical symptoms that might lead the individual
to believe he might be under extreme duress from
panic, anxiety, or depression: fatigue, exhaustion, heart palpitations, chest pain, rapid pulse,
dizziness, faintness, distorted vision, hyperventi-
lation, aching muscles, cramps, stiffness, irri-
tability, depression, insomnia, nightmares, loss
of memory, lump in the throat, nausea, diarrhea,
depersonalization, increased sensitivity to light
and sound, stiff neck, burping fluids, numbness,
tingling, tinnitus, jitteriness, tension, sweating,
trembling, facial twitching, frequent urination,
apprehension, unwanted thoughts, a fear of going crazy.*

A fear of going crazy?

Bev placed the paper down, his mind caught in a
whirlwind of confusion. *Am I . . . ? Could I possibly
be . . . ?*

"No!" he screamed, slamming his fists on the desk.
He stood angrily, clearing the contents of the desk with
a reckless swoop of his arm. "This is insane! I am not
possessed by a fucking demon!"

*Well, there's some major league strangeness going on
here, Bev. You start feeling all sorts of fucked up, then
you go to a party where an archaeologist priest pins*

*you in conversation about demonic sacrifices at the lo-
cal church and his past history regarding an ancient
demonologist called Allieb who sacrificed and ate children in an effort to summon demons from hell, and lo
and behold, your now-missing daughter happens to
leave her front door open and here you are snooping
through her shit and what the fuck? she's into the
same demonology crap, and after an hour of poking
around, Allieb's in your face again and so is a more ex-
plicit explanation to all the terrible things that have
been happening to you . . .*

No . . .

He stood from the desk, feeling light-headed, listening closely but not hearing voices or feeling that
scratch-scratch-scratch of fingers along the surface of
his skull. He careened slightly to the left, gripping the
closet door for support. The room was eerily silent save
for the ticking of a clock in the living room and his
rapid breathing. He peered into the closet. Deep in the
darkness, beyond the initial barrier of books and magazines, he saw something: a hulking figure against the
rear wall. He hesitated, not wanting to explore any further for fear of what he might find next. But he'd felt a
nagging temptation to dig, to unearth additional
secrets—just as he had while gripping the envelope
with his name scrawled on the front—the envelope
that had remained in his back pocket for twelve hours
until Kristin coerced him to open it. With a frown, Bev
hunkered down in the entrance to the closet and
shoved aside a pile of books.

Against the back wall was a small metal trunk.
Black, with two bronze clasps at either end and a flip
lock in the center. He cleared the closet floor of the remaining articles—some books, a few pairs of shoes,

empty shoe boxes, a dusty purse—then gripped the plastic handle at one end of the trunk and pulled. *What's in here?* He dragged it out of the closet against the wall alongside the entrance to the room. First, he undid the side clasps, then quickly scoured through the desk drawers in search of a key to the flip lock. When one wasn't found, he opted for a letter opener, which aided him in busting the lock after a dozen jabs.

He opened the trunk.

My God . . .

Nineteen

He sat there, motionless, sagging with the sudden enormous weight of the contents inside the trunk. He swallowed hard, the painful remembrance of Julianne surging back to him with the ferocity of a point-blank gunshot. He reached down and picked out a few articles of Julianne's clothing, a maternity blouse she'd worn while pregnant, a pair of faded jeans, some T-shirts that when held to his face seemed to retain—imagination or not—a bit of her scent. There were a few other articles of clothing that Bev didn't remember at all, black T-shirts and a hooded knit robe and sash. Digging further into the contents of the chest, he discovered a multitude of keepsakes: a silver pendant that Julianne had worn, a small jewelry box with a few of her rings, a necklace, two pairs of sandals, some love letters she'd written Bev while they were dating. Farther down: a silver crucifix, a small worn Bible, a shoe box containing some odd artifacts: tarot cards, a silver pendulum, tea leaves wrapped in clear plastic, a Ouija board planchette. *Odd.*

Beneath the box were some photos of Julianne holding a baby Kristin, and one of the three of them sitting on the grass by the lake in Alondra Park . . . Bev didn't remember the photo or when it was taken, but could see something odd about Julianne's face. She looked serious, even *scared*, her grin downcast, brow furrowed, sharp eyes pinning him from the past. He flipped through a number of photos of his long-lost wife, wondering why Kristin had never shown him any of these items she'd saved: Julianne smiling at the kitchen table, another of her breastfeeding Kristin, of her posing playfully on their bed, of her . . .

Christ almighty . . . please, no . . .

In his trembling hands he gripped a photo of Julianne wearing the black robe he'd just removed from the trunk. Hanging around her neck was a silver pentagram, fettered by a silver chain that had glinted in the camera's flash. Her face was partially shrouded by the hood, one eye lost in shadow, the other ignited by the glow of the white candle she held.

Jesus Christ, no . . .

Bev let the photos fall from his numb grasp, sudden nausea consuming his body, tears sprouting from his disbelieving eyes. In a matter of seconds his entire life as he'd known it had taken on an entirely different perspective, one darkly veiled in baleful shadows and churning iniquity. Evil had suddenly embraced him, its terrible secret now out in the open. Was his wife, twenty years past, a member of some demonic cabal? His daughter, full of giggles and smiles and diabolical knowledge, following in her mother's footsteps?

Michael Laimo

Where did you get this stuff, Kristin? How did you get it? You were only a baby when your mother died. Only a tiny innocent baby . . .

Bev leaned back against the desk. Breathing heavily. Cries came uncontrollably as his mind drowned in a whirl of utter confusion. Of fear. The world had taken on a hard, grainy texture, like old film passing by in a flickering, slow-motion nightmare. A sudden odor filled the air, of something horrid and unspeakable, and Bev, blaming his tired imagination, used his last bit of fortitude in an attempt to ignore the feelings of horror consuming him. He leaned forward. Reached back into the trunk. Pulled out another yellow envelope. Opened it. Inside, a locked diary. The small leather-bound booklet had weathered with age, making it easy for him to tear the tiny clasp away without having to break the lock.

Written on the inside, in Julianne's handwriting, he read:

JULIANNE MATHERS
MY DIARY

As he had yesterday with the envelope, and just minutes earlier with the trunk, he hesitated exploring further, second-guessing his strong desire to unearth answers to his mounting dilemmas. Still, a morbid curiosity rose in him, and he gripped the first page of the diary, realizing that he'd already come too far:

October 17, 1984

Bev and I had an argument tonight about money, and about Kristin not getting the proper attention we wanted to give her. Bev told me he wanted to work two jobs, and I told him that if he did, then I'd never see him, and he'd never have any time with Kristin, and then I'd be home alone all the time with the baby, like a single mother, and that's really not acceptable as far as I'm concerned. She needs her father as much as I need a husband.

I left the apartment in a bad mood—I'd needed to get out of there for a while. Staring at those walls can make you crazy! I went to Alondra Park and sat in the moonlight, feeding the ducks. Suddenly, a man appeared next to me. I'd never heard him approach, and he really startled me. But then I looked at him, and ... well, I should have been frightened, but for some reason I wasn't. He smiled, and at once I felt a kind of kinship with him, as though he'd come to deliver some answers to our problems.

Bev remembered the night. Julianne had told him she was going to the park. He'd stayed home with Kristin, who'd cried inconsolably. Eventually, she fell asleep after a bottle, and so did Bev, in front of the television.

He did. He told me his name was Al-lieb ...

The diary trembled in Bev's hand. He knew where this was going. It wasn't going to be easy.

> ...and at once I was hypnotized. Maybe it was his striking eyes, or his mesmerizing accent. Or his imposing posture. He said, "Julianne Mathers, I know what you need." I'd asked him how he knew my name, and he told me he had the knowledge of the sun and stars, and that he'd use it to bring me and my family riches and happiness. My common sense told me that I should've walked away, but there I was, ignoring my better instincts, following this stranger into a limo parked a short walk away. We rode in silence, and I'd never felt more relaxed in my life. The car took us to a large house, a mansion I suppose, with a circular driveway and dark rooms lit solely with candles. Allieb led me into a study, where I sat on a red velvet sofa. He made a flame appear from his palms, and then he showed me sights I never thought imaginable. In a dreamlike vista, right before my eyes, I saw Bev on a stage performing rock music in front of thousands of people, and of Kristin, grown up, adoring her rockstar father, writing reviews of his concerts for Rock Hard Magazine.
>
> When the vision was over, I asked him how he did it. It had seemed so

real! He told me that there were many more sights to see, that he'd make sure Bev would gain great musical talent—a talent he could use to earn a lifestyle of fame and fortune. I asked him how, and he told me.

And then I went home, thinking that things were going to get much better for us.

The entry ended. He turned the page and read on quickly:

October 21, 1984

I met with Allieb for the second time last night. I told Bev I'd joined a "Mingling Moms" group where women could get away from the trials of home and gossip about our spouses and children. I'd heard about the group but never really joined. I went to go see Allieb instead. I kept telling myself, this is for the good of Bev, for the good of us. Our family. Still, I felt bad about lying to him. But he'll never know, especially once he's up on that stage playing guitar and singing to sold-out crowds.

The limo picked me up at our meeting spot at the park. I was asked to change into a black robe with a hood, which I did, and was then blindfolded. I was driven to the mansion, where I *was led into a cold room. I could feel the presences of many people watching me, but I didn't know for certain there was anyone there until they started chanting. An organ played a dark, dissonant tune, kind of like the beginning of Pink Floyd's "Shine On You Crazy Diamond." I was led to a spot somewhere in the middle of the room. I should have been nervous but I wasn't. Allieb was next to me. He whispered, "You will earn success and riches beyond your wildest imagination. Is this what you desire?" I told him, "Yes, for Bev, and for Kristin. I want it for them." He told me to drop my robe, and unexplainably, with no reluctance, I did, and in all my nakedness I stood there, unknowing as to where I was and who was in the room with me. The chanting commenced, and that is all I can remember, until this morning, when I awoke with blood on my hands and lips.*

Bad. This was very bad.

Bev noted the date of the following entry, nearly three weeks later. He read on:

November 3, 1984

I am quite normal at home. I am relaxed, and calm. It's a side effect of the . . . of the, well, I suppose it is Allieb's influence that has me able to appear as though this second life I'm leading is nothing more than a dream, or fantasy. Because of this, I haven't been able to write any of my experiences down, as Allieb made me swear to Belial that should I utter a word of my participation of the masses to anyone, then something terrible will happen to me or my family. But I am consumed with guilt. Although I remember only snippets of my experiences at "In Domo," these brief memories are enough to know that I have done wrong, that I have entered a realm far above and beyond my capacities as a human being. That, really, I am damned. I believe I have sold my soul to evil, and have received nothing that has been promised to me in return. Bev is showing no promise of musical prowess. I cannot elaborate any further as to the memories of my experiences at "In Domo." There is too much pain, both mental and physical. I can only pray that God can forgive me for the decisions I have made, and hope that He will spare me any further agony.

Drowning in tears, Bev fanned through the rest of the diary. A newspaper clipping drifted out, poignantly familiar. Julianne's obituary. He picked it up and gazed at it, at the strikingly familiar date of her death: November 5, 1984. Two days after the last entry in the diary. *Jesus.* Scanning the pages again, he found no additional notations. He screamed and flung the diary into the closet, a piece of history best shunned. "How could I have not known! How could this have happened!" He fell back against the desk, fists on brow. Trembling. Crying. Knowing that from this point forward, his life would never be the same.

His cell phone rang. Hell's Bell, tolling his arrival.

He fumbled it out of his pocket, answered it. His voice, cracking: "Yeah . . ."

"Bev, it's Rebecca." Her voice, a pensive whisper.

He stayed silent. Didn't know how to react, what to say. "Rebecca . . ." he managed.

"You heard, didn't you . . ."

Confusion. Then: "Heard what?"

"Jesus, Bev . . . you didn't hear . . ."

"Hear about what?" The words bounced off his tongue with no meaningful direction or intent.

"I have some very bad news."

Finally, a burst of lucidity. *Could it get any worse?* Bev straightened up, grasping some wits. "What is it?"

"It's Jake."

"What about him?" he asked, but by the somber tone of her voice, he knew. He closed his eyes, readying himself for the blow.

"He's dead."

Twenty

He gazed back up at the clock. The cracked face read 3:44. In the hall, a disturbance. "There are two more!" someone shouted. Footsteps shuffling, and then silence. Soon thereafter, a knock upon the door.

"Enter," the man said.

Slowly, the door creaked. Through minimal space appeared an unfamiliar face. A male, in his thirties. Short, but muscular. A fresh bruise on his right eye. "God wants you," he told the man.

"How many more have arrived?"

"Two. One by calling, one by intervention, with high activity."

There were two by intervention. "Intervention? Do you have his name?" the man asked, wondering. *Could it be him?*

The messenger shook his head.

"What does he look like?"

"Older. In his fifties. Bald. Overweight."

Not the thirteenth. Not yet. "Where is he now?"

"In his cell. Like the others. It was a bad scene. Took six of us to get him down there."

The man nodded. Silent. His thoughts, racing with emotionally driven fear. *It's really happening.* He remained composed, adeptly guarding his true subjective state: hopeless grief buried in a windowless world. "The thirteenth?"

"Not yet."

"Who is your God?" he queried the messenger.

"Allieb" was his response, smiling emptily. His eyes glared, two black orbs swimming in turbulent waters. He bowed.

"Go and pray. And prepare. Legion is near." A stab of familiar pain beset him. He rubbed his throbbing chest, a habitual gesture. The pain subsided.

The messenger nodded. "God would like to see you," he repeated, eyes laden with sudden fear.

Hesitation, grief, and fear. "Then . . . then I shall go and speak with Him," the man answered, turning away, trying to hide the restless burden in his features. The door closed and the messenger was gone.

The man sat on the edge of the bed, thoughts of looming plague and pestilence tormenting his agonized mind.

He diverted his thoughts to the past . . .

His fears told him one thing; his hopes, another. The man and his wife delivered their son to the doctors. Specialists, as internists had been unable to help him. The boy lay on an examining table, arms to his side, legs jutting from the white gown he wore. The doctor pressed his glands.

Allieb swiped angrily at him, yanking the dangling stethoscope away. He screamed, kicked, punched, flailed, swore, tore at his own face and drew blood in spots. Numerous attempts had been made to treat the boy, and finally, with no alternative, they sedated him. Seventy-five milligrams of Thorazine. Three doctors were needed to assist in holding him down while the injection was administered.

For two weeks they kept him at the hospital, in a private examination room under constant sedation and surveillance. The doctors discussed a variety of ailments with the parents: epilepsy, schizophrenia, severe chemical imbalances in the brain. Tests were run: EEGs, X-rays, lumbar taps.

Everything appeared to be normal.

Soon thereafter, and quite unexplainably, Allieb returned to a normal state. Calm and composed. They quickly weaned him off the drugs. Counseled him and ultimately found a tired young boy who, through tears of remorse, pleaded to go home. Although baffled with this sudden turnaround, the doctors and his parents accepted this startling recovery with open arms. Their final analysis: *Your son is seeking attention in very extreme ways. He wants something, and will go to any lengths to obtain it. There's nothing wrong with him that requires any additional medical attention. We're prescribing Ritalin for him. It's a stimulant to help counteract his apparent depression and his hyperkinetic behavior. Remember, he's been through a great deal of trauma during these early years. The move from one country to another. You mentioned that his parents were killed in war. We really don't know for certain all the atrocities he's encountered. Now he's paying the price, and unfortunately, you are too. Take him home. Love him. And allow the medication to take effect. In three weeks, we suspect that he'll be the loving little boy you've always hoped for.*

Three weeks later, Allieb killed his mother.

The man wiped his tears, opened the nightstand drawer, removed the silver cross and kissed it, then placed it in his pocket for protection. "Jesus, help me," he muttered to himself.

And paced from the room to answer "God's" call.

Twenty-one

"Dead . . ." Bev answered, feeling unsteady.

"He drowned in the pool." Rebecca's voice: weak, staggering.

"This can't be, Rebecca." His voice was a harsh whisper.

"It is . . . and Bev, we were the last people to see him alive." She sobbed, grief fracturing her voice. "He was bombed, and he was stumbling. But he was also passed out, right? He *was* passed out! So how? How could this have happened?" Rebecca: desperately searching for rationale.

Bev sensed the terror in her voice. The phone trembled in his hand. Rebecca's anxious breaths shot into his ear like hisses from a steam engine. "Where'd you hear this, Rebecca?"

"From the police."

"The police?"

"They were here today."

"There? At your place? Why?"

"You remember the priest from the party?"

"Father Danto."

"He was staying at Jake's house. The cops showed up at my place around one this afternoon and told me that after performing mass this morning, he went back to the house and found Jake floating facedown in the pool. He called them and I guess he told them the names of some the people he'd met at the party. Bev . . . I had to tell them about us."

"So, what did you tell them?"

"The truth. That we put Jake to sleep. In the living room. On the sofa. And then . . . slept together, at the house, and that you left in the morning, about thirty minutes before I did. I told them the truth. I had to . . ." She wept.

"Rebecca . . . you did the right thing." He wanted to tell her to relax, but knew it to be a lofty command, given the rise of surrounding events—events she knew nothing about. "I'm sure the cops will want to speak with me, too, and I'll tell them exactly what happened. We did nothing wrong, Rebecca. Saw nothing. It was just a terrible, unfortunate accident. He probably woke up in the middle of the night and just stumbled outside. He *was* completely drunk when we last saw him."

Jake's dead . . . My God.

Bev's dream filtered back to him, slowly, like freeze frames in a movie: the Jake-demon on the shoreline, *drowning in the shallow lava . . .* He shivered, a cold pervasive draft suddenly surrounding him.

"I just can't believe it," Rebecca said.

I can't either . . . and I can't believe the cops are questioning us. There's got to be more to this. He gazed

144

at his hands, at the wounds somehow obtained in the middle of the night—wounds that had nearly healed over in a matter of hours. *How did I get these?* he wondered, and then, *How are they healing so fast?*, dismay and utter confusion dissecting his lucidity. He recalled the dream and the wires that had jutted up from the lava, and in this moment of conspicuous defeat, lowered the phone and gazed around the room, at the strange books, at Julianne's diary strewn on the floor of the closet, wondering why, all of a sudden, his world appeared to be falling apart.

He raised the phone back to his ear.

"Rebecca?"

A wave of interference interrupted the once-clear signal. In seconds, it returned, and Rebecca was gone.

In her place, a different voice: *Bev . . .*

Sharp. Clear. Unmistakable.

Julianne.

Body trembling. Heart slamming. Breath, short and stagnant. His voice, trapped behind a horrendous lump of dread. Tears, sprouting tensely from his eyes.

He tried to stand; his legs wouldn't let him. Finally, on his knees: "Hello?"

Interference, and then another voice.

"Come to me, Bevant."

Deep, with an accent.

A sudden strength rose in him, induced by fear of the unknown. He stood, head reeling, knees unsteady. "Who is this?" he demanded. He recalled the voice in his head, just prior to visiting the doctor. *It's the same voice.*

The voice remained silent. He could hear a raspy breathing coming through the line.

"What do you want with me?" he shouted.

The line went dead.

"Hello? Hello? *Fuck!*" he screamed, slamming the phone on the desk. He stood motionless, listening to the resonating echo of his voice as it faded away into the eerie silence of the afternoon—an afternoon that had become gray with intimidating storm clouds, imminent thundershowers, and the ghosts of days present and past.

Finally, he staggered from Kristin's office, leaving the tainted evidence of his newfound past behind. In the kitchen, he located a glass and drank some water from the sink, swallowing past the dry lump in his throat—past the shocking truth of his former life, now an open wound to agonize over; the remembrance of Jake Ritchie, who had instantly become a fixture of the past; the lonely, still, dark recollection of the evils he'd experienced that could very well pale in comparison to those the future had in store.

He began to cry. *The scratching, the voice, the out-of-control feeling, the insects, the dark man, the invitation, the face in the mirror, 6:00, being followed, Father Danto, Rebecca Haviland, Julianne's voice, Jake . . . oh poor Jake . . .*

It's too much . . . too much.

He fled outside into the afternoon.

Leaving his cell phone behind on Kristin's desk.

Twenty-two

4:45. Bev arrived back home. He pulled his car into the detached garage. Shut the ignition, thankful for no episodes. He took a deep breath, held it, then blew it out. He was home. *Thank God.* Safe. For now.

He trembled uncontrollably as he staggered from the car, stepping across the graveled driveway. *This is what having a nervous breakdown feels like . . . That's it, I'm having a goddamned nervous breakdown. None of those things were real. The voices in the phone, the face in the mirror, the fingers in my head. Not real, not real . . .*

He peered down the length of the driveway, toward the street. Concerned. Frightened. If things played out as promised—*threatened*—a limo would be here in an hour and fifteen minutes to pick him up. *Something else to worry about.*

He turned.

Fifteen feet away, at the bottom of the steps, stood a man.

The dark man, here to deliver another message . . .

Under normal circumstances, Bev might have assumed this to be a fan. One of the older crowd, trying desperately to hang on to his youthful years, hunting down his fave celeb's address and parking out front with hope of catching a real-live glimpse; it wouldn't have been the first time. But, as Bev made his approach, he saw that this man was *too* far ahead in years to be reaching for times gone by. He was pushing sixty, clothes apropos for a man of this age who'd possessed no common fashion-sense: baggy slacks; a glen-plaid blazer hanging loosely upon his slender frame. Cheeks: gaunt, sallow, and spiritless. Thinning hair, a wisp combed over. Mustache, coarse, gray, and nicotine-stained.

Not a fan.

The press?

I ain't that *famous.*

The man extended his hand tiredly, spoke in a harsh, asthmatic tone. "Why do rock stars all seem to age beyond their years, despite their riches?"

"I'm not rich," Bev answered pensively, taking his hand. "Just look at my digs."

"Not overly impressive, I suppose. But not too shabby, either."

"Who are you?" Bev folded his arms defensively across his chest.

"Please forgive my sense of humor. It has earned me some trouble in the past."

"If you're looking for trouble," Bev replied playfully, "then you've come to the wrong place."

"Oh, no, of course I'm not." The man waved away

the thought as though refusing another drink, then reached into his shirt pocket and revealed a billfold, which he displayed to Bev. Bev scanned it casually. In it, a detective's badge. And beneath, his name: Frederick Grover. Bev gazed back up at the detective, trying not to appear suspicious. Impossible, given his jaded appearance.

"What can I do for you?"

The detective grinned. "I do hope I'm not inconveniencing you, Mr. Mathers. I rang the doorbell and no one answered. I was on my way out when I saw you drive up, so I thought I'd wait."

"Where's your car?" Bev asked, looking around.

"Parked at a distance. Part of the procedure."

"This is about Jake Ritchie, isn't it?"

The detective's demeanor changed, his posture stiffening into a more serious pose. "I'm very sorry about your friend," he offered, eyes narrowed sorrowfully.

"I'd heard he drowned."

The detective grinned solemnly. "Information does travel fast, doesn't it?" He hesitated, grinned blankly, then added, "Being the bearer of such terrible news is not one of the perks of my occupation."

Can it get any worse? Bev thought again. "Well, I already know all about it, so it saves you the displeasure this time around."

The detective breathed out, closed his eyes, and shook his head. "Actually, there's something you don't know, Mr. Mathers."

"What? What is it?"

Grover hesitated, then breathed out and asked, "Do you know of anyone that might have had an issue with Mr. Ritchie? An argument, perhaps? You know—did he have any enemies at all?"

"Jesus, was Jake murdered?" Bev, suddenly shocked, added, "He was, wasn't he? That's why you came here, isn't it?"

Grover nodded. "He *was* murdered, Mr. Mathers."

Bev leaned back against the rail leading up the steps to the front door. Rubbed his forehead, then ran a trembling hand through his hair. "Oh my God . . . Rebecca didn't say anything about him being murdered."

The detective pocketed his hands and jingled some coins. "That's because she doesn't know."

"You didn't tell her . . ."

"No."

"So then why are you telling me?"

"You were close to Mr. Ritchie. Rebecca Haviland— a lovely girl, by the way—from what I gather, was only a recent acquaintance of his. So I thought that maybe, well, maybe you might know someone . . ." He hesitated, pinning Bev with serious eyes.

Bev shook his head vehemently. "No, no. Jake was as lovable as he was obnoxious. He was well-liked by everyone, despite his harsh sense of humor. I mean, I don't know of anyone that's ever held a grudge with him. Ever."

The detective's eyes swam inquisitively over Bev from head to toe. He turned away to cough, lungs wheezing. Finally, he asked, "You smoke?"

Bev nodded, reached into his pocket, and retrieved his Camels, realizing at this moment that he didn't have his cell phone. *Kristin's.* Offering one to the detective, he said, "Sounds like you've had your share."

"Thirty years' worth," he answered guiltily, taking the cigarette and lighting it. "Too late to turn back. You, on the other hand . . ." He pointed the cigarette at Bev before taking a deep drag.

"Thought you said I've aged beyond my years."

The detective laughed. "See, I told you my sense of humor always gets me in trouble."

Bev eyed his watch. 5:00. "Listen, if you have any questions—"

"Oh, yes," Grover interrupted. "I'm sorry. I'll be quick and then I'll be gone." He glanced up the steps as if looking for someone else to appear from the house. "Since you and Rebecca were the last ones to see Mr. Ritchie, and you both stayed at his place last night . . . well, I was wondering . . . do you know if anyone else might've stayed there as well?"

"That I know of? Just the priest. Father Danto."

His face tensed, as if he'd just caught a foul-smelling whiff. "And we can pretty much dismiss him as a suspect, no?"

"Don't really know the man."

"Well, he is a priest, and he did retire early, from what I gather anyway, and he performed a mass this morning, so he *could* have gotten up sometime during the night to commit the crime, but it doesn't seem all that likely, since he's the one who called it in."

"I spoke with him at the party. He was a gentleman."

Grover nodded in agreement, then asked, "At what time, approximately, did you and Rebecca retire to bed?"

"Uh . . . one A.M., I suppose. Thereabouts."

"And you spoke to Mr. Ritchie prior to going up. Correct?"

Grover seemed to be running circles around the truth. He had some facts in his head and was comparing notes, just like the good detective he was. Bev had no choice but to play along. "Yes, well, he was totally drunk. We carried him, me and Rebecca, from the kitchen to the living room. Put him down on the couch. He was snoring in seconds."

"And then you went to bed."

"Correct."

"Any reason you didn't come home last night?"

"I had a bug problem. Exterminators were supposed to spray."

"And Father Danto?"

"Upstairs."

"For certain?"

"As far as I know. I saw him go up but didn't see him come down."

"But you said you were in the kitchen at some point."

"Yes."

"So it's possible that Father Danto might have come down while you were in the kitchen. Or he might've come down *after* you went to sleep."

"Possible, I suppose."

Grover waved a hand in the air. "Not that any of that means anything. The man is a priest, after all."

Bev nodded, feeling suddenly uncomfortable—as though he were being interrogated. He blew out a gust of air and waited for Grover's next question.

"It would take a very strong man, or men, really, to move Jake in his condition from the sofa in the living room to the pool out back. That's got to be, what, a hundred feet? And Jake, he's pushing three hundred."

Bev nodded. "Rebecca and I moved him about fifteen feet, and it was as far as we could take him, and he was still awake and on his feet, barely. We just guided him along." The detective nodded, placed the cigarette in his mouth, then dipped a bony hand into his jacket pocket and removed a pad and pen. He jotted something down.

Grover removed the cigarette and said, "So it stands to reason that either Mr. Ritchie was carried by, say, a couple of strong men, or got up himself and went out back."

Bev, gaze fixed on the pad, asked, "Detective, what happened to Jake?"

"Murdered. Yes, he was murdered in a very despicable way."

Bev's thoughts immediately triggered back to the party, to Father Danto's words: *A crime was committed at the rectory last night. One of a most deplorable nature.*

"Not just drowned?" he asked, wondering suddenly if Jake's death had anything to do with the sacrifice at the rectory.

"No . . . Mr. Mathers, not just drowned. Murdered. I know you're a busy man, and I'll let you go soon. Just tell me one thing . . . just out of curiosity . . . you play guitar, yes?"

"Yes, I do . . ."

"I've been dabbling a little myself. But not your type of music, no. More of the fifties stuff. You know, Chuck Berry, Roy Orbison."

"That's great," Bev answered, feigning interest.

"I was wondering—what kind of strings do you use?"

"What kind of strings . . . ?" Bev felt a terrible sensation in his body, like an electric jolt. He pulled his gaze away from the detective and sent it across the driveway.

"Just curious, is all."

"Part of the investigation?" Bev asked.

"Maybe. Then again, maybe I'm just seeking some tips from a pro."

"Ernie Ball," he answered abruptly. "Nine-gauge."

Grover jotted the information down.

Like a sudden draft through a window, Bev felt the scratching sensation in his head. Slightly, as though only one or two fingers had returned to their digging schedule. Panicking a bit, he gripped his temples in an urgent manner. At once, the fingers receded.

"You okay?" Grover asked.

"No, not really. I haven't been feeling well of late. Migraines or something. Doctor tells me it's all nerves."

"Sorry to hear that." Grover's suddenly tense face showed genuine concern. "The wife has had some problems over the years. Panic attacks. They stick with you, despite all those medications. Rest and relaxation—now, that's the ticket."

"Just what the doctor ordered," Bev answered, smiling, somewhat relieved with the lighter tone of conversation and the fact that the mind-fingers had recessed.

"Well, I believe we're about done now," Grover said. "Just one more thing . . . anything you can tell me about Mr. Ritchie? Anything you can add that might help me?"

Bev gazed down to the cement walkway, thinking of Jake and not yet accepting the fact that he was actually dead. He looked back up, giving the detective a mournful glance. "Jake was the best. Loving. Caring. He had an obnoxious side that'd definitely irk you if didn't know him, especially when he drank, and especially if he was coming at *you*. But he wouldn't hurt a fly."

"All bark and no bite, as they say." Grover smiled and returned the pad and pen back into his jacket pocket. "That'll do. Thank you so much for your time, Mr. Mathers. If you hear anything, please, call my office." He handed Bev his card.

Bev nodded. "You're welcome."

Grover began to walk away, then turned and removed the pad and paper again. "If I think of anything else, may I call you?"

Bev nodded. "Of course. I only use a cell phone. I'll be home all night."

Grover jotted down the number Bev gave him, then raised the pad. "Thanks. Hope you're feeling better soon. And . . . you have my deepest condolences."

Bev looked down and nodded. "Thank you." Above, gray clouds filled the sky, darkening the late afternoon. "Detective?"

Grover turned.

"How? How was Jake murdered?"

Grover waited, then dropped the bomb: "Strangled. With a guitar string."

Bev shuddered and watched as Grover padded down the length of the driveway, turned out onto the sidewalk, and disappeared.

Bev looked down at his hands.

The scars were completely gone.

Twenty-three

Five minutes later, Grover was seated behind the wheel of his unmarked car, using the ashtray to snub out the cigarette Bev gave him. He noted the brand on the filter. Camel. He reached into the glove compartment and removed a small yellow clasp envelope. Opening it, he dropped the cigarette butt inside, then sealed it and placed it on the seat next to him.

Bev Mathers smoked Camels.

A single butt from a Camel cigarette was found by the pool. . . . Of course, this could mean anything, really. Bev or even someone else might have gone outside for a smoke and stamped it out on the deck. Totally circumstantial. But then there was the matter of the guitar strings. Ernie Ball, nine-gauge. Grover had learned that guitar strings were classified by their thickness in thousandths of an inch, and that the entire set was categorized using the measurement of the high E-string, the first and thinnest string. Jake Ritchie had been choked with a low E-string, the uppermost and thickest string on a guitar. Its gauge was measured out at .042 of an inch, the common thickness for a low E-string in a set that started with a .009-gauge high E.

The brand: Ernie Ball.

Grover took a deep breath, then waited in the car parked a hundred feet away from Bev Mathers's apartment. From this position he could see the front door, and watched Bev standing at the foot of the steps with the pain-filled hunch of a man of sixty.

Grover decided to stick around for a bit to see if maybe Bev would head out.

He rubbed his brow with tired fingers and dreamed of retirement.

Damn rock stars.

Twenty-four

He roamed the hallways of the mansion, coursing an accustomed path. Passing multiple doors. Many of the rooms were occupied. Others empty, their dwellers busy in preparations, missing, or dead. At last count there'd been forty-three fervently devout disciples, not including the vehicles, which by this evening would total thirteen. The congregation was very strong and very willing. Allieb was in power and held them in his reign. God help their tainted souls.

At the southwest corner of the house, the man used a key to unlock a paneled door. He opened it and followed the sequestered steps upward toward the highest room, a sole bedroom set in a large cupola. His moving shadow fell across the small landing at the top, bathed in white light blazing from an emergency beacon in the ceiling. Here, a door sat waiting. From behind the door droned the low caustic snore of an animal: a bull perhaps, or a sow. He hesitated, then slowly reached forward. The very moment his hand came in contact with the brass doorknob, the growling from within halted. In the sudden stillness, the man wavered. He swallowed past the dull razors in his throat, then tentatively entered the room, drawing back slightly from the icy cold air and horrific reek that assaulted him.

He tried to hide his repugnance as his gorge rose and his eyes teared. He turned and faced the monster that had once been his adopted son—the boy who'd grown into a young man and who'd accepted his calling from below to become the ungodly thing in this room. Allieb was kneeling naked in the center of the bare room, the wood floor beneath him fouled with feces, bile, and vomit; head and neck, jutting sideways to face his stunned father who'd never imagined a horror this severe: black and yellow eyes, bulging in their sunken sockets, pinning the human man before him with irrational corruption and blazing prowess, with true regard, and yet with a vindictive bitterness rigidly set into a fiendish mask. The man gazed helplessly at the straggled matting of hair covering his son's head; at the skeletal limbs ripped with tendons and blue veins; at the swelling abdomen and ulcerated navel; to the horrid sludge tiding out from beneath his grotesquely writhing body; and then back to his eyes—eyes that pinned and shifted to observe the man entering the room. The door slammed shut behind him. The blinds in the mostly empty room opened on their own accord, allowing pallid slits of light to enter.

"My God, my savior," the man put forth, his tone weak and prayerful. He startled at a sudden scraping sound emerging from behind him. He jerked his head around. A chair was sliding swiftly across the floor. It stopped just behind him. His heart slammed mercilessly against his chest.

"Take a seat . . . *Father*," Allieb demanded, voice inconceivably deep and strident.

The man stepped back, and gently sat, arms guiding himself downward. He crossed his hands in his lap. Waited.

Allieb crawled forward through the puddle of sludge, eyes glimmering ferociously, mucus seeping thickly from his nose. His mouth opened absurdly wide, revealing dark brown stumps for teeth. A craggy black tongue fell out, lolling uselessly across his chin. He released a series of menacing barks, then stopped suddenly, hateful gaze pinning the man who sat waiting. "Legion is near," he uttered, voice lustful and dominating.

And the man answered, "Excellent . . . my God."

"We've nine now," Allieb slurred, crawling even closer. "Three more are on the way. All by calling. I seem to be doing a praiseworthy job, no?"

"Indeed," the man answered.

"You've been commanded to intervene!" Allieb bellowed. "Have you not performed the duty that has been required of you?" He shifted his body back, exposing a scab-ravaged chest and full erection that seeped green fluid. His skin glistened with sweat and blood. His head and neck pranced subtly, like a lizard's.

"I have," the man said, remaining motionless. "One has already arrived through intervention." If not for his relationship with Allieb, he might have been served his death for not properly completing his task. Should the demon discover his true intentions . . . well, then death would be imminent. *Please, do not read my mind, do not read my mind . . .*

"So I see . . . I *am* communicating with the thirteenth. I'm sure you are pleased with this show of charity from your godly prince." A girlish giggle.

"Between the two of us, Allieb, we should find success."

"Allieb is dead!" the thing hissed, eyes bulging, searing with contempt. He seethed for a moment, breaths quick and shallow and seemingly amplified as though circulating through a respirator. Then the anger transposed itself into a hideous grin, deep, guttural laughter following. He added, quite composed, "I am one with my father now. *Belial,* you foolish one." He reached down and stroked his engorged erection, as though aroused upon simply uttering his own demonic designation. The staff appeared to grow darker, thicker.

The man nodded, eyes shuttered and trembling, silently denouncing his slipup. "Of course, of course."

"The thirteenth must arrive in the time of Legion." Allieb gestured manically, hands groping for unseen objects in the air, eyes darting as though attempting to follow their irregular paths.

"Midnight tonight," the man answered. "He will arrive before that, I promise you, my Lord."

The demon sniffed the air. The mucus dripping from his nose shot back in like a runner. Laughter. Then: "Show me your credence, and I will show you salvation." Something contemptuously feigned flickered in his black irises.

Is this a riddle? the man thought.

"Perhaps it *is* a riddle, Daddy," Allieb answered in his boyhood voice. He grinned smugly, then uttered, *"Anthropomorphitus blasphemia divinitas."*

The man sat stupefied. *Don't pray, don't pray, don't pray.* The demon waited, fixing him with a contemptuous stare. The man spoke: "The thirteenth will arrive in time for Legion."

"Very good, Papa. Very good." Allieb smiled, black tongue licking spittle over blistered lips. He giggled playfully, childlike.

The man waited. He prayed to be dismissed, hoping this time Allieb would hear his thoughts. He planted his eyes on the entity before him—his son's features were still there, contorted horridly by the demon presence within.

"I'm bored," Allieb said, blowing out a gush of putrid air. "Ask me something."

"Ask you something . . . ?"

"Anything you want." Then, in a sharp English accent: "I'm feeling charitable today. Sometimes I amaze myself with my altruism. We demons aren't supposed to do that, you know. What would dear Satan think of me now?"

"Satan . . ."

"The thirteenth . . . but you know that already . . . *Father.*" Booming laughter emerged from his mouth, vibrating the floor beneath the chair and rattling the blinds on the windows. The man gripped the chair's arms fiercely, nails digging half-moons into the wood. Allieb slithered backward, kneeling back down in the fouled puddle. His demonic face contorted, the room filled now with the pungent stench of urine—with a wave of heat like a blast from a furnace.

His head fell forward between his knees, where he began to perform fellatio upon himself.

The man sat stunned. His flesh raised into goose bumps, icy nails tickling his nape and bringing the hair on his back to stand as a puddle of urine and liquid waste seeped out from beneath Allieb. Abruptly, the blinds rolled shut, seemingly bringing an end to their conversation. The man quickly rose from the chair, watching Allieb's head bobbing rhythmically, deep rolling snorts and hisses rising as his stride increased. The man stood unmoving as the act escalated, uncertain if he'd been granted permission to depart. Allieb's body began to shake, rippling as if insects crawled beneath his skin. Horrid curses and grunts spilled out from his plugged mouth.

Unwilling to further witness this vulgar display, the man reeled from the room, nearly fainting, immediately setting himself to continue his clandestine mission as his ears rang and his breath escaped his lungs in short, strangling gasps.

In the hallway, the man listened as Allieb's groans of pleasure rose. A booming roar exploded as he climaxed, momentarily silencing the mansion.

Then dreadful silence.

Soon, the bustle of activity returned.

Attempting to gather his composure, he proceeded down into the cathedral. Seatless. Dimly lit. The altar had been fully prepared, thirteen pentagrams posted on the columnar supports, marking thirteen positions, one for each vehicle. Tears filled his eyes, and he turned and staggered away, trying to erase the looming thoughts from his mind. Ghostly fingers prodded the back of his neck, cold and unrelenting. In the antechamber to the cathedral he heard bells tolling from some faraway point. From the basement below loomed agonizing screams, the sounds of creaking woods and clanging chains, of hissing snakes and snorting bulls and bleating pigs.

Michael Laimo

The man shuttered his mind and coursed from the antechamber, through the many halls, to his room. Once inside, he gripped the silver cross in his pocket. It felt . . . different. Its texture had changed. He raced into the bathroom, shut himself inside, and pulled it out.

The silver had rusted to a dull, muddy brown.

The man closed his eyes and prayed to Jesus Christ.

He knows. Allieb knows.

There is no likelihood for good to prevail.

Twenty-five

Jake's dead, Bev thought, falling into yet another state of utter disbelief. He stared at his hands, at the palms, where the scars used to be. Not eight hours earlier, he'd awoken with a series of deep red gouges running across his palms—thin, bleeding, burning, *as though guitar strings had been ripped across them*. He thought back to his dream from last night. The lava. Jake standing at the shoreline alongside Kristin and Rebecca, then pouncing forward, falling into the lava and burning away. *Dying*. And at that precise moment, thin metal wires had jutted up from the lava and wrapped themselves around his hands, digging deeply into his flesh.

He rubbed his eyes, terribly confused. *Jesus, what the hell is going on?*

He looked up toward the front door of his apartment, at once cursing his decision to return home, despite its seeming his only logical move. He felt awful, the horrors of the preceding events pushing him toward insanity. The world, once composed of fame, success, and fortune, had been shattered and was now drowning in misery and wailing for help. He stood his ground at the foot of the steps, mind boiling with imbalance and indecision. He gripped the iron handrail and thought hectically of Kristin, of Jake, and even of Father Danto, who, Bev believed, might be connected to all the freakish events taking place. *He was in my dream, too. I remember it. He'd said, "There are two souls invading you, a man's and a beast's. It is the man's soul that torments you. Follow the beast." But what does it mean?* Bev thought of his own gathering disorder: the scratching, the voices, the hallucinations, the loss of control. Where was it all coming from? Was there some deep-rooted cause? Was it guilt? Remorse? Or something more clinical, like fatigue, anxiety, or depression, as Palumba so explained?

Or . . . is it what the texts in Kristin's office conveyed? Is it what Danto talked about in my dream?

Is it . . . demonic invasion?

Shuddering with uncertainty and fear, Bev eyed the steps, and despite his sudden need to rest, again second-guessed his decision to return home, given the menacing circumstances: the arrival of the mystery limo, now less than forty minutes away. Who knew what additional horrors it would bring? He considered leaving, going to Alondra Park and staying there until six-thirty or seven. Sit near the lake, meditate, try to ease away the discomforts of the day. *I could return home long after six—long after the limo is gone. Shit— should've made this decision an hour ago! Then I wouldn't have had the displeasure of contending with Detective Frederick Grover. Who knew?*

It's not too late.

Too tired . . . I just want to go inside and rest.

But . . . what if the limo comes and then doesn't leave? What if it continues to wait outside long after six o'clock? It might just wait all night . . . He decided that it didn't matter, because he had no intention of getting into a limo at all—that is, of course, if one actually arrived. If it *did*, well, then he'd just lock himself in his house—maybe even call the police. *Yes, just call the cops,* he told himself. *Make a scene. They'll have no choice but to leave.*

But . . . what if the people inside the limo rush the house, break down the door, snatch me before I'm able to make a call?

That's anxiety speaking, Bev.

Jesus. Too many factors at play. Endless angles to consider. Eventually, Bev convinced himself that he needed to rest, and that coming home hadn't been a bad decision at all. The limo wasn't here yet, and when—if—it finally came, all he'd have to do was lock himself inside for the night. Keep a stakeout from his kitchen window.

All alone. Just Bev.

And the bugs.

Shit. He'd forgotten about the beetles. That had happened more than twenty-four hours ago—Jesus, it seemed like a century. He frowned, wondering with reluctant curiosity if the exterminator had indeed come. Had been able to alleviate the situation. *They better have.*

Wearily, he climbed the concrete steps to the landing.

Taped to the front door was an envelope.

His heart joggled in his chest. His breathing fell short. *No, not another envelope.* With numb fingers, he felt out the invitation in his pocket. Still there.

He ripped the envelope from the door and quickly eyed the return address: *Huxtable Exterminating.* Relieved, he reached inside. Pulled out a yellow piece of paper. An invoice. On it, scribbled pieces of information:

SERVICE CALL—$65
SEARCHED ENTIRE APARTMENT, INCLUDING
BEDROOM CLOSET AT CUSTOMER'S REQUEST.
NO SPECIMENS FOUND. NO EVIDENCE OF
INFESTATION AS DESCRIBED BY CUSTOMER.
NO CHEMICALS APPLIED.

No specimens found? "Are they fucking kidding me?" Angrily, he slid his key into the door. He gripped the doorknob and received a shock, then turned it and went inside.

Immediately, he felt a chill. The air: colder than outside. A slight stench filled the room, something familiar. *Smells like . . . like burning wood. Must be the insecticide.*

No . . . no chemicals were applied.

The apartment was just as he left it: a sullen mess, the bed unmade, towels piled on the bathroom counter, the jeans from where the first beetle emerged heaped on the bedroom floor. He tossed the invoice on the bed, then gave the apartment a full sweep. A smothering tension rose in the air.

He saw nothing out of the ordinary.

He looked at the open closet, tentative, not wanting

to investigate but knowing that if he wanted to stay here tonight, he'd have to. With one hand on the edge of the bed for support, he leaned down on one knee and peeked inside the shadowy recess.

Plenty of shoes. Folded shirts. A couple of fallen wire hangers. But no bugs.

Slowly he stretched a reluctant hand into the closet. His skin crawled as it came in contact with the dusty wood floor. Using his thumb and index finger, he pinched the corner of a strewn shirt and quickly dragged it out in a motion that suggested the shirt might be on fire. He stood up, holding the shirt at arm's length. Shook it.

No bugs.

He tossed it aside. Then he reached back into the closet and grabbed a pair of jeans from the pile on the hamper, slowly unfolded them.

Nothing.

He took a deep breath. *Did I hallucinate the bugs? Like the face in the mirror? Or the bug in the sink?* Then he hunkered back down, accelerating his campaign to unearth *something*. He removed a pair of shoes, shook them, tossed them aside. Then a pair of sneakers. No bugs. Breathing out, he leaned back down, pressed his head against the floor, and peered at the back wall of the closet, where yesterday the insects had been *swarming*.

No beetles.

He stood back up, confusion besetting him yet again. He shifted his eyes around the room. Saw absolutely no evidence of insects.

Scratching his head, he padded soundlessly into the studio room, as though trying to sneak up on someone.

Oh my God.

He halted. Stared incredulously at the sight before him, at once trying to sort out his emotions. Disturbing. Unnerving. Puzzling. He couldn't believe what he was seeing.

Bev had two large Marshall amplifiers in the apartment, each housing four sixteen-inch speakers. Both of them, usually pressed tightly against the foam-padded walls, sat inexplicably in the middle of the room, one stacked atop the other. The ten guitars he kept here, five Les Pauls, three Martins, and two Fender Stratocasters, were out of their cases and on the floor alongside the cabinets, arranged in a starlike pattern. Stereo wires formed a circle around the pattern, completing what appeared to be a pentagram shape.

Last night, someone sacrificed a goat on the lawn outside the rectory. It had been decapitated, its carcass gutted and impaled on a large crucifix. Its entrails were laid out into a pentagram shape beneath the cross.

Very tentatively, he paced about the room. On further inspection, he noticed that other items had been moved. Two collapsible chairs, usually folded and stored in the hall closet, were open and stacked against the wall where the amps usually were; CDs had been dumped from their tower into an open guitar case; a pile of two-inch recording tape lay atop the console, purloined from its steel reel and strewn indiscriminately like ticker-tape ribbon.

Amid it all, something caught his blank and uncomprehending eye.

On the floor.

Black. Shiny. Bulbous. Skittering across the carpet on many legs.

"Son of a bitch!" Bev cried. He backed up and watched the horror: a four-inch beetle racing across the carpet into the one-inch space between the floor and the studio closet.

A moment of indecisive horror passed. Gingerly, Bev stepped over a guitar, flesh from head to toe writhing dreadfully on his bones. He stood in front of the closet, tense and waiting.

He placed a shaking hand on the knob. It was icy cold.

Scratch, scratch, scratch, from behind the wood door—tiny nails picking away along the edge of the jamb. *Sounds like . . . like the scratching in my head . . .*

Scratch . . . scratch . . . scratch, in his head.

Scratch . . . scratch . . . scratch, from behind the closet door.

Slowly, he twisted the knob.

The latch made an audible *click.*

The scratching from within abruptly ceased, as though someone had pressed the stop button on the tape recorder from where they'd surfaced.

He pulled the door open. Slowly at first, and then all the way.

The closet was completely empty. Everything he'd ever stored in it was gone. Including the beetle. An odor purled out. Something foul. Like a current of burning sulfur.

"What the . . ."

Digging, digging, digging.

And with the sensation in his head came horrible pain. He fell to one knee. Squeezed his head, yelled out. His body twisted at the waist, then slammed to the floor; it was as though he'd been physically thrown by some malevolent force. His heart palpitated irregularly; he could feel it trying to escape his rib cage. He could feel many things, his throat shrieking, a sensation of falling deep into his body, into the churning acids of his stomach. He could sense his mouth and lips moving, could hear wicked moans emanating from his throat . . . but he maintained no control of these actions. His arms and legs flailed spasmodically as his back arched up, then smashed down violently onto the carpet, over and over, quickly and frequently. He heard himself shrieking nonsensical expletives: "Fuck! Fuck! Fuck!" over and over again. Unseen hands prodded his body, fingers digging into the place where skull met brain.

And then it stopped.

He could hear himself breathing heavily. He could *feel* it as he rose from the dark recesses of his gut, back into his mind and body familiar. He staggered up. Stumbled from the studio, into the kitchen. He gazed out the window.

Black limo. In his driveway. Lights off. He gazed at the clock on the kitchen wall. Exactly 6:00. *Where did the time go?*

In his head, the voice: *Come to me, Bevant.*

He gripped the sides of his head. The pain had filtered away, leaving behind a sharp, resonating tone that trailed the deep voice like a stream of exhaust from a race car. It had come through clearly, as though the digging in his skull had finally produced a hole through which the voice and tone could travel.

Staring out the window, toward the waiting limo, he whispered, "Who are you?"

Your friend, Bevant.

"My friend . . ."

Your friend.

"What is your name?" His tone was oddly calm, despite the impossible fear. His eyes searched all corners of the room.

Low, raspy breathing.

"Are you in the limo?"

Come to me, Bevant.

"You didn't answer my question. Are you in the limo?"

A horrible wail filled Bev's head. Bloodcurdling; piercing; the sudden presence of a being making itself known in his body. It held his soul, dragged him away from the conscious realm of his awareness, then hurled him back with a quick, calculated thrust. A timely show of power. He screamed, fell to his knees. Gripped the sides of his head. *"What do you want from me?"* he screamed, staggering back into the bedroom. The moment turned into a sepia-toned slow-motion nightmare: Bev hurling himself on the bed, writhing, tangling the blanket and sheet, his tongue thrusting uncontrollably from his mouth, which gasped and grimaced and spat a melee of odd noises that could only escape the throats of animals: oinks, clucks, neighs. He could feel his eyes rolling into the back of his head, and on the black canvas of his inner lids he could distinctly see the roiling lava and the torn limbs and bones of human corpses. He screamed, *"Stop it! Stop!"* An icy cold wind plunged through the room, knocking pictures off the wall, blowing the blanket and sheets from the bed. The unspeakable presence then left Bev, and he remained breathing heavily on the bare mattress, soaked in sweat, exhaustively convinced of his bodily possession.

In the walls: hideous laughter.

He remained curled on the bed for a minute, maybe more, seeking out—and not wanting to find—the presence of the malevolent spirit within. Then, slowly, he rose. Looked at himself in the mirror: trembling; dark circles around the eyes; skin sallow; hair matted. In a panic, he careened to the kitchen window, looked out front again.

The limo waited.

In his head: *Come to me, Bevant.*

Twenty-six

Detective Frederick Grover breathed in the car's interior darkness and watched with curiosity as the limo waited, lights out, in Bev Mathers's driveway. Only moments earlier it had pulled in, perhaps a minute or two after Grover had decided that nothing of further interest was going to happen at the Mathers apartment.

He adjusted his rearview mirror to show the road behind him. Apparently, Mathers had lied about staying home all night, and now Grover wondered if someone else might be showing up in addition to those in the limo. The presence of the limo meant that there might very well be some ritzy plans for Bev Mathers, something he presumably did not want the detective to know about. Grover frowned . . . something smelled wrong here. He shifted his position on the seat slightly, getting a better view of the limo and its dark windows. As of now, no one had emerged. The driver had probably cell-phoned Mathers, alerting him of the car's arrival.

Grover closed his eyes for a moment, then mentally reviewed the chain of events. Jake Ritchie's death had been tied to the desecrations at St. Michael's, that much was for certain. There'd been the pentagram at the crime at the rectory, patterned with the entrails of the animal. Ritchie had been nearly decapitated with a guitar string, he too gutted, his intestines shaped into a pentagram twenty feet away in the grass. Still, there'd been no blood present anywhere in the house—not even a spot, according to the forensic team working the scene. Which meant, most assuredly, that whoever committed this particular crime had left immediately thereafter, perhaps cleaning themselves off in the pool before fleeing. Bev Mathers had allegedly awoken in bed, alongside Rebecca Haviland—this they both cor-roborated. So the more-than-likely scenario here was a methodically planned group degradation and killing—not uncommon, considering the cultlike nature of the crimes—that may have included Bev Mathers and maybe even Rebecca Haviland. Was Bev Mathers in-volved in some sort of demon-worshiping cult? The de-tails haunted Grover's mind: the priest, Father Thomas Danto, had had a great deal of experience in de-monology and devil worship, as confirmed by some of the guests who'd overheard his conversation at the party. He and Mathers and Ritchie had engaged in a lengthy discussion on the black arts, the priest doing most of the talking. Should the police be sniffing Danto's trail as well? Perhaps. But then again, his in-nocence seemed overly apparent, given his willingness to offer information from the onset. *And, for Christ's sake, he's a priest!* There were fingerprints found at the scene of the crime at the rectory, none of which belonged to any of those in residency, Danto included. At the scene of Ritchie's murder, shreds of skin and blood were found on the ends of the guitar string that was used to choke the victim. Grover took notice: Neither Danto nor Mathers possessed any visible lacerations on their hands. Still, something seemed amiss.

Grover let out a deep breath, keeping his eyes on the motionless limo. He rubbed his forehead. Light rain started to fall, and he used the wipers to clear the windshield. He waited, fifteen minutes or more, staring at the limo, staring at Bev Mathers's apartment. Waiting for something to happen.

He rubbed a solid knot in his jaw with his thumb, eyeing the quiet scene and knowing, just knowing—call it gut feeling, or detective's intuition—that something would happen very soon.

Yes, he thought, *something is going to happen very soon.*

Twenty-seven

Come to me, Bevant.

Bev fought back, biting his tongue, drawing blood. He lurched away from the window, raced back into the bedroom, feeling partially in control of himself once again—the evil embodiment seemed distant. Still, in his head, the voice chattered, over and over, calling his name, and he beat it back with his fortitude. He yelled, threw a frame and then a vase across the room in utter defiance of that which pursued him, the shattering and the clanging sending jolts of lucidity into his brain. In a desperate longing to flee, he opened the back window, catching a suddenly cool draft, wet and penetrating against his skin. His shirt billowed in the wind, the rain starting to fall freely from the darkening skies. He peered down; the woods stretched out, perhaps a half mile's worth before they let out onto the freeway. He could hear the collective roar of the distant rush-hour traffic. He released the ladder, realizing now that running to the highway gave him no opportunity for shelter. To the north was the shopping mall. To the south, additional homes.

He had friends in those neighborhoods. Jake was one of them; but he was dead. *Dear God, Jake.* So who else? He clambered out of the window and landed on the soft earth, then stared up into the darkening gloom of the woods, keeping his thoughts away from the waiting limo, away from his familiar world, wondering where he could possibly go and what might happen when he got there.

II

LEGION

My name is Legion, and we are many.
—Mark, 5:2–5:9

In Hell, anything can happen.

Twenty-eight

Gripping the rusted cross in his closed palm, the man cried, his prayers deep and intense, begging for mercy. *He knows, he knows,* he realized with dismay, trying desperately to shutter his true thoughts, to keep them masked by false pretenses: an honest willingness to proceed with the Legion. He placed the rusted cross in his pocket, then lay down across the limo's seat and peered at the clock: 6:14 P.M. Will the thirteenth be captured now? Only Allieb—*Belial*—knew for sure. The man prayed that the intervention would prove successful, as his very soul was at stake—who knew what tortures Allieb would inflict upon him? Still, he had strong doubts. *The demon has spared me so far, despite my shortcomings and his apparent knowledge of my ongoing faith in God. I can still believe, even after all this time, that he has an affinity for me because I am the boy's father—even putting aside the lack of a bloodline. I have stood by Allieb, although I fear he knows that my allegiance to him is a cover while I plan for his demise.*

Rubbing his eyes, he stretched out on the seat and sought sanctity in the blackness of his closed lids. Instead, he found only harsh memories: three weeks after returning home from the doctors—after they'd promised that Allieb would be okay . . .

Again Allieb refused his medicine. He remained in his room, unwilling to allow the presence of his pestering parents. He howled like a wolf and crawled into the darkness of his closet, remaining eerily silent behind the closed door, save for his chanting and tapping out of odd rhythms against the wall. He cared little for food; the raw vegetables and meat he demanded at times were his only nutrition.

His mother and father opened the closet and pleaded with him to take the pills. He leaped forward and swatted at his mother's hand, the pill bottle flying from her grasp, showering capsules everywhere. She cried, imagining sharp talons swiping at her from the tenuous wrist of her adopted child—a child who'd never shown her an ounce of the love she'd been willing to give. She prayed for something terrible to happen, a quick and sudden death, taking him away from her to end all misery. He'd read her ungracious thoughts, and his response was brutal. Sharp poundings resonated from the walls, like the fists of giants attempting to break through their cement bonds. The boy screamed, mouth twisting in agony and dread, his child's voice temporarily escaping its unseen barrier, pleading for mercy.

The man yelled at the boy, the woman shrieked, falling back against the wall in a near-faint. She crawled for the door, tried to escape the sudden chaos: inanimate objects in the room, leaping through the air, hurled by unseen forces; the lone window, slamming open, sharp wintry gusts blowing in; the curtains, swept from their rods, sailing about the room like ghosts. There was a loud crash, the door slamming shut before she could reach it, the sharp cracking of the wood splintering away from the brass hinges. The man stood solid ground, gasping dreadfully at the insanity as the poundings grew heavier, cracking the ceiling, the walls. The furniture in the room: two end tables, the bed, a bureau, heaved and rocked in erratic semicircles, carving gouges into the wood floor. And the boy, here, fully possessed by something otherworldly, now hiding, back in the closet amid his tattered things, laughing in a deep and strident voice, eyes bulging in an ashen face, the closet door slamming open and shut and open and shut, revealing to his horrified parents a now-bloodied torso, slashed at repeatedly with a straight razor gripped in his white-knuckled hands, blood pooling out in a glistening red wash, dousing his body.

The woman screamed, "No! No!" and then, "Do something!" directed to her husband, who stood trembling, paralyzed with shock. The man stepped forward toward the closet, beseeching Jesus Christ through weak-willed prayer. The closet door fell off its hinges with a deafening crack, revealing in full the horror within. The boy, flinging the straight razor toward his father's feet, lubricating his penis with the blood seeping from the wounds in his chest, masturbating furiously, exhibiting an impossibly-sized erection, blackly engorged with blood. "Come suck my cock, Daddy," he growled, voice seething with malignancy, while his features contorted into something repulsively vile, seemingly layered with undulating scales.

"No!" screamed the woman.

The boy crawled from the closet, trailing his feces behind in a slug track. His eyes were a distinct hue, reptilian, green irises ringed with yellow, the odor rising from him hideously foul, strangling the room. In an instant of fear, the flying objects in the room fell from the air in scattered heaps. The poundings in the wall stopped, bringing the room into eerie silence—silence, save for the sobs of his parents as they sought each other's arms for security and comfort.

The boy kneeled, hands stroking his engorged erection, laughing deafeningly in that horribly deep voice that wasn't his. "Let me fuck her, Daddy! Let me come on her tits!" A bellow of malevolent howls followed, his penis spitting copious amounts of semen as both parents cried inconsolably.

The parents remained a single passive unit, arms embracing each other's bodies as the horror commenced, the boy, laughing . . . laughing . . . laughing, tongue lashing out and gushing blood as his teeth chomped down upon it. The woman, in a maniacal state of fear, rushed the boy, screaming "Stop!" in throat-tearing fury, her hands shaking, grasping at his bloodied body, the boy releasing the grinding howl of a monstrous being, spouting his ferocity toward her, reaching up, grabbing her ears and shoving her face into the spew on the floor; her forehead split open, blood splatting out into the wicked mixture. "Swallow my jism, you fucking whore!" Allieb yelled, his evil eyes pinned on his father, who remained frozen in fear, a witness to his wife's barbaric thrashing. Allieb smashed her face repeatedly against the floor, over and over and over until it was a massive bloody pulp of indistinguishable features. The man, breaking his terrorized inaction, finally lurched forward, and was sent back with a splintering blow across the face. He slammed against the wall in a haze, a storm of horrid visions and sounds coalescing into an outrageous vista of mad realism, his gaze reaching past the fervent torture toward his son, who had twisted his mother's head unalterably around so that the neck was a twisted purple rag bursting with blood-soaked flesh.

"Come play with me, Daddy," sniggered the foreign voice.

Openmouthed, heaving, disbelieving, the man stared unblinkingly at his son's lunatic face: the torn bloodied lips, the thick, pale skin, the snakelike eyes, until he crumpled down into a black-filled heap of bitter nothingness.

The man started awake, rubbing his eyes. He looked at the clock. 6:28. He'd nodded off—for only a few minutes, it seemed. Still, the memory played out once again in its entirety, all the way to its horrid finale. He remained lying on the seat, breathing heavily, waiting . . . waiting.

Waiting for the Legion to arrive.

Twenty-nine

With his hands on the steering wheel, Grover sat up straight, eyeing the limo with great interest as it began backing out of the driveway, sans Bev Mathers. Foot on the brake, he turned on the windshield wipers and shifted the car into drive. The limo arched out into the street and slowly drove north up Hillage Avenue. Grover checked the rearview mirror.

Through the rain-spotted rear windshield, he noticed a silver Jeep Cherokee parking at the curb across the street, a few houses back. The driver's-side door opened and a woman emerged. Shielding her head with a newspaper, she started walking briskly up the sidewalk. Ahead, the limo rounded the first corner onto Donnell Avenue. Grover returned his sights to the road, slowly pulled away from the curb, and followed.

* * *

Bev waited, a few minutes seeming an eternity, unwilling to take the first step. It had felt as though one step might equal a fall into an inescapable chasm, one that would keep him buried in his agony for eternity. He gazed forward. The trees were thick, trunks staggered like soldiers, their roots reaching underfoot in serpentine loops, a threat to take him to the carpet of bristling foliage.

Then a voice in his head: *Bev?*

This, in the muffled distance: a woman's voice.

Julianne . . .

In fear, Bev raced away, dodging trees and foliage, swinging his arms, pushing aside drifting rain-spotted twigs.

Again, Julianne's voice: *Bev? Is that you?*

Bev ran, lungs cold and heaving. In the looming darkness, he lost his footing and fell. Mud slathered his hands and knees. He scrambled up, twigs poking his skin, rain dousing his entire body, sending chills deep into his bones. Bits of bark and wet leaves clung to his clothes like appliqués.

Bathed in semigloom, he moved east across the thickest stretch of woodland Torrance had to offer. He caught brief glimpses of the darkening sky filtering in through the treetop patches; rain continued to fall upon him.

And the voice in his head called to him. *Bev . . . wait . . .*

Despite the rain, the crickets were out, their ceaseless cries piercing Bev's strained psyche; on and on they trilled, like the incessant beckon of a phone left off the hook; neither pine nor elm nor brush could absorb the racket as it lanced into his head, finding the nerves of his bones and joggling them until his blood began to boil. He caught a palmful of thorns and nearly screamed out in pain, but choked it down for fear of pinpointing his location to anyone who might be out here seeking him.

Jesus, what am I thinking? Out here? Looking for me? That's absurd! The limo is in the driveway. Yes ... but then, what about the dark man? He'd managed to find his way backstage ... and followed me at the beach as well. Might still be following me. And the detective? He has his suspicions. Might've seen me making my escape down the fire ladder. After all, I did have blood on my hands.

Didn't I?

I didn't kill Jake!

Julianne's voice: *Bev ... where are you going? Wait for me!*

With the onset of the showers, a pacific wind ensued, restlessly tossing the upper reaches of the trees about, creating a staticlike sound that grew stronger as he moved deeper into the woods. This, in combination with the crickets, made more than enough noise for Bev to wonder if he'd ever hear anyone approaching him. But not enough, he felt, to shroud the noisy twigs and underbrush snapping beneath his footsteps.

He continued on. Running. Stumbling. Breaths short and spurting as he advanced trancelike through the woods, hearing only the crickets and the wind, his footsteps and his own mind trying to make sense of the horrifying events that had taken place over the past two days. *This is what it's all come to. All the success, a single in the top twenty-five, and here I am running through the rain-soaked woods like a man who's lost his mind. Lost his mind ...*

He heard something. Not the voice in his head. Not

his feet against the woodland floor. He pressed his body against the trunk of an elm, hands embracing the rough bark, waiting for what seemed an eternity, listening attentively and peering into the surrounding woodland in search of what he thought could have been a voice.

Bev . . . I'm right behind you.

"No! It can't be!" he yelled, and he darted away, continuing east and veering slightly to the right, following a thin, matted trail mostly free of brush. He trampled weeds and grass. Loose stones struck his ankles. He fought exhaustion, making decent progress nonetheless and realizing suddenly where his deepest instincts were taking him. He kept his eyes peeled on all sides, taking advantage of gaps in the woods to check that no one was following him. He pictured the place he was now heading in his weary mind, and wondered if it would provide the much-needed sanctuary he so recklessly, and suddenly, sought.

He continued on for another five minutes.

Then froze.

He heard it again.

A scraping sound. Raspy.

He crouched down next to a bush, looked left, right, up, down. Saw nothing. No one.

Only the wind. The crickets. *My mind's playing games with me. It is only some animal. A squirrel, perhaps a dog. Not the scratching in my head.*

Maybe it's the demon inside of you?

He waited. Thirty seconds. A minute. Nothing. Still, he felt strongly that something might be back there, hiding in the woods, watching him. His inaction brought pain: stiffness in the bones and muscles. Weariness. He wanted to scream.

Then, suddenly, footsteps. Nearby. Heavy, labored breathing. And a voice. *Her* voice. Julianne: "Bev, please, wait . . ."

Bev remained frozen in his crouch. Tears sprouted from his eyes. *Julianne, my dear wife . . .* He covered his face with his muddy hands, hearing the approach of tentative footsteps. When he took his hands away, he saw sneakered feet alongside him.

"Julianne?" he whispered, looking up, heart escaping his chest.

She knelt down alongside him. Labored breathing. Then: "Bev . . . what's going on? Why are you out here running?"

His eyes fell upon her.

Rebecca Haviland.

Tears poured from his eyes, half out of relief that it was someone he knew, someone he could trust, half out of disenchantment because he'd thought the woman whose voice he'd heard would be his long-lost Julianne, back from the dead to comfort him.

That's an insane mind thinking . . .

Rebecca stood, helping Bev to his feet. He leaned against a tree, hands rubbing his face, smearing mud about his worn features, eyes darting crazily back and forth.

"Bev . . . are you okay?"

"My God," he wheezed, hands on knees, lungs heaving for air. "No . . . I . . . I don't know." Through the cast of gray weather and his dose of tears, he gazed at her imploring features and saw so much of Julianne, even more so than the night before when they'd made love. His heart pounded ferociously. He asked, "What the hell are you doing out here?"

"Following you."

"Why . . . ?" He fought to catch his breath.

She breathed heavily for a few moments, then said, "Bev . . . we were talking on the phone earlier, about Jake. We got disconnected . . . I tried calling you back, but I couldn't get a signal. Eventually—it took me a long time—I got through, but you never answered. I was very worried . . . concerned that you . . . you might've, well, that *something* bad might've happened."

Bev shook his head. "I was at Kristin's place when you called," he whispered laboriously, still out of breath. "I forgot my phone there." He coughed hard and spit onto a patch of moss. A string of saliva hung from his bottom lip.

"I'm so sorry, Bev . . . but . . . I had to find you, and talk to you . . ." She started sobbing, her words breaking up. "I was so shocked and scared when I heard about Jake . . . I didn't know what to do, and when I couldn't get back in touch with you, I had to come by your place, talk to you about it, but when I got there, I got worried. Something looked wrong. The front door was ajar. I knocked a few times and called your name, but you didn't answer, so I went in and looked around and saw that your bedroom window was open and the rain was coming in, so I walked over to shut it, and that was when I saw you, running into the woods. I called you, but you didn't stop, so . . . I just . . . I just came after you. I'm sorry, but I didn't know what else to do . . . I thought something was wrong, that you . . . well, that you might be really upset over Jake, that you might . . . might hurt yourself."

"You went out the window?"

She nodded. "I'm sorry . . . it's just that I feel something . . . an unexplainable connection to you. I can't help it. All I know was that I needed to find you." Shivering, Rebecca wrapped her arms around her body. "What is it, Bev? What's happening?"

"Jake . . . he didn't drown. He was murdered."

Rebecca gasped. Her face fell white. She gripped her cheeks with nervous, probing fingers. "My God, Bev, when did you hear this?"

"A little more than an hour ago. A detective came by and questioned me. Told me that Jake had been choked to death with a guitar string."

Rebecca's eyes grew wide, her body swaying unsteadily. "A guitar string? Bev . . ."

Bev shook his head defiantly. "No, no, I didn't kill Jake, and I don't know who did." He thought of the gouges in his palms that were no longer there, and ran his hands through his wet hair as if to wash away any remaining evidence. He looked at her. Their eyes locked, and he almost told her about the scars that had miraculously healed over.

She stood her ground, arms crossed, waiting in tempered silence. "What, Bev? What is it?"

Shivering, he stepped forward. "Come with me." He grabbed her hand, eyes darting about the woods. "I'll tell you everything when we get to where I need to go."

"Where's that?" she asked, following his lead.

He didn't answer.

Thirty

Slowly, Frederick Grover followed the black limo in and around the neighborhoods as it wound its way up into Hollywood Hills. Here, your net worth was estimated by the altitude in which your home sat—the size of the homes grew bigger as the air grew thinner. Grover stayed back, maintaining a low profile while keeping the limo in his view at all times; the rain had darkened the skies, creating a gray sheet between them, keeping his unlighted presence cloaked.

The roads curved. The distance between the homes expanded. Finally, the limo made a left turn and stopped before an iron-gated mansion. The driver, unseen from Grover's position at fifty yards away, reached out and punched numbers into a code-entry box. The gates opened automatically, allowing the limo access. Upon the car's entry and disappearance behind the eight-foot hedges, the gate closed. Grover inched his car up to the corner, positioning himself between a gap in the hedges. He shut off the ignition. Watched in darkened silence as the limo rolled up a long curving driveway to the entrance of the house: eight-foot twin Gothic doors bathed in misty crimson lights. Besides the driver, one person emerged. They were both dressed in black robes. Quickly, they entered into the mansion.

Grover grabbed the radio handset in his car, cleared his throat, then called in his location and asked for details on the home's residency.

Officer Renee Saunders took a few seconds, humming as she waited, then answered, "Got a name. James Thornton. No other info. No priors. What's this about?"

"Checking a lead on the ritual murder."

"Need backup?"

Grover looked at the house, thought about it, then answered, "Nah, I'll be all right. Probably nothing."

Instead he told Renee to send Officer Rose over to the rectory at St. Michael's Church. "Let's take a shot and see if the priest is there. If he is, have Rose question him more thoroughly." When asked why, he replied, "I have my suspicions," to which she replied, "Smart-ass."

He lit a cigarette, smoked it to the filter, then put on his hat and emerged from the car, keeping his eyes on the iron gates.

Thirty-one

Bev stopped, breathing heavily, trying to allow the dizziness to fade. Rebecca, in tentative silence, watched him carefully, seemingly prepared to pick up the slack should he collapse from the exhaustion threatening to take him down. In silence, he pressed on, pulling Rebecca along, coerced by the sudden desire to find answers to the mystery abruptly dismembering his life. Along they went, heading east, Bev nearly startling with panic at the sound of every twig snapping under their footsteps: his mind, contriving the presence of those in the limo, standing at an arm's length away, reaching out to take them both by their throats once and for all. *What would Dr. Palumba say about these exaggerated responses to so many common noises?*

At one point, Bev asked Rebecca, "When you arrived, was there a limo in the driveway?"

"No," she answered, leading Bev to believe that the occupants within had known he'd fled and had moved on to pick up his trail. Soon, he knew, they'd find him.

With his rolling thoughts, and his desire to flee the darkening woodland, Bev raced forward as quickly as possible, pulling Rebecca along, sidestepping brambles and roots and copses, at last nearing the edge of the woods.

The trees thinned. In the distance he saw a few homes, each separated by a stretch of trees providing a natural privacy for the residents.

"You know where we are?" Rebecca asked.

"Yes," he answered. "Just follow me, and lay low."

Looking nervously about, he slowly made his way from the purple shadows of the woods into the backyard of one of the homes, Rebecca following tentatively behind. The house was quaint, a shingled ranch with a circular brick patio and sliding doors. A pair of French windows looked out on either side of the doors, the curtains drawn.

They stepped forward, out into the open; the rain had strengthened and fully saturated their clothes. Cupping their hands around their faces, they quickly scampered to the side of the house, then made their way into the street, standing up as nonchalantly as possible upon reaching the curb. Bev tried to brush his clothing free of the mud and bark, an ineffectual effort, then looked up and down the short neighborhood block. He saw no one.

Luckily, with no one present to witness their evasive behavior—thank the rain—they were able to dart eagerly across the street into the backyard of another house, where they crouched along a row of azaleas in an effort to blend into the environment.

"Why are we doing this?" Rebecca asked suspiciously. "Why are you trying to hide?"

"I told you—I'll explain later."

"Is it the cops, Bev? Are they after you?"

"No . . . please, just bear with me."

He pressed on in an evasive manner, Rebecca following Bev's method of "dart and dodge" in the more visible areas. They wandered for twenty minutes in this fashion, traveling for nearly half a mile until they found their way into the open parking lot of the place Bev was headed—the place where he felt the answers to his crisis might be found. At one point, he never thought he'd make it. But now, he was thankful to be here.

St. Michael's Church, on Caliendo Street.

Thirty-two

The man heard the expectant knock upon the door. He gazed at the cracked face of the clock, stiff neck slowly craning. Eyes watering. 6:47. "Enter," he said morosely, the numbers blurring.

Three bodies stepped in, all donned in black robes. Their faces remained shrouded amid the dusky shadows of the room, golden candlelight flickering against the wall behind them like specters. With them, an odor of excrement and of blood—already, they'd bathed in preparation for the event.

The figure at the forefront of the trio shook his head ruefully. "God wants you."

The man frowned and fidgeted. The demand had been anticipated. *Allieb knows I have failed yet again to bring in the thirteenth.* "The car . . . is it still out front?" he asked, standing, tugging at his sleeves.

"Yes," a male voice replied from within the dark void

in the hood, unseen gaze following the man's path to the closet.

My hesitancy. My fear . . .

He shoved past the hooded trio and exited the dark room. Impetuously, he paced the halls, past the empty rooms whose occupants kept busy in preparation. He reached the stairs and climbed them to the uppermost landing, where, behind the lone door, Allieb prepared for the Legion. The man approached the door and raised a tentative fist to knock as false hope prodded his wearied heart. From behind the door ascended the tempered breathing of a sleeping boar. A foul odor emerged.

Sweat running down his brow, he moved to knock. Then, suddenly, he decided against it. He took a deep breath.

I am in communication with the thirteenth, you know.

He placed the side of his face against the door; its surface was icy cold. "My God," he whispered, "where is he now? The thirteenth. I shall again go out . . . this time I will not fail to bring him to you."

From behind the door, the snoring escalated, carrying with it an impossible echo. Then Allieb's voice, low and coarse, whispering in his mind: *Find the priest, and you will find the thirteenth.*

The man backed away, skin rippling with gooseflesh. For the first time in years, he smiled.

The priest . . .

Thirty-three

Grover stared through the wrought-iron gates, up the length of the driveway to the parked limo sitting stoically beneath the crimson glow of the house lights; rain battered the car's glossy finish, igniting the ebony glare, making it appear as though it had been caught under flames. He gazed curiously at the keypad entry set into the stone pillar, then at the gates themselves. He stepped forward and reached through the slats, searching blindly for a latch. He didn't find one. Shielding his eyes from the rain, he peered up at the fancy cathedral spires running ten feet high. In script, the wrought-iron bars twisted and curved to form the words: *In Domo*. Meant nothing to Grover. Might be Latin for "Welcome," he thought, although he doubted it. Grabbing two slats, he pressed against the gate. It made a sharp *clack!* sound and swung forward, creaking anciently on its hinges—a sound not unlike the growing wind that buried chills deep beneath his skin. He slipped through, careful not to shut it all the way.

The land at the forefront of the house was no more than an open courtyard, a double-wide driveway intersecting it like a vein. Twenty feet in front of the house, it split into a circular shape with a cement fountain at the center. On the opposite side of the fountain (atop which a trio of gargoyles embraced), the two ends of the driveway met. Here the limo sat like a sleeping dragon before the twin Gothic-engraved doors.

Despite the shield of looming darkness and rainfall, Grover felt vulnerable at this position: standing before the gates where a security camera might be aimed. He leaned down and scooted to the left, onto the grass, where he hunkered down before the hedges, making his best effort to blend into the environment. Here an awful odor arose, and he wondered if a swamp might be nearby, although it seemed unlikely in such an affluent area.

He waited, contemplating the grounds, trying to ascertain his motives for coming here. What did he expect to find? He gazed at the mansion, with its massive architecture and flaring red lights. Dark clouds shifted ominously behind the highest point—a rounded cupola—revealing a cold slice of moon that cut through the poor weather like a failing beacon. Inside the house, the windows were covered with black curtains or sheets, yellow light bleeding from the billowing edges in thin, wavering strips. He caught glimpses of hooded people inside. Grover stayed low, listening for noise. Heard only the pelting rain, which continued to strengthen and batter. A low-lying mist seeped in from around the corners of the house. *And that smell . . . there is a swamp around.*

He swiped his eyes with a sleeve, wondered who lived here and why they'd come for Bev Mathers, only to leave without him. It didn't seem to make sense—unless, of course, Bev *had* decided to stay home after all, as he'd indicated earlier, and at the last minute had canceled his plans to join his rock-star chums for a party of guitar playing and pot smoking. Maybe it did make sense after all? Maybe . . .

But then, why were those people wearing hoods? Because they're devil worshipers and this is where Bev Mathers comes for black mass! Herein lies the answers to the crimes!

It hadn't started with the goat, or Jake Ritchie. There had been ten other "sacrifices" before them, all cats or dogs left exposed in public venues so the offenders could duly make their dark statement known: a pentagram formed of mutlilated flesh at the scene of each crime. Following these sacrifices came the slaughter of the goat at the rectory. Grover took a deep breath, both concerned and frightened. The people responsible for these events had played—were still playing—a very dangerous game, one that had accelerated with the ritualistic murder of Jake Ritchie. What was next? Did it end there? Now, staring up at this threatening mansion, Grover felt convinced that he'd stumbled upon a headquarters of some sort, a place where iniquities were plotted—and within dwelled those blameworthy for abhorrent crimes. His heart rate increased.

Suddenly, the doors to the house opened. Yellow light spilled outside, a dark, lithe figure emerging from its glare. Grover pressed back into the hedges and watched as the hooded individual slowly came down the wide porch steps and entered into the back of the limo. Another cloaked figure emerged and settled behind the limo's wheel. With its headlights cutting into the wisping fog and rain, the limo edged around the fountain and moved slowly up the driveway, wet pavement squelching beneath its tires. Grover turned away and hid the white of his face and hands in the hedges, shivering in the cold wetness, until the limo exited the grounds. He waited, a sudden downpour pelting him, the gates humming electronically as they closed after the car left. He gazed out through a branching space in the hedges, watching with dismay as the limo turned the corner and disappeared.

He twisted around, gazed back at the mansion, wondering if he'd been locked onto the grounds. A few moments passed, and in this time he felt no alternative but to take a closer look at the looming edifice. He stood up. Stepped away from the hedges, walking slowly— now shrouded in near-darkness and knee-deep fog— toward the hulking residence. Nearing it, he could ascertain unclear noises coming from behind the blockade of stone walls: a throbbing rhythmic beat, like a great heart; the errant knocking of something heavy, a mallet on wood perhaps; the tolling of a bell; the muffled voice of someone shouting.

Rain soaked his body, sending a numbing chill deep into his bones. Soft grass and mud mashed beneath his feet. He angled his path toward the left side of the house where a narrow strip of lawn disappeared into an unlighted backyard surrounded by eight-foot hedges. Here the windows were also curtained over in black, many of the lights out behind them.

Suddenly, from behind, hidden in the seep of fog, came a low, guttural snort.

At once, the chill of the rain seemed to amplify. Something fluttered around his ankles. He started with

205

fear, kicking his feet rapidly as he looked down. The fog parted mysteriously around him.

He was standing in a tall patch of weeds.

He heard a shuffling noise. He turned, pressed back against the slime-covered stone of the house, pulling his escalating fear away from the glowing red eyes emerging from the fog-shrouded darkness.

From the nodding bulk of a head.

From the heaving body and jutting bristles of hair.

From the hooves that dug madly into the mud.

Here, parting the fog and ascending from the gloom, black-skinned and bleeding from its head, was a pig.

The eyes, seemingly on fire with cunning and intelligence, contemplated Grover. Its head nodded aggressively up and down, and its pointed hooves slapped the wet earth. It produced another harsh grunting noise, and a spray of mucus shot from its nose. Its head then stilled, eyes peering accusingly at Grover.

Pressing himself against the house as hard as possible, Grover shooed at the large animal, but to no benefit. The thing was *immense*—the size of a small cow. *Aren't pigs supposed to be small and pink and cute?* he thought idiotically. The animal continued snorting, inching closer and closer, discharging a mound of dark steaming excrement, the immediate stench of which slammed Grover in the face like an explosion.

"Git!" he whispered aggressively. "Git away!"

The pig stayed put, head bobbing violently back and forth. It rose up on its hind hooves and slammed back down, spraying up mud and grass. Terrified, Grover slithered along the edge of the house, then darted off toward the gates, doing his best not to skid on the slick grass.

The pig squealed and pursued, its weight thudding

against the soft earth. Grover could feel the ground vibrating beneath his feet. He splashed in a patch of water. His shoes, sodden and heavy, lost their hold and came out from under him. He slammed down, water splashing about him, hands breaking his fall and sinking into the muddy earth.

The pig was right behind him, clawing at his heels, snorting savagely. Something tore into his Achilles tendon, and he howled in pain. Twisting, he saw the demonic red eyes glowing angrily at him, its snout rising up, baring brown stumps for teeth that attempted to gnaw him once again.

In a maddened state, Grover crawled toward the gate, glimpsing with utter dread and dismay the rising fog that traveled no farther than the boundary of the wrought-iron fence. He reached the gate, pulled himself up on his knees, and yanked it violently.

Locked.

He turned. The pig was there, sharp hooves bearing down on him, slicing deeply into his thrashing legs. Grover cried out as it knocked him to the wet driveway, teeth biting brutally into his wrist. He kicked and flailed, tried to push it away, but couldn't so much as shift its heaving bulk. The pig released its jaws, rose up, blood dripping from its snout. It came down on Grover again, slamming his waist, the sharp agony of something bursting inside his body paralyzing him. It lunged at his head, rough snout slathering his face wetly as it gnawed crazily into his neck, front hooves pinning his chest, tearing his clothes, teeth digging deeply into the thin flesh of his throat, a horribly demented snorting sound rising fiercely in his ears. Grover, gasping for air, managed to jerk an arm free. Dug his nails into the pig's back, which only inflamed the animal further. He pounded on the pig's head. It released its death grip, exposed its teeth, then lunged forward and slammed its heaving bulk atop Grover's head. Blackness consumed the detective as two hundred pounds of rolling black pig flesh filled his mouth and nose. He tried to fight the massive weight overwhelming him but was helpless beneath its brutal influence. He attempted a breath, but found the crushing force of the pig's weight to be definitively stifling. His strength waned as darkness filled his oxygen-deprived brain. His thoughts and knowledge escaped his mind as permanent damage set in. His thrashing waned. His eyesight went black and he fell silent and still, surrendering to the terror-filled night.

Thirty-four

Intemperate sheets of rain swept against Bev's face as he stood in the center of the empty parking lot; the deluge, caught in the wind's hazy grasp, dulled the world to a starkly gray tone. Hand cupped around his eyes, he gazed toward a clutter of elms alongside St. Michael's Church, their branches casting leaves across the blacktop.

Muscles aching, he gazed at Rebecca, then grasped her hand and moved forward onto a cement path leading toward what he hoped would be his salvation. He gazed at the intimidating structure, wondering if he'd be greeted with further agonies or sanctification. This uncertainty brought about a queasiness in him, lungs clutching for air in quickened bursts. His heart and mind soared with suspicions of imminent panic and emergency.

In an effort to calm himself, he gently pressed a hand

to his chest, held his breath, then lurched toward the church, pulling Rebecca along, feeling weak and somewhat vague, as though he were in a strange, sodden dream. *No, Bev, your dreams are forged of fire and of sulfur, of demons and the demoralization and destruction of those you love.*

That's no dream. That's the real world.

He climbed the church steps and pulled open the large oak doors. Instantaneously, he gagged. Shrinking back, afraid to enter, he sucked in powerfully, attempting to gain control of his galloping breaths. A pressure at once filled his head in that area where the *scratch-scratch-scratch* had once been, as if the infamous ghostly fingers within had finally broken free with a duty to explore the other side of his skull.

He dropped to one knee. Grasped his temples.

"Bev?" Rebecca asked, holding his hand tightly. "What's wrong?"

Ignoring her, he gritted his teeth, mentally forcing the hole in his mind closed, seemingly shutting the fingers in.

Isn't a house of worship supposed to be welcoming? Its imaginary arms open wide at any hour to embrace all those sinners in need of a temporary Messiah?

He stood on shaky feet. Silently staggered across the threshold, into the church's vestibule. He straightened, taking deep breaths, mentally willing away the horrid wooziness attempting to take him back down.

"Bev . . . what is it?"

"Let me be for a minute," he whispered painfully.

He stared about the vestibule—at the bulletin board with its church activity announcements; the threadbare rug and pinewood architecture. Once his eyes adjusted to the warmer interior, the dizziness faded and he wiped the wetness from his face and started forward, into the church.

A gray marble holy-water basin came into view at the entrance to the nave. Bev shivered, cold fear and nervous denial straining him. With unfamiliar trepidation, he walked to the small marble bath and forced his fingers into the lukewarm water. His heart pounded. His hand trembled.

And then it burned.

In pain, he quickly plucked his hand out of the seemingly scalding water. He gazed curiously at his fingers. Reddened. Lightly blistered. He gritted his teeth, then caught his escaping breath and crossed himself.

Nausea returned to him like a palpable force. He shivered with unexplainable disgust and derision. A harsh burning sensation surfaced on his brow, as though someone had snuffed a cigarette out on his forehead.

"Bev! Jesus, your forehead! It's . . . it's turned bright red. It looks like it's *burnt*."

Dismayed, he pinched his lips and looked away, feeling confused and embarrassed and frightened. He advanced away from her, into the church, fists clenched nervously at his sides. Trying to ignore the throb of pain on his head, he gazed at the surfeit of Gothic architecture surrounding him. The columnar supports, vaulted ceilings, arched doorways, all seemingly constructed as a reflection of the heavens. Above, dome-shaped fixtures cast ghostly yellow auras across the ranks of pews, leading beyond the sanctuary to the altar.

Shrouded in shadows, the altar was a shrine of blessed figures and religious statuary, molded from porcelain and painted with the finest hand. Gracing the wall behind the altar hung a great crucifix, twelve feet high, intricately carved in wood, extraordinarily detailed. Gazing upon it, Bev could feel the pain carved and painted upon the face of the crucified Jesus: the thorned head; tortured eyes in search of the heavens; mouth contorted passionately. *I share your agony.*

Rebecca came alongside him and grabbed his hand. Together, they paced down the center aisle, their wet footfalls squeaking hollowly throughout the empty church. Bev ran his free hand along the wooden pews, keeping his eyes pinned to the wooden Jesus, to its heavenward gaze and bloody wounds, to its straining, sinewy muscles and tattered loincloth.

Like magic, a row of candles at the front of the altar came alive.

Bev and Rebecca halted. They looked haphazardly into the nearby pews, then glanced back to the nave. Nothing.

Bev riveted his sights back upon the crucifix and the dozen burning candles.

Out of the shroud of darkness on the altar, a figure appeared.

A sudden gust of wind gripped the outside door—which had been left open—and slammed it shut. The jarring noise and Rebecca's resulting wail reverberated around the church like a pair of warring souls.

"Are you all right?" the man said.

Bev blew out a breathful of anxiety, his heart settling like a surfacing balloon.

Father Thomas Danto.

The priest leaned down, toyed with a knob on the candle basin that lowered the flames, then made his approach, head thrust forth, shoulders hunched.

Watching him, Bev released a plaintive sigh. "Father . . ."

"Bevant Mathers. I've been expecting you. Come with me. We have much to discuss."

Thirty-five

Slowly and deliberately, the limo coursed the dark roads of Hollywood Hills, rain pelting the windows like strewn needles. The wipers, slapping incessantly, barely cleared the view of the driving storm. Wincing, the man lifted his left leg over his right, then peered at the LED clock on the limo's back dash. 7:58 P.M. He sat erect, staring out the tinted windows at the passing houses, praying openly in his mind without fear of being heard.

I have been communicating with the thirteenth, you know.

He grew restless as the limo braked and slowed, oncoming traffic splashing jarring swells against it. Lightning flashed above, igniting the premature night every twenty seconds. *Perfect conditions for Legion*, the man thought. *More odds stacked against us.*

He closed his eyes and sighed. Thought of what lay ahead.

And, at the same time, once again, recalled the past . . .

He opened the door. Standing on the porch was a man in his thirties. He wore a gray Windbreaker and a cap.

The man nodded once.

"Father Danto. Thank you for coming. Please, come in." He stepped aside, allowing the priest entry into his home.

The priest carried a worn canvas bag, which he placed at his feet. The two men stared at each other for a moment, having only once spoken on the phone. Their gazes meshed as magnetic opposites, one laden with grief and desperation, the other, intelligence and understanding.

"Reverend James Thornton," he said, breaking the charged silence. He offered his hand. A gentle rush of electricity passed between them as they shook: a bond, at once created in a union of forces.

From somewhere above or below, horrid wails arose: the voice of the boy, rattling the house's windows. The lights flickered; a stench of sewage blew in from the vents.

"He knows you're here," Thornton said, clutching his cheek nervously.

Danto nodded, eyes searching the room. He cocked an ear, perceiving something . . . something familiar. *Intimate.* "Give me a few short moments to prepare," he requested, senses still assessing the environment.

"Of course," Thornton said.

"The bathroom, please," Danto said.

Thornton showed the way, across the living room. The priest glanced down as he paced across the stained carpet. He entered the bathroom, shutting the door behind. Silence dominated from within. Thornton still wondered how the priest knew of Allieb, his phone call yesterday coming so suddenly and unexpectedly. *A gift from God*, he could only presume, asking no immediate questions of the holy man. In minutes, Danto emerged from the bathroom, dressed in a black robe, brown wooden rosaries, and a silver cross. He handed a worn Bible to Thornton.

"You say he is your son?"

Thornton nodded. "Adopted."

"From Israel . . ."

"Yes, that is correct—"

"And he goes by the name of Allieb."

This repeat discussion from yesterday drew heavily on Thornton's curiosity. "How do you know of this?"

Danto peered around the room, a glint of intensity in his eyes. "I followed him here." He gazed knowingly at the basement door. "Let us begin right away."

The priest stepped aside, allowing Thornton to lead the way. The minister, hesitant and staring at first, swallowed hard and ushered the priest to the triple-bolted steel door. As he unlocked the dead bolts, he remarked, "He killed my wife."

The priest nodded, as though he'd already known.

The door creaked open, darkness and rancid air beckoning them. From below, a sharp pounding began, and a loud taunting voice ripped through the air. "The children taste delicious, Danto." Then, in an almost sensual tone: "Wanna try some?"

The priest stared down into the darkness, motionless, nodding his head with recognition. "It *is* him. Allieb. The demonologist."

"Come to me, Danto." The sharp poundings

216

stopped, and were immediately replaced with a rattling of chains and ensuing animalistic barks.

Thornton leaned forward, pulled a tiny chain dangling from the ceiling, which ignited a bare bulb at the bottom of the steps. Danto hooked his arm through Thornton's, then nodded. Slowly, they walked downstairs, gripping their Bibles tightly. The growls below segued into a series of grisly laughs, then tapered down into complete silence as the two holy men reached the bottom step.

The air here was cold, filled with dread and things gone afoul. The two men stared blankly at Allieb. The ten-year-old boy was sitting on the cement floor, naked in his own feces, thick link chains wrapped about his wrists and ankles, fed through heavy eyehooks screwed into the cinder walls just beyond his reach. He leaped forward, the muscles in his limbs straining as they fought their bonds, the skin beneath the chains red and raw. The boy snarled, baring his teeth, black tongue flickering in and out of his bleeding lips. His penis stood erect, strangely large, mottled with purple bruises. This aggressive conduct lasted a minute, until Allieb fell silently still against the cinder wall, stomach ballooning up and down, wolfish eyes contemplating the two men as they stared him down in silent prayer.

Alongside the boy lay a human femur bone, stripped clean of its flesh.

He killed my wife . . .

The boy-demon smiled wickedly. "Let us play," he growled.

Thirty-six

Still holding hands, Bev and Rebecca followed close behind Father Danto as he guided them across the altar through a doorway leading into the rectory. The hard aroma of fresh paint hung thickly in the air, stinging their nostrils.

"They just finished cleaning everything," he said. "Took three coats to cover the bloodstains. I'm the only one here right now. Everyone else will be moving back in tomorrow morning." Rebecca, unaware of the crime that had taken place at the rectory, looked around questioningly, eyes wide and skittish.

They crossed through a short hallway into an empty reception area. To the left rose a set of carpeted steps, leading into darkness. Danto flipped a switch on the wall in the foyer, bringing light into the second floor. They climbed the stairs, angling into a hallway lined with closed doors. Danto fished a key from his front pocket, unlocked the second door on the right, and guided them inside.

The room was meagerly decorated: an aluminum-framed twin bed alongside a small end table supporting a shaded lamp and telephone. On the opposite wall were an easy chair and a small television. Like the rest of the rectory, the floor was carpeted in dull blue, a cotton curtain in a near-matching color shading the room's only window. Sheets of rain slashed the dark pane.

"Can I get you some water?" Danto asked.

"Please," Bev replied; Rebecca nodded also. Danto retrieved three plastic bottles from a small icebox next to the room's lone window. He handed one to each of them and drank from the third.

"I need to call my daughter," Bev announced abruptly. He walked over to the end table, grabbed the telephone handset. Quickly, he punched in Kristin's apartment number. No answer. Then her cell. Again, nothing. After six rings, he left a harried voice message, then nervously set the phone back into its cradle. He blew out a deep, anxious breath.

Saw her getting into a limo last night. 'Bout seven or so. Last I've seen her.

Rebecca asked, "Kristin . . . is she okay?"

He shrugged. "I don't know." Trying to shake the troubling thought from his mind, he turned his attention to Danto. "You said you were expecting me."

The priest nodded. "Take a seat," he said, motioning to the bed. Danto sat down on the edge of the easy chair. "There is much to discuss, and little time to do it."

Bev and Rebecca shared the foot of the bed, facing the priest. In the pause of the moment, Rebecca asked, "Bev . . . what's going on?"

Looking toward the floor, Bev attested, "I don't know . . . there's been some terrible things happening over the last couple of days. I came here hoping . . ." He looked at Danto. "Hoping to get some answers."

Danto, staring intensely at Bev, as though searching for something *in* him, replied, "You did good, Bev. You've come to the right place."

"Well . . . what is it, then?" Despite his demanding tone, the question had been asked with a bit of hesitance. In the back of Bev's mind were the various texts on demonology he'd read while poking around in Kristin's office, and one essay in particular that had gone into great detail with respect to the symptoms of an individual possessed by a demon. It appeared now, given those texts, plus Danto's proclaimed expertise at the party and his apparent knowledge of Bev's situation, that Bev might indeed be harboring a spirit of some malevolent nature, as crazy as that sounded. He closed his eyes and rubbed them, cursing silently to himself, wishing his assumption to be wrong. "I'm getting the impression you know what's happening to me—and might even know why." He opened his tired eyes, staring at Danto.

"I do know, Bev," Danto replied. "It would help if you told me everything that's been happening to you."

Bev nodded, feeling a sense of frustration despite his measured understanding of Danto's point of view; he wanted answers, and he wanted them *now*. He took a sip of water and realized that his experiences over the last forty-eight hours might very well shed some additional light onto the situation, especially to a man who had a good deal of prior knowledge and facts rolling around in his head.

So he started from the very beginning, divulging every last detail.

Danto remained silent, staring at Bev with disconcerted eyes, as though waiting for him to add a few more important details. Finally, Bev asked, "What do you make of all this?"

The priest nodded in earnest. "I make much of it." He looked at his watch, then leaned over, pulled the curtain aside, and peered out the rainy-wet window. "The hour is getting late. We have much work ahead of us, and so little time."

"Work? What work? Father, please . . . can you give me a bit of insight here before I completely lose my mind?"

The priest grinned ruefully. "You are not losing your mind . . . in a clinical sense, that is. But there *is* something dire happening . . . something that is affecting not only you but a number of other people as well. At this very moment, there are other innocents out there—unoffending folks like yourself—that are experiencing all the same terrible symptoms. And many at this point, I might add, to a much greater degree."

"Jesus, are you trying to tell me that it gets worse than *this*?"

"Afraid so."

"Please, Father, what is it? What's happening?" In a dark corner of his mind, however, he already knew. *It can only be speculated as to what an individual may experience while under demonic possession. At first, they may feel suddenly ill, nauseous and dizzy . . .*

Danto leaned forward. "Does the word *Legion* mean anything to you?"

Bev and Rebecca shook their heads in unison.

Danto blew out, looking white and nervous, as though he'd raised a subject that would bring about great pains. He leaned forward, elbows on knees, again glancing at his watch. "There's a story in the Bible, one that tells of Jesus's miraculous calming of a great storm that had filled Jerusalem's homes with sand, subsequently absorbing all the city's holy waters. After performing his miracle, Jesus traveled into deserts of Gerasenes in Israel and met a man there claiming to be possessed by thirteen demons. This man was unsettled, naked, and had been living in a tomb, under guard by many men. He claimed to have broken the chains that had bound him and had escaped by frightening away those who were watching him. When Jesus asked the man his name, he replied, 'I am Legion, for we are many.' Jesus then commanded the demons out of the man into a herd of thirteen swine feeding on the hillside. The possessed herd ran down the hillside into the desert, where they buried themselves in the sand and remained out of contact for years. Soon, the holy waters returned and the pigs drowned, so it is said. This, as the Bible relates, is the first story of God's conflict with evil. And it is a powerful one, too—the demons had realized that they could not defeat the son of God, having elected to be placed into swine instead of the abyss, where they would remain for eternity. *This* was one of God's first mistakes, sparing the demons—it is assumed that there would not have been a temptation of evil today if the demons had been sent into the infernal abyss.

"It is known in the Church that regardless of the passage of time, demonic forces will *always* oppose that which is good. These thirteen demons *knew* that Jesus's coming would hinder them from performing their evil wills. So, to avoid permanent exile, they chose to sleep within the pigs, knowing that eventually they would be released.

"The demon-swine remained sequestered until, years later, one man, Allieb, sought to release them unto the world, offering them the bodies of thirteen children into which they could escape the drowned swine. But Allieb had ulterior motives. As a master demonologist, he raised the soul of his father, the demon Belial, then made attempts to subsequently draw the remaining demons from the children's bodies into his own body. By doing this, he aimed to gain immense power over the world by sharing his own soul with the thirteen demons once released by Jesus Christ. Allieb had been successful to a certain degree, but was ultimately murdered for his crimes before the entire transition could take place. He was buried in a tomb in the Negev Desert, where his body remained for over two thousand years."

"You mentioned this at the party last night."

Danto nodded. "But there are additional details you must know."

Bev nodded.

The priest continued. "By chance, in '67, during the Six-Day War, while I was studying at the University of Archaeology in Jerusalem, Allieb's tomb was uncovered. As I'd mentioned, a young boy had been found hiding inside. I didn't realize it at first, but it became apparent to me, after my six months of study of the tomb and its history, that Allieb's soul might've been released into the six-year-old. Once I discovered the exact nature of Allieb's history, I felt no choice but to follow the boy (who'd uttered very few words upon his rescue, his professed name being one of them: Allieb) to America, where he'd been adopted by an American minister and his wife. I eventually located the family and kept close tabs on the boy until . . ." Danto paused, sipped some water, then said, "Well . . . let's just say I'd been correct in my deduction. Within a few months of my arrival, the soul of Allieb had completely taken over the boy's body and had immediately begun summoning the thirteen demons. This poor boy, whose true identity had never been discovered, had *become* the two-thousand-year-old Allieb. But . . . the boy's body had not been strong enough to absorb the soul of the ancient demonologist *and* the demonic souls—he was to have brought the demons into individual human vehicles first, which he failed to do. This would have weakened the souls, allowing Allieb to more easily absorb them into his own soul. It can only be assumed that the soul of Allieb, two thousand years in waiting, had ignored his father's counsel and had impetuously commenced with the drawing."

Danto took another sip of water, allowing Bev a moment to ask, "How do you know all of this—that the boy had become possessed by the soul of Allieb, and Belial?"

"And a number of other demon spirits as well," Danto added.

"Right."

He stared at Bev. "Because I exorcised the souls from his body."

The two men, priest and reverend, moved to opposing sides of the boy, out of his grasping reach. Eyes filled with hostility peered up at them. A dense lull suffocated the basement. Then the boy stroked his erect penis, chains dangling from his jerking wrist. Thick yellow ooze seeped from his urethra. "Suck me, Father," he cooed playfully, then barked, "Choke on my jism!"

"Who are you?" Danto asked, making the sign of the cross on himself.

"You know, proud Papa."

"Allieb. The demonologist?"

"Maybe," the boy growled.

"Or are you one of the thirteen demons?"

Allieb seethed. "I am in full control of the dark souls . . . all thirteen!"

Danto thought, *He's lying.* "Show one to me," he asked.

The boy yanked on the chains and barked like a dog. White foam appeared on his mouth.

"Was that one of the demons?"

The boy cowered, sniggering, eyes yellow and peering up through crust-laden lashes.

The priest and the minister kneeled down and prayed aloud, exchanging verses from the Bible over the boy's depraved laughter. *"Deliver us from the evil!"* The boy howled with specious merriment, louder, louder, drowning out their forceful supplications. Upon completion of the first set of prayers, Danto removed a vial of holy water from his pocket. He removed the cap and showered the boy. Wails of pain filled the room; the boy, writhing on the cement floor like an injured insect, the veins in his arms and legs swelling like balloons; his tongue, dangling from his mouth, dripping thick white saliva. An eerie chorus of anguished voices sprouted from his widening mouth.

And they prayed and flung the blessed water at Allieb: *"Take thy unclean spirit and condemn it into the abyss for eternity!"* The boy hissed like a reptile, oinked like a pig, honked like a steer, arching his back into a U shape so that the rear of his skull nearly touched his reaching heels. Items flew across the room and collided against the ceiling and walls: a paintbrush, a plastic bucket, tattered rags.

"No power to the enemy! Lord, hear our prayers!" The boy's body snapped back into shape, his head making hard contact with the cement floor. Blood gushed out in a shocking spray. "Jesus!" Thornton yelled, the boy rising suddenly off the ground, the manacles clanging harshly in the curdling silence. He levitated for an indeterminable amount of time, canine eyes doused in blood, staring through the two men as they continued praying aloud, dousing the boy/beast with holy water. His limbs strained, continued to fight their steel bonds, his mouth open and choking, hunks of brown phlegm spurting out.

They continued their prayers: *"Lord, Jesus Christ, take back this beast planting Satan's debris, and drive it into the abyss to rot for eternity!"*

The boy fell to the floor in a crumpled heap. He twisted his neck around and peered up at the men with dark, baleful eyes. The voice of a grown man emerged from his lips. "The demons are leaving . . . but *I* still remain."

There was a sudden, horrid stench as liquid feces exploded from the boy's rectum. Danto screamed, *"Be gone, befouled spirit, and take thy demons with you!"*

The boy tilted his head down, quiet and unmoving. His eyes rolled maniacally in their sockets, like eggs in boiling water. Thornton watched intensely as his adopted son choked and coughed, spasmed uncontrollably. His limbs twisted into impossible angles, the bones popping and snapping, the red skin stretching. The room grew icy cold, the feces on the floor vaporizing, filling the room with putrid steam. The lone lightbulb flickered, brightened, dulled.

"Return to the depths of hell and wallow in Satan's wasteland!"

In the grown man's voice, the boy uttered brokenly, "Satan refuses to join . . . he disputes the Legion . . ." Tears sprouted from his eyes. "Beelzebub is gone . . . Baphomet . . . gone . . . Rex Mundi . . . gone . . . Satan has retrieved his brethren. Damn him . . ."

A grinding noise filled the room. Deep laughter emerging from the sudden wind whipping about. Cracks ran along the cinder walls, white light seeping from within the running crevices. The wood beams in the ceiling splintered. The boy reached for the heavens, arms raised high, grasping the air. The white light seeping from the cracks in the walls filled the room, taking with it the warring souls escaping Allieb. Harsh, tortured screams deafened the two men as they fell back from a sudden, unseen blow, attempting prayers amid the encompassing din of escaping evil.

"God of heaven, God of earth, God of all creation, we implore you . . ." Danto commenced his prayers, watching in near blindness the blackened shadows of the demons spilling from the boy's mouth and ears and eyes and rectum, nearly tangible forms winging across the room, caught by the white light and wholly absorbed. Seven entities in all, fighting their way out over a span of nearly two hours, combating the light that seized them, screeching in agony. Every second was fought with prayers and showers of holy water, while

Allieb's frail, naked form jerked and jolted and spasmed as the demons vacated.

And when the shadows ceased and the white light faded back into the cinder cracks, Allieb the demonologist remained frightened and alone, possessing a young boy's body too weak for achieving his purpose.

"*The power of the Lord, Jesus Christ commands you,*" the two holy men shouted, Bibles in hand. There was a sudden howl from the boy. Then he curled up on the ground and began sobbing in the feeble tone of an injured ten-year-old. He twisted his neck, gazed up at them, eyes human, appealing, full of tears.

"Where am I?" he asked, looking down at his fouled naked self.

Thornton kneeled down, facing his son for the very first time. "You are home, my son. You are home."

"It had appeared he was back, the boy Thornton was meant to adopt—the boy who had lost his parents in the war and hid in the tomb."

Rebecca, slack-jawed, asked, "Did he remember anything?"

Danto shook his head. "He'd told us that the last thing he remembered was seeing his parents being killed and thrown onto a heap of bodies—it was as if he'd been in a coma and had woken up a year and a half later. Of course, we discovered later that he was lying . . ."

"Okay . . ." Bev said, frowning, holding the priest's gaze. "What does all this have to do with me?" Bev, riddled with gooseflesh, feared that Danto might reveal that *he* was now possessed with the spirit of Allieb. He tossed the thought from his mind, shuddering at the possibility.

Then thoughts of Julianne's diary filtered back to him: *Allieb was next to me. He whispered, "You will earn success and riches beyond your wildest imagination. Is this what you desire?" I told him, "Yes, for Bev, and for Kristin. I want it for them."*

"This all has to do with my wife. Julianne. What she did years ago. Doesn't it?"

Danto nodded sorrowfully, then held a gentle index finger up. "Soon after Allieb's exorcism, I realized that the soul within the boy's body was still that of the demonologist." The priest's eyes turned toward the rain-spotted window. "You wouldn't have thought it at first. He sounded just like a ten-year-old boy. Acted like one. But there were signs. First, he refused to change his name, leading me to believe that the exorcism had been only partially successful. Yes, the demons had been driven out, but the soul of the demonologist still remained in full control of the boy's body, influencing his thoughts. I could see it in his eyes. I could *feel* it. Eventually, as he aged, it showed in his appearance. His eyes were jet black in hue, possessing this internal radiance that was difficult to pull away from. His skin . . . it stayed as white as bone—he never went out in sunlight. His face had grown oddly angular, the chin pointed, the nose sharp, his brow ridging out over his eyes. He'd shaved his head and grown a jet-black goatee, keeping it neatly trimmed. He looked like a demon, one that had somehow taken on a human perspective—much like the ancient demonologist himself as artistically rendered in the texts discussing his history. The resemblance was remarkable.

"I could see that Allieb was playing a big charade, remaining internally incognito, at least to Thornton, convincing the minister that he was his 'human' son. All this time I'd tried desperately to stay in close contact with Thornton, making hopeless attempts to convince him that the exorcism had not been successful in driving out the soul of the ancient demonologist. But the minister disregarded me, distanced himself—this was Allieb's influence, I knew, who, as far as I could tell, had taken full mental control of his father.

"By the time the boy had reached his early twenties, he'd earned a small fortune through the foretelling of numbers, exploited by both him and his father in gambling venues, Reno, Atlantic City, Vegas; here you could plainly see the power of his influence on the minister: the once-religious man, desperate for an escape from evil, ultimately drawn back in—swayed by prosperity earned through deceptions and lies. With his rapid fortune and powerful charisma came long lines of followers, who'd gathered nightly at his new home, a mansion in the hills he'd coined *In Domo*, which, roughly translated, is Latin for 'at home.' The parties there were rampant, famous for their debauchery, laden with sex and drugs and alcohol: the subsequent rewards of participation in Allieb's black masses."

Sex and drugs and black masses . . . dear God, Julianne.

"The stories flew over what went on up there, and many people strove to be invited to his events, hoping for participation in what were rumored as 'self-indulgent orgies of limitless proportions.'"

Bevant Mathers, your presence is requested for an exclusive gathering . . .

Hey, Dad, maybe you'll get lucky and it'll turn out to be one of those ultrasecretive high-class sex romps. You know, orgy of the stars!

Bev felt in his pocket. Shuddered. The invitation . . . it was still there.

"The house, *In Domo,* is fairly isolated, like most of the homes up in the hills. Everything that went on up there was kept under heavy lock and key. No one ever complained, and no one ever investigated his doings, as far as I could tell; perhaps it had been Allieb's influence over the house itself: a shield of protection armoring it from interlopers. Most important, however, were the people whom he invited inside; once they had a taste of the excesses within, no other way of living seemed possible. Eventually, these 'partygoers' would be coerced into joining his cabal through initiation. They'd move into the house, not permitted to leave after they had engaged in the rites. It was purported that if someone contested Allieb's influence and tried to leave, they would disappear suddenly, or tragically die."

Bev's jaw dropped. "Julianne. The accident."

Danto nodded. "Once the cabal grew to a healthy number, the black masses increased in scope, enacting every cruelty, perversion, and defilement known to man. Most of the cult members had relished in it. There were others, however, who were able to break their trances. They eventually resisted Allieb's rule and attempted to flee *In Domo.* They were quickly taken care of."

Danto continued, "He's been up there in the Hollywood Hills mansion for the last twenty years, growing stronger, wiser, perfecting his black arts and waiting for the ideal time to begin summoning the thirteen demons again."

Bev said, "Julianne had gone up there. To the house. I read about it in her diary."

Danto, eyes filled with compassion, said, "I know. She along with many others over the years. And then she tried to flee."

"And this is why I'm experiencing all these horrible things?" Bev asked.

"Yes."

"How? What's happening to me? Please, tell me."

Danto, looking suddenly glassy-eyed, said, "The time has come to commence. And you, Bev, must lead."

"Lead? Lead what?"

Danto hesitated, then in a voice just above a whisper, said, "Stopping Allieb's Legion of demons."

"Ohhh, you've gotta be kidding me."

"I'm not."

Bev shook his head vigorously, in sudden denial. "No . . . no . . . why should I believe you?"

Rebecca, drawn of color, said appealingly, "Bev . . ."

He shushed her with a raised hand. "Tell me, Father, why should I believe all this?"

"Bev, I understand where you're coming from. The last few days have been very hard on you, and if I were you, I'd have trouble believing everything I've just heard. But . . . you read your wife's diary, about what she did all those years ago. There's no doubting that. And . . . your daughter—"

Bev stood up, instantly red-faced. "What about Kristin?"

"Bev, please, based on what you told me, the literature and research in her room, and the limo that came for her . . . she is in danger. Allieb is very powerful. He knows that Kristin is Julianne's daughter. He knows that you were her husband. There's great power in bloodlines, and he is using it to his advantage."

"Which means what? That I'm possessed by one of the thirteen demons?"

Danto nodded. "As I mentioned, two thousand years ago Allieb utilized the innocence of children as vehicles for the demonic souls, one by one transferring them from the children's bodies into himself through the consumption of their bodies. Once inside of him, he used his demonological proficiencies to corral them for his own personal use, to gain supreme knowledge, strength, and omnipotence. The demon spirits themselves had willingly joined forces within him in a union of great power—Allieb had given them a taste of freedom from exile, and they relished in it, now an army of forces with the demon Belial in the forefront." He paused, then added, "But . . . one demon had protested having his minions overtaken."

"One demon?"

"The Devil himself. Satan."

Bev shook his head. "Father, I—"

"He—Satan—had been responsible for Allieb's demise two thousand years ago, creating a persuasive force in alerting the people of Jerusalem of his massacre of their children, an unlikely move for the Devil. Allieb had proved a worthy adversary of Satan, giving Him a reason to fight using whatever means necessary. Satan had also protested Allieb's attempt twenty years ago—I realized this because I heard it pass through the boy's very lips following the exorcism. Now . . . He appears to be doing it again."

"Satan? Protesting Allieb?"

"Yes. But Allieb is much stronger now, more powerful, more confident. He has been preparing for this confrontation for twenty years—he is now ready to clash with the Prince of Darkness. Bring Him in. Corral Him inside his strengthened body along with the other demons. To create within him the ultimate power, one that not even God himself can defeat."

"This is serious," Rebecca said, mesmerized.

"It is. You see, Allieb is once again using human vehicles to transport the thirteen demons from the underworld into his own body. He began the process a few weeks ago, each person handpicked by Allieb himself to be used as a vehicle. They were given invitations to a party—"

Invitations . . . "Father—" he interrupted, instantly stunned. "I got one . . ." Bev reached into his pocket and pulled out the envelope. He opened it, handed it to Danto.

Danto took it and gazed at the words on the beige parchment. Nodded. "This invitation, along with Allieb's telepathic influence, has already drawn in twelve relatives of past cabal members—members who'd unwittingly sacrificed their lives for another's benefit. In your case, this would be Julianne: At an impressionable and stressful time in her life, she'd been easily persuaded by the young Allieb, promised good fortune for her husband and daughter as long as she heeded his demands. Eventually, she got what she'd hoped for—but, unbeknownst to her, wouldn't be around to see it. Of course, that was all part of Allieb's master plan, to sacrifice the family member of a future vehicle; in time, he would ultimately call upon those on the receiving end of the 'good fortune' to take part in the grandest ritual of all: the summoning of the thirteen demons. You see, the strongest vehicle for demonic transport is one who has lost a family member to demonic sacrifice. Bev, that would be you."

Bev rubbed his face, focused on a cross hanging on the wall. Nausea purled in his gut, and he had to look away.

Danto added, "It's a grand plan. One that has taken years for Allieb to complete. And now the time has come." Danto leaned away and peered out the window again.

Rebecca, white-faced and shivering, asked, "Why did he use invitations?"

"Allieb never leaves *In Domo*. Also, as mentioned, once you become a member of the cabal, there is no leaving the house. Allieb has only one reliable servant, but he wasn't strong enough or influential enough to go out and physically haul all these people in. The man who's been following you is Allieb's only trusted aide: Thornton."

"His adoptive father?" Bev asked.

"Yes. He's the one who gave you this envelope." Danto handed the invitation back to Bev, who stuck it back into his pocket.

"My God . . ." Bev was stunned.

"Bev, listen to me carefully. Twelve of the thirteen vehicles, now wholly possessed by demons, have been brought into *In Domo*. Allieb and Thornton . . . both of them have been struggling for the past couple of days to bring you in—Allieb telepathically, Thornton physically—but have been unsuccessful because . . . because the demon inside you is resisting them."

"Resisting. You mean . . . Satan."

"Yes . . . the ritual cannot be accomplished without

the thirteenth. The first demon, Belial, has already been brought in. Allieb has assumed Belial as his primary personality—as father and son, they are virtually inseparable. The other demons are waiting in their vehicles, elsewhere in the house, for the drawing to commence. But, without Satan's presence, the ritual cannot be wholly completed: If the Devil remains free, outside the Allieb's body, He will ultimately retrieve them."

"Jesus," Bev said, running a hand through his hair. "How is it that you know all of this?"

"Thornton," the priest answered. "He contacted me a few weeks ago. Allieb had used his father for the harvest—after nearly twenty years in isolation, the man had been released from his prison at *In Domo* to locate the thirteen people who would be utilized as vehicles for the demons. Allieb had begun his summoning once they'd all been sighted. Soon thereafter, the invites were sent out. It was a lethal combination: an invite to spur curiosity and temptation, and a form of telepathic communication to instill fear and break down resistance. It's worked with everyone so far . . . except you.

"Additionally, Thornton, once free of his prisoner's shell, in combination with Allieb's preoccupation with the prospective vehicles, had fallen away from the demonologist's trance. It was at this point, almost immediately, that he became conscious of the danger that existed and realized no alternative but to oppose his son's intentions. He contacted me, revealed to me everything in great detail, and we both agreed that the person harboring the soul of Satan would prove to be our only chance to defeat him."

"Me? Harboring Satan? I can't buy it . . . it's absurd." A sharp sudden pain jabbed his neck and back, as though he'd been punched. From the inside.

"Bev, please. I am explaining all this to you so you can understand. You will be brought to *In Domo,* and you will be brought into ritual. Satan is lying in near dormancy within you, contesting only Allieb's influence upon you—"

"C'mon! I'm in a damn church right now. How come Satan isn't freaking out?"

In his mind, an image of a clawed hand reached out from the hole the ghostly fingers had created. It gripped the edges of his skull and pulled . . .

"Bev, the holy water . . ." Rebecca remarked. "The burn on your head?"

He looked at her accusingly, ignoring the looming sensations in his body and mind. "You're buying into this?"

She shrugged her shoulders, eyes watering. "I just—"

Sweat broke on Bev's head. *Hot flash.* "And how is it that both Thornton *and* Allieb want me at the house?" Bev asked. "That doesn't make sense either."

"Allieb wants you so that he can draw the Devil out of you, into him. Thornton wants you for opposing reasons: to keep Satan inside of you so that He may oppose the demonologist. Thornton wants to get to you first so he can prepare you for the battle ahead."

"Prepare me? What the hell does he want to do with me?" A surge of dizziness filled his head. He closed his eyes and rubbed them, trying to fight it off.

"*We* want to give you a chance to live, to save God and mankind by allowing Satan complete use of your body so that he may oppose Allieb here on earth. It sounds crazy—Satan being used to save God—but it's true. You see, if Allieb succeeds in harvesting Satan, then He would exist no more. His powers and abilities would be absorbed by the demonologist for his own personal use here on earth. Allieb, in a sense, would *become* Satan, and would control the Legion of demons inside of him. So, in this situation, Satan would opt for the lesser of two evils, so to speak."

"This is absurd," Bev muttered, shaking his head in denial. A burning sensation rolled in his stomach.

"Look, Bev, it was no accident that we met at the party. About a month ago, Thornton hunted your location down and established as to when you'd be returning home. That was when Thornton alerted me. Knowing that you'd be our only chance of defeating the Legion, I tracked you down through Jake Ritchie, whom I befriended—and don't think that Jake's sudden interest in the church wasn't somehow influenced by his forthcoming demise; he knew *something* was going to happen. Also . . . the sacrifice at the church. This was an attempt by Allieb to try and deter me, but it didn't work."

"The sacrifice . . . is that what happened to Jake, Father? Was he sacrificed?" Bev looked down at his hands, unblemished, free of any scarring. Suddenly, images of pain and murder suffused his mind, of a drunken Jake dying at his hand. He closed his eyes and drew in deep breaths, trying to wash the vision away. It would not go.

"In order for the demon to enter a vehicle's body, a sacrificial ritual must be performed, whether it be an animal or human. Up until Jake's death, there had been twelve sacrifices made by way of Allieb's influence on the person used for harboring the demon. Through the power of dreams, Allieb set each ritual into motion. The person involved would commit the crime unbeknownst of their actions—it would be done while they were asleep."

Bev rubbed his eyes, shuddered. Looked at his hands again. His skin crawled. "My God . . . I killed Jake, didn't I?"

Danto nodded. Rebecca began to cry. Stood. Pressed herself against the wall, wobbling, sobbing uncontrollably. "What's going on?"

"Additional sacrifices will be made before, during, and after the drawing of the demons. This concerns me . . . we don't know where Kristin is."

"Kristin?"

The priest stood abruptly. Looked out the window again. A sudden wash of light ignited the raindrops on the glass. "The car . . . it is here. We all must go now."

"What car?" Bev stood again, despite the persistent dizziness trying to take him down. He shoved the priest aside. Looked out the window. In the rectory lot outside, headlights cut into the rain-filled darkness.

Rebecca, hands over her mouth, eyes suddenly swollen with tears, looked back and forth between Bev and Danto. "What is it, Bev?"

Bev shot Danto an enraged glance, his head and body feeling hot, as though he'd been caught in a blast of steam. "You're in on it! You and that damned Thornton guy. Jesus, you're a priest, for Christ's sake! Whatever happened to appealing to God for a duel with the Devil?"

"Bev, please understand . . . Thornton and I are working together to help you. If you do not work with us, you will be killed, that much is certain. And so will everyone you love, including Kristin."

Downstairs, the front door to the rectory opened. A man's voice called in: "Hello?"

Bev paced back and forth in the small room. Shaking. Frightened. Running his hands through his hair. His senses felt suddenly heightened, as though he possessed antennae clutching at the environment, telling him that he was wholly exposed to the approaching menace, like vulnerable prey. "Jesus, I just don't know what to believe."

"Believe *me*, Bev," Danto implored. "You have the knowledge inside of you now. Use it to fight evil!"

Scratch . . . scratch . . . scratch . . .

Bevant . . . come to me.

Bev grabbed his head. "It's Allieb . . . *he's back!*" he yelled. "God, it *hurts!*"

Bev's legs wobbled. He staggered forward.

Danto grabbed Bev by the arm. "We must go now. Come on."

Something inside Bev tried to push his body away from the grasping Danto. His world spun around him, the drab colors of the room swirling into pallid gray tones. He felt hands clutching his shoulders, leading him out of the room into the musty hallway, body hitting against the wall, his waning balance nearly sending him to the floor. He did his best to stay still, feeling his mind being probed by the ghostly fingers, the voice within calling, *Bevant, come to me. Bring your demon with you.* Bev shook his head hard, a flood of awareness assaulting him, shoving the invading entity away.

A sharp, sudden vision leaped across his mind, that of parting flames and a dark monster rising up from a sea of boiling lava, black-skinned, eyes aglow with emerald flames, serrated horns curling out from a mis-shapened, bulbous head. It reached its sharp-clawed hands out toward Bev, snorted a gush of visible smoke from its widening nostrils, green and sulfuric; a harsh burning odor infiltrated Bev's nose, and then the grunting demon sank back down into the boiling sea.

Hands groping for support, Bev stood in the hallway, breathing heavily, his eyesight returning to the real world. He looked at Father Danto. Standing beside him: Rebecca.

"What's that smell?" she asked, eyebrows arched with distress. "Something's burning."

"It's me," Bev answered, almost automatically.

"You fought him off again, Bev. Allieb."

Bev stiffened. He placed a supporting hand against Danto's shoulder. His heartbeat quickened, skin riddled with gooseflesh as a chill of horrible fear invaded his body. He stood immobile, staring at the floor, stunned with disbelief.

"Bev?"

He looked at Rebecca, her face taut with fear, revulsion, horror. Shook his head. The black beast he'd witnessed rising from the lava of his dreams—it wasn't imaginary. It was *real*, appearing as though he were actually there with it.

In Hell.

"It wasn't me," he whispered, taking a single step forward. "I didn't ward off Allieb. It was Him."

Bev fell forward, his strength suddenly giving out, Rebecca and Danto each supporting him as he collapsed. Despite his immediate loss of motor skills, he could feel his eyes rolling into his head. He could feel his body being dragged across the carpeted hall, thumping down the steps, one at a time, until they reached the bottom.

A strange man's voice: "What's wrong with him?"

Bev's eyes rolled forward, the man before him coming into focus: standing in the foyer, staring at them, eyes filled with suspicion.

A cop.

Thirty-seven

The limo coursed the darkened streets of Torrance, pacing slowly through the torrential downpour. The wipers slashed at the driving rain, the man seated in the back using their incessant beat as a semihypnotic cadence for prayer.

Will God really fight alongside Satan? he'd recently asked the priest.

We can only pray so had been his answer.

He shivered, shifting his position, the black leather upholstery of the limo's seats squeaking hollowly beneath his weight. He peered up at the blue digital readout of the limo's clock, set in the ceiling's dash. 7:34.

He swallowed a dry, uncomfortable lump in his throat. Tried to rub away the pain in his temples. There seemed no hope for solace. The feelings assaulting him were nearly unendurable, and he wondered how he'd made it this long after breaking his hypnotic bond with

Allieb. *Drive. Passion. The will to live.* He felt over-whelmed with guilt and shame, compounded with anger and resentment, even pain. Yet, at the same time, he'd never felt so purposeful, despite the discomforts plaguing him. He had a mission to accomplish: the B-movie hero about to take on a seemingly undefeatable monster threatening the world with its evil. Christ . . . the whole scenario, it seemed so made up, like the imaginative writings of a horror novelist; but . . . this was no creative release—this was *real* life, and he, Reverend James Thornton, was playing the part of the meek little turtle reaching its head out of its shell in attempt to attack the ever-menacing giant.

Despite his limitations, he possessed a great deal of knowledge about his enemy, every tidbit of vital information gathered from the very mouth and actions of the entity he sought to crush. He collected every last detail and shared them with the only man capable of understanding the sheer magnitude of the circumstances. The only other man who would stand beside him in his very own turtle shell, unafraid to expose himself and take his best shot.

Father Thomas Danto.

He peered out the rain-soaked window, wondering how it had all come down to this. He'd wanted to father a child. But it had not been God's will; some things were never meant to be, and his sterility had guaranteed his childless future to be one of them. Still, with much regret, he'd challenged God's preference, seeking his progeny beyond man's natural intentions. The punishment of doing so had been severe: At once his life was glutted with evil—an evil that had thrived in his home like maggots on a corpse.

A deafening clap of thunder shook the car. Lightning

ignited the gloomy night. Above, the streetlamps flickered and went dark. The golden lights within the surrounding homes vanished. A gentle trickle of electricity danced across his skin, the hair on the back of his neck standing on end.

In his mind: faraway laughter. Deep. Caustic. *Eager.*

God help me, he thought. *God help us.*

Then, knowing that righteousness alone would not be enough to defeat the ultimate in evil, he prayed to a different God. *It's okay that I'm doing this,* he attempted to convince himself. *It's just like fighting fire with fire. It's the only way to win.*

He folded his hands in prayer.

And looked down.

Satan, help us.

Thirty-eight

The lights inside the rectory blinked. Somewhere upstairs, a clock alarm started tolling.

The cop, a middle-aged man wearing a mustache and full uniform, kept his eyes pinned on the suspicious trio—they narrowed as his hand covered the gun at his hip.

"He isn't feeling well," Danto exclaimed, eyes nervously probing the room's walls.

Bev, eyesight flitting in and out of focus, did his best to maintain his composure, a task not so easily secured. His legs were painstakingly numb, bordering on powerless, as though nearly devoid of blood; and he had no choice but to crumple into the supporting arms of Rebecca and Danto. Closing his eyes, he drew in long deep breaths, begging his strength to return. A third set of hands seized him beneath the armpits, pulled him over toward a love seat in the foyer. He settled down into the soft cushions, eyes gradually open-ing, taking in the swirling blur of colors that had be-come his world. He thought, *I—I've never lost my vision like this. Never . . .*

Danto had said: *It gets much worse than this.*

He could hear the cop speaking into his radio: "This is Rose. . . . I've got three people here, all of them sus-pects in the Ritchie murder. The Haviland girl, the priest, and the rock star, Mathers. Yep, will do. Out."

"What is it?" Rebecca asked the cop.

"I need you all to take a seat on the couch."

"Are we under arrest?"

"Not yet."

Bev's focus began to return, the swirling colors fad-ing out. He tilted his head upward, toward the cop, de-spite the sudden pain. An intense numbing sensation rained down on his body: pins and needles picking at the tips of his nerves, unearthing them like roots, caus-ing his body to jerk in crazy spasms.

"Shit . . . is he having a seizure?" Rose asked loudly, taking a step forward.

Danto stood up. Faced the cop defiantly, searching his tired mind for an excuse. Arms spread, he said, "I . . . I need to bring him to a friend. He mentioned something about . . . about medication that he needs."

Rebecca was gently rubbing Bev's face, her touch cool upon his hot wet skin. "Bev," she whispered. "Please, take control of your body, please."

My mind . . . the scratching is gone. Yet there's something else in here. No fingers, no voice. It's an en-tire entity. I . . . I can't take control because I am no longer in command of my body. I'm leaving and I'm not coming back . . .

Another claw, reaching out from the hole in my skull . . .

Bev closed his eyes. Felt his conscious mind sinking down into the bowels of his stomach. His body was instantly overcome with vertigo, waxing and waning as though he were on some crazy free-falling ride until his consciousness hit bottom, splashing up in a pool of stinging acids. He lay there breathing heavily, sweating in the intemperate heat, helplessly lost in a strange world that was dark, flat, wet, and vacant. In a few moments, when the dizziness passed, he sat up. His hands sunk wrist-deep in churning acids. He looked around, saw himself bound by deep darkness and squealing echoes, as though he were in some monstrous cavern.

He waited, hearing only the distant echoes of voices leaching in from beyond the walls of the cavern—from outside the constricting confines of his body: Rebecca, calling his name, gently tapping his face; Danto, arguing with the cop, pleading for their release; the cop, a doomed stranger, calling for an ambulance.

Bev felt a sudden sense of dread piercing his recoiling mind. He took a few deep breaths and soon his strength returned, along with the power to carry on.

He struggled to his ethereal feet, looking out into the infinite darkness of his inner body. From far away, he heard a thunderous sound, like an approaching army of horse-driven soldiers. A storm rolled in the distance, menacing black clouds stirring, hauling in with them the flaming lava, flowing rapidly toward him like a crashing tide, covering everything in their hostile wake. The boiling surge hit him hard, crashed over his head, filled his lungs as he fell helplessly back. He felt himself drowning in the sudden depths, arms and legs flailing, barely able to wade through the wide-ranging tide.

Then, as quickly as the tide came, it thinned, and he pulled himself up above its searing surface. The storm seemed to have vanished, the lava now calm and un-flowing. Bev stood waist-deep in the char-blackened muck, coughing up smatterings of the hot flow.

He remained motionless, gasping for air, looking out over the endless panorama of waste and scorching filth. A coagulation of bubbles fired up, and from amid the turmoil emerged the black-scaled horned creature he visioned earlier. Nine feet tall, muscular arms raised high, reaching for the charcoal sky before a massive span of tenebrous wings. The Devil roared in a pitch previously unheard by human ears, a wail of a thousand burning souls firmed into a single, agonizing wail.

With green reptilian eyes, the Devil—Satan—stared at Bev.

It grinned, acid pooling on its broad lips. A thick forked tongue flickered out from between them.

And then it leapt at him.

Thirty-nine

The lights flickered. This time they went out.

Darkness filled the room like a tangible force, Bev's body jerking uncontrollably in response, waist arching, limbs thrashing, the hot stench of burning sulfur seeping from his pores. His teeth clenched, lips whitening from the pressure, dampened screams attempting to sift their way out from behind his compressed mouth.

Deep in his bowels, Satan hurtled toward him, pouncing in a seeming attempt to crush his weakened soul. Bev recoiled, fell back into the lava, the monstrous thing upon him like a chameleon's tongue. Scales flaring. Reptilian claws grasping. Muscles swelling. Lungs blowing out its malevolence in hot stinking currents. The Devil grinned down at him, jowls rife with straight razors jutting bloodily from shredded jaws, green-glowing eyes fixed intently on

Bev. Despite its colossal form, its hideous scowl, the Devil exhibited a visage of childlike amusement, an outward response to its encounter with the soul of the body it now inhabited. But soon, the wicked smile disappeared from its repulsive face and it roared deafeningly, an awesome span of batlike wings expanding from its back, quivering as its body prepared for flight. The wings beat against the sweltering air, producing a fierce gale of wind that knocked Bev back down into the lava. Bev gazed up at the creature as it soared up and away like a rocket toward the upper reaches of his mind.

Bev writhed in agony, Satan thrusting his might upon his physical body. He could feel every painful sensation inflicted upon him as the Devil commenced with the possession: fingers and hands cramping; burning coals peppering his face and chest; reptilian claws cleaving into his brain, wrenching into his organs, twisting, shredding, threatening to disembowel him as his soul wallowed powerlessly along.

Despite the disconnection with his body, Bev could feel his eyelids opening, but was unable to see anything around him. He could feel his muscles expanding, the blood rushing through them. He could feel the burning agony of his skin stretching. Still, he had no control of his body. The Devil had assumed full command, his body no longer weak and feeble, but now outrageously strong. He doubled over as his stomach swelled, the skin splitting across his abdomen, blood trickling out in rivulets. Bev could feel the Devil filling every vessel in his body, assuming every muscle and tendon.

He could feel the beast heave his body to a standing position. Reach his arms forward. Grab the stunned cop by the throat. He could feel his right arm swinging, a powerful fist connecting with the cop's face, removing his jaw in a horrifying shower of teeth and blood. He could hear Rebecca and Danto screaming in the darkness, Rebecca trying to flee the scene as the cop lay dying before her, Danto unsure of his actions, following Rebecca, yet wanting to stay . . . wanting to communicate with the Devil occupying Bev's body.

All of a sudden, Satan reappeared before Bev, breathing heavily, ribbons of fire and slime dousing his scale-covered body. He grinned, then raised his awesome arms and sank back down into the lava, providing Bev with an opening to rise back up into his mind, to retrieve the body that was once his.

In an instant, Bev found himself looking back out through his unfocused eyes. He could see only darkness and the slight form of the cop who lay jawless and bleeding on the carpet. He fell to his knees, crying from the physical and mental pain that had besieged his mind and body like a swarm of rats finding their sudden release from behind a rotting wall. His body felt illogically heavy and stagnant, as if he'd just been birthed into a treacherous world, one incongruent to the place he'd spent his entire physical life.

In the not-too-far distance, he heard Rebecca sobbing.

Close by, Danto's voice: "Bev?"

Having no strength to speak, Bev nodded, seeing only shifting shadows in the gloom.

"It was Him. Wasn't it? Satan."

Bev nodded again.

"We must go," the priest said, grabbing Bev gently by the arm.

This time, Bev didn't have the strength to nod. He fell down onto the sofa and curled his body inwardly, where he remained trembling uncontrollably.

Forty

The limo pulled into the church parking lot. Stopped. Thornton slid across the seat and got out, palms wet with nervousness.

Tapping on the driver's-side window, he instructed the chauffeur to unlock the trunk, then hurried around to the back of the car, raindrops pattering all about him like tiny footsteps. Inside, he retrieved a yellow halogen flashlight and a dozen plastic ties, which he shoved into his pocket. Gripping the flashlight in his right hand, he paced across the empty parking lot, his long shadow thrown forward by the rain-filled splay of the limo's headlights. He eyed the church despondently, its steeple aiming darkly toward the heavens, occluded from the billowing storm.

He circled around the side of the church, making his way across the small lot leading to the rectory.

There was a police cruiser parked outside.

He looked toward the six oak doors lining the two-story brick building. One door was wide open. On the curb, fifteen feet from the open door, stood a woman. She was soaking wet, crying into her hands. He paced quickly toward her, determined footsteps splashing water.

"Where's Father Danto?" he yelled, grabbing her shoulder roughly. She startled, wrenching away from his sudden grasp. Sobbing, unable or unwilling to speak, she backed away, pointing feebly toward the open door. Thornton tossed her a look of expressionless curiosity, then hurried up the walkway, following the flashlight's sprawling beam into the rectory.

Within its pallid glare, Thornton made out three figures in the lightless room, two of them moving, one lying motionless on the carpeted floor. The beam wavered from his shaking hand, eventually finding Thomas Danto. The priest was positioned before another figure curled fetally against the sofa's armrest. The prone man was jerking peculiarly. Danto peered up at Thornton through the tops of his eyes, then at the floor, then back at Thornton. "Don't look," he uttered nervously, but Thornton aimed the flashlight down anyway, glimpsing a uniformed police officer, the lower portion of his face gone, a dark glistening puddle spreading three feet out from his injury.

"My God . . . what happened here?" he asked uneasily, his rational mind answering him truthfully: *Bev Mathers is wholly possessed by Satan.*

Without answering, Danto instructed, "Help me get Mathers out of here."

Thornton stepped around the dead cop and assisted in pulling Bev up, each man shouldering his deadweight. "There's a limo out by the church."

They staggered forward, hauling Bev across the foyer and outside into the pouring rain. Despite Bev's loss of consciousness, he continued to spasm and flail, making it difficult for Danto and Thornton to maintain a firm hold on him. His skin was boiling hot to the touch; his eyes, partially open and glassed over; his long hair, matted against his face and neck. They carried him down the walkway, knees buckling, Bev's feet dragging between them. The girl was still outside, although farther away, now twenty steps into the parking lot and backpedaling.

"Rebecca!" Danto yelled. "Go tell the limo to come here."

She remained still, weeping, head shaking, palms flat against her cheeks.

"Move!" Danto yelled, and she wailed and staggered away, rain and wind beating against her.

The men waited at the curb, alongside the police car, each struggling to keep Bev standing. A series of groans issued from his blue lips. Gooseflesh riddled his soaked skin. In the distance, the two men saw Rebecca feebly waving the limo over, which at once appeared around the corner of the church, bypassing her, rainwater parting beneath its tires. She kept her position at this distance, head shaking, clearly unsure as to her next move. The car stopped before them, engine humming impatiently, steam tendriling from the hood.

Using one hand, Thornton yanked open the rear door. Using every last bit of strength, he and Danto heaved Bev's body into the back seat. Once inside, Thornton clambered over him and pulled his twitching legs across the seat so that his entire body was completely inside the car. Danto climbed in and strapped Bev into a seatbelt, while Thornton fettered Bev's wrists and ankles with the plastic ties.

"We need to get the girl," Danto said. "She has to come with us."

"Who is she?"

"Mathers's girlfriend. Rebecca Haviland."

"She knows?"

Danto nodded.

Using an intercom built into the car's rear dash, Thornton instructed the driver to "get the girl." Without delay, the car swung around—Bev's body bobbled, his upper half tilting over the shoulder strap, leaving behind a wet smear on the black leather—and halted before a rain-soaked Rebecca. Danto pushed open the door. "Get in."

She hesitated, shaking her head.

"C'mon!" he yelled.

She looked around, apparently seeing no alternative, then obediently climbed in and slid toward the front of the long seat, away from the two men and Bev.

Thornton opened up a small compartment in the bare wet bar and removed a hand towel. He tossed it to her. "Here . . . dry your face."

Sobbing, she grabbed the towel and hid her face in it, rubbing her eyes vigorously, pressing her body against the partition dividing the car's interior.

The limo sped away from the church, back onto the roads leading toward Hollywood Hills. They rode in pensive silence, all eyes precariously glued on Bev's form. His belly rose up and down like a balloon, generating murmuring growls as he breathed. His skin had paled into a colorless hue, features twitching madly. He made involuntary jerking movements that startled all those in attendance.

Rebecca eventually asked, "Where are we going?"

Her question was answered with blank stares.

"And what's going to happen to me?" She closed her eyes and massaged her forehead, the look on her face one of unguarded abandonment. She drew in a lengthy, quavering breath, then was calm, eyes bouncing back and forth between Danto and Thornton.

Danto answered, "We're going to need your help."

"With what?"

A moment of silence passed between them. Then Thornton answered, "We don't know. Yet."

Bev waded through the lava, its searing flow determined in guiding him forward. The depth of the lava had dropped from his chest to his ankles, the shoreline now only feet away. Eventually, he reached the coast, burnt black sand sifting through his char-blackened toes. The Jake-demon's body lay only a few feet away, washed up on the beach in a drift, its scales and feathers circling it like a foul moat, flesh partially decomposed, maggots the size of slugs twisting within the fleshy circles of decay. In each skeletal hand was a pig's hoof, black and swollen and covered in fresh blood. The only unscathed ingredient on the Jake-demon was its face, eyes peering up at Bev, rolling madly in their sockets. "I fucked her, Bev, that little piece-of-ass daughter of yours. You oughta try her, my man. She's as tight as a trap." Incensed, Bev lunged forward and slammed his foot down on the Jake-demon's head. It burst like a piece of soft fruit, eyes gushing vitreous fluid, brain matter spurting from the crushed skull, pooling on the sand. He pulled his foot away. The flattened mass of flesh and bone wriggled and writhed. Ambling out of the eye sockets came two large beetles, followed immediately by a dozen more. And then a dozen more upon those. They scattered in all directions like dropped marbles, shining blackly, legs flicking and kicking as they amassed in ranks, a few running up his smoking legs, others fleeing into the fiery surf, instantly perishing upon contact, thin trails of pungent smoke rising into the putrid air.

He turned away from the dead Jake-demon, running against the tide. Farther along the beach he saw more bodies. He raced over to them. Kristin, Rebecca, Julianne. They were all here. Dead and rotting, their cadavers dismembered and twisted to outline a pentagram in the sand, arms and legs and torsos forming the star, their entrails circumventing it, shaping the perimeter.

"Bev."

He darted around. Danto and Thornton were here, both dressed in black hooded robes, holding large rusted crosses. Beetles raced across their faces; they didn't seem to notice.

"The time has come, Bev," Danto said, a beetle emerging from his mouth. "The Legion is sound, but so are you. Satan is your stronghold. The only thing that can destroy evil is evil itself."

A deafening roar filled the air, the world around them shaking. The lava receded, whirlpooling like water down a drain, the black sands churning beneath them as a monstrous entity emerged, a hideous creature with dark flaring scales and glowing black eyes spotlighting the writhing braids of hair atop its head. Bev stared at the great black beast whose long yellow claws reached forward, dripping venom that sputtered as it hit the ground.

It grinned a mouthful of sharklike teeth, a bulking wart-ridden tongue lapping across them. "Legion," it growled. From within its chest a face suddenly formed, a man who'd taken on the appearance of a snake, the face elongated, eyes like diamonds, the snout two holes in a single drop of cartilage. The face, breaking through the membranous skin, gazed at Bev, a black, forked tongue flicking in and out, tasting the air.

"The demons are joining us," the black beast pronounced, petting the looming face in its chest. It sank back down into the blistering lava, releasing a vile howl that echoed throughout all of Hell . . .

Bev awoke, his body lying prone to those who held him captive. Two silhouettes appeared in his blurred sights, nodding, talking to him. The words were muffled, unintelligible. A third figure emerged, shouting, crying, the barely audible voice higher in tone. Imploring. He tried to move a hand toward the voice, but could not. He felt a hand grasp his. Squeeze. It felt reassuring. Comforting.

He tried to move. Other hands pressed down on his shoulders. Grabbed his wrists. Forceful, yet reassuring. He followed their lead and kept still.

Then closed his eyes and fell back into darkness.

Forty-one

Slowly, the limo made its way into Hollywood Hills, shouldering each turn carefully behind the muted span of its headlights. Thankfully, the driver had been prudent in his technique—the storm had increased in intensity. Rain fell in relentless layers, sheet lightning igniting the environment every ten seconds, booming thunder riding its heated coattails.

Despite his swooned state, Bev had put on an alarming show of unrestrained movement for Danto, Thornton, and Rebecca, who herself had spent a good deal of time trembling and moaning. She'd complained of feeling "sick as hell," and had subsequently thrown up in the towel Thornton had given her. The car took on a sickening stench from Rebecca's vomit and Bev's perspiring stink of sulfur, forcing Danto to open the windows despite the slashing rain fighting its way in. He felt a pitter of sickness in his stomach but was able to hold it down.

Danto looked over at Thornton, who himself, despite his experiences at *In Domo,* looked gray and greasy and about to heave. Danto was about to tell Thornton that he didn't look well when Bev started bellowing like an injured dog.

Bev's eyelids darted open, revealing only bloodshot whites, webs of yellow pus oozing out from beneath the upper lids. He snarled, baring his teeth, tongue flickering in and out of his cracked and bleeding lips. He fought hard against his restraints, neck bulging, muscles and veins swelling like balloons.

"Jesus Christ!" Rebecca yelled, pressing herself against the partition. *"What's wrong with him?"*

Danto shot a frustrated look at her. "Didn't you hear a damn word I was saying earlier?"

"Is it . . . *Satan?*" she asked, cowering.

"It is Bev's soul fighting the Devil's presence, and the Devil is winning the battle."

She sobbed uncontrollably, covering her face, peeking through her trembling fingers. She pulled her knees up to her chest and hugged them despondently, staring at Bev.

Danto looked out the window, feeling desperate and weak. Rain and blackness met his nervous gaze . . . except for the large house on the corner whose pale red lights cut through the stormy night like beacons. The limo turned up the hill and stopped, facing the imposing dwelling built of bricks and arches and spires. Iron gates and eight-foot hedges met the idling car like sentinels.

The driver reached out, fingered a keypad set in a stone column. The gates opened.

Bev bucked and thrashed and hissed maniacally. He pulled against his restraints, the attached seat belts allowing only a few inches of slack. The lights inside the car flickered, brightened, then went out. A tiny trail of smoke surfaced from the overhead lamp. Bev's eyes rolled forward, green and radiant in the darkened interior, pinning them with an almost playful attitude, the corners of his mouth turned slightly upward. Then his body stopped fighting, and suddenly, he was still: composed, alert.

The car lurched through the gates. Wet gravel crunched under the tires. Danto heard Thornton say, "Oh my God," and quickly shifted across the seat to where the minister was peering out the rain-spotted window. He lowered it, rain immediately pelting both their faces.

Alongside the driveway on the grass lay a man's body. He'd been eviscerated, bowels strewn about his twisted body like streamers, white and slick from the drenching rain. His jacket and trousers were shredded and bunched up around his neck and ankles, exposing his gutted midsection. His head was bowed toward them, the face untouched by his attacker. As the limo went by, Danto said, "I know this man. He's a detective. He came to the rectory this afternoon." He quickly closed his eyes and embarked on a hushed prayer, while Thornton fell back despondently against the seat.

"It is just the beginning of the sights we are about to see," Thornton pronounced solemnly.

The car circled around the fountain to the forefront of *In Domo* and stopped. The driver emerged and raced lithely up the front steps, keeping his hooded gaze away from them. Danto, Thornton, and Rebecca watched as he opened the twin doors and disappeared inside. They glanced hesitantly at one another, then over at Bev.

Tense and waiting, the rock star stared back at them, hair a tangled mess, lupine eyes aglow in the crimson gleam of light from the house. Emotionlessly, he shifted his gaze out the window and began humming a slow, tuneful chant in Latin: *"Magnus es, domine, et laudabilis valde."* His voice took on an eerily melodious and merry tone, contrasting the harsh, baleful gaze; the mucus seeping from his nostrils; the string of blood and saliva wavering from his lips. His head rocked tenderly back and forth, then, as the song ended, slumped down lifelessly, eyes rolling upward into the sockets. His lids shuttered.

Danto saw Rebecca inching forward on the seat. "Whose voice was that?" she asked, her voice weak, troubled.

Thornton lowered his head and replied, "Satan's."

The lava receded far into the distance, clouds of ash rolling in from the bloodred skies of his bowels. Soon thereafter, black rain fell upon Bev, cutting burning holes in his skin like needle shots of acid. The bodies of those he loved had mysteriously vanished from the shore, now replaced by two massive iron ovens filled with bone and ash. Cauldrons the size of small cars surrounded the ovens, spilling over with the melted flesh of those boiling inside their rusted bulks. The piles of ash in the ovens shifted and dropped down onto the beach. Beetles emerged from within, showing the way for additional horrors: bloody arms, severed at the elbows, clambering out of the ovens, doused in gray ash, led by clutching hands whose fingers raked madly at the sand. Like crabs they circled the ovens and cauldrons, strings of tattered flesh and blood straggling at the detached ends like shreds of seaweed. They massed together, emulating hungry rats in a sewage duct, gray-coated and throbbing, rabidly falling over one another. Soon they stopped rising from the ovens. The hand-led arms immobilized. They stood on end, palms turned up, facing Bev, then began to sway hypnotically, giving him the impression that they were sizing him down. He stared back at them, dumbfounded. Without warning, the arms fell back down and came at him, fingers darting furiously across the sand with purposeful intent. He turned to move but could not so much as budge—in what first appeared to be paralysis, he gazed down to find two sets of hands securing his ankles, locking him in place. More hands immediately reached him, clawing angrily at his legs, rending his skin away in soft, gouged lumps, his seared flesh tightly wedged beneath the hardened yellow nails. His knees buckled and he fell, parting the black sand. Like rats on a carcass, the arms climbed all over him. He clawed at them, feeling every distinct scratch of pain.

Forty-two

"We'll bring him directly to my room," Thornton said.

"Where is Allieb now?" Danto asked, wiping the rain from his eyes. He peered into the car at Bev, who was in a trance, head bobbing, legs jerking, lips quivering and spotted with thick white spittle. Long red welts had appeared on his arms, neck, and face.

Thornton gazed up at the house. Rain slashed at his face. "He knows we're here with the thirteenth, and is probably making his way down to the cathedral. The congregation is there now, I can hear them praying." He paused, then added, "I have to go soon."

Danto, unable to detect anything but the pattering rain, asked, "And what of the other demons?"

"In the basement."

"Are we to bring Mathers there?"

Thornton shook his head. "That's what Allieb wants . . . we must keep him separated from the rest of the demons. Satan will emerge in full power at a time when Allieb's weaknesses can be exploited."

"When is that?"

"During the drawing of the twelve demons; we must wait until the demons have been wholly absorbed by Allieb. At that point, Satan can retrieve his army all at once."

Thornton crawled back into the car and retrieved a small knife from the bar. Danto held Bev's arms as he cut the plastic ties securing his ankles.

The two men pulled Bev out of the limo, clutching his slumping body beneath his bound arms. Rebecca exited the car and seized him from behind, fingers curled tightly through the belt loops in his jeans. Together they lugged him up the cement steps through the twin doors leading into *In Domo,* nearly falling down in the vestibule.

Before them was a second set of open doors that gave way to a large sitting room. The room was barren save for a threadbare Oriental rug. Danto felt a blunt tingle wash over his body, as though a gentle electric shock had passed through him. In this moment, a strong gust of wind blew in and grabbed the doors, closing out the storm with an eerie slam against the frame. Once the doors were shut, silence captured the moment, allowing Danto to hear the distant chanting filtering in through the colorless walls.

Carrying Bev, they staggered clumsily into the sitting room and gently let him down onto the rug. There he remained, unconscious, squirming in his bonds like a worm out of earth.

Danto took a few long deep breaths, then eyed the barren interior. An aching pain tightened his shoulders, back, and neck. In addition to a sudden headache, he thought he might be bleeding, but realized the warm wetness was rainwater dripping down his back. Using a sleeve to wipe his brow, he paced a few feet away from Bev, shoes squeaking wetly against the wood floor, listening . . . listening to the droning prayers, the voices, men and women alike, lost and pleading for either death or salvation. There was an odor in the air, like incense at mass, only more pungent. It lived here in the walls of this evil house, he realized, as though the framework had been constructed of timber from a building whose plaster walls had burned away in some terrible blaze. He circled the room, looking at the shuttered doors and lone staircase that disappeared up into the darkness, contemplating the task at hand—the extraordinary spectacle about to be witnessed—and wondered if he'd ever perform another mass, ever relish in another offering of body and blood, ever carry out his duty in the confessional again.

He stopped walking and closed his eyes, rubbed them, feeling a suddenly unexplainable desire wash over him—a *wanton* hunger: Suddenly, as if under the influence of some strange exotic drug, he wanted to taste the lips of a woman, to hold a feminine body, caress it, plant his gathering seed into it—a conduct he'd been devoutly able to ward off since his early twenties. And with these thoughts came further lustful yearnings he never knew to exist: the desire to copulate with multiple partners, men and women and children alike; the want to pleasure himself through masturbation. *Jesus!* He instantly hated himself for these hideous emotions, the vow of celibacy he'd taken all those years ago now murdered by these dreadfully impulsive urges. He gritted his teeth, shook his head, muttered, "No, no, no . . ." Tears burdened with grief and anger and fear sprouted from his eyes. He fell to one knee, fist slamming his thigh in frustration.

Thornton stepped over and knelt beside him. He placed a gentle hand on his arm. "Thomas, listen to me carefully. This place you are in, it is *pure evil*. It tempts its visitors with shameless desires and does not yield until you surrender your soul to them. Listen to me— do not give in to these baseless enticements. You *must* ignore them. If you don't, they will grow dominant inside of you." He grabbed the priest on the shoulders, shaking him slightly. "Thomas . . . I beg of you, be strong. Listen to your inner faith. Allow it to guide you. And by this, I do not mean your faith in God but the faith you have in yourself to rise above the temptation. If you do this, the evil attacking you will not flourish."

Danto looked at Thornton, at his worn features, the tired lines creasing his tensed-up brow. He had no choice but to trust the man, despite his sudden, inexplicable reservations. He knew that if he were to be left here unaccompanied in this portal to Hell, he would perish under the crushing hand of evil.

Thornton would guide him, not unlike the way he himself had guided the minister all those years ago with the young Allieb.

He swallowed past the dry lump in his throat, focusing his sights on Thornton, and then on the twitching figure on the floor that was Bev Mathers—now possessed by Satan. The image alarmed him, and he thought suddenly, *What has become of me?* completely mindful of the horrible truth: that he, Father Thomas Danto, had been wholly convinced to use the Devil to combat evil. *Fight fire with fire.* A wave of panic struck him like a lightning bolt. Christ, no! It made no sense! It went against his every sworn conviction. Still, unfathomably, he felt no alternative but to take this course of action—a course of action that would force him to participate in a clandestine ceremony of demonic ritual and worship. He rubbed his face with his palms, trying desperately to extinguish the utter insanity from his mind.

A moment of alarming silence passed. He pulled his hands away from his face and looked at Thornton. He felt instantly sick. Nausea purled in his gut. His mind reeled in spastic circles of confusion. Utter disgust washed over him, forcing him to shake his head and backpedal away from Thornton.

"Thomas? What's wrong?"

The tears continued pouring from his eyes, distrustful words firing from his mouth like shotgun blasts. "You're evil . . . all *evil*. Ah . . . I cannot believe I allowed you to convince me of this. I must rely on my strength in God! In *God!*" The words came from his lips uncontrolled, adrenalized, and he couldn't determine whether they were a result of reason or of mutiny—his mind seemed incapable of making such a rational decision.

"No, Thomas, no . . . listen to me, please." Thornton's voice was surprisingly calm and consoling, full of sense and wisdom despite the matter's urgency. "The evil thriving here is lying to you, it's trying to confuse you; psychological attack is its most powerful weapon. I should know, I was under its command for nearly twenty years." Danto peered up at him, the minister's words working their way into his head. "Please, listen to me—as difficult as it may seem, I know what is happening to you. You must be strong. Pay no attention to what your mind is trying to tell you."

Danto kept still. He closed his eyes, searching for

serenity as Thornton continued his speech, his voice gentle and reassuring, and at the same time authoritative. It triggered in him something wholly enthralling, as though he'd suddenly rediscovered himself and his passion. *This is what it might feel like to be born again.* He pushed away his pain and listened, the minister's words flowing seamlessly into his hexed mind like a stream of water into a funnel. Suddenly, the evil thoughts were gone, now camouflaged by metaphoric images of paradise: sunsets, songbirds, blue skies, the gentle crashing of ocean waves, palm trees swaying in a cool wind. His legs began to tremble. His sights, now open to the dim world, beheld traces of light at the end of the long, dark road ahead. Thornton and Rebecca stood before him, peering curiously into his face. Behind them, Bev Mathers lay motionless on the floor.

"My God . . ."

"Are you okay, Father?" Rebecca asked.

A strange vagueness beset him. "Jesus, what just happened to me?"

"You fought off evil, my friend."

He nodded methodically, as though aware of his feat.

"And, I regret to say, you'll be doing a lot more of it very soon."

Danto shivered, silently contemplating Thornton's warning, then pointed toward Bev. "Is he okay?"

"No," Thornton said. "He needs our help."

Danto blew out a long, nervous gush of air. He walked past Thornton and Rebecca. Kneeled next to Bev. "What's next?"

"We bring him to my room."

The sands vanished, as did the ovens, and the cauldrons, and the attacking arms. In its place settled the yielding walls of his stomach, encompassing him like a massive organic capsule. Straight above, the black hole of his esophagus wound into the dark heavens like a tornado's funnel, the dense toll of his heartbeat impregnating the nightmarish surroundings. Winds blew, carrying with it the tortured screams of those burning in the tide. Fires shot up like reptile claws, pulling the tortured souls back down into the unendurable agony of the lava. Bev stood, turned around, and beheld a ghastly sight: a multitude of torture devices bursting up from the blistering landscape of flesh like morays from their lairs; an iron maiden, a rack, a bath of boiling excrement, glistening with gastric acids. Within each of the devices, Rebecca, Kristin, and Julianne met their fates. The mechanisms functioned on their own accord, planting the souls of his loved ones into the soils of pure agony: the nails of the swinging maiden perforating Rebecca's nude form, blood geysering from her fresh injuries, her face punctured into indescribable muck; the rack, tearing Kristin into two wriggling portions, her midsection slopping its innards out in steaming masses; the cauldron's contents alive with the bones of its past beneficiaries, consuming Julianne as she attempted to claw her way out from its blazing contents. Bev screamed, but the howling wind absorbed his voice. He reached for them but could not move—the walls of his stomach oozed up and swallowed his feet.

"Bev, you little turd," came a deep voice behind him. Bev turned. The Jake-demon was there, perched ten feet away atop some huge, glistening organ. It had massive wings now, folded flat and quivering against its feathered body. The blustery wind whipped at its feathers, dozens coming loose, flying wildly about it *like a storm of flies. It stood staring at Bev for a drawn-out period of time, its face transforming into some kind of man/bird hybrid, lips extending out into a black beak, a high ridge reaching out above the brow, the top of the head elongating to a rounded point. It opened its beak impossibly wide. A swarm of black beetles spilled out over the straight razors lining its jaw and raced across its body, in and out of the gaping pockets of decay lining its midsection, and off into the vile landscape. It removed a clawed fist from beneath its right wing, waved it in the air, then swiped it across the glistening purple surface of its fleshly throne. The pain struck Bev as though a knife had been plunged into his liver. He collapsed to the floor, writhing in agony.*

The Jake-demon held up a rendered slab of the bleeding organ in its fist. "I should char your face and prick and slit and gouge every morsel of your being."

"You . . . need . . . me," Bev stammered through the pain, realizing the demon before him to be the Devil in disguise.

The Jake-demon laughed. "I don't need you, pissant. I need your lowly human form. You are nothing but a speck of shit on a sow's ass." The Jake-demon laughed. "Ah, but it appears that mankind needs a worthy opponent to battle my army of beasts. Hmmm, a nice little symbiosis of sorts. Like the bird that pecks the bugs off the bull's back. Everyone wins." The Jake-demon howled like a wolf, eyes glowing greenly, then took a bite out of the scrap of organ in its claw. Bev doubled over in agony. Instantly, the Jake-demon disappeared in a sudden explosion of white fire, the flames' spires grabbing Bev like hands and hurling him across the acidic ground. He closed his eyes, feeling the acids of his stomach splattering against his face. He tried to shift his weight, but his body throbbed shrilly, ribs aching screamingly, the searing heat squaring up the whole agonizing effect to unquantifiable proportions.

There he lay, waiting for Satan's blow to silence him forever.

But the beetles hit him first, hundreds of tiny feet scattering all over his body.

He screamed and screamed until he fell away into darkness.

Forty-three

The three of them lugged Bev through the badly lit halls, his body feverishly hot, as though he'd been sitting too close to a fire. Jewels of sweat burst across his skin. His eyelids were once again wide open, revealing trembling irises and blood-saturated whites. His mouth hung open like a drawer, pools of saliva pouring out. "It's burning, it's burning me," he moaned, his body twisting in their grasp.

"Hold tight," Thornton said. "We're almost there."

As Thornton had speculated, they passed no one in the halls, thankfully, and in a few minutes were in his room.

They carried Bev to the bed and placed him down. He wriggled and twitched, skin flushed red and hot. His head arched back, exposing an Adam's apple that undulated like a pogo stick beneath his skin. Dark red welts had formed where the plastic ties chafed against his skin. His eyes were shut again.

Pulling his gaze away from Bev, Danto scanned the distressing space: the moldering rug; the stained mattress sitting crookedly atop the rusted frame; the mildew-coated tiles in the decrepit bathroom. A rancid stench rode the air.

Here the distant chanting in the walls was louder, their close proximity to the cathedral now evident. Thornton closed the door, then gazed forlornly at Danto and Rebecca, his dark face drawn in impending panic. He rubbed the stubble on his chin. In this moment of inactivity, Rebecca staggered away into the bathroom and vomited again, the choking sounds befitting the miserable surroundings. Danto felt bloated and tender, but fought back his urge to join her.

"What now?" Danto asked, feeling strangely inept despite his knowledge of the situation. *Must be the house,* he thought. *It's distracting me.* Rebecca emerged from the bathroom, pale-faced and haggard. She positioned herself on a chair in the corner of the room and buried her face into her hands.

"We need to distance ourselves from Mathers," Thornton replied, knotting his fingers together nervously. He walked to the nightstand, removed a bottle of whiskey from the space below, and single-handedly manipulated the top off. He took a drink, then offered the bottle to Danto. The priest refused. "Satan could emerge at any time to take on the Legion. We must not be in his presence when this occurs. As long as he is here, away from the other demons, we have a fighting chance." Thornton rifled through a pile of clothing on the floor and located three black knit robes. He handed one to Danto and one to Rebecca. "Put these on."

Rebecca stood up shakily, holding the robe, sobbing.

"Get ahold of yourself!" Danto yelled nervously. She began to cry louder, uncontrollably, like a scolded child. The priest quickly donned his robe over his clothing, then grabbed the robe from her and held it up for her to slip into. She hesitated, doubtful eyes darting back and forth between the two men. Thornton approached her and grasped her hands roughly. "If you want to live, do what we say."

She shook her head pleadingly. "Please, I just want to leave here. I don't belong here." Her voice was weak and puny, like a child's.

Thornton stepped aside, hand waving toward the door. "Be my guest. If you make it out the front door, you *will* end up like that man we saw on the front lawn. I can promise you that."

She peered down, looking sick and terrified, as though she'd just witnessed her own murder and had lived to tell about it. "I . . . I *can't do this*." Tears of frustration exploded from her eyes. She twisted her neck back and forth in a slow and methodical fashion, as if trying to work out some kinks, then looked back at Danto. He nodded reassuringly, feeling like a liar. She pulled back her gaze and released her hands from Thornton's grasp, then shiftlessly shrugged into the robe, sobbing the entire time.

"Satan is listening," Thornton said, peering at Bev's twitching form. "He will emerge at a time that is most advantageous to him."

"What of Allieb?" Danto asked.

"The demonologist is wholly consumed with the drawing. Belial is guiding him, and will ensure success in possessing the remaining demons. Both Allieb and Belial are confident that Satan will show little resistance and follow his army."

Thornton paced to the nightstand and opened the drawer. He retrieved a vial of holy water and a large hook key, both of which he pocketed, and then the crucifix that had recently turned from silver to rust. He held it tightly in his fingers, kissed it, then asked Father Danto to bless it. The priest took hold of the small rusted charm, pressed it against his chest, and recited a silent prayer. Afterward, he kissed the rough metal and handed it back to Thornton.

Holding the cross out like an offering, Thornton sat on the edge of the bed, alongside Bev. "This cross has protected me for twenty years. May it shed its miracle upon you, my brave brother." He kissed the cross one last time and lodged it into Bev's back pocket.

At once Bev's body began to tremble. An icy breeze swept the room, causing gooseflesh to ripple across his exposed skin. A pleasant aroma rose up, that of perfume; it was coming from Bev.

"It's all your fault I'm dead."

A woman's voice, surfacing from Bev's throat. Soft-spoken. Gentle.

"You had to adopt the boy, didn't you?"

Thornton's mouth fell open. "My . . . God . . ."

It was the voice of his wife, twenty years dead at the hand of the young Allieb!

Bev's head rolled toward the minister, eyes open and filled with sadness, the face contorting into something nearly feminine. "You promised you would take care of me, protect me. But you didn't. You let the boy kill me. And now I'm in here, in Hell, with the rest of them."

Thornton buried his face in his hands. "No, no . . ."

"I'm fellating a wolf, and it tastes wonderful. Would you like to try it?" Tendrils of green mist seeped from Bev's mouth.

"No!" he screamed, lurching away.

Danto came to his side. "Heed your own advice, James. Clear your mind of the evil."

Thornton nodded. Shaken. He wiped his tears with his hand, then turned and looked back at Bev, who was again unconscious, rocking gently from side to side.

Rebecca's cries had stopped altogether. She emerged from the corner of the room, out of the shadows, mumbling something unintelligible. Her eyes were lost behind a glossy haze. Danto, concerned more with her abrupt silence than with her breakdown, paced over to her. Gently, he grabbed the knit hood of her robe and pulled it up over her head.

"Come . . . we must go now."

She looked at Danto and nodded, suddenly composed.

He shuddered. Something . . . there in her eyes, behind the glossy haze; an intelligence, deep in the blue that he hadn't noticed before. It unnerved him.

"I will lead you both to the cathedral," Thornton said. "Then I must leave you both for a time. Do nothing and say nothing, and you will not be noticed. Understand?"

Danto and Rebecca nodded in unison. Thornton opened the door and slipped free of the room, Rebecca following close behind.

Gripping the doorknob, Danto turned and looked at Bev one last time. The sole light in the room brightened, flickered once, then went out, bringing the room into darkness.

From amid the gloom, Satan's green eyes stared back at him.

He closed the door.

Bev opened his eyes. The acids burst like mammoth blisters against his skin. The pain was excruciating, and he grunted insufferably, his voice torn to shreds from the harsh vapors assaulting his throat. He pressed his hands into the organic floor and leaned up. Looked around. Saw nothing but the dark bloody vista of his bowels; an infinite landscape of colon, kidneys, liver, and pancreas: all of his organs glistening like mountains in the distance, still functioning properly despite the supernatural stress placed upon them. He could hear the intemperate winds of his lungs howling down from the blackened heavens, carrying to him the agonized voices of the damned moaning from their eternal tortures. He looked around at his immediate surroundings, everything blurring into dull blotches of gray and pink. For the first time since coming to Hell, he was alone. He fell to his knees, then lay back down in the acids. There were no more games to be played. Satan had finally assumed absolute control of his mind and body. He breathed in the thick, putrid air, and prepared himself for the agony about to be thrust upon him in the war of the demons.

Forty-four

Danto, Thornton, and Rebecca trod wearily through the empty halls of *In Domo,* their footsteps heavy, echoing hollowly. The chanting grew louder with every footstep forward. Danto could feel the pulsing rhythm of it in the floor.

"There has been a recent surge in the population here at *In Domo.*" A haunted expression came into Thornton's eyes. "I can only assume that Allieb needs these bodies as sacrifants for the demons, and as well, to act as his witnesses to the drawing. There's strength in numbers, and the congregation he's assembled will act faithfully to his needs." The trio turned a sharp corner and continued down a doorless hallway lit dimly by a queue of exposed lightbulbs. "You are going to see some terrible things; the most important thing is that you do not react to the unfolding events. Just follow along with the ceremony, quietly and obediently; do not draw attention to yourself, and speak to no one. Should you create any kind of disturbance, Allieb will assume you have broken the trance and will consider you a threat."

"Trance?" Danto asked.

Thornton stopped walking, turned to the others, his face contorted with pain. A stifling quietness filled the hall. He whispered, "During the ceremony, you *will* feel moments of mental recklessness. Your mind will play tricks on you, leading you to believe that there are no means of thought other than the evils psychologically imparted upon you. You *must* resist these feelings—they won't be any different than the impressions you felt upon arriving here. Allieb has diverted much of his energy into the drawing, and will continue to do so, thereby diluting his mental hold on everyone and making these sensations easily combatable. Some of those in the congregation will undoubtedly find the strength to sever their psychological bond with him; I can only imagine the fear they'll feel upon 'waking up' in the middle of Hell." He rocked his gaze back and forth between Danto and Rebecca. "Be strong. It is all I can ask. You don't want to fall victim to Allieb's fury."

Danto nodded, then peered at Rebecca, who remained oddly silent, gazing past Thornton toward the end of the dark hall. Her blue eyes glimmered in the shadows, despite having no source from which to derive their glow.

"Rebecca?" Danto placed a hand upon her arm. "Are you okay?"

She faced him. Gone were the fear and pain and tears from her features, now replaced with a prepared, almost smug grin on her face. "I am."

She looks different, Danto thought. *Something isn't*

right with her. Has she fallen victim to the grasp of evil?

The chanting grew louder. Thornton rolled his eyes up toward the ceiling, contemplating the all-encompassing mantra. Danto watched him conscientiously as beads of sweat trickled down the sides of his angular face. "The Legion is near. Satan, help us."

The insanity of his statement hit Danto like a speeding truck, and a surge of anxiety riddled his body. He took a series of deep breaths in an attempt to calm the sudden, naked loathing he had for the seemingly inescapable state of affairs. He followed Thornton's moving shadow into an adjacent hallway, where a charge of red light splayed across their footsteps, emerging from a large columned archway not ten feet away. Here, with no barrier to mute the sound, the chanting voices amplified.

Danto eyed the entrance to the cathedral, gripping his cheeks and wiping the sweat from his lip. There would be no turning back now. The Legion of demons was about to commence, and he would be here to witness it. The only uncertainty was whether he'd live to tell of his experiences.

Quietly, they stepped forward and stopped at the end of the hall, just beyond the arch. Thornton turned toward Danto and Rebecca. Both remained frozen, Danto's mounting fear and aversion keeping his feet glued to the wood floor. They adjusted their hoods, hiding their faces as much as possible. Thornton pointed toward the center of the room, mouthed *Follow me*, then paced through the archway, his near-silent footsteps absorbed by the murmuring chant of the congregation.

Side by side, holding hands, Danto and Rebecca followed the minister into the cathedral.

* * *

In the acidic pits of Hell, Bev Mathers screamed and cried and wailed in immeasurable agony, his voice one of countless millions paying their respects to the Prince of Darkness. Above, he could hear the rustle of his body as it morphed into something otherworldly, his hands and feet altering, his body shifting bizarrely. When he gazed down at himself, he saw a ghostly image of what his physical body had developed into: yellow claws, thick like daggers, bursting from the tips of his fingers, blood trickling from the lesions; skin, thick like leather, blue veins flowing like branches beneath the milky surface. He tried to scream, but his familiar voice had vanished, exchanged for a strident wheeze barely recognizable by his own ears. He felt his body rise up from the mattress, and the dizzying lumber of it as it staggered across the dark room: Satan, familiarizing Himself with man's physical form. Bev couldn't physically see through his eyes. Yet he maintained a delicate link with his mind, hearing all that Satan could hear; seeing all that He could see; perceiving a thin account of His meandering thoughts as they formulated a plan to take Allieb down and retrieve the twelve demon hostages. His body stopped. Bev listened. Beyond the moan of the wind, he could hear Satan's steerlike breaths oozing from his lungs . . . and then the deafening roar of the beast, a physical being now walking the earth for the first time in more than two thousand years.

Forty-five

Oh my God . . .

The first thing that struck Danto was the sheer size of the cathedral; he hadn't expected the room to be so expansive. Roughly the size of his own church, the room ran at least two hundred feet from corner to corner. It contained no furniture and other embellishments, which exaggerated the room's intimidating size and added to the dark, looming threat it sustained. Flat black paint covered every inch of the area—the floors, walls, ceiling, and columnar supports—creating a suitable camouflage for the hundred-plus black-robed attendees circling the midpoint altar. Dozens of perched candelabra were set up equidistantly throughout the room, igniting everything in a ghostly yellow radiance.

Unlike the rest of the house, the cathedral had been meticulously attended to. Along the opposite wall ran a balcony perhaps eighty feet long, etched columns at every six feet fitted with three-foot pentagrams. Lining the balcony's edge at equidistant points between the columns were glossy black chalices, burning with sulfur, yellow smoke oozing from their rims like boiling milk. The altar itself was an impressive display: Dressed entirely in black cloths, the platform it rested on spanned fifty feet from end to end, lined with burning candles whose black wax glowed eerily in their flickering light.

Thornton led Danto and Rebecca to the circle of hooded subordinates, breaking the line to allow them a connection. Danto grasped a woman's hand to his left, her palm and fingers petite and callused. His right hand held Rebecca's left; she in turn latched on to the hand of another incognito member of Allieb's cabal. No one paid them any attention, it seemed, and Danto and Rebecca both aimed their frightened gazes toward the floor, impersonating the postures of all those in attendance.

Danto clenched his teeth to keep them from chattering, realizing with trepidation that Thornton had already slipped away from the circle. Through his pursed lips, he took a deep breath and began whispering the repetitive chant: *"Anthropomorphitus blasphemia divinitas."* The congregation droned on and on, with no end in sight, and after every sixth repetition, they would stop and acclaim their loyalty to the dark side: *"Hail Allieb. Hail Belial."* Every so often, Danto would squeeze Rebecca's hand to reinforce his support, but she would remain absolutely still, moving not even a hairsbreadth.

Keeping his gaze down, he continued patiently with the event's progression: a dark affair that seemed to last forever. He wondered how long it would carry on before the actual drawing of demons began.

Before all Hell breaks loose . . .

The chanting commenced for an indeterminable amount of time, the Latin phrase repeated over and over again until it had embedded itself deep inside his head. Eventually, no one else moved into the locked circle and no one moved out—the ring was complete, it seemed, every member of Allieb's cabal now in their respective positions. After an interval eulogization of *Hail Allieb, Hail Belial,* an unexpected roar abruptly broke the chant, pervading the cathedral as though a crash of thunder had found its way inside the house. Danto felt the floor vibrate beneath his feet, the harsh, multilayered tone proving its possessor's origins to be not of this earth.

Now Rebecca stirred a bit, her hand and arm trembling with noticeable fear. To Danto's left, the woman remained motionless, grip cold and steady, head bowed, seemingly tranced and unaffected by the monstrous presence. A cold blast of air filled the room, tousling his hood, sending chills down his spine. The flickering candle flames swayed in all directions, showing no particular route from which the draft had come. The air seemed to thicken. His head began to pound, keeping him from falling deeply into the persistent trance. He waited in distressed silence, peering up through the tops of his eyes at the circle of black-hooded individuals who dutifully waited for the first phase of the drawing to commence.

Away from the cathedral, Thornton walked a narrow hallway leading toward the west wing of the mansion, its indirect length lit by only one exposed bulb in the ceiling. Although he'd traveled through this hallway many times in the past, he still managed to bypass the only door dividing its length.

Bathed in near darkness and easily overlooked, the door offered access to Thornton's final destination.

The basement.

He stopped. Turned back and faced the door. He folded his hands and said a prayer: this time to God, begging for His forgiveness.

He grabbed the rusted doorknob; a tiny shock struck his damp hand.

He closed his eyes.

Turned the knob.

He opened the door and peered down the length of steps, their distance steeped in murky darkness.

Without hesitation, he drew a deep breath, then proceeded down the stairs. About halfway down, he noticed a vestige of red light being thrown up from somewhere below, enough to allow him sight of his feet as they tackled the rest of the wooden steps.

The basement was strangely silent, given the circumstances.

He reached the bottom landing. Shuddered.

Then turned into the basement.

He could remember being down here only once before in all his time at *In Domo,* two weeks ago, upon Allieb's capture of the first vehicle, a thirty-year-old man who carried the demonologist's self-proclaimed father, the demon Belial. Thornton himself had escorted the man down here, locked him in a cage, and hurried away before his remorse in doing so made him act out of character—a single tear or thought of regret might have raised the demonologist's suspicions of him. Afterward, Allieb demanded that Thornton steer clear of the cellar and focus his efforts on the gathering of the vehicles.

He knew . . . he knew all along my intentions to destroy him. Why didn't he stop me then?

The basement had once been home to Allieb's array of torture devices, many of them utilized to carry his primitive experimentations to new horizons. Years earlier, an excess of chains, whips, racks, and swings had been installed at various places in the cement playing field, exploited during *In Domo*'s untried years. If one looked closely, the ghosts of Allieb's past debauchery could be seen in the bloodstains on the porous cement floor. Later, under anticipation of the drawing, Allieb had his workers remove many of the devices and mount cages against the walls, thirteen in all, that would be used to detain the vehicles upon their capture; despite Allieb's awareness that Satan wouldn't allow His own vehicle uncomplicated entry into one of the cages, he placed it there anyway . . . a bit of wishful thinking, and perhaps brash confidence, on the part of the demonologist. The cage remained empty alongside the enclosure that had once held the demon Belial's vehicle.

The other cages were a different story altogether.

Thornton put a hand up to his mouth in an attempt to stifle the scream trying to flee his lungs. There was an appalling odor in the air, a palpable discharge of feces and rot that assaulted him like a blow from a fist. The surging heat down here was intense, and yet when he paced forward, deeper into the dungeon, pockets of icy cold air parted the heat like a knife through soft butter.

The basement was huge, nearly the size of the cathedral sitting directly above his head. The cages were staggered throughout, anchored to various places in the walls.

The shadows within each of the cages were eerily silent and motionless.

He could hear them breathing, a chorus of tempered growls, like dozing animals in a zoo. Within a few of the cages, he could see the ghastly glow of their eyes contemplating him. In the others, dark misshapened silhouettes.

God help me.

He paced to the nearest cage, on his left.

Peered inside.

His eyes fell upon a naked child, perhaps five or six years old, curled fetally against the cinder wall. He gazed at the twitching arms and legs that looked like whittled broomsticks, skeletal and wasted; the head, bowed down between the folded legs, displaying a straggled mess of hair; the purple lesions covering the translucent skin like leeches. Despite the vulnerable appearance, the demon-child righted its head and spread its legs, revealing its long-lost femininity. She peered ferally at Thornton, then sniggered in a deep, masculine voice, emaciated hands clawing the rear wall as though trying to get away.

"The wolf is mine," she growled. "You . . . can't . . . have . . . it." Distrustful yellow eyes peered at him. She faced the wall, clawing more furiously. "No! No! *You can't have it, you bastard!*"

Thornton made the sign of the cross. Behind him, all around him, the other demons began to stir from their slumbers, their untamed drones mounting into sputtering snores. He peered fearfully over his shoulder, then slowly reached into his pocket and pulled out a vial of holy water. The girl-demon shot him a fierce glance, her eyes gleaming, pinning him in utter repulsion. She was now scraping at the wall ferociously, screaming: *"The wolf is mine! You can't take it away from me!"*

"Who are you?" Thornton asked, his voice barely a whisper.

"I'm the pig that feasts on child!" The girl's lips were now cracked and bleeding, the mouth bowed into a grotesque frown, blood pouring from the nose in a stream.

Danto raised the vial, recited a prayer: "God, Lord of all creation, I call upon your might to cast this demon aside like a thorn, make it fall from Heaven behind your power. Strike terror in this beast laying waste in your firmament so that it may not arise again from its burning . . ."

The child howled. From behind him, a few of the sequestered demons snorted loudly, like a herd of unfed pigs. The ghostly red light in the room brightened, and Thornton could not establish the source from which it came—it appeared to emanate from thin air. He raised the vial of holy water, covered half the opening with his index finger, and sprinkled the contents at the demon.

The demon wailed a thousand voices of agony as it climbed the cement wall and perched itself in the upper right-hand corner of the cage, where it writhed and recoiled in fear and pain. "Stop! Stop! You baaaaastard!"

Thornton listened to the other demons in the room, who were now awakening from their slumbers. He turned and gazed at the moving forms in the cages, the shifting shadows, the eyes glowing at him from within, like jackals in the night. The room grew suddenly frigid. The hair on his arms stood on end. His breath unfurled from his mouth in a cold, hazy plume.

He gazed back at the cage. The girl-demon inside had collapsed to the floor, where she writhed like a salted slug, the eyes bulging grotesquely from their sockets. A string of gibberish sprung from her lips, interspersed by deep, croaky breaths.

"Who are you?" Thornton demanded.

"Fuck you!"

He sprinkled more holy water upon the girl. She bellowed in terrible agony, a deep chorus of voices screaming the name of the demon inside her: *"Abbadon! Abbadon!"* Like a springing insect, the girlish figure bounded up from the floor and crashed against the front bars of the cage, reaching her ravenous arms toward Thornton. He backpedaled from the filthy, groping fingers. The girl-demon bellowed, barked, snorted, her marred face pressing between the iron bars like a monkey at a zoo.

Thornton swallowed past the burning lump of fear in his throat, thinking back to the exorcism that he and Danto had performed on Allieb more than twenty years ago. It had taken two men—one an experienced priest—over five hours to complete. And, although it had driven the demons out, it had not fully purged the soul of the demonologist, and perhaps the soul of Belial, from the boy's body. Feeling a wave of sudden hopelessness, he halfheartedly sprinkled more holy water at the girl-demon, shouting weakly, "Be gone, Abbadon, back to the fires of Hell from whence you emerged!"

The girl-demon hurled herself to the cement floor; somewhere inside her, a bone snapped. She writhed there in absolute pain, howling monstrously, choking, jerking spasmodically as hunks of bloody phlegm sputtered from her mouth. Thornton, vision swimming in a blur, cringed as her jaw cracked loudly and then, in a horrifying display, dehinged itself, forming an open maw one could easily fit a fist into. Her tongue slumped out in a limp heap, spilling saliva.

Yet still the words came, clearly defined in their hideous tone, despite her motionless lips: "The girl is mine, you fucking charlatan. Be gone!"

He dropped his gaze to the floor, wholly defeated; his efforts . . . they were utterly futile, he knew, and in spite of any valiant effort would go unrewarded. The demon would persist, maintain its hold on the vehicle with all its power and might, for it realized the rewards of its labors would soon be attained: freedom from Satan's domain in the bowels of Hell, with a place on earth alongside the throne of its new prince, Allieb.

Thornton realized his intentions to be noble—in theory, exorcising even one demon would very well prove itself successful in weakening Allieb's war against Satan. But, given the time and energy and forces needed to accomplish such a daunting task, it made the idea impractical.

But . . . there was one other option, lying on a dark shelf in his mind. It was the reason he did not invite Danto—or anyone else, for that matter—to join him in facing up to his son. Looking at the demon-child, and realizing there were others like her that would fight to the bitter end, he realized that no other alternative existed but to rely on one evil to defeat another.

Fight fire with fire.

With a ghastly wheeze, the girl fell into a fitful slumber, eyes closed, thick mucus running from her nose.

Thornton capped the vial and placed it in his pocket, then paced away from the cage, eyes searching the floor as he rubbed his throbbing head. His brain . . . it felt as though it had begun to waste away, a feverish heat and clawing pain dousing his mind and body, despite the cold air.

A sensation of grasping fingers scratched on the surface of his brain.

Then a voice: *Father . . .*

Allieb.

Time was short; the demonologist had left his lair and was hiding somewhere nearby, waiting to commence with the drawing. Thornton moved away from the cage to the right side of a wooden rack. He gripped a black metal hook embedded in its grain, then leaned down to pick up a thick steel chain from the floor. He eyed the chain nervously, running the cold links through his trembling fingers: each one a sin waiting to be committed. With the chain looped around his hand, he staggered back to the girl's cage in blinding silence, wobbly from the conscious sin he was about to commit. He gazed at the slumbering demon, then turned around to survey the looming basement.

In the other cages, glowing eyes stared back at him.

Slowly, he removed the hook key he'd taken from the nightstand in his room. Gripping the chain in his right hand, he slipped the key into the lock on the girl's cage. From behind, a chorus of growls emanated, like a tribe of baboons howling over the presence of a nearby hunter.

The blood howled in his veins, filling his ears with a numbing deafness; he screamed in an attempt to fill his soul with an overwhelming sense of hatred. As the weakness in his body ascended into hate-filled strength, he flung open the door to the cage, raised his strengthening arms, and brought the steel chain down onto the head of the girl-demon.

Her wasted body flung sideways and slammed against the rear wall, spilling an obscene trail of blood on the floor. A deafening wail erupted from her unmoving jaw, a monstrous bellow of pain and torture and defeat as impending death fell upon the twitching vehicle that held the demon Abbadon.

The only way to defeat evil is through evil itself.

Fight fire with fire.

In a mad state, Thornton leaped at the girl. He brought the chain down on her skull, again and again, crushing it into a soft mass. Behind him, the demons howled in a fury, all of them thrashing against their cages, an obscene ensemble performing their hellish symphony. The cacophony beat against Thornton's ears, and he dropped the chain and fell to his knees before the girl's body, hands pressing against the sides of his head. The demons continued wailing. The agony sliced into him like heavily hammered nails, his skull feeling as though it were being chiseled away from the surface of his brain, clawed hands reaching from within to take hold of an unexplored world.

And then, abruptly, the demons ceased their wicked chorus, bathing the cellar in complete, menacing silence.

Still in the cage, feeling the hot threading seep of blood against his knees, Thornton pulled his hands away from his head. He opened his eyes. Tasted bitter blood in his mouth, licked his lips nervously as he surveyed the quiet basement. A few feet away, the cadaver wheezed as putrid gases made an escape.

The red light was still aglow, faintly igniting the shadows within the cages and the reflective gleam of their watchful eyes. The sounds that had saturated the basement moments earlier had completely ceased to exist: the fits, the growls, the snorts, the roars. Not a single breath could be heard. Thornton stood, paced hesitantly from the cage, wondering, *What did I do? My God, what did I just do?*

With a hard, nearly impassable lump in his throat, he stepped deeper into the basement, passing additional cages and the glinting eyes from within that followed him as he went by. As he moved forward, the red light strengthened, glowing strongly from the cinder wall at the opposite end of the cellar. The air felt suddenly dense, as though it were congealing. A harsh, deathlike odor materialized. Thornton stopped, stared hypnotically at the crimson radiance, eyes ferreting out a faint gray form taking shape at its core. His gaze shifted briefly toward the two closest cages beside him. He locked eyes with one demon—a bald, middle-aged man pressed against the bars, hands stretched out, fingers groping the air just inches away from his face. It opened its toothless mouth and produced a catlike hiss, tongue darting in and out swiftly.

Thornton turned away from the possessed man and refocused his sights upon the dark gray shadow developing inside the red light.

In his pocket, he fingered the vial of holy water.

In his head, a scratching sensation, and then a familiar voice: *That won't help you against me, Father.*

He shuddered, realizing his unconditional defeat, knowing that the only way to save Bev Mathers, Thomas Danto, and Rebecca Haviland was to separate himself permanently from them; that Allieb had known all along his adoptive father had severed his trance, had "switched sides," so to speak. But Allieb had also seen no threat in his father's knowledge of the drawing of the thirteen demons, and that no matter whom

Thornton recruited in a battle, it would prove a fruitless effort; that, despite this lack of intimidation Thornton represented, he would still pay a dire price for his betrayal.

But now Thornton had killed one of the vehicles, thereby releasing Allieb's hold upon one of the demons. Unless all thirteen demons were absorbed by Allieb, then a threat *would* exist for him. With no vehicle to lock in Abbadon, Satan could easily retrieve his demon soldier, fuse its strengths with His own, and strike heavily against Allieb as he lured the remaining demons into his body.

Thornton closed his eyes and recited a silent prayer to God. When he opened them, the red light had vanished. He stood in the pitch black—a darkness rivaled by its silence—feeling the sinister gazes of the demons upon him.

And then, from behind him, a deep, throaty voice, more animal than human: "Father . . ."

Thornton turned. Standing there, bathed in the piercing yellow glow of his eyes, was Allieb. He'd grown even more monstrous since Thornton's last encounter with him in the attic. Thornton gazed helplessly at the beast that was his son; at the straggled matting of hair covering his head; at the skeletal limbs jutting stiffly from his emaciated torso, covered with thick, scaly skin; at the swelling abdomen and the eight horrid teats wriggling from it; at the short lupine tail that swung lazily across his bare buttocks; and then, back to his eyes—eyes that shifted to observe the man standing miserably before him.

Thornton moved to speak, but the words failed to burrow past the mound of fear in his throat.

Allieb stepped forward, eye-to-eye with the man who

had adopted him over thirty years earlier. He released a horselike snort, the gush of putrid gas spilling from his lungs nearly unendurable. "Who is your God?" he asked Thornton, his voice strident, demanding.

In a quick flick of the wrist, Thornton removed the vial of holy water from his pocket, flipped the rubber stopper off with his thumb, and splashed the entire contents on Allieb, shouting, *"The Lord, Jesus Christ, is my God! Damn you to Hell!"*

A hellish din ensued, the demons rattling against their cages furiously, deafening howls joining together into the shriek of a thousand hurricanes, Allieb himself raising his arms high, a blinding glow of red light emerging from behind his broadening body, a roar gunning from his lungs, deep and colossal, hitting Thornton like a tangible force, knocking him to the ground. Allieb, panting, towered over Thornton, his thick, scaly skin oozing where the holy water had struck him, bloody and seeping with pus. He grinned, his mouth rife with black stumps for teeth; eyes sharp, reptilian, peering vindictively down at him.

"Does your God approve of your conspiracy with the Devil, dear *Father*?"

Thornton remained on the ground, lips trembling, reciting a silent prayer: *Dear Lord, please deliver me from this servant of evil . . .*

Allieb laughed. In the cages, the demons mimicked his mirth—a symptom of blind adoration. "Your soul is mine, Father. Or shall I say Abbadon's."

Allieb raised his arms. From behind, the door to the cage of the dead girl slammed open, then closed, then open. With a screeching fracture, it tore free of its hinges and flew across the basement, colliding with the cinder wall. With a quick thrust of his claw, the demonologist grabbed Thornton by the neck and pulled him close. A thick string of hot spittle fell upon his cheek.

"Jesus is weeping, Father."

Thornton's lungs gasped for air. He felt his consciousness slipping away, falling down, down, down, his very soul plummeting into the depths of his bowels.

In his boyhood voice, Allieb began to sing a Latin-phrased hymn: *"Magnus es, domine, et laudabilis valde."*

And as Thornton fell into Hell, he could hear the distant tune of the demons singing along.

Forty-six

Deep in the entrails of Hell, Bev Mathers finally slept. In his dreams, he saw Julianne. She stood beside the lake at Alondra Park, waving to him, telling him to come over to her. Kristin was there too, as an adult, sitting on the bench alongside her mother, petting a white swan. They were both smiling, offering mountains of reassurance to Bev that everything was going to be all right. Bev approached them, tears of joy filling his eyes. He stood before Julianne, his wife, looked into her adoring eyes. He took her hands. They felt . . . rough. With trepidation, he looked down at them and saw that he held two lizard claws. Repulsed, he threw them down, then looked at her with fear and disgust. She smiled. "What's wrong, dear?" she asked, her voice carrying a gentle, comforting lilt. From the corner of her mouth, a swan's feather appeared, its downy white tainted with a thin streak of blood. It trembled in the gentle breeze, then swept away over the lake. "Honey? What's wrong?" she again asked. Bev jerked his gaze from the fluttering feather, then backed away from her, feet squelching in a puddle of sizzling acid. He looked over at Kristin. The swan in her lap was now dead, its gut shredded open, the innards dangling like streamers. She was petting it soothingly. "Daddy, come to us," she requested, the generous smile on her face cloaking something sinister. "No," he muttered, shrinking back. "No." A deep rumble emerged from Julianne's mouth. When he looked at her, her eyes were green and glaring, the pupils shaped like diamonds. "Allieb's attempt at Legion has begun," she said, her voice low-toned, monstrous. "You are about to experience agonies you never thought imaginable. Be strong, and you shall be spared." At the finish of her words, Julianne collapsed to the floor in a dead heap, as did Kristin. The serene environment melted away, its illusion giving way to the fiery acids of Hell. Bev, once again imbued with unendurable pain, screamed and screamed until he crumpled back down into the burning lava.

Silence filled the cathedral, the circle having remained at a standstill since Allieb's concealed roar put an end to the congregation's perambulatory chant. Through the tops of his eyes, Danto chanced a forward glance toward the altar. The candles burned brightly, the hooded participants on the opposite side keeping their shrouded gazes down. His grasp on the hand of Rebecca, and that of the woman to his left, had gone numb. His feet ached, his knees quivered. He fought to simply stand.

Suddenly, a low monotonal hum pervaded the room.

The six-second vocalizations repeated six times at the same even pitch, and were immediately followed by a series of loud, echoey poundings that sent vibrations deep into the framework of the house. Danto could feel the tremors racing painfully from his feet straight up through his body, into his throbbing head. After the poundings, the hum returned; this time the pitch waxed and waned, composing a dark, droning melody. The flames on the candles rose nearly six inches, flickering like ghosts. The hum stopped and the poundings resumed, the entire house shaking under their authority. Amazingly, everyone in the circle remained stoic despite the looming danger. Danto squeezed Rebecca's hand. Gently, she squeezed back, soothing Danto's fear of being left alone amid this chaos.

Alone.

Where is Thornton?

As the hummings and poundings continued, Danto noticed a rimmed serving plate being passed along the circle of partakers to his left. He watched as a man retrieved the plate, bowed gently toward the altar, then removed something from it and placed it in his mouth. The act lasted not ten seconds before being repeated by the next individual. Danto swallowed hard, remembering what Thornton had told him before coming here: *Do not react to the unfolding events. Just follow along with the ceremony, quietly and obediently, do not draw attention to yourself, and speak to no one.*

The plate eventually reached the woman next to Danto. She disconnected her cold grasp from his, removed what appeared to be a host, bowed to the altar, and placed it in her mouth. She then handed the offering to Danto.

Danto took it from her. He peered down at the contents.

It was half filled with irregularly shaped hosts.

They were brownish red in color.

It was at this moment that he realized what he was about to put into his body, and he shuddered with revulsion. These hosts were made with flour . . . and blood. Whose blood, or *what's* blood, he had no guess; he *did* know that this act indicated a "beginning phase" of Allieb's black mass.

The drawing—it was near.

He removed one of the hosts from the plate. It was misshapened, thicker and heavier than one of God's usual offerings: a thin, tasteless wafer composed of flour and blessed water. He trembled, did his damnedest to erase his mind of the offense that was about to be committed.

He placed the host in his mouth.

His head rushed. His tongue twinged from the sharp coppery taste. Nausea rolled in his gut, and despite the lack of saliva in his mouth, he swallowed the pasty wafer down before his stomach could shove it back up.

Eyes closed, he stood there momentarily, gripping the plate tightly, trying to rid his mouth of the lingering aftertaste. A restless murmur rose among the participants. He soon realized his hesitation, and quickly passed it to Rebecca.

She performed the ritual like a pro, accepting the host with no noticeable uncertainty, then promptly handed the offering to the participant on her right. In minutes, everyone attending the congregation had taken part in the communion, the near-empty plate returned by a cloaked member to the foot of the altar.

Time passed sluggishly. A harsh burning ball carved a hole in Danto's gut. He swallowed hard, stifling the acids crawling up his esophagus.

Moments later, a faint red light formed at the center of the altar, seeping up along the edges of what appeared to be a trapdoor in the platform. At this point, the people closely monitored the light as it grew brighter, its beams reaching out along the edges of the rectangle-shaped access.

The door jostled, then gradually creaked open, an inch at first, releasing the crimson radiance in a lustrous surge. The door opened further. The shafts of light expanded, spilling out brightly. From within its brilliant and oddly silent depths, bleating could be heard: anxious, animalistic. A dark figure soon appeared, staggering from the access, the door bobbing up and down now as the form climbed its way out onto the altar. In the face of the light, it was hard for Danto to distinguish what was emerging from beneath the altar, other than it might be some kind of animal. Once it was completely out of the hole, the door slammed back down to the floor of the altar, shutting out the blinding light, thus revealing the animal to be a large black sow.

The animal, although unleashed and free to run riot, staggered irregularly about the platform until deciding upon the support of the altar to nestle itself protectively against. Here Danto could see the pig's injuries: a bloody snout, seemingly knifed or bitten in a scuffle; deep, glistening slashes across its hide; blood-covered hooves; a broken leg dangling behind it like a storm-damaged branch. It remained still and shivering, huffing noisily.

Danto's breathing increased, Thornton's words haunting his fears: *You are going to see some very un-*

pleasant things . . . Amazingly, the circle remained still, and wholly silent; Danto hadn't realized until now that he was once again holding hands with Rebecca and the hooded woman. The labored huffing and puffing of the swine echoed about the room, sending harsh shivers down his spine. He listened to the pig's discordant suffering until the room was once again shocked into attention with the deafening slam of the trapdoor flinging open against the platform.

The red light shot up from the access like a geyser, shafts reaching vigorously to the ceiling, crooked beams splaying out across the entire congregation, igniting Allieb's startling entrance into the cathedral.

Allieb climbed out of the hole onto the altar, sinewy arms rippling, eyes glimmering ferociously. In a daunting display, he opened his mouth staggeringly wide, his weathered black tongue lolling out, lapping saliva across his lips and chin. Facing the circle of worshipers, he shook his body like a wet dog, then released a series of menacing barks, causing some of the participants to visibly flinch. He turned, gazed down at the cowering pig, then leaped to his feet and raised his hands high, eyes facing the black heavens.

In a deep, lustful, dominating voice, Allieb roared, "Legion . . . is . . . here!"

The congregation replied in unison: "Hail Allieb. Hail Belial."

The demonologist climbed atop the altar, hands and feet gripping the edges like talons. He stared into a rising flame, then removed the candle and held it out before his face; the flickering glow ignited his reptilian eyes, as though they were charged with electricity. He recited to the congregation: "*Anthropomorphitus blasphemia divinitas.*" The worshipers, Danto and Rebecca included, repeated the phrase. Danto had no clue what it meant, relying on ignorance as his only protection against the dark prayer. Allieb, staring into the flame, spent the next few minutes swaying and mumbling inaudible prayers to himself. Upon finishing, he licked the flame, drawing it into his rough, skeletal body, then threw the candle to the platform. It rolled alongside the cowering sow, which snorted in fear and pain.

Allieb stepped down from the altar, turned to face the pig. He recited another Latin phrase, to which the congregation replied, "Release the demons from Jesus's sow."

Allieb delivered a series of low mumbling phrases, many of which were in Latin, some, however, in a tongue Danto could not recognize. After each, the congregation responded in prayer: "Release the demons from Jesus's sow."

Finally, Allieb recited in his deep, hoarse voice: "Unto earth the demons shall walk within my body, amidst my very soul." He pressed his chest out, from which the eight ulcerated teats wriggled erectly from his chest. The sow, seemingly entranced, staggered from its hiding spot beneath the altar. It nestled up against the demonologist's chest and began to suckle one of the nipples.

A time passed where nothing but the sound of the suckling pig could be heard. Danto waited in uneasy silence, wondering, *Dear God, where is Thornton?* and then, *What of Bev Mathers? Where is he?*

Suddenly, a sirenlike squeal filled the room. Danto shook away his anxious thoughts and brought his sights back to the altar, where Allieb had drilled his pointed fingernails deep into the abdomen of the sow.

The pig thrashed and bucked maniacally beneath Allieb's unyielding grasp, hooves slamming determinedly against the wooden platform, snout biting at the air, horrid bleats escaping from within. With a show of silent strength and power, Allieb split the pig's stomach open. Bones cracked; muscles tore; the gaping cavity pumped its innards onto the platform.

A nauseating odor saturated the room, that of excrement and blood. Allieb leaned down before the twitching sow, rumbled, "Come to me, my demons. I have released you from Jesus's pig."

And then something incredible happened, nearly causing Danto to scream out in disbelief and disgust. Beetles the size of mice wriggled out of the pig's ragged wound, black chitinous exoskeletons staggering aimlessly amid the spilled viscera. Allieb reached down and one by one gathered up thirteen insects in total, gingerly placing them atop the black cloth of the altar. There they remained nearly motionless, side by side, antennae swaying hypnotically, tasting the air.

Once the beetles had been gathered, Allieb shoved the dead pig under the altar with a swift kick of his foot, then faced the altar. He prayed in an indecipherable tongue, during which Danto squeezed Rebecca's sweating hand. He chanced a look at her but could see no more than her nose and a few strands of hair escaping the cloak of her hood. Gently, she squeezed back, keeping her gaze forward, as though to say, *Don't worry, everything is going to be all right.* Danto, returning his sights to the altar, found her calm composure somewhat unnerving given her near breakdown just hours earlier. He shuddered, took a deep breath in through his lips and slowly released it from his nose, trying to calm himself despite the jarring circumstances.

Allieb turned and faced the congregation. "Legion has begun," he seethed, leaning down and pulling open the trapdoor in the platform. This time no red light exploded from within.

Instead, after a few minutes of prayerful silence, a human hand emerged, gripping the edge of the opening. Then, soon thereafter, another hand, immediately followed by an arm. A second arm appeared, and it was at this moment that Danto felt a numbing, unbearable fear wash over him, a wave of utter defeat as the man reached his head out of the hole and howled his demonic fury over the congregation.

It was Thornton. He was possessed by a demon.

Allieb reached down and with both hands grabbed the onetime minister by the neck and jerked him out of the hole with a quick, rippling thrust. Thornton's body slammed to the platform just as the door came down on his right leg, which was still halfway in the hole. He howled, jerking his head up and down, body flailing with trembling fury. The altar began to vibrate, then tipped lazily back and forth, spilling a couple of candles, whose flames were immediately extinguished in the pig's blood on the floor. The beetles, remarkably, remained still. Allieb, still gripping Thornton by the neck, yanked him free of the trapdoor. It slammed down, Thornton's broken shinbone twisted sickeningly behind his body. Once Thornton was free of the hole, the rocking movements of the altar subsided.

Wholly deadened and straining to block it all out, Danto averted his gaze from the altar, first toward Rebecca, then around to the other incognito members of the congregation, whose hidden gazes were also shifting slightly behind their darkened cloaks. Facing the floor, he found no choice but to pray for his life: *Lord, grant me the strength to see the light of tomorrow. I beg of you to hear my prayer.*

Allieb shot an attentive glance in Danto's direction, clearly perceiving his traitorous thoughts. Thornton bucked and thrashed beneath his grasp, as though sensing his distraction and using it as an opportunity to escape. Allieb responded by tightening his grasp on the minister's possessed body. Hulking over his prey, the demonologist commenced with the drawing: "Come into me Abbadon," he demanded, voice hideously deep, layered with the monstrous voice of Belial. "Escape Satan's undying grasp upon your soul and walk the earth with us, my child. The time for Legion is here!" The house shook as though in the grasp of an earthquake tremor. Danto and some others peered around anxiously as cracks formed in the black walls, spilling out gray beams of light that pinned the bucking Thornton.

Allieb kneeled before Thornton's trembling body. Thornton, whose eyes had taken on a canine glow, offered the soul of the demon within to Allieb: "Father . . . take my flesh and eat of it, for this is my body."

Allieb fell upon Thornton and launched a clubbed fist deep into his sternum, blowing it apart. From within, he promptly ripped free his still-beating heart. Breathing heavily and seemingly entranced, the demonologist stared indulgently at the seeping heart in his grasp.

Danto watched with horror, his mind feverishly thrashing, taking all logical knowledge and hope and tossing it out the window; it wasn't supposed to be like *this*. His pulse raced at an unfathomable speed, depleting him of all faith, each fear-induced heartbeat in his chest feeling like a shovel's burrow into the soil of his very own grave.

Thornton's body crumpled, limp and silent on the bloody platform. From within the gaping hole in his sternum emerged a leaching black shadow, dense and impenetrable, moving through the air like a waft of smoke into the still-beating heart in Allieb's grasp. Allieb opened his eyes, grinned ferally, and whispered hoarsely, "Welcome, Abbadon, my child." A loud cracking sound issued from the possessed demonologist as he freely dislocated his jaw. He opened his mouth wide and shoved the entire heart in, swallowing it whole in a single jerking motion, like a monitor lizard gulping down its prey.

The moments that followed were wholly intimidating. Allieb remained still, statuelike, jaw hanging obscenely, the whites of his eyes gleaming evilly at a nondescript point in the black room. A thick green mist rose up from Thornton's lifeless body and circled the altar like ghostly fingers. Danto glanced warily around the room, at the partakers who remained in their fixed positions, many still entirely tranced, others, it seemed, beginning to fall away from their hypnotic states, given their restlessness; they all remained composed despite the overpowering events. Allieb still had a hold on his followers, thank God.

Thank Satan.

Forty-seven

Pain.

Agony.

Bedlam.

And it would never end. There was no such thing as death in Hell. Existence was ongoing, torture and mortality an unadorned illusion to absolute realism; all that could be known was the eternal continuation of life, permeated with all of death's agonies. Bev lay in the churning acids, experiencing one fatality after another, his very own beheading, his very own body, hung, drawn, and quartered. The agonies would come, and persist, and then, when the act of torture was complete, he would lie writhing in the pit of his own stomach acids, in the aftereffects of his most recent torments, only to have new ones served to him time and time again.

Then, suddenly, they stopped. The tortures. He

waited for an indeterminate amount of time. When nothing happened, he slowly and skeptically rose up from his place in the shallow lava and looked out across the vista of his entrails. As though caught in a whirlwind, his mind climbed up in an unforeseen release of his soul, and for a few strikingly daunting moments he was back in control of his body, looking out through his eyes once again—not his eyes, but the eyes of the Devil, the beast that had not only assumed psychological control of his mind but had physically invaded his human form as well, molding His own grotesque appearance upon Bev's body. Bev peered at his dark surroundings, this giant step into the real world feeling as foreign as his very first sampling of Hell. His head felt heavy and cumbersome, as though weights had been soldered to his skull. He was standing in a dark, musty hallway, awaiting Satan's assessment of the situation. The Devil's decision to strike against the Legion of demons might occur now, or later, or there might be some preparatory measures awaiting him. Who knew? Bev leaned against the wall, feeling the heaving bulk of his alien shape against the chipped paneling. He peered down at himself from this unaccustomed, dizzying height, at the reptilian claws jutting from his unrecognizable hands and feet; at the black, flaring scales covering every inch of his massive body; the visible ridge jutting out over his eyes; the swell of his strapping chest; the flaming breaths that seared his lungs as he began to panic. "What have I become?" he muttered aloud in a voice that was barely human. He looked left and right, along the shadowy passage that disappeared into darkness. He stood there waiting, hoping that he wouldn't be required to assume responsibility for the Devil's form.

Would he?

Then, in his head, a voice, one truly powerful and indomitable. Unlike the demonologist's wavering, distant attempts to ensnare Bev into his cabal, here was the voice of Satan in absolute command of Bev's mind, body, and soul. His power was awesome, unmistakably superior to that of Allieb's.

"What do you think of your new body?"

"Is this really me?" Bev asked.

"For now . . . for now."

"Why are you showing me?" It pained Bev horribly to speak through a throat that had been so hideously transformed.

"I'm feeling a bit charitable at the moment. Of course, that can all change at any given second."

"The Legion . . . has it begun?"

"Yes."

"The pain . . . the tortures . . . please, no more, no more."

"Mere child's play."

"When will this be over?"

"Maybe never. I haven't decided yet."

"Please . . ."

"Perhaps after the war."

"The war?"

"Once it's won, your life will become useless to me. Dead or alive, it doesn't matter."

"Please . . . please let me live . . ."

"Are you certain you can handle life after witnessing so many horrors?"

"No, I'm not . . . but I want the option to try."

"If you perform your duty well, then perhaps . . . but it all depends on my mood at the moment. You know, I can erase your mind of the memories."

Bev swallowed hard, his saliva feeling like drips of fire in his throat. "I was told the Devil tells a fortune in lies, and should never be trusted."

"Hmm . . . very good advice," Satan replied. He paused, then added, "Your daughter Kristin . . . she is here."

"Kristin . . ." Bev replied, vaguely remembering the library of puzzling items he'd discovered in her apartment. "Where is she? Can I see her?"

"I don't think she would take too kindly to seeing you in such a . . . Satanic state," the Devil chortled, low and cocky.

"Just tell me, then . . . is she okay?"

All of a sudden, Kristin's voice filled his head, distant, echoing: "Daddy, please, help me. Help me . . ." A series of fearful sobs followed, then quickly faded.

"Kristin!" Bev yelled, unable to shift his unwieldy body. Bev looked deep into his possessed psyche. His heart, still full of its emotion, dropped like a lead weight. An overwhelming feeling of loss and pain beset him. Satan sniggered.

"That wasn't her, was it? It was you."

Ignoring Bev's question, Satan replied, "Do not let her distract you from the task at hand." Then, in a swift and abrupt gush of power, the Devil rushed Bev's soul and tore it free from its place behind his eyes, quickly reassuming full control of his body. Bev fell away, plummeting down through his esophagus, past his lungs, back into the pit of his stomach where the stirring acids sloshed beneath his collapsing weight. After hitting bottom, he leaned up, looked up toward the whirling black hole in the space above, feeling the pains of his body morphing completely into Satan's monstrous form.

314

Echoing from the black heavens above, Satan's voice rained down on him. "The time is now to put an end to Allieb's childish game."

Allieb removed himself from his self-induced catatonia, limbs twitching, eyes rolling back, threatening in their focus. He spoke in three tongues: "Abbadon has joined us."

The congregation replied: "Hail Allieb, hail Belial, hail Abbadon."

The demonologist, his body suddenly larger, more stalwart, now greenish in hue, leaned down and jerked open the platform door.

Hovering over the black gaping hole, Allieb summoned the next demon, his befouled voice robustly layered in triplicate: "Come to me, Beelzebub. Escape Jesus's pig and walk the earth's firmament with your brothers."

An elderly woman crawled spiderlike from the depths of Allieb's dungeon, eerily agile despite her feeble appearance. Danto recognized her as a longtime member of St. Michael's parish, and stood as still as possible as she cackled in a fairy-tale witch's voice and splattered the floor with streams of thick vomit. Her clothes hung in tatters from her pink, flabby body; her white hair stood on end as though caught in a swell of static electricity; her eyes were starkly black, glistening, staring intently at the crowd as she leaped from the hole and licked her fingers with feline precision. In a muscular swoop, Allieb grasped her by the hair and dragged her flailing body across the platform, reciting a vile prayer that only he could understand. And then shouted, "God will fall! Satan will fall! Humankind will bow at my feet!"

Danto's blood raced, his will roaring desperately for support. He watched with inescapable dread as Allieb completed the drawing of Beelzebub, ripping away the woman's frontal lobe with a single swipe of a claw and swiftly ingesting it in hypnotic prayer.

Soon thereafter, the demonologist roared his frenzy in four tongues.

And the congregation replied: "Hail Allieb, hail Belial, hail Abbadon, hail Beelzebub."

The drawings continued unremittingly, each one lasting longer and proving more challenging than the next, despite Allieb's growing physical form: his seven feet in height; his hulking physique rippling beneath a coating of snakelike scales; the black horns that spiraled out from his head like those on a goat; the tail emerging from the small of his back that now touched the floor, spaded not unlike his penis, which itself dangled black and wetly to his knobby knees.

But what appeared to be an escalation of strength and power on the outside fell in harsh contrast to his noticeably diminishing abilities to perform. It became obvious to Danto that the demonologist was weakening on the inside. While each drawing had been successful up to this point, Allieb seemed not to have the strength to execute them with the unrestrained dynamism he'd exhibited on Thornton.

The platform and altar were littered with the discarded remains of nine vehicles: Thornton, three adult males, two adult females, two teenage boys and a teenage girl. Each body lay twisted, partially cannibalized, mutilated beyond recognition. Tendrils of steam rose from the obscene display like evaporating mists materializing from sun-shower puddles.

In addition to Allieb's dazed performance, his hold

on the occupants had also waned. The circle began to falter upon the drawing of the fourth demon. Two individuals had broken their trances and consequently swooned upon sighting the unforeseen butchery laid out before them. Others simply collapsed from exhaustion, their mindless states still dependant on their physical capacities. One man who had shed his robe and tried to flee the room discovered his heart on the receiving end of a large wooden spike that had been telekinetically ripped from the wall just beneath the balcony. With members falling away, the circle tightened, bringing those still standing closer to Allieb's daunting pursuits. Now, with the hours gone by and nine demons drawn, roughly twenty-five percent of those once positioned steadfast in prayer lay on the floor, either dead by Allieb's hand or unconscious.

The disorder of the situation had afforded Danto an opportunity to shift his body at times, enabling him to gaze at Rebecca's face. Her eyes remained bright and unwaveringly true to the complicated tasks at hand, only once peering back at Danto with a confidence and glow that unquestionably hadn't been there before. *She's stronger, as though she's become a totally different person, one entirely capable of handling this situation. And . . . she even* looks *different . . .*

She *did* look different. Her face had changed—only slightly, but enough for Danto to notice the slight shift in her cheekbones, the gentle arching of her brow, the curvature of her eyes, the definition of her jaw. And, of course, her demeanor: the fear that had previously dominated her behavior had vanished, only to be replaced by a poised self-assurance that seemed to demonstrate a hint of insight to the unfolding events.

During the drawing of the tenth demon, Bael, Allieb

collapsed to the floor after devouring the eyes of the human vehicle. He remained writhing amid the carnage, seemingly oblivious to the events at hand. Here, Danto broke his connection with the circle and faced Rebecca.

She seemed to stare right through him, her eyes ostensibly greener, her skin paler with a blush of red at the cheeks. She looked totally different now, lips fuller, nose a bit smaller, hair a lighter shade of brown.

"Rebecca," Danto whispered. "What's happening to you?"

Her gaze came into focus, for a moment contemplated the wailing demonologist, then looked Danto straight in the eye. At once he felt mesmerized, as though she held some higher form of power he could never identify with. The world seemed to spin around him, everything set into a blurring whirl . . . except her face, which instantaneously fixed itself into an aura of positive light and came alive with the personality of someone other than Rebecca Haviland. In an ethereal voice that clearly wasn't hers, she said, *"Thomas, your job is not yet complete. Go back into the circle and allow the events to play themselves out. Do as I say, and you will be protected by the One who has looked over you your entire life."*

And then the reeling environment came back into focus, nearly sending Danto to the floor. He grabbed Rebecca's arm to keep himself from collapsing, regained his balance, and dutifully placed himself back into the circle before Allieb rose up and commenced with the ceremony.

A whirlwind of emotions inundated Danto—of uncertainty, of wonder, and of awe. Would everything be all right? Somehow Rebecca had retained a bit of otherworldly influence, an unwavering conviction that the situation would conclude as they'd hoped and prayed for; that despite all that had gone wrong up until this point, good would ultimately prevail over evil. Yes, Danto thought, somehow she knew this. And damn, he believed her.

More time passed. Hours, it seemed. Every nerve and vessel in Danto's body pleaded for a respite. The muscles tightened in his face and body, bringing about stabs of excruciating pain. Still, he remained fixed in the circle that had been reduced to half its original size. Additional participants collapsed under the strain of events; others, killed at Allieb's hand upon their attempts to flee the cathedral. Soon, dozens of bodies littered the floor of the cathedral. It looked like a human slaughterhouse. In retrospect, it was just that.

Allieb eventually completed the drawing of the twelfth demon, Baphomet, but it had taken him a tremendous amount of time and effort to accomplish the monstrous task. The demon had been riding the body of a young muscle-bound man whose soul had seemingly found the will to struggle against the evil spirit inside, making Allieb's task enormously difficult; the man's personality continuously broke through that of Baphomet, screaming in his agony and fighting for his life, breaking the possessive flow that Allieb needed to accomplish the task. Even with Baphomet's compliance to walk the earth via the Legion, Allieb seemed not to have the fortitude to keep the demon present long enough to complete the drawing. The demonologist remained on his knees the entire duration, slapping his spaded tail against the wooden platform and praying in a chorus of twelve grotesque voices: his, and those of the eleven demons within.

In the end, it appeared that the vehicle holding Baphomet could handle no more physical abuse. The possessed man eventually grasped his chest and collapsed to the ground after an intense warring of souls that shook the house and brought a few of the wooden pentagrams on the columnar supports crashing down. The platform collapsed, pulling the altar and the surrounding carnage to the floor. In the middle of the bloody sea, Danto spotted one of the beetles on its back, stuck in a puddle of gore, its chitinous legs swiping frantically in the air. The possessed man groped through the chaos, growling like an injured dog, pawing at the gory mess. He aimed his glowering sights toward Allieb. The demonologist must have been rationing his strength for this moment; with alarming alacrity, he pounced and drilled his blackened teeth into the man's arching neck. A deafening wail filled the room as the man's body collapsed inwardly, the eyes sinking back into their quickly rotting sockets, muscles dwindling to slimy clots, limbs curling fetally against his shrinking body. As his flesh and blood were altogether extracted by Allieb, the skin of his face stretched out tautly against his skull, leaving behind a hollow rictus grin that sputtered and coughed its very last efforts to breathe. In the end, the black soul of Baphomet oozed out of the man's body and covered Allieb like a membrane, which the demonologist quickly absorbed through his flaring scales.

Once the drawing was complete, Allieb pulled away from the withered mass of skin and bone of Baphomet's vehicle and buckled back against the broken platform. His eyes rolled up into his skull, lumpy whites eerily stark against his blood-doused visage.

Body shifting and twitching into a greater monstrous form, he commenced with a spellbinding prayer.

And the congregation replied: "Hail Allieb, hail Belial, hail Abbadon, hail Lucifer, hail Rex Mundi, hail Ashtoroth, hail Dantalion, hail Malphas, hail Gadon, hail Gaap, hail Beleth, hail Bael, hail Moloch, hail Baphomet."

After the prayer, the room fell into eerie silence. Danto peered nervously about, his heartbeats tremulous and staggering, his breath lost amid the slaughterhouse in front of him. Finally, the whole scene hit him. It tore at his sanity, filled his senses like a tangible force: the spectacle of the bodies, the pungent stench of their seeping fluids, the sounds of their escaping gases, the bitter taste of metal in the air. He was a partner in death, in sin—no escaping the horrid truth. The revulsion factor flew off the chart, to a point where nothing seemed to matter anymore—humankind, butchered, bled, flayed, skinned, and devoured.

Still, with all that, he could never prepare himself for the horrors to come.

The candles on and about the altar had been extinguished, eliminating much of the light in the center of the room . . . but there was still enough of a glow to witness Allieb's inconceivable transformation. His body began to palpitate, his anatomy morphing into a beast never before beheld by human eyes: arms and legs elongating—tearing—into arachnidlike appendages, the scales on them flaring widely, green blood spouting from the spreading crevices. The joints on his arms and legs cracked and swelled like balloons and eventually ruptured, discharging arcs of oily black fluids. His chest and back broadened, the scales shedding away to reveal the skin beneath, pink and premature. His jaw and brow developed hideous simianlike characteristics, while the horns on his head grew longer, curvier, bursting bloodily from his swelling skull. This beast, once a human being who had at first become possessed by the spirit of the ancient demonologist, was now possessed by twelve of Hell's most powerful demons—Satan's army, corralled into a single vehicle, for the first time in all of history able to walk the earth and take advantage of its worldly pleasures.

A little piece of each demon had made itself present in his physical manifestation.

Allieb screamed, in either agony or triumph. It seemed not to matter. Its eyes rolled obscenely beneath the bloody slab of brow protruding from its head as it clambered on all fours out of the gore toward the wavering circle, trailing jagged splotches of blood behind. It shook its hulking head heavily, back and forth, tail thick and slapping the puddles of humanity on the floor. When its scream ceased, a low, unintelligible groan issued from its sizzling maw.

And still it morphed gruesomely further, crawling low-bellied to the ground, dragging its udderlike teats, legs and arms indistinguishable from one another, sprouting thick insectine hair. A row of broad protruding spines ran along the length of its back. It pulled itself through the carnage, toward the waning circle, which at this point had lost all its cohesiveness; those who remained did so out of fear and not by hypnotic power. Many individuals had shed their hoods and were gazing about in utter confusion; clearly, this was the first time these people had found themselves released from Allieb's influence since coming to *In Domo*.

Those conscious members in the room, perhaps fifty in all, backpedaled away from the emergent beast, many reaching down and snatching the closest thing to a weapon they could find. Danto grabbed Rebecca by the hand and led her to the only doorway leading into the cathedral, but others were already there, yanking furiously on the large oak doors that wouldn't budge.

From Allieb, repulsive growls emerged.

Danto spun around and gazed at the beast that had become Allieb, as much reptilian and arachnid as it was simian, with only the slightest hint of the human form it had once retained. With alarming rapidity, the thing raised its grotesque head, bore open its jaw, and leaped at the nearest member of the congregation, a twenty-something man whose insubstantial efforts to fend off the creature with a candlestick went unrewarded. The beast buried its teeth into the man's waist and wrenched him violently, the gash opening, opening, opening, quickly exposing the glistening meat of his stomach. It dragged the body back toward the slaughter pit, then jerked its huge head back and launched the body fifteen feet through the air. It slammed into the wall of the cathedral, leaving behind an obscene splatter before plunging to the ground.

Screams erupted from those still present to witness the beast's actions. Its transformation still hadn't yet reached a final stage, it seemed. The thing kept growing, expanding, shifting, reaching an intimidating height of twelve feet. Ribbons of organic matter fell away from it, bloody fibers interweaving with bloody fibers, knitting themselves together into thickly coupled tendons. Elaborate tattoolike patterns drew themselves on the bumpy black and pink skin, expanding tautly over the exposed sinew and muscle. All Danto could do was squeeze Rebecca's hand and wonder, *What next?*

The beast lunged about the room, seemingly testing the resiliency of its new body. People screamed, cowered, huddled together against the walls. It rose up on two legs, raised its other four segmented extremities high, and gripped the edge of the balcony twenty feet in the air. Shafts of red light burst from the spreading slits in its skin, beaming about the room like lasers and panning the recoiling occupants. People screamed as the light washed over them. A single beam lanced over Danto's forearm. He screeched, gazing at the smoldering burn it left behind. He shook his head back and forth, in pain, in confusion, wondering furiously if he'd live to see another day.

Where is Bev Mathers? Was Thornton wrong in his assumptions? Is this how it's going to end?

Soon, the beams of light coalesced into a solitary pole that burned the floor before a single hooded occupant. The beast that had been Allieb bounded back down on its six limbs and advanced upon the individual, treading through the tendrils of smoke rising from the smoldering wood. Those nearby screamed and scattered like rats. The light bursting from its skin faded, then extinguished itself as the creature settled expectantly before the cloaked being.

It remained utterly still, breathing heavily, staring down at the individual. Currents of green smoke geysered out of its palpitating snout. It grinned ferally, lowing like a steer, thick strings of spittle seeping from its maw, searing as it hit the floor.

Then, in the voices of one man and twelve demons, it spoke: "Reveal yourself."

The person trembled with unimaginable fear.

With a calculated swipe of its middle right appendage, the beast clawed away the person's robe, exposing the individual's identity.

The first thing Danto saw was her hair, long tresses flowing down past her shoulders, covering her face. Then her jeans, fitted cleanly upon a youthful figure, a solid black T-shirt completing the common outfit. She cowered, arms folded tightly against her chest, then jerked her head away from the looming monster, revealing a tear-filled face to Danto.

His mouth fell open, but he could not draw a breath.

Kristin Mathers. Bev Mathers's daughter.

The beast reached down, grabbed her by the neck, and drew her in against its hulking chest; white fluids burst from its wriggling teats, dousing her face. She coughed and choked. Everyone in the room responded in horror, men and women alike, wails arising from every direction.

In what appeared to be his complete form, the beast that had been Allieb held Kristin close in its spiny extremities, as a mother monkey would her baby.

It then raised its head and roared in thirteen fiendish voices a single, demanding word:

"SATAN!"

Forty-eight

The guillotine sliced down on Bev's neck for the third time in as many hours, his head rolling away from his body, the pain registering just as intensely as it had the first two times. It took a few seconds for the sting to kick in, which was instantly followed by a tremendous agony localized across his entire throat. He gasped like a landed fish, the odor of something rotten filling his nostrils. Strangely, he maintained his sense of smell, and even his sight, although it quickly turned blurry on him. Something inside his brain exploded, sucking away what remained of his vision, and then the odor infesting his nose. Once that was gone, his mind triggered the survival synapses in his brain, allowing him to remain alive for what might have been two minutes. Then death came, followed by a respite of blackened silence. A wave of dizziness washed over him, and soon thereafter Bev found himself whole again, mired in the shallow sea of acid, staring at the black heavens of his stomach beneath the looming shadow of the guillotine.

In the distance, a voice shook the universe: "SATAN!"

He scrambled to his knees and looked up toward the black hole of his esophagus, afraid as to what might happen next. His world shifted from side to side, his body moving rapidly through the halls of In Domo under the dominion of Satan.

Then a scream, seeping in from the outside world, through the horrible walls of his universe, his personal Hell.

Kristin. Satan had not told a lie after all. She was here! Bev stood, looked up, all around, pursuing another sign of her presence, but heard nothing. Outside the walls of Hell, he could feel his heavy body moving quickly, arms scraping the walls, feet slamming down, splintering wood. Bev realized now that the tortures had ceased. Had Satan finished playing his games? Was the war about to begin?

Suddenly, the lava began to rise, first to his knees, then to his waist. It sloshed about him, a result of his physical body moving resolutely under the guide of Satan. He waited, listening, hearing nothing but his heartbeat as it pounded furiously in his chest from the heavens above.

Then a figure appeared before him, rising from the lava.

Julianne.

She stood naked, peering at Bev, her features unaffected by the extreme environs. She spoke in her very own voice, and it brought tears to Bev's eyes hearing *her speaking to him for the very first time in more than twenty years:* "Bev . . . a duty will be required of you very shortly. As you perform this duty, keep in mind that I am here to protect you. This . . ." *she said, looking around,* "is all my fault, and I've made a vow to protect you from the one that aims to hurt you."

Bev tried to move toward her, but the flow of the lava against him was too strong, holding him in place. "What is my duty?"

"Find the boy, and wake him from his slumber. This is the only way to defeat the demonologist. He has gathered immense power from the demons in his possession, and will soon secure his invincibility. Should Satan be drawn before the boy is awakened, then all will perish. Including Kristin."

"Kristin . . . is she here?"

Julianne nodded, then began to sink back down into the lava.

Bev reached out to her. "Wait! What boy?

As the lava reached her neck, she replied, "The one whose body the demonologist possesses."

The beast carried Kristin to the center of the cathedral, to the spot where the altar once stood, positioning itself amid the carnage. Kristin cried inconsolably, keeping as still as a threatened soldier, only her eyes moving about the room, searching for a hint of salvation amid the ensuing hell. The beast stood nearly motionless, transfixed on the twin doors, waiting, cradling its prize.

In the distance, Danto could hear a series of muffled poundings: slamming footsteps drawing near, shaking the room, vibrating the walls and floor like a colossal heartbeat. *Bev Mathers,* he hoped. He grabbed Rebecca's hand and crouched down in a spot against the wall, in full view of the beast and the door. He wrapped his other arm around her waist, forming a tight ball of dread between them. From the corner of his eye, he noticed her face . . . It had changed even further, not only physically but in persona as well: the eyes, staring, unblinking, seemingly motivated by something otherworldly, unaffected by the imminent evil.

You will be protected by the One who has looked over you your entire life . . .

The poundings grew in volume, approached threateningly closer. The beast waited, staring at the door, menacingly fervent, clutching Kristin tightly. Grinning anxiously.

At one point, the beast leaned down and licked its huge tongue across Kristin's face. She wailed with horror.

Danto trembled, feeling his bowels threatening their release. "Jesus Christ," he uttered, palms against his ears, trying to drown out the approaching footfalls. "What in God's name is going to happen?"

Rebecca replied, "Something amazing."

Satan's footsteps shook the walls of Hell. The lava swelled about Bev as he anxiously awaited his call of duty.

From beyond his confines, he heard the Devil's pounding gait cease. Then, after a moment of restless silence, a deafening crash resounded as something was crushed to pieces beneath His destructive hand.

* * *

Danto panicked as the door exploded inward, shards of wood showering the room, raining down everywhere. He squeezed Rebecca tightly, more for his own comfort than to provide for hers, watching with terrifying awe as smoldering dust settled in the doorway.

The Devil made His entrance.

"My God, it's Bev," he uttered, amid the cries and shouts of others.

The monster that was Bev Mathers took a giant step into the room, stopped.

Looked directly at the beast clutching the girl.

Danto's breaths were involuntarily cut off; with everything that had occurred tonight, he still couldn't accept the evil image before him: the Devil, Satan, here and now riding the body of Bev Mathers, who, in the face of his hideous appearance, still maintained much of his own human features: the deep brown eyes, tiny nose, shoulder-length hair, and full-lipped mouth, all very much apparent despite being besieged by the Devil's own wicked characteristics: deep red skin darkened with blotches of ebony, a muscle-bound build nearly eight feet tall from the tip of His rattling tail to the uppermost points of His serrated horns. Although He was naked and glistening, a few strips of Bev's clothing dangled from the shoulders and waist of the gruesome being, like strewn service station rags. The two monsters stared each other down in threatening silence, the room filled with palpable tension, impenetrable in its malevolence.

The beast Allieb squeezed Kristin mockingly, and Danto winced, feeling her anguish. She howled in pain, her efforts to squirm away utterly futile. She looked so frail and tiny in the arms of the beast, like a baby bird in the jaws of a crocodile.

Satan gazed at the girl, and Danto urged his weakened mind to question whether Bev was in there somewhere, peering out behind the eyes of the Devil upon his daughter, poised to clash with the one creating the utter chaos that had become his existence. He wondered, and prayed . . .

From the churning lava, Julianne rose up again; this time she had been wounded by the heat, black smoldering patches charring her skin, her hair falling away in searing clumps, her eyes reduced to globs of yellow jelly. Again Bev tried to move, but skeletal hands rose up from the fiery depths and held him firmly in place. In the distance, beyond the confines of his body, he once again heard Kristin screaming for help. He looked at Julianne, pleading for an answer. She spoke to him, every other word in her own feminine voice, the others in Satan's grating tone. "The demonologist is growing stronger, and I am growing weaker. Hurry . . . find the boy and wake him. Do not allow the demons to influence you. Their abilities to charm are powerful. I will do my best to watch over you."

He reached out to her, but she instantly vanished, as did the entire landscape of Hell. The universe went black as he rose up into the echoing heavens, through the inner workings of his upper body, toward his head . . .

Danto watched with amazement as the Devil dropped down to His knees and bowed, hands spread out in

submission to the beast. The beast appeared to grin
through the monstrously misshapened visage of inflam-
mations, lesions, and teeth. With a quick jerk of its extremities and a triumphant howl, it forcefully cast
Kristin aside like a piece of trash, Satan's apparent surrender eliminating its objective for her. She somer-
saulted through the air and slammed against the floor,
rolling toward the wall, where two daring members of
the congregation quickly scooted over and dragged her
away from the scene.

The beast took an assertive stride toward the Devil.
A series of prayers erupted from its sodden jowls:
deep, animalistic, a chorus of thirteen voices chanting
in an unknown language. Suddenly, from the pores of
Satan seeped a thick black cloud like those that had
emerged from the other vehicles. It gathered around
the head of the Devil like a swarm of flies, then quickly
flew from His throat into the awaiting mouth of the
beast. The beast fell to its knees, heaving, choking,
drawing what it believed to be the soul of Satan into its
body . . .

*For the first time in what seemed an eternity of pain
and torment, Bev Mathers sensed a taste of freedom.
He felt himself free-falling into complete and utter
darkness, the painlessness of the act bringing about a
sensation of ecstasy and of power. Eventually, as
though tethered to a parachute, he slowly drifted down
and landed in a different world, a new Hell.*

*He at once became aware of himself teetering on the
edge of a stone walkway: a path built of deep blue
granite that disappeared into a churning crimson panorama of immense magnitude. He took a step back and
centered himself on the path, then gazed at the infinite*

landscape surrounding him as a cool gusty wind that stunk of burning leaves dried his skin and tossed his hair.

Carefully, he began to follow the labyrinthine path, perhaps three feet wide with crumbling edges that shed its fragments into an abyss of black and red eddies.

Keeping himself steady, trying his damnedest to avoid looking down for fear of dizziness, he paced the path determinedly, making a series of turns at the scores of intersections he encountered. During his travels, the entire environment lurched at times with a threat to toss him off the path, into the bottomless abyss. When this occurred, he would kneel down and grasp the crumbling edges and wait until the movements ceased.

Eventually, he sighted a massive edifice constructed of towering columns and arches. He raced toward the distant structure, peering at its intricate architecture, the Gothic pillars and etched parapets, knowing somehow that it was here he would find the boy . . .

The beast Allieb peered up at the Devil. Danto watched with great fear as both Devil and beast climbed up on two legs, glaring furiously at each other. Something was wrong. The Devil had not surrendered His soul . . . He seemed to have thrown His adversary a curveball instead—Danto realized this because all of a sudden the features of Bev Mathers no longer existed upon the Devil's face; the visage of something purely bestial was now there: the face of Satan Himself, glowing green eyes, straight razors for teeth bursting from bloodied gums, long pointed nose, braids of hair vining about the two great horns emerging from His head.

The beast Allieb trembled, then coughed and choked agitatedly, as though he'd consumed something rotten.

Satan glowered, then spoke in a deep booming voice. "Use my minions to gather the alien, or use them to defy me. What is your choice?"

The beast howled its deafening fury, thirteen voices flung forth like lightning bolts. Its body contorted, jerked, trembled with rage. *It's been tricked,* Danto thought, watching with panic as the bellows of the beast blasted off his own corroded sanity, tempting him into nothingness. The beast slammed its clawed appendages against the floor, the poundings jolting the entire room. The walls splintered, dust from the ceiling raining down everywhere, multiple cries of frustration lancing about the room like specters.

The beast howled piercingly in its multitude of voices, then leaped wrathfully at the Devil.

From somewhere high above in the agitating heavens, Bev heard a monstrous howl. The world shook violently around him. He shuddered, kneeled down, and latched his fists onto the disintegrating lip of the path. Once the violent shaking ceased, he carefully stood back up, regained his balance, and wandered unsteadily until he reached the access to the colossal edifice. He entered between the towering columns, racing quickly along a series of granite corridors, tracing the cold walls with the tips of his fingers and seeking out something unique amid the dark banality.

After a seemingly endless number of twists and

turns, he came into a wider corridor, dimly lit from the shifting blue and red heavens that cast watery light down through the structure's ceilingless heights. This corridor was different from the rest: Here were a multitude of closed stone doors denoted with odd symbolic carvings. Somehow he knew that this place was where he needed to begin looking for the boy. He paced inside the heavily inscribed passageway, glanced up toward the sky, then stopped and stood readily before the first door . . .

The two beasts collided, creating a thunderous sound like that of two crashing automobiles. They locked their arms in battle and fell sideways, skidding across the cathedral and crushing the far wall, opposite Danto and Rebecca. Three members of the congregation fell victim under the battling weight of the monsters, their bodies instantly trampled and torn apart in the mêlée. Danto grasped Rebecca tightly, eyeing the splintered door only feet from the waging beasts, then the few people who were able to bravely make their escape. Others, Danto and Rebecca included, kept a safe distance from the waging beasts. He quickly peered over at Kristin. She was lying on the floor alongside the two men who'd dragged her unconscious body to a spot beneath the shadows of the balcony.

Roars erupted, shaking the walls, the floor. The fighting monsters twisted furiously, jaws tearing flesh, the growls of numerous animals emanating from their throats, permeating the room.

Rebecca yelled, "Not that door! No!"

Danto peered curiously at her.

She stared blankly at the battling fiends, body shaking hysterically, sweat beading on her skin like drops of rain.

"What is it, Rebecca? What?"

"It's the wrong door!"

Bev placed his hand on the door. Pushed it.

The heavy door opened of its own accord, scraping loudly against the stone floor. He peered inside.

Beyond the threshold, in the distance of a large columned room, squatted an unimaginable beast, part human, part canine, part machinery. Upon sighting Bev, it instantly pursued him, utilizing its eight human legs that jutted at various angles from the sides of its abdomen. Jutting in and out of its upper torso were a series of transparent rubber hoses that glimmered and flashed with sparks of electricity, creating a semitranslucent glow beneath its biological parts: a dog's head crudely stitched upon a man's swollen neck, jaws snapping at the air with feral anger as its two foremost limbs groped in Bev's direction. Bev remained paralyzed beyond the threshold of the door, watching with terror and awe as thick black liquid began rushing through the tubes; as blue spittle sprayed from its biting chops; as it howled in horrible fury.

Not that door! Close the door!

The voice in his head was unmistakable: Julianne.

He immediately reached in, grabbed the stone edge of the door, and pulled it shut a split moment before the demon arrived at it. He heard a loud collision, then furious scratches on the other side of the stone barrier as the demon attempted to claw its way out. Bev backed away from the door, pressing himself against the cold granite wall.

Suddenly, the roars ceased. A moment of silence passed, then the voice of the demon emerged, calmly pleading, "Let me out, rock star, and I'll show you the way to the boy."

Find the boy and wake him . . .

Bev pulled away from the wall. He rubbed his face, then stared at the door. He swallowed, feeling a sudden want to obey the demon, to open the door back up.

Find the boy and wake him . . .

He took a step forward. Reached out and touched the door.

In his head, Julianne's voice: No, Bev! Not that door! Don't open it!

"Open the fucking door, you slime!" the demon howled.

Bev drew his hand back as though shocked with electricity. "No," he uttered, trying to shake the confusion from his head. He wondered suddenly: Why can't it open the door by itself?

His curiosity was answered by Julianne. This time her voice wasn't in his head but beside him. "It's Allieb's place for Gadon," she said. Bev waved his hand through the air, trying to touch her words. "The demon doesn't want to flee the room; it will lose its freedom from Satan should it emerge from the sanctuary Allieb has bestowed upon it. But . . . it will pull you in if you let it. Allieb knows you have invaded him and would be very grateful for your capture. Move away . . . I will guide you to the right door."

Tears filled his eyes. He backed away from the door. Then turned and staggered crookedly down the hallway, the room feeling as though it were pitching sideways. He journeyed past an endless succession of huge stone doors, all of them alive with curious charm, tempting voices, and anxious scratches. "How do I know I can trust you?" *he cried.* "You might be another of Satan's lies."

Her voice filled his ears as though she were standing right beside him. "Bev . . . the accident. When I was killed . . . you looked into the car coming at us, remember? A moment before it hit our car? The girl behind the wheel . . . she had no face."

He relived the moment for the millionth time. "Yes, I remember," *he answered, the vision still horrifically jarring after all these years.* "How do you know this? I never told anyone."

"It was Allieb that killed me. It was his influence behind the wheel of that car, empowering the young girl who was near death from his tortures."

"My God . . ."

"Would Satan ever reveal such a truth to you?"

From behind the numerous doors, the eerie whispers grew in volume: "Bevant . . . come here, come to us . . . open the door . . ."

"Ignore them," *Julianne's voice demanded, appearing to stop before a door from which no voices emerged. On its surface: an engraving of a scarab.*

Bev stopped, stood before the door, overcome with emotions of sadness. "Julianne . . ."

Her voice was back in his head. Wake the boy, Bev. Wake the boy. Wake the boy . . . *until it faded away to nothing.*

Crying, he grasped the air for her voice but found nothing. He consequently turned and faced the door.

He pressed a hand against the cold stone. Bits of soil and sand fell away from the edges.

The door opened.

He stepped into the small room.

* * *

"Rebecca . . ." Danto shook her more forcibly, but she seemed enraptured, trembling furiously now that her consciousness was returning. The nonsensical words had stopped spilling from her mouth—her speech had been mostly indiscernible, given the chaos unfolding in the room. But he was still able to make out a few snippets. What did it all mean?

Wake the boy . . . the girl . . . had no face . . .

Bev paced quietly over a drift of sand toward a single wrought-iron bed, perfectly centered in the barren space. Lying atop a bare mattress was a boy. Perhaps six years of age, he was curled in a fetal position, sleeping peacefully. Bev stood over the bed and peered down at him. Dark curly hair, olive complexion. Simple features: thin lips, smallish nose, thick eyelashes. His entire body was slender, ribs pressing through the fine veil of skin on his torso. His stomach rose slightly with every breath he took.

Bev sucked in a deep breath of putrid air, then placed a gentle hand upon the boy's shoulder . . .

A loud crash jarred the room. The beast Allieb backpedaled from Satan and collapsed to the floor, against the wall, spiderlike appendages flailing madly, strings of gauzy weblike matter swathing his claws. Both monsters had gained a share of injuries, black and green blood seeping from various wounds. Satan stood His ground, heaving laboriously, harsh eyes glaring at the beast that detained His minions.

The beast gazed back up at the Devil. It gagged, then frantically inhaled, dragging gulps of fetid air into its lungs. It tried to stand, but had lost all balance and slammed back down to the floor, like a shot elephant. Alongside it, perhaps ten feet away, a candelabra fell, its flames taking to the splintered wall; Danto thought it extraordinary that none of the other hundreds of candles had started a fire yet—many of the flames had been extinguished in blood. The beast Allieb twisted its head up toward Satan and howled furiously.

And that was when Rebecca stood up and ran toward it.

The boy's eyes flickered, then opened. Stared up at Bev. Just a boy, Bev thought, an innocent pawn in such an evil game. Bev held out his hand. "Come with me."

The boy leaned on one elbow and took Bev's hand. Without a sound, he struggled up and sat on the edge of the bed. He looked at his desertlike surroundings with blank curiosity, then peered at Bev. Waited.

Now what? Bev wondered, waiting for Julianne's voice to offer instruction. It did not come. "Follow me," he finally said, seeing no other alternative. "We must leave here."

The boy stood. Quickly, and rather miraculously, he followed Bev, who had to remind himself that this was the soul of the boy, not his physical body. They paced through the sand and exited the room into the blue granite hallway with its intricate architecture and dark circular carvings.

Slowly, they began to pace back through the corridor, returning the way Julianne had guided Bev.

From above, he heard her screaming voice . . .

* * *

"Open the doors, Bev! Release the demons!" she screamed, drawing stares from all those that still remained in the room, both beasts included. "You are safe now that the boy is awake!"

The beast Allieb shouted, "No!" in a singular human voice. *Is it losing its hold on the demons?* Danto wondered. Satan circled Rebecca, eyeing her suspiciously, but left her alone to perform whatever strange duty had been called upon her.

Rebecca screamed again, "Open the doors! Now!"

Allieb bounded forward, swiping her with a single pointed claw. She fell back, blood gushing from the open gash rendered across her chest.

Danto pressed his hands against his eyes, incapable of witnessing another atrocity. He cried out hysterically, head shaking furiously, his depleted mind trying desperately to shake the vision of Rebecca's falling body—to come up with some sort of logic behind the madness.

He could reason nothing, just a tidal wave of hopelessness as it crashed down upon him: the monsters, the slaughters, the blood, the flames, the *evil*.

He thought, *It is hopeless. Utterly hopeless.*

Bev had heard her voice from the heavens like a message from God: "Open the doors, release the demons!"

Without waiting for any further instruction, he pulled the boy along the corridor and raced to the closest door. He pushed it open, then backed away, holding the boy close to his chest.

Inside, just beyond the threshold, was an unimaginable monster, part swine, part human, a genetic splicing of man and pig that stood on two legs and pawed the air with a pair of heavy hooves. Its heaving body, thick and pink, was coated with a mass of corkscrew-shaped appendages that thrust in and out, coiling and recoiling in a mesmerizing display. Bev hoisted his gaze and saw that they covered its face as well, smaller in size but no less astonishing in their propelling movements. The demon, eyes glowing red, returned Bev's stare, then peered curiously at the boy, putrid snout sniffing the air.

"Look no further," Bev instructed, quickly guiding the boy away from the pig-man, down the corridor. Fifteen feet away, on the opposite wall, was another nearly identical door. Bev placed a hand against its crude carvings and pushed.

Inside, another beast, this a black dragon with wings the span of a small airplane and a tale aglow with dancing flames. It snorted fire, then plodded forward toward the open door, rocking its tail and leaving a trail of charred patches behind. Bev and the boy screamed, pulled their sights away from the monster, and quickly moved on.

They came to a third door. Pushed it open and at once stood transfixed with awe at the fiendish evil within: a leaping imp the size of a small dog, with chattering teeth and barbed wire for hair. It quickly bounded from the room, intercepting Bev and the boy before they could turn away. It peered up at them with black bulbous eyes the size of eight-balls. "So . . . the boy is awake," it offered in a thin, whiny voice. "I must return to the master now. Oh dear, I can't imagine the punishment he has in store for me!" It clapped its little hands, then leaped like a flea and attached itself to the wall, huge eyes still fixed on them. Like a chameleon, its skin turned the blue color of the wall, making it look like a cement gargoyle on a Gothic manse's ledge.

The previously released demons had settled in the corridor outside the doors leading into their sanctuaries. They remained quiet and brooding and staring, seemingly waiting for something to happen.

"Why aren't they touching us?" Bev asked the boy, the air feeling suddenly warm. "Is Satan going to take them back now?"

The boy gazed up at Bev and spoke in Satan's rasping tone: "Because they are under my control now. Allieb has been defeated . . . yet again."

Bev peered at the boy, curiously unafraid, knowing quite well that in Hell, anything can happen. "Will his soul remain here?" he asked, remembering the tale Danto had recounted in the rectory about the demonologist's soul not being exorcised from the boy's body all those years ago.

"This time I believe I'll bring him with me. My demons would enjoy a human soul to play with."

Then something unforeseen happened. One by one the released demons began to howl, shriek, and shudder. Their bodies turned black and withered into inky billows of smoke that geysered up and away into the roiling heavens like blasts of steam. The remaining doors holding the other demons suddenly crumbled away from their arches, the demons within faltering out as though dragged by invisible hands, each one duplicating the nightmarish conversion before vanishing into the skies as if caught in the furious winds of a tornado.

As this went on, all Bev could do was watch and wait. And wonder why one door had remained closed.

The far wall fell victim to the leaping flames, black smoke beginning to permeate the room. The beast was undergoing a second transformation, this time ostensibly regressing back from the complicated monster he'd become into a lesser being, one taking on more and more of his original human form as the observable features of the demons inside him shrank away into mere hints of their former selves.

A grinding noise filled the room. Danto, hunkering over Rebecca, shot a wary glance toward the Devil. His eyes were closed. He was sitting in the corner of the room, chortling deeply, claws folded beneath His chin. A sudden wind sprang up, fanning the growing flames, whose spires began to stroke the ceiling. Cracks ran along the wall beneath the fire, spilling crooked beams of blinding white light. The wooden girders in the ceiling splintered, glowing embers raining down on the shuddering Allieb. It reached up, its newly returned human arms raised high, grasping at the blistering air. The white light blasting through the flames enveloped Allieb and started to absorb the warring souls escaping him. Harsh, tortured screams deafened Danto as he used his arms and chest to cover Rebecca's writhing body, attempting hopeless prayers amid the encompassing din.

"God of heaven, God of earth, God of all creation, I implore you to protect us . . ." Danto shouted, watching in near blindness the blackened shadows of the demons spilling from Allieb's mouth and nose and ears and eyes, tangible forms winging across the room like soaring eagles, caught by extending bolts of blinding light, and wholly swept away until they were no more: eleven entities in all, yielding to Satan's power. Allieb's withering, damaged form jerked and

jolted and spasmed, his body now free of the demons. Satan remained in the corner, now curled into a tight ball, head bobbing uncontrollably, thin beams of brilliant white radiance emitting from the cracks of His eyes.

The fire began to spread across the balcony. Danto dragged Rebecca over to Kristin's location at the rear of the cathedral, blood gushing from her wound. Both women were unconscious and incapable of escape. The two men who had watched over Kristin were gone, as were many of the others. Danto considered fleeing himself, when he noticed Allieb standing up, now nearly human in form. His eyes, however, were still fully demonic, yellow and piercing, his skin blue-veined, virtually translucent.

The demonologist's fiery gaze pinned the priest with incensed recognition.

Danto shuddered. *He remembers me . . . he remembers that I exorcised him all those years ago.*

All of a sudden, Rebecca's eyes darted open. In her agony, she screamed: "Bev! The last demon! Belial! He's still inside!"

And all Danto could do at that moment was recall Thornton's words: *Belial. Allieb. Close in name, they are virtually inseparable.*

"Bev! The last demon! Belial! He's still inside!"
Holding the boy close, he stood before the last door. Pressed a hand against it. It wouldn't budge. "How?" he screamed, searching the heavens for an answer. When none came, he cast his gaze down at the boy. "How do you play into all of this?"

The boy shrugged, filthy face silent, peering away embarrassed. His hair billowed in the wind.

"You need to get your body back . . . How are we going to do that?"

The boy stayed silent.

From behind the door, a loud, jarring crash, followed by a hideous roar. Bev peered all around. They were alone; the demonic souls had vacated Allieb's body.

"All the demons . . . they must be gone before I can repossess my body," the boy revealed.

"How? How do we get this demon out?"

The boy peered up at Bev, eyes glassy, blank. "Exorcism. That, or . . ."

Allieb stood on trembling legs, his body nearly that of the man he once held prior to the drawing of the demons. Despite his awareness of defeat, the ire in his possessed face still aimed to exact revenge on those he felt responsible for his failure.

The priest. Danto.

His body was a tapestry of scars from the transforming changes it had undergone: skin ripped to shreds, bleeding profusely, meaty strips dangling like streamers; hair disintegrated into a weblike matter; muscles torn and eviscerated, bones jutting crookedly, as through the consequence of improper healing.

He stared at the priest. Grinned. "Care to sprinkle your holy piss on me again, Father?"

Danto cowered, a hand on each of the women lying prone to Allieb's potential wrath; Kristin was still motionless. Rebecca writhed as though in seizure. "May the Lord Jesus Christ strike—"

"Fuck you and your Lord!" he howled. "Belial, my father, is with me . . . He chooses not to return to the Devil's domain!"

Danto trembled, perceiving a slight movement behind Allieb.

Allieb grinned, moving forward, feral breath hot and stinking in Danto's face. "Why don't you cop a feel on the ladies while you've got your hands on them? You know you want to—you've whacked off in the privacy of your holy rectory more than a few times, thinking of those hot bitches and the lapping tongues they display for you during communion. You know you have, *Father*."

Suddenly, Satan appeared behind Allieb. The demonologist sensed His presence, darted around, but all too late to defend himself from the Prince of Darkness.

Satan, now towering over Allieb's human form, seethed, "Give me back my demon."

"Or what?" Bev pleaded with the boy.

"Death."

"Which would mean that you would have to die, too?"

The boy nodded, then said, "I've been dead for a long time already."

Suddenly, the Hell around them quaked. The walls of the towering edifice crumbled down and vanished into mountains of blue dust swept away by the wind, revealing the demon Belial, who, like Bev and the boy, seemed just as stunned to have had the world disintegrate into nothingness.

The skies turned from red to gray. The clouds of the churning storm split open, revealing a chasm like a gaping wound. From within, a giant clawed fist emerged, reaching down and snatching Belial from his place in Allieb's concept of Hell. The claw twisted and turned while holding the howling demon, then pulled back into the gray void that the environment had become, and disappeared, taking the demon with it.

With no forewarning, Satan thrust His fist into Allieb's chest until it burst through his back. It remained there, finalizing its deadly intention, gouts of gore and splinters of spine rupturing as it twisted and turned. Allieb choked, coughed, strings of blood spewing from his mouth. Satan pulled His fist back, red spouts arcing onto the floor.

Allieb collapsed into a trembling heap.

Kristin had come to. She was crying, gazing hysterically at the fire that was spreading throughout the room. She sat up in a panic. Danto moved to her and grasped her arm, then looked down at Rebecca, whose eyes were still open. Her ashen face was still that of . . .

"Mom?" Kristin said. "Oh . . . my God . . ." Kristin loomed over Rebecca, who was barely conscious, blood pouring from the wound in her chest, drenching her midsection. "Mom . . . Mom!" Tears exploded from her eyes. She shook uncontrollably, blue veins of sorrow and disbelief swelling in her neck. "It's my mother!" she yelled, swollen eyes pinning the priest whom she'd never met.

"The fire . . ." Danto replied, pulling frantically on her arm. "We must go!"

She jerked away. "I recognize her from the photographs!" she sobbed.

"It's not your mother!" Danto yelled, eyes now burning from the smoke wafting toward his face.

"She's alive . . . we have to get her out of here!"

Danto, his gaze bouncing frantically all over the

burning room, reluctantly agreed, despite knowing their efforts would be in vain: Rebecca's fate had already been sealed, her purpose to carry Julianne's soul to the drawing and guide Bev through fulfilled.

Danto heard an odd voice, like amplified words on a backward-running tape. He turned.

Kristin looked up at the priest, then past the twitching body of the demonologist, toward Satan. The Devil was kneeling before Allieb, palms turned upward in prayer. From Allieb's eyes came thick funnel-shaped shadows, coalescing into a single swirling ball floating ghostlike in front of His face. It began to spin, like a tiny tornado, then shot forcefully into the gulping mouth of Satan. The Devil fell back in His first outward display of vulnerability.

The burning house began to shake, as though caught at the epicenter of a massive earthquake. The ceiling splintered, threatening a full collapse upon those still in the room: Danto, Rebecca, Kristin, Allieb, and Satan. The murderous poundings produced huge holes in the walls, wood splinters exploding outwardly toward the now-burning bodies at the center of the cathedral. All this while, the entity that had been Satan regressed into Bev Mathers, body spasming crazily, the great horns shrinking back into his skull, the tail thinning, transforming into segmented bone and vanishing into his spinal column like a retracting tape measure. His bones creaked noisily, muscles stretching with the ghastly sound of tearing cloth. His countenance reverted from Satan's grotesquery into Bev's familiar persona, the bones of his skull shifting pliably beneath his paling skin. And the groans: emanating from his throat, they started as deep growls but eventually tapered down into those of a man in bitter agony. In a matter of a minute, Bev Mathers had rematerialized, lying naked and shivering on the wooden floor of *In Domo*.

Danto and Kristin hurried to him. His eyes fluttered, then peered up at them. "Where am I?" he managed.

"In a burning house," Danto yelled over the crackling flames that were approaching them. "Can you walk? We've got to get out of here."

Bev stretched out his limbs—they were swathed in clear goo. He winced. "I think so."

"C'mon," Danto said, helping him to rise. Kristin supported him from the other side, an arm wrapped tightly around his waist. She grimaced, in a great deal of pain herself. Bev looked at her curiously. "Kristin?"

"I'll explain later," she answered.

"Let's go," Danto shouted.

"Wait . . . what about Mom?" Kristin held back.

Mom?

They all turned.

Saw Allieb.

He was still alive.

Despite his wounds, he had risen to his knees. He was teetering back and forth, peering down at the gaping hole in his chest, trembling hands trying desperately to shove back in the stew of his escaping organs. When he brought his gaze back up, they could see tears soaking his eyes.

His human eyes.

He began to whimper, not in the strident voice of a demon, nor even that of a man's.

He wept in the high-pitched intonation of a young boy, one perhaps six or seven years of age.

Recovering some strength in his body, Bev broke

away from his easing support and tottered unsteadily toward Allieb.

"Bev . . . don't," Danto pleaded. "It's a trick!"

Bev replied confidently, "No, it's not." He approached Allieb, took his bloody hand, and locked his gaze. Recognition filled his tortured eyes.

"Thank you," Bev said. "I am forever grateful for your sacrifice."

Allieb sobbed, then blurted through his distorted lips, "I don't want to die. I'm too young . . . I want another chance . . ."

"What is your name?" Bev asked.

"Ah . . . Ahmed," he sputtered, blood squirting from his mouth. He trembled once, then collapsed to the floor in a suddenly lifeless heap, guts unfurling from his injuries.

Danto hurried over and grabbed Bev by the biceps, tugged.

Bev did not move.

His eyes were suddenly pinned on the female body six feet away. He pulled away from Danto, stumbling anxiously to her. He kneeled down beside her.

"Oh my God," he said.

Julianne.

Danto and Kristin rushed forward and stood alongside him, also staring down at her.

Her eyes were half open. A steady flow of blood pooled from her mouth. She shivered uncontrollably and gasped, "Bev . . . it's over . . ."

He ran his hands through her matted hair, then along her cold, wet face. He grasped her flaccid hand. "Julianne . . ."

"Go," she said. "Live your life in peace. It is over . . . I have redeemed myself."

"You have," he blurted, sobs filling his throat. "Thank you, thank you, my love."

And then she stopped shivering, eyes staring lifelessly into the void. Bev turned and looked up at Danto. "My wife," he said. "She was in there with me. She helped me find the boy. She, too, has made the ultimate sacrifice."

The priest motioned that it was time to leave.

When Bev looked back down, it was Rebecca Haviland who lay dead on the floor.

Danto added, "And so has Rebecca."

With no time for introspection, Bev stood up on weakened legs. He gazed momentarily at Rebecca and thanked her as well.

Then, along with Father Thomas Danto and Kristin, he hurriedly fled the burning walls of *In Domo*.

Forty-nine

Someone had taken the limo. No surprise.

Danto spotted a black robe at the edge of the fountain. He retrieved it and handed it to Bev, who shrouded his nakedness despite its being soaking wet. The robe looked familiar to him. *There was one in the trunk in Kristin's office.*

The front gates were open, thankfully, although they still had to pass by the detective's riddled corpse, which had been rained on and pecked at by crows for a good part of the night. *I know this man,* Bev thought, seeing pieces of recognition in his battered face.

They exited the gates. From the road, they could see the flames quickly spreading throughout the house, the windows filling with a glimmering orange glow.

As quickly as possible, they fled *In Domo,* making it

353

only three blocks before sirens could be heard in the distance. They hunkered down behind a row of hedges as fire engines and police cruisers passed them by on their way to what would undoubtedly be coined in the papers as a "mass cult suicide."

"How are you doing?" Danto asked Bev, his voice an expended, raspy whisper.

"In pain. My joints."

"We should get you to a hospital."

He shook his head. "Just need some rest."

A moment of uncertain silence passed. Then Danto said, "About a mile from here is the Hollywood Hills Motor Inn. Can you make it?"

"Do I have a choice?"

Danto shook his head. "I don't think so. Kristin, can you make it?"

"Bad headache, but I'm okay," she said calmly, gazing warily at her father.

"Let's go, then."

As inconspicuously as their exhausted pace would allow, they gradually passed through the dark and quiet streets of Hollywood Hills. The journey seemed endless, their gaits slowed by pains and injuries. They kept mostly to the sidewalks, crouching down and hiding behind trees and bushes when fire trucks, ambulances, and police cruisers sped by. Danto led the way, continuing in a downhill direction, passing fenced-in homes on either side of them whose mostly dark, silent windows were a welcome relief from the night's overwhelming events. Danto kept glancing over at Bev, whose face sat in grim expression, the pain evident in his features. Danto searched for something intelligent or comforting to say, but elected silence instead, unable to formulate an idea as to how Bev was actually feeling.

They reached the lower perimeter of the neighborhood. Here the roads thinned a bit, the homes and cars shrinking in size and stature. Eventually, they came out onto Hunter Avenue, a main thoroughpass segregating Hollywood's blue-collar district from the affluent community of multimillion-dollar homes.

They crossed the double yellow-lined road and paced along the uneven shoulder, sidestepping stones and overgrown patches of crabgrass. A hundred yards ahead sat the rear parking lot of the Hollywood Hills Shopping Center. They could see the clock tower arching above Pasquale's Food and Drug. It read four A.M. They paced across the lot, bypassing a trio of empty Dumpsters. Thankfully, not a soul or car was in sight at this hour. The entire journey had taken them perhaps fifty minutes, but felt like hours.

"This way to the motel. The two of you wait outside. I'll go in and get us a room . . . I'll use my clergy ID."

They hurried as quickly as possible across the front of the small lot, toward the motel. The building had seen its prime years ago, with rusted gutters and chipped paint in colors that might be considered retro these days.

Kristin and Bev sat in an alcove near the front office, facing an out-of-order soda machine. Danto limped away and knocked on the screen door to the office. A tiny bell chimed as the door was opened. A young Hispanic man let him in.

Bev moaned, "I'm so thirsty. Tired. How did I make it all the way down here?"

Kristin, seeming to ignore his complaints, said, "What happened to you, Dad?" She eyed him guardedly, suspiciously, chewing a nail. "How did you get like you did? You were *possessed* by . . . by something."

"Possessed . . . no . . . I don't know." He rubbed his hands roughly through his hair. "I . . . I can't remember much, other than I . . . I . . ." A jarring thought suddenly came back to him, Satan's voice, revealing to him: *I can erase your mind of the memories . . .*

And soon thereafter, even that memory faded like dissolving salt from his searching mind.

Bev shook his head. His mind felt blank. Devoid of conscious thought.

"Daddy? Are you okay?"

"I'm . . . so . . . tired," he mumbled, rubbing his eyes, his hair, too tired, refusing to divulge the lingering memories of his otherworldly communication with Satan, his fleeting memories of Hell. He pulled his hands away from his eyes, looked at her, the view of her face shifting in and out of focus. "Kristin . . . what . . . what were you doing there?"

She grabbed her head suddenly.

"What's the matter?"

"My headache . . . it feels . . . *weird*. It feels like a . . ."

The door chimed again. Danto emerged with a key and three plastic bottles of water. "Number six," he said, pointing. "Second room on the right."

Bev and Kristin stood, both of them wincing in pain. They followed the priest around the bend, two doors down. They entered the room. Kristin and Bev immediately collapsed on the musty bed. Danto locked the door behind them, then disappeared into the bathroom.

Danto spoke a few words from behind the closed door.

Bev didn't hear him.

Sleep overcame him.

Dark, dreamless sleep.

Fifty

Bev awoke.

He sat up. The first thing that fell into his emerging sights was a half-filled bottle of water on the nightstand. He leaned up, grabbed it, sipped it. It was warm.

He gazed around the gloomy room. Kristin, lying on the bed. Then the priest, Father Danto, asleep in the chair, head tilted sideways, feet propped up on the edge of the bed.

A chill ran through him. He shuddered.

He gazed at the clock: 9:33 A.M.

Kristin awoke suddenly. She sat up quickly, looked around the room, then took the bottle from his hand and gulped it. "I just had the strangest dream . . ." she said.

Bev looked at her, his thoughts in a jumble. He ran a blood-caked hand through her tangled hair. Ignoring her, he said, "I remember the house, the fire, the people. Where were we? What was I doing there?"

Danto came awake. He immediately leaned up, eyeing Bev incredulously. "You don't remember?"

Bev looked at the priest. "I remember there was some sort of trouble . . . it all had to do with the cult." He gazed tearfully at Kristin and said, "Jesus, Kristin, were you a part of it?"

She scooted next to him on the bed. She folded her legs in front of her and stared into his eyes. "No, I wasn't." She looked at Danto, then back at Bev. "I guess I need to explain everything to you."

Bev and Danto waited.

She took a deep breath, then spoke. "A few years ago, I was going through some of Mom's things. Looking at her pictures. Reading some of her letters to you. Things like that. While going through her jewelry box, I found a small hidden compartment beneath the velvet liner. Inside was a key, plus a note discussing how she'd committed a terrible sin and that the only way to liberate herself was to 'bury her poisoned past,' as she'd explained. On the back of the note was a crude drawing of a map. It pinpointed a spot in Alondra Park where she'd supposedly buried something beneath a tree she'd carved her initials on. I was curious, so I went to find it.

"I located the tree. It was in a mostly untraveled area, in the north woods of the park. Sure enough, as the note indicated, her initials were carved there in the bark; I'd almost missed them, as they were mostly worn away and barely visible. I'd brought a spade with me and began to dig alongside the tree, below her initials.

"About a foot down, I found a box."

Kristin took a sip of water, then continued. "I dug the box out. It was pretty big, made of metal, about eighteen inches long and six inches deep." She gestured with her hands to demonstrate how big it was. "Using the key I found in the jewelry box, I unlocked the clasp and opened it.

"Inside I found a diary, as well as some drawings and other keepsakes and notes that revealed what appeared to be Mom's participation in a demonological cult. As disturbed as I was to discover this, I was also instantly obsessed . . . I had to find out as much as possible about this cult, its history, its current activities.

"I spent the better part of two years researching the cult and its leader, Allieb. It was all I could do to learn about what Mom had done, how she was drawn in to the point where she felt no choice but to totally surrender herself to it. From the very start of my research into the cult, I recorded all my findings, soon realizing that all the data I'd gathered would make for an incredible article.

"I'd quickly learned that there was a great deal more to Allieb and his cult than just textbook demon worship. According to some of the information I gathered, I determined that in due time a momentous event would take place, a ceremony of grand proportions that would purportedly raise a true demon spirit. Once I confirmed the existence of this forthcoming event, I knew that I had to be there for it. So I infiltrated the cult."

"The things I saw in your office, Kristin," Bev inquired. "The papers, the drawings . . ."

"All research materials. Dad, I didn't want to tell you about my research right away because I didn't want you to worry. I never thought in my wildest imagination that the event would turn out like it did—I thought it was going to be something like a séance."

"You got a lot more than you bargained for," Danto remarked.

Bev looked confused, eyes bouncing back and forth between Kristin and Danto. "Like what?" He rubbed his forehead vigorously. "Jesus, why can't I remember anything? I mean . . . I *was* there. I can sense it. I remember the house. But . . . I can't remember what went on."

Kristin grabbed her forehead, rubbed it furiously. "God, my head hurts."

Danto stood up. "It's better that you don't, Bev." He stretched his body, then took a sip of warm water.

"What do we do now?" Bev asked, rubbing his eyes, his thoughts a gray void, allowing only flashes of memory through.

"First . . . we need to get something to eat."

"And then?"

"And then we figure out how we're going to answer the slew of questions that will be asked of us."

Bev stood, stretched his legs. His bones popped, but didn't hurt as much as last night. His body, although still slightly bent at the joints, had nearly rehabilitated itself.

Kristin went into the bathroom. Ran the water. When she came out, she said, "What about the news . . . maybe there's something on about the cult and the fire."

Bev went into the bathroom. He relieved himself, then scrubbed the dried blood from his hands. Over the running water of the sink, he heard light, tinny music filtering in through the bathroom door.

"News is on Channel Twelve," he heard Kristin say.

He dried his hands on a towel, then opened the door and went back into the room.

What he saw on the TV stunned him.

His face, staring right back at him.

It was a color press head shot, taken prior to the start of his U.S. tour. Danto, Kristin, and Bev all stayed silent and motionless as the announcer droned:

". . . forty-three-year-old Bev Mathers is now considered at large, armed, and dangerous. For those of you just tuning in, rock musician Bev Mathers is being sought for the murder of his manager, forty-four-year-old Jake Ritchie, which took place at a party being thrown by Ritchie at his Beverly Hills home on Saturday night. Mathers presumably fled after detectives questioned him about the murder on Sunday. Mathers is also suspected in the murder of a police officer at the St. Michael's Rectory. Officer Larry Rose was called in to question Mathers's suspected accomplice, Father Thomas Danto, a priest at St. Michael's Church. After calls to Rose went unanswered, police went to St. Michael's Rectory, which was also the site of a ritualistic animal sacrifice earlier in the week, and discovered the murdered body of the officer inside. What makes this story even stranger is that the detective who'd questioned Mathers about Ritchie's murder, Frederick Grover, has been listed as missing. His family reported him to the Missing Persons Bureau last night after he failed to return home from work. Also at large is Father Thomas Danto, Mathers's suspected accomplice, and a resident at the rectory where Officer Rose was murdered. And now we've just learned that Bev Mathers's daughter, Kristin Mathers, has also not been seen since yesterday afternoon. She, too, has been placed on a missing-persons alert with respect to this mystifying case. Police believe that Mathers and Danto may also be responsible for the rash of cult activities that have taken place in the L.A. area over the last few weeks. If you've seen Bev Mathers, Kristin Mathers, or Thomas Danto, or have any information as to their whereabouts, please call authorities immediately. They are considered armed and dangerous. I repeat . . ."

The screen flashed an assortment of recent photos showing Danto, Kristin, and Bev. The announcer segued into a capsule of Bev's career before leading back into the murders and Bev's suspected involvement.

"Turn it off," Bev said. "I didn't murder Jake or the cop. What is this all about?" *Jake's dead? Dear God, what's going on?*

Danto shut the television. He faced Bev, his expression deadpan. "Bev, you need to turn yourself in."

"For what? I didn't do anything!" His legs felt suddenly numb. He fell back down on the bed, trembling uncontrollably. He held his face in his hands and began to cry, shoulders jerking up and down.

"Bev . . . listen to me . . . you were possessed by the soul of the Devil. This evil that was inside you . . . *it* murdered Jake. And that cop."

"No! What? No! This is outrageous!"

Kristin, too, began to cry. "Daddy . . . please." She wrapped her arms around him. He hugged her back, squeezed tightly, at once resigning himself to the fact that he may very-well be going to jail for the remainder of his life—that this would be the last time he'd ever touch his daughter again.

He pulled away. "If I was possessed by something, and if it made me do these terrible things I had no control over . . . then how can *I* be the one responsible?"

Danto shook his head. "There's no logical way you

can explain it to the police. I can back you up . . . but no one's going to buy it."

Tears filled Kristin's eyes. "What are we gonna do?" she cried, her voice edging on panic.

An idea crossed Bev's mind. A way out of the mess. *Could it work?*

"Kristin . . . I need you to get me some clothes and some food. I'm going to leave here, leave L.A."

"How?" Danto asked. "How can you hide from the authorities?"

"Tell the police that we were all a part of the cult. Tell them that you haven't seen me since you fled the fire, that . . . that you believe I was killed as a part of the ritual, and that my body burned in the house. They'll assume me dead amongst all the bodies. There's no way they'll be able to identify everyone in there."

Danto nodded. "Not a bad idea. Just might work."

Kristin hugged Bev. "Stay right here, Daddy. I'll be back with some clothes and food for you."

"You have any money?" Bev asked.

She stopped.

Danto said, "I'll go. Kristin, stay here with Bev. I'll be back in fifteen minutes."

She rubbed her face nervously, then nodded and sat next to Bev on the bed, holding his hand. "Will it work, Dad?"

Bev nodded. "It has to."

Danto gazed at them. Then he turned and opened the door.

A gun was pointed in his face.

Someone shouted: *"Slowly, put your hands on top of your head."*

Bev sat in shocked silence as the police rushed the room. They pulled Kristin away from him, leaped on him, twisted him around, and cuffed him at gunpoint as he lay facedown on the bed.

He closed his eyes, listening to the officer shouting in his ear: "Bev Mathers, you are under arrest for the murder of Jake Ritchie. You have the right to remain silent. Anything you say or do . . ."

Fifty-one

Bev sat in the guarded jail room, opposite his attorney.

Dave Collins wore a blue suit and red tie. Sweat coated his forehead. Bev twisted uncomfortably in the metal chair, handcuffs chafing his wrists.

"How did they know we were there? At the motel?"

"The kid working the desk recognized Thomas Danto when he checked in. The story had been all over the news for most of the night."

Bev shook his head. "I didn't do it."

"Bev . . ." Collins said, the frustration evident in his tone. "Your prints were a match to those found at Ritchie's murder scene. They were also everywhere in the rectory—they were in the cop's blood, for Christ's sake. Listen, do us both a favor—tell me the truth. There's a mountain of evidence against you. My only suggestion is a plea, which will get you life. Otherwise, given the nature of the crime, prosecution will seek the death penalty."

Bev stared blankly at the smooth gray surface of the table. "What about Danto?"

"Exonerated. Prosecution is using him as a witness."

"And my daughter?"

"She's our star witness. Right now she's blaming it all on the cult—not sure how that will help us, but it's a long shot we have no choice but to take."

Kristin . . . thank you. "Can I see her?"

Collins nodded. "She's outside." The lawyer stood and exited the room.

Moments later, a police guard escorted Kristin into the room. Despite the stress of everything, she looked good. Made up. Black skirt. Tan blouse. Very professional. A visitor's pass was tacked to her belt.

She paced across the room and sat across from Bev.

He moved to take her hand.

She resisted.

"Kristin?"

She stared intensely at him, then turned and eyed the guard. The guard stared back.

"Kristin?" Bev whispered.

She looked back at him. Grinned.

Not *her* smile. Still . . . there was a strange familiarity to it.

And then she spoke.

In a whispering voice that wasn't hers: "Come to me, Bevant."

Bev's mouth fell. His heart slammed against his chest as his mind was instantly inundated with every minute detail of the events that had taken place over the last few days. He shuddered, then rubbed his chest furiously.

He gazed back at his daughter.

Not his daughter.

Allieb.

"Where is Kristin?" he asked, trembling.

Allieb grinned. "In here . . . with me."

"No . . ."

"If you want to see Kristin again, come with me. Or . . . you can spend the rest of your life in jail."

"Kristin . . ." *In here . . . with me.* Then he asked, "How?"

"What is your decision?"

Bev nodded. "Let me see my daughter."

Her face shifted a touch. Suddenly, she returned, her feminine voice falling from her lips. "Daddy . . . Daddy, is that you? Please. . . . please, *help me.* I don't want to go back down there!"

Her countenance shifted back, and Allieb's personality returned. "Well . . . what is your choice?"

"I remember . . . Satan told me that He was going to take your soul."

Allieb smiled, Kristin's lips thinning ever more slightly than usual. "Don't you know by now that the Devil is a liar?"

Bev swallowed. *Kristin needs me.*

"It's your only way out of here."

Her words struck him like a bolt of lightning: *I don't want to go back down there.*

"Okay," he said.

He felt a slight scratching in his head. As though a fingernail were digging in the thin space between his skull and brain.

An odor of burning limestone filled his nose.

Blackness filled his sights, and then he felt himself

falling down, down, down, deep into the bowels of Kristin's body, where she awaited him, burning in the torturous acids of her stomach.

In her very own personal Hell.

DEEP IN THE DARKNESS
MICHAEL LAIMO

Dr. Michael Cayle wants the best for his wife and young daughter. That's why he moves the family from Manhattan to accept a private practice in the small New England town of Ashborough. Everything there seems so quaint and peaceful—at first. But Ashborough is a town with secrets. Unimaginable secrets.

Many of the townspeople are strangely nervous, and some speak quietly of legends that no sane person could believe. But what Michael discovers in the woods, drenched in blood, makes him wonder. Soon he will be forced to believe, when he learns the terrifying identity of the golden eyes that peer at him balefully from deep in the darkness.

RICHARD
LAYMON
BLOOD GAMES

They meet for one week every year, five young women, best friends since college, in search of fun and thrills. Each year they choose a different place for their reunion. This year it's Helen's choice, and she chooses the Totem Pole Lodge. Bad choice.

The Totem Pole Lodge is a deserted resort hotel deep in the woods with a gory, shocking past. Helen has a macabre streak and she can't wait to tell her friends all about what happened at the lodge and why it's now abandoned. But Helen and the others are in for a nasty surprise. The resort isn't quite as deserted as they think. And not all the gruesome events at the Totem Pole Lodge are in its past. The worst are still to come. . . .

WOUNDS

JEMIAH JEFFERSON

Jemiah Jefferson exploded onto the horror scene with her debut novel, *Voice of the Blood*, the most original, daring, and erotically frightening vampire novel in years. Now her seductive, provocative world of darkness is back.

Vampire Daniel Blum imagines himself the most ruthless, savage creature in New York City, if not the world. He once feasted on the blood of Nazi Germany and left a string of shattered lovers behind him. But now the usual thrill of seduction and murder has begun to wear off. Until he meets Sybil, the strange former stripper whose mind is the first he's ever found that he cannot read or manipulate. . . .

___4998-8 $6.99 US/$8.99 CAN

DOUGLAS CLEGG
NIGHTMARE HOUSE

There are places that hold in the traces of evil, houses that become legendary for the mysteries and secrets within their walls. Harrow is one such house. Psychic manifestations, poltergeist activity, hallucinations, and other residue of terror have all been documented in Harrow. It has been called Nightmare House. It is a nest for the restless spirits of the dead.

When Ethan Gravesend arrives to inherit Nightmare House, he does not suspect the horror that awaits him—the nightmare of the woman trapped within the walls of the house, or the endless crying of an unseen child.

Also includes the bonus novella *Purity*!

- -